THE
SONG
DOG

JAMES McCLURE

THE MYSTERIOUS PRESS

New York • Tokyo • Sweden

Published by Warner Books

 A Time Warner Company

MYSTERIOUS PRESS EDITION

Copyright © 1991 by James McClure
All rights reserved.

The Mysterious Press name and logo are trademarks of Warner Books, Inc.

Cover design by Michèle Brinson
Cover illustration by Wendell Minor

Mysterious Press books are published by
Warner Books, Inc.
1271 Avenue of the Americas
New York, New York 10020

A Time Warner Company

Printed in the United States of America

Originally published in hardcover by The Mysterious Press.
First Mysterious Press Paperback Printing: August, 1992

10 9 8 7 6 5 4 3 2 1

To Don Wall

1

*L*ike a cat she was quick and her hand slapped and the
mosquito spread red on her thigh.

"Christ, he'd done well out of you," he murmured.
"Look at all that blood . . ."

"That's never *my* blood," she said, flicking away the dead
insect. "I didn't give the little bastard the chance! Must've
been yours."

"Can't be," he said. "I'd have felt it also."

They lay back on the bare mattress. They lay side by side,
no longer touching.

He was glad of this: he was hot, the sweat streaming.

"Phew!" she said, and they both laughed, before falling
silent.

Outside, mangrove frogs croaked; a crocodile slid with a
lazy splash into the estuary; two owls hooted, one high and
one low.

Oh, ja, he was hot, bloody boiling, but awash with
well-being. Even better, he seemed able to think straight
again, now that she had stopped crowding his mind with
voluptuous conundrums; now that he had all the answers to

how each and every part of her young body felt, and to what she cried out when she came. Her hoarse cry had made him come also, that very same instant, and he looked forward to hearing it again, once they'd rested awhile.

Then the candle flame, fast running out of wick, began to fluster, and this sent a tremble through the shadows it cast. Some shadows were long, looming right up the unpainted wooden walls of the room; others slunk across the floorboards into untidy corners that were heaped with fishing tackle and dirty clothing. Soon, even the exposed roof of river rushes overhead appeared to be moving uneasily, undulating in that wavering light.

And he found himself going back over the events of the day, astonished, in a numb, remote sort of way, by how suddenly he had succumbed to a temptation fiercely resisted for five years or more, ever since he'd first known her. A temptation so strong that in the end only the words of a crazy black bitch had stood any chance of holding him back from the brink, from what he feared would be his eternal damnation. Beware, Isipikili, the spearhead in your veins and where you next plunge it! Beware, Isipikili, for the songs I hear are of death, and how my old heart mourns! But, great mother, he had replied, all my songs are of death, so what can you mean by this?—and he had been afraid when she refused to answer him. Yet, after long hours without eating and only one brandy, it had taken no more than the lightest of touches, brushing the back of his hand, for him to dismiss all this as the usual mumbo jumbo, meaningless, without context, and how easy the rest had been, how natural, how good and life-giving, a joyous thing happening between two unhappy people that nobody else would ever know about.

He raised himself on an elbow. "Whose blood?" he said, looking again at the vivid smear left by the mosquito.

She, her eyes closed, shrugged.

"Listen," he said, " a mozzie who's sucked up that much blood doesn't fly far—he's too full."

"How would you know, hey?"

"It stands to reason. So where did it get that much blood?"

"Is it really a lot?"

"Look for yourself!"

Her eyes languidly opened. "You mustn't frown like that," she chided. "Makes your eyebrows meet in the middle, spoils your good looks." And she touched a fingertip to his forehead.

"You're certain that your bloody cook boy isn't still here? That there's no one?"

"How many more times?" she said. "Like I told you, I gave him the night off and he went to get drunk at his uncle's. Ach, he'll never be back before morning at the earliest."

He twisted round to look at the shuttered window. "That mozzie must've come from somewhere close by," he said. "I know, what about poachers?"

"That'll be the day!" she said, and laughed. "No poacher ever comes within ten miles of this place—no kaffir in his right mind would ever dare to! You-know-who has given it too much of a reputation."

This made him glance at the bruise on her right shoulder: a big, lilac bruise that clearly showed three knuckle marks. He had found such evidence of brute violence curiously titillating earlier on, but now it troubled him.

"Ach, come on, why the face?" she said, taking his hand and making it brush her right nipple. "There," she said, "do you see how quickly it says hello to you?" She cupped his hand over her other breast, squeezing it. "Ja, nice," she grunted, "only do it harder, hey? Harder!"

His hand remained limp, his gaze back on her thigh. "You'd think," he said, "a mosquito so loaded down like that would just want to sit somewhere quiet and digest."

"So what? Maybe that's what he thought he was doing when he landed on me, only I was too—"

"But where did he come from, so fat?"

"Jesus!" she said, shoving his hand away. "What's the matter with you? You're the last person I would ever expect to act like he had a guilty conscience!"

"It goes with the job."

"That I believe!"

"No, what I meant was, being on your guard all the—"

"Just shut up a minute," she said.

And she reached out for her cigarettes on the orange crate by the bed, lit one and inhaled long and deep. The smoke drifted slowly from her nostrils, drawing his attention to the droplets of sweat on her upper lip, and to the beauty spot just to the right of it. From so close up, it was revealed as no more than a small mole from which two tiny hairs sprang, but it still gave him a small thrill for some reason or other—just as he liked licking the imperfection of her slightly protruding navel, neat as the knot sealing a pink party balloon.

He touched his tongue to it again, on sudden impulse.

"Don't stop," she said, her free hand moving to hold his head there. "And stroke me. Stroke me the way you did when we first started . . ."

He began, facing the darkening bloodstain there beyond her plump, tawny mound on the surprising pallor of her thigh; a mark as vivid as a splash on the white tiles of an autopsy room. His eyes closed and he stroked more swiftly. His hand skimmed lightly over her breasts and then down, dipped and rose gently, flattened out along her smooth flank, and paused only when it reached the coarsened skin of her knees. Back again. Down again.

"More," she said, her cigarette hastily crushed out on the orange crate. "More . . ."

There was no need. He was hardening against the movement of her insistent hip, and the great dizziness was again taking hold of him. Soon, he knew, he'd move round, mount her, strive for that ecstatic moment of release which would be sudden, like the give of a stiff trigger-pull, and he'd see her arch up, cry out, and then slump back, a deadweight beneath him.

She stirred, moving her legs wide apart. "Now?" she whispered.

"Just wait," he whispered back, his hand skimming light as a feather, faster and faster.

She waited, her whole body beginning to tremble.

"Ja, now!" he said, rolling over to kneel between the

clench of her thighs, his back to the window. "Quick, take it and—"

A cough sounded right behind him.

"A croc," she said quickly, closing her fingers around him, making him feel ridiculous: a saucepan grasped by its handle. "Just a stupid old croc—they sometimes make noises like that."

He pulled away, sitting upright. "A croc?" he said, as though the word were entirely new to him.

"Ja, you know," she said, "only a crocodile—I'm sure of it. Sometimes they like to come up and lie in the gap under the house. Don't ask me why." She was trying to draw him down again.

The space beneath the floor was hardly a gap, he thought, having noticed it earlier on his way across the dunes. The wooden piles supporting the house were easily tall enough to allow a fully grown man to crouch, eavesdropping beneath that floor, turning a deathly pale.

"Listen," he said, his voice uneven, for it had dropped very low, "there're ashtrays everywhere in this place. Does, er, you-know-who also smoke? Well, does he?"

She nodded. "Ja, but he hasn't a—"

"How many?" he hissed. "How many a day? Lots?"

"Ja, quite a few—maybe thirty, forty. He—"

"Be quiet!" he said. "Be dead quiet and lie still!"

"Honestly!"

Yet she lay still, apart from the slight jiggling of her right foot. He listened hard. He wondered if he should reach for his revolver, there in its shoulder holster where his clothes were neatly laid, underpants uppermost for a quick getaway. The candle flame dimmed and then flared in its death throes. He felt very, very excited.

"Well, at least *someone's* still interested," she murmured with a sigh, taking hold of his extreme hardness to thumb its slippery tip daintily.

And he could see that her own state of arousal had been heightened too. Her eyes now had a strange look in them, a stare that was snakelike in its fixed intensity. It made him twitch against the softness of her palm.

"Ja, it's time you stopped imagining things," she said, her thumb even busier. "Do you honestly think that ten minutes ago either of us would've noticed a mozzie biting us? Jesus, it must've thought it'd landed a ride on a bucking bronco! I bloody did!"

He laughed out loud, very loud, astonished to learn what a wonderfully dirty mind this young girl had. "Not bad for my age, hey?" he said, joining hands with her. "But that was only the curtain raiser, remember!"

"Oh, ja?" she said, raising herself to him.

The second cough came from directly below them, abrupt and chesty.

Her skin goose-pimpled. It goose-pimpled all round the blood smeared on her right inner thigh, and he actually saw this happen.

"Oh, no!" she said. "You've gone kerflop!"

"Shut up!" he said.

A giggle took hold of her. "Gone KER-FLOP, just like that!" she sputtered. "One second, it was looking me—"

He struck her, frantic to halt her noise, and hit her perhaps a fraction too hard with the edge of his hand, as he occasionally did with people.

"You okay?" he said.

She said nothing, her blue eyes wide open.

"We could be in bad trouble," he said, dropping his voice even lower. "Stop fooling round . . ."

Those blue eyes were unblinking.

"Jesus wept," he said. "A joke's a joke, hey? Reach over and pass me my gun—you're the nearest."

A strange warmth enveloped his knees. He glanced down; her bladder was voiding. Recoiling violently, he landed on his feet beside the bed with a loud thud.

Cough

The two owls hooted, one high and one low.

"You bastard!" he exploded, snatching up his revolver.

"YOU BASTARD! I'll get you for this! FUCKING GET YOU!!"

And, not thinking, not caring, but berserk, he hurled his empty holster aside to go charging, stark naked, from the room. He knocked over chairs, barged a table aside, and went crashing, shoulder-first, through the fly screen over the front door, before taking a wild, windmilling leap from the verandah to the ground below.

Where he landed badly and fell, sprawled facedown, with his left hand over the toe cap of a fishing boot.

He whimpered.

Just once, never having felt so vulnerable before, and froze.

It went on and on, that wait for the unimaginable. That craven grovel in the stinking, filthy mud beside the estuary. Until something slimy suddenly slithered over his right calf, making him flinch involuntarily and jerk his hand—the fishing boat toppled sideways.

It was empty.

"Oh, Christ . . ." he sobbed, getting clumsily to his feet and having to stoop to pick up his gun again. "All for what, hey?"

Because he just *knew*, even before looking around him, that he would see nobody in the vicinity, nothing untoward under the house.

The moon reappeared at that moment, slipping free of a sea cloud, and its cold, steady light confirmed at a glance just how right he was: the place was totally deserted. And when he heard a sort of cough, he was able to turn in time to see a huge crocodile heave itself into the estuary from a nearby mud bank, plainly outraged at having its peace disturbed.

"You bastard," he said weakly, and tried to laugh.

But no sound came. Because, in his mind's eye, he could still see her so vividly, her hair seemingly askew like a wig, her breasts not rising and falling. Perhaps a nightmare hadn't just ended—perhaps it had barely begun.

"Rubbish!" he said to himself, starting up the wooden

steps to the verandah. "Time you stopped imagining things! It's concussion—that's all! Do you hear me?"

He drew open the fly screen in a much improved frame of mind. First of all, he would find a big bucket of cold water and dash that over her, then light her one of her cigarettes. There was bound to be a bucket somewhere in the kitchen, probably under the sink. Then he would fetch her a towel from the bathroom, a big, fluffy one—on second thoughts, perhaps he'd best fetch the towel *before* bothering about the cigarette. Ach, no, she was all right, she was fine: she had just struck a match to light a fresh candle.

Or so he imagined, for a millisecond, when there was a sudden flare of light from the room where he'd left her. A sudden flare that blossomed instantly to a blinding brilliance, filled with hurtling particles of glass, wood, fishing tackle, dirty clothing, mattress, bone, tissue, and a great deal of blood that wasn't his own.

The explosion itself was heard up to twenty miles away.

2

Lieutenant Tromp Kramer of the Trekkersburg Murder and Robbery Squad was in no mood for a confrontation with fifteen head of dozy kaffir cattle. So instead of braking and waiting until they moved leisurely off the dirt road ahead, he swerved out into the veldt and went round them, shedding a hubcap in the process.

"Yirra, Lieutenant!" protested Detective Sergeant Bokkie Maritz, bracing himself against the dashboard. "Please remember this car was booked out in my name, hey?"

"I won't forget, Bok," said Kramer, accelerating hard over the corrugations, which hammered the shock absorbers unmercifully.

"I mean, it is *almost* a new car," added Maritz.

"True," said Kramer. "Any of those candies left?"

He had never encountered barley sugars before—never having had an associate prone to car sickness before either—and was finding them very much to his taste, especially now his cigarettes had run out. That was one of the hardships a man faced when traveling through Zululand, he'd learned: as many as thirty miles could go by without even a trading store.

"Er, there's actually only one barley sugar left," Maritz disclosed reluctantly. "And to tell the truth, I'm beginning to feel a tiny bit queasy again. Perhaps if—"

"Ach, don't bother to take the paper off—I can undo it for myself, ta," said Kramer, taking a hand from the wheel.

"No, I'd rather!" said Maritz, hastily ripping off the wrapper before passing the barley sugar over.

Kramer flipped the sweet into his mouth, crunched hard just once, and swallowed.

"Worse than a dog," Maritz muttered.

"You said?"

"Nothing, Lieutenant—nothing! I was just thinking what a hell of a business this was. According to Colonel Du Plessis, Maaties Kritzinger had only—"

"Bok, didn't I say I don't want to discuss the case?"

Maritz nodded. "Ja, but I can't help—"

So Kramer diverted him by jerking on the handbrake as they entered the next bend, high above a great, brown river, and sent the Chevrolet skidding in a four-wheel drift that slid them sideways on into the straight.

"*Bus!*" screamed Maritz.

"I see it, I see it," said Kramer .

And then he had to go all the way back to the start of an official communiqué he was trying to compose in his head:

7 August, 1962

Dear Colonel Du Plessis,
Cognizant of the fact I was transferred from Bloemfontein to your Division in Natal only twenty-three days ago, I nonetheless hereby make application for an immediate further transfer. Never, in all my born days in the South African Police, have I met such baboons as you and your little band of arse-creeping half-wits—and as for Trekkersburg itself, God knows what our forefathers thought they were doing, fighting the bloody English for it! Three

weeks in Trekkersburg should become, in my opin-
ion, the new sentence for aggravated child molest.

So far, so good—even if it did have a few rough edges, he
thought, and looked forward to seeing the expression on Du
Plessis' face.

Bastard!

Inadvertently, Kramer had just caught a glimpse in his
mind's eye of the Colonel standing where he had first seen
him at five-thirty that morning: scratching his bum over by
the big window in his office at divisional headquarters.

"Ja, Colonel?" Kramer had said, walking in without
knocking. "What's the problem—apart from the fact some
stupid bugger's just woken my landlady to tell her you
wanted me down here, chop-chop . . . ?"

Du Plessis turned, his shriveled neck protruding like a
turtle's from the oversize collar of his uniform tunic. "Ah,
Lieutenant!" he smarmed. "So good of you to be so quick!
Poor Captain Bronkhorst has been worrying that you would
find it difficult to adjust to our little ways, but your
promptness leaves me no cause for complaint—none whatsoever. Promptitude is what I like to see in an officer! That,
and loyalty, too, of course. Loyalty and promptitude."

"Ja, ja, but why did the Colonel send for me?" asked
Kramer, already growing edgy in the buffoon's presence. By
the sound of it, Du Plessis wasn't so much in need of a
homicide detective as of a devoted spaniel with a bloody
alarm clock.

"Terrible tidings!" said Du Plessis, suddenly very grave,
and left the window to move behind his huge desk. "Terrible,
terrible tidings," he repeated, slowly lowering himself into
his seat in what Kramer had come to think of as the
hemorrhoid crouch. "From afar," Du Plessis added, wincing
as his weight settled.

"How far?" asked Kramer.

Du Plessis opened out the brown docket on his blotter.
"From Jafini, way up in Northern Zululand," he said.
"There's been a double murder some fifteen miles farther east

at a place called Fynn's Creek. Two adult persons, both white, one male and one female; explosive device suspected, motive as yet unknown."

"Uh-huh . . . When?"

"Just after midnight. Or twelve-eighteen this morning to be exact, because that's when the station commander at Jafini heard a loud detonation and went out to investigate. It took him until four-ten to pinpoint the scene of the explosion, and by then he—"

"Ja, but you still haven't told me what's so terrible about it, Colonel," Kramer interrupted, impatient with detail at this stage. "Were the deceased known personally to you or something?"

"Astute, very astute," murmured Du Plessis, with a smile as fleeting as a nun's wicked thoughts. "Yes—and no, I think is the answer to that. The male personage butchered in this despicable, cowardly fashion was none other than Maaties Kritzinger . . ."

Kramer shrugged. "And so?" he said, aware that a very much stronger reaction was being expected of him, but at a loss to know why.

"Detective Sergeant Martinus Kritzinger?" prompted Du Plessis. "Head of the CID at Jafini? Who once played fullback for your own home province, the Free State?"

"Oh, a cop—now I get it," said Kramer. "Never heard of the bugger. Who was his lady friend?"

Du Plessis bristled. "A fellow officer dies in the line of duty and that's all you can say?"

"At present, ja," confirmed Kramer. "There's plenty of cops I wouldn't leave a lame cat alone with, so I tend not to prejudge."

"*Prejudge?*" echoed Du Plessis, and swallowed hard before giving an unhappy chuckle. "Ja, Captain Bronkhurst has informed me you, er, have inclinations to be a bit of a freethinker on the quiet. But, take my word for it, Maaties Kritzinger was one of the best. In fact, I can't remember an occasion when he didn't bring me a nice piece of fresh venison on his visits here to headquarters, never mind the season. And once it was a whole, entire box of mussels that he'd gone and got off the rocks personally!"

"Shit, Colonel."

"Exactly! As I say, one of the best—it's just too bad you two can't ever come face-to-face now, because then you could see yourself what a great bloke he was."

"Ach, we'll come face-to-face all right, never fear, sir," said Kramer. "What mortuary's he in?"

"No, no, I meant really get to know him!" Du Plessis turtle-snapped, and raised a pointing finger. "And you *do* prejudge, you know! That remark of yours regarding his 'lady friend' *was quite uncalled-for*. God Almighty, man, the fellow was married and he leaves four poor little kiddies, not to mention a police widow. I'm going to get a memorial fund started, it's such a tragic case."

"Then who was the white female involved?" asked Kramer.

Du Plessis glanced at his notes. "Annika Gillets, wife of the game ranger at Fynn's Creek," he said, "who was absent at the time. Hans Terblanche, the station commander at Jafini, is still trying to get in touch with him, to tell him what's happened."

"Perhaps he knows already, Colonel."

"Sorry? You mean the husband?"

"Uh-huh. How old was this Annika?"

"She'd just turned twenty-two, the same as my—ach, no! You're not starting that nonsense again! Listen hard and get this into your thick head: Maaties died in the line of duty, like I told you. There was *no hanky-panty* involved. Understand? Anyway, his body was found miles away, his gun still in his hand."

"No hanky-panty," Kramer repeated with as straight a face as possible, adding the phrase to his small collection of Colonelisms. "Only how many miles away was his body found? Must've been one hell of an explosion to—"

"Ach, you know damn well what I mean, Lieutenant! She was *inside* the house and Maaties was *outside* the house, making his approach, gun in hand, obviously aware that things were—"

"He was alone?" asked Kramer.

"Of course—Maaties always preferred to work that way."

"He didn't even take a boy with him?"

"No, never. Maaties said a Bantu was more trouble than he was worth, and besides, he himself was fluent in Zulu, so what was the need?"

"Hmmm," murmured Kramer.

"Just who are you criticizing, hey?" Colonel Du Plessis demanded. "Captain Bronkhurst tells me you're a definite loner yourself—and you won't even work with *white* fellow officers unless you're forced to comply. What kind of attitude is that?"

"Hell, my Afrikaans and my English are fluent, Colonel," replied Kramer, taking a cigarette from the Lucky Strike packet in his shirt pocket, "so, as you say, what's the need?"

"I hope you're not going to light that," Du Plessis said sternly. "I've a strict no-smoking rule in my office—I'm a church elder."

"Uh-huh," said Kramer, placing the cigarette in a corner of his mouth. "But as I was about to say, it seems—"

"No, as *I* had already started to say, Lieutenant, I have decided to send you forthwith up to Jafini to take charge of this investigation. It's high time you got to know the full extent of the division, not so? Besides, I'm happy to report that Captain Bronkhurst speaks very highly of your deductive powers."

"Sir?" said Kramer, who had just spent three weeks in Trekkersburg having the arse bored off him by routine inquiries that needed no deductive powers whatsoever. "I'm amazed."

"Modesty is also something I value in an officer!" said Du Plessis, showing his dentures. "The full details will be made available to you when you reach Jafini, so I need detain you no longer—it's quite a drive there. Bokkie Maritz is already waiting with a car in the vehicle yard."

"Bokkie, Colonel?" said Kramer. "What's that fat idiot got to do with anything?"

"I'm sending him with you to assist, of course. Pretoria will expect the paperwork to be kept up-to-date, and while one does that, the other can be out—"

"But Maritz's a total clown, Colonel!" objected Kramer, lighting a match. "The bloody last thing I need is a—"

"Lieutenant," Du Plessis said, cutting him short and glaring at the match flame, "Bokkie Maritz has served me well and true for the past eight, nine years, and I will not have my judgment questioned—especially not by someone who's hardly been here five minutes!"

"My point exactly, Colonel. Why—"

"You heard what I said about not smoking in here?"

Kramer nodded, watching the match burn down toward his fingers. "But why send me, when I'm still a new poop? Why not someone with more rank, with more local knowledge and—"

"Listen," Du Plessis, intent on the flame, too, "I don't know how your previous superior did business, but when I give an order, I expect—"

"I bet there could be more to this than meets the eye," said Kramer, as the flame reached just above his thumb. "Has Captain Bronkhorst some special reason for not—"

"Never mind that!" exploded Du Plessis, poking a ruler angrily at the match. "Blow it out! Blow it out this instant!"

"On my way, Colonel . . ." said Kramer, taking note of that curious little slip, and lit up, using the same match, as he stepped from Du Plessis' office.

The Chevrolet, now down another hubcap, started up yet another steep ascent. But at least cattle had begun to give way to goats, and the sky ahead looked more interesting, being piled high with giant white clouds, heaped like the pillows in a hospital storeroom. Kramer had spent many happy minutes in just such a storeroom back in Bloemfontein, making friends with a student nurse who never gave her name nor wore underclothes. It surprised him how often he had been reminded of this lately, since his transfer to Trekkersburg.

The city that lived with its legs crossed.

"Tell me, Bok," he said suddenly. "Where do you reckon the bodies will have been taken? They don't usually have state morgues out in the bush—well, not where I come from. A hospital, maybe?"

Bokkie Maritz nodded. "Ja, a hospital's more likely. I'd guess a nuns' mission one."

"Oh, wonderful," said Kramer.

"Okay to talk now?" Maritz inquired cautiously. "Only I thought you'd like to get some proper background on poor old Maaties . . ."

"One of the best, Bok."

"Oh, so you know that, do you? Ja, very definitely, one of the best."

"And?"

"Well, always laughing and joking. Hell, Maaties had the typists at headquarters in fits by the time he left to go home again."

"Bit of a ladies' man, is that what you're saying?"

"Hell, no! They liked him, that was all. He'd show the snapshots of his kiddies, and things like that."

"What sort of wife did he have—a good-looker?"

"Hey? How should I know?"

"She was never in any of these snaps he showed round?"

Maritz frowned. "Can't say I can remember one with her in it," he admitted.

"Hmmmm," said Kramer. "Look . . ."

They had just topped the rise, and beneath them lay a wide, green plain, given over almost entirely to sugarcane. So much green seemed unnatural after the barren, bread-colored landscapes Kramer was used to, making him think of mold to be scraped away with a knife.

"That must be Jafini—over to the far left," Maritz exclaimed, motioning toward a smoky smudge some distance to the north. "Man, we've made excellent time, hey? The Colonel is going to be very impressed with us!"

"Bugger him for a start," said Kramer.

3

*I*t was a good thing the brakes on the Chevrolet worked like dropping a battleship's anchor. Without them, it could have proved all too easy to overshoot a dump like Jafini completely. Here one moment and gone the next; a brief blur of tacky shopfronts ending just before the red-brick, tin-roofed police station, half visible behind a high hedge of Christ-thorn, with a bleached South African flag drooping motionless from the stunted flagpole in its front garden.

Maritz, caught off guard by those brakes, became temporarily wedged beneath the dashboard. "Yirra, Lieutenant!" he gasped. "What happened? Did some kiddie run out in front of us or something?"

"Cigarettes," Kramer said. "You go on ahead—I'll catch you up in a minute . . ."

And he climbed out of the Chevrolet to look about him. Jafini's one and only street seemed to have about a dozen businesses in all, run mostly by Indians. There was a bakery, too, and a hole-in-the-wall branch of Barclays Bank, manned on only Tuesdays and Thursdays, plus a small, red-brick

Anglican church. A pair of distant petrol pumps suggested that Jafini boasted a one-mechanic garage, but he wasn't about to take bets on that.

Instead, he loped across the road and went into the Bombay Emporium, inhaling deeply. Kramer had always relished the warm, prickly smells of trading stores—the only kind of shop he'd known until he was eleven—and still marveled at the sheer, mind-boggling variety of their contents. The Bombay Emporium did not let him down. It carried everything from hurricane lanterns to sewing machines, from miles of cheap cloth in great bolts to plows and battery radios, plus at least nine varieties of tinned sardines. On the crowded shelf of cigarettes and pipe tobacco, he saw, for the first time in years, the little cotton bags of shag his father had smoked to excess, so crude it came complete with tobacco stalks. Good stuff, that shag: it had given the old bastard the long, lingering, thoroughly horrible death he'd deserved.

"May I help you, sir?" the Indian storekeeper called out hesitantly, over the headdresses of the bare-breasted Zulu women first in line.

"Lucky Strike—make it a whole carton," said Kramer.

The storekeeper looked agonized.

"Ach," said Kramer, reminded that his mother tongue was rarely understood by nonwhites in this godforsaken province of Natal, and repeated himself in English. "A carton of Lucky Strike cigarettes—no, better make it two."

The storekeeper wrung his hands, "Would it were possible, sir! Gracious me, yes! But you see, sir, the better brands are not often being requested, sir, so stocks—"

"Luckys, damn it!" said Kramer. "Many as you've got."

As the shopkeeper hastened away into a back room, someone new joined the silent line of typical country bumpkins still waiting to be served. This latest arrival was a cheeky-looking Zulu that Kramer felt sure he'd seen somewhere before, and this bothered him, because that "somewhere" could only have been Trekkersburg, two hundred and more miles to the south. Impossible. After all, the whole point of the Pass Laws was to keep coons confined to particular clearly defined areas, and they weren't meant to waltz round the country like they bloody owned the place. Yet this one certainly did, sauntering in jauntily with his hands in pockets, like a bloody Chicago gangster, and as blacks weren't permitted to watch such films, this alone suggested that Short Arse might be worth further investigation.

Short Arse: a good name for him, decided Kramer—until the bastard's pass book revealed his correct particulars. Hell, he couldn't be much more than five-six, well beneath his own shoulder height.

"Very sorry, sir—won't be many more moments!" the Indian shopkeeper emerged to say, before disappearing again.

Kramer took another look at the waiting, silent line, straight off the local native reserve. Most were dressed in whites' castoffs or, in the case of some females, in what now passed for traditional Zulu costume, it seemed: a bead-bedecked headdress, lots of copper anklets, even more crude, copper bracelets, a short, pleated skirt, and—if they bothered with a top at all—a plain, white singlet. Short Arse had on an old sports jacket, turned inside out to show off its satin lining, plus a pair of riding britches with a front flap, now outmoded. By way of contrast, the coon in front of him was wearing the pinstripes of a posh lawyer—or the public hangman, come to that, Kramer having seen him once—plus a pair of massive rugby boots. That was a point: unlike anyone else in the line, Short Arse's footwear looked the right size, even though his were only cheap tennis shoes, and this set him subtly apart from the others. It also posed a few interesting questions: how fast was Short Arse on his feet, how often—and *why*?

Short Arse turned to stare at something back out on the street, tantalizing Kramer with a rear view of that alert, cannonball head. He tried to will it to turn just enough to show that profile again. Contrary to what most people outside the SAP said—"They all look bloody alike to me!"—Kramer had never experienced any such difficulty. Hell, telling actual monkeys apart, that was different: you didn't have the infinite variations afforded by moustaches, beards, eye size, jawline, nostril width, and so on. But any breed of kaffir, to the trained eye, presented a few problems. Even so, the back off a head wasn't much to go on, and then he began to have doubts about his initial reaction. He noted the two small pigtails braided from the close black curls above the left ear, and had to admit they rang no bells. He also failed to make anything of the yellow kitchen matches being used to keep open Short Arse's pierced earlobes.

"Sir . . . ? Your very generous purchase, sir," said the Indian shopkeeper, placing a brown-paper bag on the counter in front of Kramer, too polite to hand it to him directly. "But first, is there anything else I can be doing for you, sir?"

There wasn't, so Kramer paid him and left, lighting his first Lucky on the way out and forgetting to give Short Arse one final look. Not that this mattered anyway, he told himself—at worst, the coon was probably just some city kaffir's country cousin.

"Lieutenant!" said Maritz, hotfooting it up the road from the police station, outside which the Chevrolet was now parked. "Lieutenant, the station commander wants to know where the hell you've got to!—his words, Lieutenant . . ."

"He can go shit in his shoes—*my* words, Bok," replied Kramer. "After a long journey like that, the next thing a man must do is go bleed his dragon."

I'm stalling, he told himself ten minutes later. Ja, there's something very weird about this whole Jafini business that I don't understand yet, and I don't think I want to. Especially when it comes to my part in it. Stalling won't help, though; I'd best get going, get the bloody job done and then get the hell out of here again, back to the Free State.

Yet, even after he zipped up, Kramer tarried, his gaze lowered in the corrugated-iron privy marked *WHITE MALES ONLY* behind Jafini police station. He was studying the state the floor was in. None of the white-males-only seemed to care much where they aimed, and had left five separate puddles. Moreover, a large patch of the cement floor was noticeably darker than the rest, as though perpetually damp, and this suggested such was the norm. Interesting, mused Kramer, for this in turn suggested one of two things about the station commander he was about to meet: either the man was a born pig, or else too gutless to insist on basic standards of decency among his subordinates.

And I bet I know which of the two it is, decided Kramer, as he crossed the parched lawn to the back door of the police station, where Bokkie Maritz was anxiously waiting for him.

"The station commander's through here, Lieutenant . . ." Maritz said, leading the way.

Cracked brown linoleum stretched the length of the long corridor, passing between scuff-marked cream walls painted green to waist height, and from the ceiling dangled unshaded light bulbs, sticky with tiny fried insects. The linoleum showed its greatest wear about halfway, where a short side passage met it at right angles. The side passage led in turn to a heavy, brown-painted door that bore a sign, in both official languages, declaring the room beyond it to be the station commander's office.

"In there," said Maritz, pointing.

"Bok, you're invaluable," said Kramer. "But have you any idea where the CID does its business?"

Maritz nodded self-importantly. "Ja, of course! They've got two offices over the other—"

"Then bugger off and start going through Maaties' desk, hey? I want a summary of all recent cases he was investigating, and when you've gone through everything with a fine-tooth comb, I want a full report typed out in duplicate—one for the Colonel."

"The Lieutenant would entrust such a task to me?" said Maritz, so flattered he was barely able to contain himself.

"Hell, whyever not?" said Kramer, who couldn't think of a quicker, yet more bloodless way of getting shot of the idiot.

Then, without knocking, he threw open the door to the station commander's office and strode in.

* * *

"Who the—!" began a startled fifty-year-old in uniform, as he looked around, a telephone receiver pressed to his ear.

"Kramer, Murder and Robbery. You Terblanche?"

The station commander nodded, covering the receiver's mouthpiece with his hand. "Find yourself a seat, hey?—I've got the Colonel on the line." Then he turned away and said, "Sorry, Colonel! Ja, it was—just arrived. Thank you, I'll remember that, sir."

I'll remember *what*, Kramer wondered, as he reversed an upright wooden chair, straddled it, and looked about him. Three gnawed chicken bones lay whitening on top of the one filing cabinet beside which slumped, on a slither of fresh black mud, a pair of filthy rubber boots. Half a packet of biscuits stood beside a cloudy water pitcher and its glass, and the window ledge was heaped with sun-faded dockets, shedding their contents. The only clean and tidy area in the room appeared to be the bottom of the large, wicker wastepaper basket.

Terblanche himself certainly wasn't a further exception to this rule, Kramer noted. Jafini's station commander had small balls of blanket fluff in his spiky, Brylcreemed hair, something similar stuck to the razor nicks in his double chin, and a streak of maize porridge running grittily all the way down his uniform tie. There was also a dead moth in his right trouser turnup, made visible by his sitting with his unpolished shoes propped on a corner of a desk so cluttered it would take a bulldozer to make an impression.

"Ja, Colonel, sir, all is arranged," Terblanche was saying, and rose to his feet, almost to attention. "Very good, Colonel—I fully understand your orders, sir. 'Bye for now, hey? 'Bye . . ."

Kramer, watching him replace the receiver, asked: "What is all arranged, hey?"

"Ach, accommodation for you and your sergeant," replied Terblanche. "There's no hotel or anything here, see? So I've fixed you up with a couple of rooms with a widow woman I

THE SONG DOG / 23

know. I'm sure you'll like her." Then he smiled shyly as he extended his huge hand. "The name's Hans—a pleasure to make your acquaintance."

"Tromp," said Kramer. "Like a Lucky?"

"Thanks all the same, but I'm a filter-tip man, myself."

Then Terblanche used a clapped-out lighter on first Kramer's cigarette and then his own, before sagging back into his chair, looking exhausted. "I don't mind telling you, this has been one heck of a day," he said, knuckling his red-rimmed eyes. "I've only just got back from Madhlala, where I had to break the news to Lance Gillets."

"That's the husband of the female deceased?"

Terblanche nodded. "Game ranger. I had a job finding him, too, until someone told me he'd been picked up by plane at Fynn's Creek yesterday to help catch a rhino for some American zoo or other. He was at the main rest camp."

"Uh-huh—and how did he take it?"

"How do you think? Badly, really badly—Annika was his world to him. He went berserk, understandably. I thought they'd have to use the knockout gun on him, same as with the rhinos, but now the other rangers have got him locked up in a guest hut, pouring neat gin down him."

"What time did this plane pick him up yesterday?"

"I didn't ask, hey?" Terblanche gave a weary, lopsided smile. "I thought whoever came from Murder Squad could catch up on that sort of finicky detail later."

"There speaks a true Uniform man."

"You're right," agreed Terblanche, heaving himself to his feet once again. "And since you're here now, ready to take over, I'd best put you in the picture as quickly as possible. Easiest would be if I took you to the scene of crime, and explained on the way—after which, I'm off home to get some sleep for a change, I can tell you!"

His face showed a grimness that Kramer recognized, having come across it in a few mirrors himself: it was the look of a man pushed to the limit of his endurance, willing

himself to grit his teeth and make one final effort before going
down in a heap, pole-axed by exhaustion.

Even so, it was odd, thought Kramer, as he followed the
station commander out of his office, that *not once* so far had
Terblanche mentioned, even in passing, his late colleague—
the otherwise deeply lamented Detective Sergeant Kritzinger.

4

Kramer and Terblanche left Jafini in a scarred, long-wheelbase Land-Rover that had been fitted with a wire cage on the back for Bantu prisoners. "The track down to Fynn's Creek is truly terrible," explained Terblanche. "It'd totally wreck that nice new Chevy of yours! You know about this bloke Fynn?"

"One of the best?" ventured Kramer.

Terblanche didn't bat an eyelid. "He was some mad Irishman, a white hunter," he said. "You know, back in the days of the early settlers in Natal. He came up this way and got in cahoots with Shaka, I think it was—anyway, the Zulu king at the time. They became such big pals that Fynn married all these kaffir maids, even started his own sub-clan with his own *impi*, his own Zulu warriors, and went completely native. Disgusting really, I suppose."

"Uh-huh," said Kramer. "That takes care of Fynn, but what the hell does 'Creek' mean, hey?"

"It's English for sort of a stream, I think."

"Ah. Colonel Dupe tells me you heard the explosion."

"No," said Terblanche, "it was my lady wife. She gave me

a shake and said there must have been a bad car crash. You know how they sound like a big bang going off, when you're close enough? But as for myself, I was out cold. Monday had never stopped, I promise you!"

Kramer lit another Lucky. "And then?" he prompted.

"And then the telephone goes," Terblanche continued. "I answer it and it's the Bantu left in charge of the station. He's heard the big bang, too, and he's panicking a bit because Sarel Suzman—my Uniform sergeant—is out patrolling in the van and he doesn't know where to get hold of him. Man, it's high time they gave us radios in the SAP, same as cops in America! Take that mess-up at Sharpeville when all those coons got shot. Now, if we'd been issued with radios, then instead of hitting a panic, they could've called for backup and—"

"Ja, ja, so what happened next? You went out looking?"

"I went to pick up a boy at the station first, and heard there'd been phone calls reporting the noise from all round, but nobody seemed to know exactly where it had come from. We drove all over, round and round. I even tried the other side of the estuary from here, where Grice's farm is, and on my way there, I spied headlights coming. It turned out to be four blokes in a jeep who'd been down on the beach, having a barbecue and a beer drink after fishing. They claimed to have actually *seen* the thing go off, a big flash the other side of the estuary, Fynn's Creek way. One said it was a bang just like you get with sticks of dynamite when they're building a dam. You know what I thought it could have been?"

"No idea," said Kramer. "Civil engineer running amuck?"

"Ach, no—no jokes. From a submarine."

Kramer blinked.

"You know," said Terblanche, "surely you've seen all these newspaper reports of Russian subs coming in along the coast? The ones dropping Commie-trained agitators?"

It was true, Kramer had seen such stories. But after only three weeks in Natal, he had already decided that the English-speaking press should, in all fairness to its readers, make liberal use of "*Once upon a time*" at the start of its news items.

"I see you've gone quiet," said Terblanche. "Because it does make a kind of sense, not so? Commie agitators with bombs and suchlike in their cardboard suitcases, landing at a time when there is already so much trouble among the kaffirs, burning their pass books and so on. Maybe the bomb went off soon after the agitator landed—you can never tell with coons, he could have been fiddling with the detonator's clock to see what time it was."

"So you've found a third body?" said Kramer.

"Well, no, but at least it's a theory."

"How about the theory that this explosion could have been accidental?" asked Kramer. "Did the Gilletses use bottled gas for cooking? Were petrol drums stored near the house?"

"Ja, Lance did have two forty-four-gallon petrol drums, but set well back—they've gone untouched. The stove was just an ordinary paraffin one that obviously never exploded."

Kramer nodded. "Besides which," he said, "the possibility of an accident wouldn't have brought Maaties Kritzinger skulking around at midnight with his gun out. Why was he doing that, do you think?"

"Not a clue, Tromp," said Terblanche, shrugging. "I've never been one to push my nose into CID business. I just read their reports every month, then put my rubber stamp on."

"Making you the ideal boss, hey?"

"Ach, no, not exactly—it's just I find it hard enough to keep up with my own job, never mind theirs, and Colonel Du Plessis's quite happy. Here it is, the Fynn's Creek turnoff: you'd best grab something to hang on to . . ."

The rough track to Fynn's Creek looked like a dozen others leading off into the vast sugar fields, so Kramer memorized a distinctive clump of stinkweed near its entrance. Then for a mile or so, the tall cane blocked the view on either side, and the bumpy ride grew monotonous. The air, however, changed, taking on a tang and curious freshness.

"It was about here," said Terblanche, "that I found an old

kaffir staggering around on his way home at close to four this morning. He said he was Moses Khumalo, the Gilletses' kitchen boy, who'd gone to get drunk with his uncle in Jafini. When asked about a bang, he said it was true, he had heard lightning strike much early on, and that his young missus, who was alone, must have been very frightened. You could tell how drunk he was from that!"

"So what did you do?"

"Ach, I left him there, and started going really fast— believe it or not, I'd somehow forgotten there was a game ranger's house at Fynn's Creek! It's a new reserve, you know, experimental, and it hasn't been manned very long. Or maybe I didn't want to think such a thing—who knows? Anyway, I went like a bullet, hey, worried about little Annika now I'd just heard she hadn't got Lance with her."

"She was known to you personally?"

"Of course! Her pa, Andries Cloete, was labor manager at the sugar mill for as long as I can remember, and I've known Annika since only so high. She . . ."

Terblanche bit down on his lip, and Kramer looked away, not wanting to add to the man's troubles. They drove on without talking for a while, entering an area like some remote corner of a bad dream. Here the sugarcane had been set on fire, presumably to get rid of its leaves and the weeds, making it easier to cut, and everything had been blackened until the red earth itself was hidden by ashes. Half-obscured figures, hooded with sacking, paused in the cane and stood very still, long cane knives raised motionless in their soot-covered hands, while they watched the police Land-Rover lurch slowly by. Kramer had never seen black men so black before, and the whites of their eyes were like the dots on the Devil's dominoes.

"Ja, you're going to hear quite a few stories about—er, young Annika, let me warn you," said Terblanche, stopping briefly to engage four-wheel drive. "But before you believe any of it, you come to me first, you hear?"

"From that," said Kramer, lighting himself a Lucky, "I

suppose what we're talking about is a real good-looker. Correct me if I'm wrong, but as soon as this Annika turned sixteen, every young bloke in the district started swearing to God he'd given her eight inches, while every mother took to swearing that, although boys will be boys, such a slut would never be welcome as *her* daughter-in-law. The usual bullshit."

Terblanche gave a surprised laugh. "Isn't it just?" he said. "You can't be as citified as you look in that suit and tie of yours . . ."

"Ach, no—a farmer's son, born and bred."

"Me, too. What kind of farm was your pa's? Arable land? Dairy herd?"

"We grew a lot of rocks," said Kramer.

Another laugh did Terblanche good, and he seemed far more relaxed as he drove on again. Perhaps, thought Kramer, the station commander was neither a pig nor gutless, but simply overworked to the extent he was playing footsie with a nervous breakdown. Not that this explained why he never appeared to use a rude word, which was always worrying in a police officer.

"You'd just left behind the drunk kitchen boy and driven on," Kramer reminded Terblanche. "What happened next?"

"Next, more headlights! Not the Jeep's, this time, but Sarel Suzman in the van, going hell-for-leather—we nearly collided! Then Sarel is out, babbling that Fynn's Creek has been blown up, and two persons killed, and he doesn't want to be the one to tell Hettie Kritzinger. 'Hey, calm down, man,' I say to him. 'Calm down and tell me how you know this.' Well, apparently Sarel had heard the bang and seen the flash himself, giving him some idea of where to look. But by trying to take a shortcut down from Murray's Bay, across that bit of beach there, he'd got in soft sand and had been stuck there for goodness knows how long. Let me warn you, that stuff can be murder if your vehicle hasn't—"

"Ja, ja," said Kramer. "And then?"

"And then, well, obviously Sarel had got to Fynn's Creek, and couldn't believe what his eyes saw there! In fact, he drove *past* the first time, he says, because he was looking out for the house from the beach—only it wasn't standing any more. Then he got to the estuary and went back and started searching for survivors. Maaties he found almost straight-away, and for a time he thought he must be the only victim, concluding Annika and Lance were away for the night. Then he found part of her hair-style, and that sent him full tilt for Jafini—in the process of which, we met up, you see."

"Uh-huh," said Kramer. "So Suzman had beaten you to it by only a few minutes?"

"Five at the most," said Terblanche, nodding. "Naturally, I issued him with certain instructions—to telephone the Colonel, and so forth—then went on to see for myself what had happened."

"How much farther now?" asked Kramer.

"Not far, man, not far . . ."

The sugarcane began to thin out and the track changed color, switching from reddish brown to almost white. Little grew on the flat landscape ahead, apart from the waxy-looking tufts of grass and a few wind-bent thorn trees, while in the distance lay a line of pale hillocks of an unusual kind, reminiscent of mine dumps.

"What the hell are those?" asked Kramer, pointing.

"Man, those are giant dunes, believe it or not," said Terblanche. "This is all duneland, this part—you know, it was once under the sea. You can even find seashells way back here."

"Don't they have bloody animals in this game reserve?"

"Birds will be the big attraction, so they say. It isn't properly open yet."

"Just birds?"

"Ach, there's a few crocs in the estuary, but let me show you something . . ."

The Land-Rover slowed down and stopped. "Over there," said Terblanche. "Do you see that clump of thorn trees about fifty yards to the right?"

"Ja, and I can also see what is probably Kritzinger's car hidden and abandoned there," said Kramer.

"You've got good eyes!" exclaimed Terblanche, sounding mildly miffed to have had his punch line stolen from him. "I haven't really enough boys to put one on guard there, but I will if you insist, hey?"

Kramer shook his head. "Forget it," he said. "Clever positioning, though, on Kritz's part. I bet that at night any headlights going along this track wouldn't touch it."

"Correct, Tromp—mine didn't. I only noticed the car this morning and Sarel says the same."

"A very cautious man, then, Maaties," said Kramer. "I see better now how he could have successfully worked alone for so long."

"Who told you that?" asked Terblanche, rather sharply, as he set the Land-Rover in motion again.

"The Colonel."

"Ach, of course. What else did he tell you?"

"About Maaties Kritzinger? That he was a father of four, an ace detective and Olympic-class arse-creeper."

"*Du Plessis* said that?"

"Not exactly," admitted Kramer. "But it was there, if you read between the lines. I just didn't want to bore you."

Terblanche smiled slightly. "What gives you the idea it might bore me?" he asked, his eyes fixed on the track ahead.

"Who was Kritzinger's main Bantu detective?"

"Mtetwa," Terblanche replied, nonplussed. "Why? What has that to do with—"

"Do you know, Hans," Kramer remarked, "you'll say the name of everyone else here at Jafini, including a kaffir's—but you never use the name of the male deceased in this matter. I find that a little strange."

The even roar of the Land-Rover's engine faltered, as though Terblanche's foot had lifted involuntarily for a moment from the accelerator. "Is that so?" he said. "Then it's easily put right: Maaties Kritzinger . . ."

"I was more interested in the reason," said Kramer.

For a long moment, Terblanche stared ahead of him, as though all his attention had shifted to his driving and he wasn't going to be drawn any further.

"Man," he said, quietly, "I don't know the reason. Ja, he thought I was slow and I was stupid, but I didn't mind that—every man is entitled to his opinion. What I did mind was him never being around to give me CID backup on jobs like the armed robbery at Mulamula yesterday. Where was he? But that still isn't reason enough, I agree."

Then he began driving the Land-Rover faster and faster, his eyes fixed on the track. "Huh! What I will always remember," he said, "God forgive me, is how I reacted when I arrived at this place last night and found his body lying out there on the sand. I wanted to grin, to laugh, shout out—only I had a boy with me, and that put paid to that. You know, despite all my prayers, all that trying to find love for my neighbor, there's a good chance I actually—ja, hated him?"

"But why?" persisted Kramer, aware one piece of a minor puzzle had fallen into place: Terblanche was obviously some kind of practicing Christian, poor bugger.

"Why? I don't know why! I hadn't even realized it until that moment—it was like a sudden feeling that came over me, there beside the house where little Annika had been blown to bits. You know what else?"

Kramer shook his head.

Terblanche gave a mirthless chuckle. "I got angry next," he said. "I got so furious! I was outraged that he'd died a hero's death of all things—now they'd *never* stop calling him 'one of the best'!"

And with that, Hans Terblanche accelerated hard, taking the Land-Rover up the side of a high dune, and then slowed to a stop. Devastated, Fynn's Creek lay before them.

5

Kramer tried not to gape and look foolish, but nothing had fully prepared him for that moment at Fynn's Creek. It was an extraordinary sight. Not just the sheer scale of it all, but that dizzy sense of being right at the edge of things.

"What's up?" asked Terblanche, puzzled. "You look like a man who's never seen the sea before!"

"No, never," said Kramer. "There's one hell of a lot of it."

"Ja, and remember, as my grandpa always used to say, *that* is only the top!"

Kramer pondered this thought for a moment, then redirected his gaze down the far side of the dune to the remains of the game ranger's house. Jesus wept, he thought, here's a mess worse than Terblanche's office.

The only parts of the house still in place were the stout wooden posts that had once supported it high above flood level. The rest of the structure lay in pieces over an area the size of two tennis courts: a flapping, smoldering, scorched hodgepodge of half-recognizable shapes. Yet there was something of a predictable pattern to it: sections of plasterboard walls had been flung far from the apparent center of the blast, but as a general rule, the bulk of an object had determined the distance it had traveled. The stove, refrigerator, and kitchen sink, for example, had moved no distance at all, plunging instead to the ground beneath where they had once been positioned.

"Let's begin with where Kritz's body was found and work our way in from there," suggested Kramer.

They climbed out of the Land-Rover and started down the dune, the fine sand immediately making its way into Kramer's shoes and thoroughly irritating him.

"We've marked the spot," explained Terblanche, "and I made sure that Sarel took plenty of snaps with his camera before the body was moved. With the sun so hot, we couldn't delay—and besides, the Colonel wanted the postmortems done as soon as possible. Doc Mackenzie had to be in court over at Muilberg this morning, but he's promised me he'll start them at three."

"At three?" said Kramer, glancing at his watch. "That means we don't have very long here."

Terblanche stopped and turned to him. "You don't want to be present, do you?" he said, his face a picture of distaste. "There's truly no need, not locally. We have this arrangement with Doc, whereby he just phones over his reports when he's finished."

"I see. Did Kritzinger do business this way?"

"Most often, ja, and —"

"Me, I go by the book, Hans, which makes it imperative for me to attend," said Kramer. "On top of which, I like to meet the people I'm working for—makes it all so cold and impersonal otherwise, don't you agree?"

Terblanche hesitated, a wary look in his eyes indicating he wasn't too sure how seriously the remark was intended. "Whatever you decide, Tromp, you're the boss," he said. "But when we're finished here, I'm going home to catch up on my beauty sleep!"

"Fine," said Kramer. "Who's this lot poking around in the mess—your entire establishment at Jafini?"

"Almost: Suzman, Malan, Mtetwa, and two of his boys. I hope I did right; I told them to start searching for clues, pending further instructions on your arrival, and to collect up Gillets' things, any valuables and that."

"Fine," Kramer said again, and they reached the outer edge of the debris.

A second police Land-Rover stood parked there, and against it leaned a big, vicious-faced coon, built like a brick abattoir and dressed in a pale yellow suit with yellow, pointed shoes to match. He was rolling himself a cigarette and at first, in an astonishing display of insolence, did not trouble to look up and acknowledge their approach. Then he raised his bloodshot eyes lazily, licked his cigarette paper, and rumbled some unintelligible greeting in Zulu.

"Now listen to me, Mtetwa," said Terblanche, "this is Lieutenant Kramer, the new CID boss who's come to take charge. So just you see that anything the Lieutenant here wants, the Lieutenant gets—okay?"

The Bantu detective sergeant looked at Kramer, flicked a salute like brushing a fly from his right temple, and began what sounded like a long complaint, again in Zulu, while making no attempt to stand up properly in a respectful manner.

Kramer scratched at his left armpit under his jacket, plucked his Walther PPK from its shoulder holster, and fired, slamming a steel-jacketed bullet into the mud within an inch of the bastard's left foot.

"*SHIT!*" bellowed Mtetwa, startled into a wild, sideways leap, his eyes popping with fright.

"Good, so you *have* mastered another language—that's all I wanted to know," said Kramer, reholstering his gun. "Just see it's the one you address me in on future occasions, hey, kaffir? Or, better still, Afrikaans."

The rest of the introductions went very smoothly after that. Kramer, however, was not overimpressed by his first sight of the so-called manpower now being placed at his disposal.

Crew-cut Detective Constable Jaapie Malan only just

topped the minimum height of five-six and breathed through his mouth, never closing it. He was the sort who wore rugby stockings with his khaki shorts, hoping this would make him appear more of a man, and yet was still having difficulty, aged about twenty-five, in getting a moustache to grow. Probably to make up for this, the squeeze of Malan's handshake was so sudden and excessively hard that Kramer imagined he spent a good deal of time locked in the bathroom, struggling to get toothpaste back into its tube.

In direct contrast, Sergeant Sarel Suzman's handshake was the almost illusory contact contrived by someone who hates to be touched, just a brushing of palms and a quick, light clasp of cool fingers. It wasn't a pretty thought, picturing what Suzman would be like should a prisoner try to wrestle with him, and he obviously had his revolver out a lot, to judge by the worn look of his button-down, leather holster. Aged about thirty-one, his blue uniform had the knife-edge creases a good wife would insist on her washerwoman making, yet he wore no wedding ring.

Lastly came the two Bantu detective constables Mtetwa had with him, whose names Kramer didn't catch and wouldn't have remembered anyway. One was skinny and the other had most of an ear missing.

"And now," said Terblanche, "I'm going to step aside and the Lieutenant here will take charge of this double murder inquiry. Okay?"

"Excuse, sir," said Suzman hesitantly.

"Ja?" invited Kramer.

"I thought this was actually a single murder, and poor Maaties getting killed was more of a case of—"

"Bad timing?" said Kramer. "Good, Sergeant, I'm glad someone is using his brains. It's important we make that distinction right at the start, or a hell of a lot of time is going to get wasted through sheer bloody emotionalism. The *target* here was clearly Annika Gillets—maybe even her hubby as well—and not Maaties Kritzinger. Got that?"

Everyone nodded.

"And by the same token," Kramer went on, "it's only by

investigating this target that we stand any chance of establishing motive—our key to who might have committed this act. Eventually, of course, that means we'll probably find out the same things that Maaties must have found out, and which brought him here early this morning. You'll get your chance for revenge then, I expect."

"Good!" said Suzman and Malan together, and there was a grunt from Mtetwa as well.

"Anyone found anything interesting yet?" asked Kramer. There was a shaking of heads.

"Any questions?"

"Er, ja, if you don't mind, sir," said Malan, tugging up one of his rugby stockings. "Is there anything special we should be looking for?"

Kramer nodded. "Means of detonation," he said. "There's a bomb expert on his way apparently, but in the meantime we can try and find out what made the thing go off. Was it lit by hand—or was there a timing device? In other words, was the murderer here in the vicinity at the time—or had he got himself off to a safe distance?"

"You want us to search for clocks and wires, sort of?" asked Sarel Suzman, looking up from his notebook.

"Ja, and don't forget one of the simplest fuses of all, hey? An ordinary cigarette gives you about eight minutes to—"

"*Cigarette?*" echoed Malan. "Hell, there's cigarette ends every bloody place here, Lieutenant! Surely, you can't expect us to—"

"But I do," said Kramer. "I want every cigarette end picked up, and I want the envelope you put it in marked with the exact position in which it was found. What was that remark, Malan?"

"Me, Lieutenant?" said Malan, who'd just muttered something and was now turning red in the face. "I never—"

"You did, so let me warn you now: any childish nonsense from you again, and I'll kick your arse so hard the echo will break both your bloody ankles—understood?"

Malan glared at Mtetwa, who was fighting off a smirk, and then gave Kramer a curt nod.

"Well, back to work, chaps, hey?" said Terblanche in a jolly tone obviously intended to lighten the mood. "Would you like to see around now, Tromp?"

It was a moment Kramer had been almost avoiding, his own close inspection of the site. Usually, at a murder scene, the trick was to look for something that seemed out of place, but here *everything* was bloody out of place.

"Why not?" said Kramer. "Starting with where Kritz's body was found . . ."

Terblanche took him to a spot a good twenty yards from where the front steps to the house still stood, attached to the wooden piles. "He was lying here on his back," he said, "with one leg sort of bent under him."

"Not much sign of blood."

"Plenty in his clothes, and it's this sea sand—soaks up everything that touches it."

"Uh-huh. Whose is the boot, about five yards closer in?"

"Probably Lance's—it's for fishing. Shall we move closer in now?"

Treading carefully, they advanced over a litter of wooden fragments and river-rush thatch, sidestepping sharp slivers of window glass.

"You'll notice," said Terblanche, "the floor of the house is only missing totally from one of the rooms, the little one at the back. The kitchen boy says it was going to be the guest room for scientists staying overnight when they came to study the birds. It just had an unmade bed in it."

"Where's this kitchen boy now?"

"In his hut back there—I told him not to go anywhere in case you wanted to question him."

"Fine. Let's take a look where the guest room was."

Kramer found there exactly what he'd expected: scorch marks at almost ground level on the wooden posts immediately below the gaping hole in the floor. "So the bomb must have gone off on the ground here," he said. "Where was the female's body found?"

Terblanche swallowed hard. "All over, really," he said.

"Then how did you identify her?"

"Er, the hand. The left hand, the one with the rings on it. Like I told you, it was a matter of being blown to bits. I don't think I've ever—"

"What was she doing in the guest room at that hour?"

"Sorry? I'm not quite with you, Tromp."

"I've seen blast injuries before," said Kramer. "You get a lot of them on the mines in the Free State. To be actually blown to pieces, she'd have had to be practically standing on the bloody thing—not lying in bed in another room."

"Well, I suppose Annika could've heard a noise in the night and come through here to the guest room to investigate," suggested Terblanche.

"Sounds logical," agreed Kramer. "Ja, you're probably right. By the way, what are these funny marks in the mud?"

"Ach, that's just crocodile spoor," said Terblanche. "I remember once, when I came over for a few beers with the builder who put the place up, there were these big old crocs under the house. He said they were there often and weren't any trouble. You just had to be careful that one didn't do a snap at your leg when you came down the front steps."

"Ja, my auntie had a fox terrier like that once," said Kramer, "until I trod on the bastard. But this I don't understand: crocodiles that live in the sea?"

"No, in the estuary—it's still fresh water, you see."

"Ah, I get you . . ."

Kramer turned his attention to the estuary for a moment. It was a silty brown, like tea with a dollop of condensed milk in it, and it had a margin of scum the same as the mouth of a sherry tramp. A little way out, some mud banks rose like small, flat islands only a couple of inches or so above the water, and on these were about a dozen crocodiles. They lay totally inert, armor-plated, some with jaws agape, their hideous teeth on show.

"At least with lizards," said Kramer, "you can *see* when the one you're up against is a bloody psychopath, hey?"

Terblanche smiled wearily. "Ours has never been an easy job," he said. "Time to go, hey?"

* * *

Heading back through the cane fields toward Jafini to retrieve his car, Kramer said nothing for a long while, but reflected on what he had learned so far. Admittedly, it wasn't much, but there were definitely some intriguing aspects to the case.

"You know, Hans, what I find most significant?" Kramer said, stirring to light a Lucky. "It's the way Kritz hid his car out of earshot of the house and then came sneaking up on foot with his gun at the ready. This can only mean he knew in advance something bad was on the go at Fynn's Creek last night—and tried hard not to give away his approach."

"Ja, that's a fact, Tromp."

"And so the big question becomes: How did Kritz come by such knowledge? Who tipped him off that some maniac was going to blow—"

"Totally beyond me!" said Terblanche. "The tip-off can't have been long before, though, or surely he'd have asked for some backup from the rest of us."

"Good point, unless he was overplaying the Lone Ranger," said Kramer. "You're positive Kritz hadn't mentioned anything to you recently that could have a—"

"No, nothing, Tromp. Of that I'm certain. In fact, I've been thinking, and it's two whole days since I last saw him, typing up a statement in his office. His family last saw him yesterday morning, since when nobody seems to have seen him at all."

"What about his sidekick Malan?"

"The same. So far as he was aware, his boss was out working on just routine Bantu cases. Nothing special."

"Hmmm," said Kramer. "Who else might know what Kritz was up to lately? Did he talk to his wife about his job?"

Terblanche shook his head. "I doubt that very much," he said. "Hettie's a nervous little thing, always biting her nails and getting stomach cramps almost for nothing. I remember the time she told my wife she hated being married to a policeman because of all the dangers and so forth. Five of us had just been stabbed to death doing a marijuana raid in the reserve."

"So Hettie will be taking this badly?"

"Too true! Doc Mackenzie's had to put a big injection in her arm to take her mind off things."

"Then what about a close friend outside the force he might have talked to? Perhaps some bloke he went hunting with?"

"*Hunting* with?" said Terblanche, glancing away from the track to look at Kramer in amused surprise.

"Ach, the Colonel told me Kritz always took him a—"

A sour laugh escaped Terblanche's lips. "Ja, I know, big pieces of venison!—only he'd buy those off the game rangers, hey? Same as he once bought a box of mussels off me, only I bet he never told the Colonel that. Made sure he kept him happy, see, so he could carry on doing things his own sweet way, which meant just about ignoring the rest of us!"

"Hmmm," said Kramer, who knew the feeling.

They reached the T-junction, where the track met the district road from Jafini, and Terblanche stopped to check for oncoming traffic. Then he turned right.

"Hey, wrong way!" said Kramer. "Jafini's the other—"

"Ach, I've changed my mind," said Terblanche. "I've got my second wind now, and besides, if you go back for your car, you could be late for the postmortems."

Kramer knew a lie when he heard one, and wondered what had really prompted this sudden about-face in the station commander. "Listen, Hans," he began, "if you think—"

"Don't worry, Tromp! I'll be fine! I bet my stomach's as tough as yours any day, hey?"

Dear God, so that was what lay behind all this bullshit, thought Kramer: Terblanche was afraid he'd be branded a sissy if he turned tail on the postmortems. Nothing scared a member of the SAP more than being suspected of cowardice, of course—bar perhaps being seen as a kaffir-loving liberal, but then that was virtually one and the same thing, come to think of it.

6

Nkosala turned out to be Jafini times about three, only it did have a civic hall of sorts, built to an imposing Victorian design out of corrugated iron sheeting and painted maroon with brown woodwork. There was also a fairly modern police station in a pinkish brick, and right opposite, the sprawling, single-story hospital had been constructed of it, too.

Terblanche drove straight round the back to an isolated building that had high, tiny windows, and stopped the Land-Rover beside a mud-splattered Oldsmobile already parked there.

"Doc's beaten us to it, I see," he said.

"A doctor who's *English-speaking* drives a heap like that?" said Kramer. "Why not the usual Merc? Isn't he any bloody good?"

"Ach, no, relax, Tromp! Doc is the dedicated type, hey? And a tip-top district surgeon, too—you ask any policeman around here. Whenever your wife or kiddies are sick, just give Doc a bell and he'll soon have them—"

"But what if they're dead?" asked Kramer. "Is he any good at telling you how and why?"

Terblanche winced. "Put it this way, I've never heard any complaints made."

"Hmmmm," said Kramer.

Back in the Free State, he'd had some bad experiences with doctors part-timing as district surgeons in remote rural areas. Some had not known much more about forensic pathology than the average backyard mechanic, armed with a grease-smudged manual from a newsstand, knew about automotive engineering. This meant, in practice, they were fine while coping with something fairly straightforward like strangulation by neck ligature, the equivalent of diagnosing when a fan belt was too tight, but God help the investigating officer if things proved any more complicated than that.

"Come, and I'll introduce you," said Terblanche. "You'll soon see there's no basis for any misgivings!"

Kramer followed Terblanche into a refrigeration room, empty except for about fourteen thousand flies, a hoist, and the acrid stench common to mortuaries, and saw two blurred figures through the frosted glass panels set in a big pair of cream doors.

Terblanche hesitated, looking very shaky. "Er, that's Doc through there and with him is Niko Claasens, the mortuary porter. Niko retired from the force about eight years ago."

"Uh-huh, but why nobody from over the road? I thought the whole cop shop would be here—can't be many white murders to come and have a gawk at."

"You're forgetting how people felt about the deceased," said Terblanche. "I, er, suppose we'd better go in now?"

"Lead the way!" said Kramer, and followed him into the postmortem room.

A moment later, he was standing stunned, unable to believe what met his eyes, and so shocked even his hearing seemed to go, making any sounds seem very distant.

"Tromp?" prompted Terblanche, possibly for the second or third time. "Doc's just said how pleased he is to meet you . . ."

Kramer looked first at the wrong person, as he realized an

instant later. Niko Claasens, the mortuary porter, still had cop written all over him, from his short, grizzled grey hair to the way his hard, steel-grey eyes deflected an inquiring glance, making it ricochet.

No, Doc Mackenzie was the smaller man, as toothy as a neighing horse. Life had trodden hard on him, giving him a bald patch like the lobby carpet in a cheap rooming house, and the rest showed in the burst blood vessels of his face. His high color was repeated in his jazzy tie, which had been cut—by the look of it—from a café's curtains.

"Welcome to Zululand, Lieutenant!" said the district surgeon. "This is an unexpected honor!"

"Ta," said Kramer, then forced his gaze back to what had shocked him so deeply.

Like the very worst sort of backyard mechanic, Mackenzie had plainly been working away with cheerful abandon, removing every part he could find some means of dismantling, undoing this and undoing that, until he'd finally ended up surrounded by more bits and pieces than he probably knew what to do with—or indeed, understood. Not a flat surface remained that hadn't some component or other heaped on it, coiled on it, or balanced on it, while the floor appeared, in motoring terms, as though someone had forgotten to drain the sump first, making it hazardous to move about.

"Ooops!" said Terblanche, correcting a slight skid as he advanced farther into the room. "You certainly don't waste any time, Doc! Tell me, how far have you got?"

"I'm on my second, and all I've got left to do now is take a look at the lungs."

"Goodness, that was quick!"

"Not much to the first PM, to be honest, Hans," said Mackenzie, picking up a clipboard that held a bloodstained postmortem report form. "Female, blah, blah, virtual disintegration, blah, blah, gross disruption of tissue, blah, blah— all of which naturally set certain limitations on any examination that could be usefully conducted. Conclusion: death consistent with large quantity of high explosive detonated in close proximity to deceased."

"There!" Terblanche said to Kramer. "Didn't I say Doc would come up with all the answers?"

"Unbelievable," said Kramer.

"Ja, and I know what you meant by that disintegration business, Doc," said Terblanche. "Man, we had a hell of a time chasing the sea gulls off, and then looking for the smallest pieces by listening for where the flies were buzzing loudest. Malan was really good at that."

"A good fellow all round," agreed Mackenzie. "Is his athlete's foot any better?"

"Ach, as you know, CID's not really my department . . ."

I don't believe any of this, thought Kramer, I just *don't*. Then, to distract himself, he turned and went over to come face-to-face, as promised, with one of the best, Maaties Kritzinger.

The late detective sergeant had been reduced to little more than a chassis and some flapping bodywork, making it difficult to decide where the effects of the explosion had ended and the postmortem begun. Even so, through half-closed lids, it was still possible to glean an impression of a broad-shouldered, stocky individual of above-average height, well muscled but running a little to fat that gleamed like butter in cross section. As for the face, it turned out there was no longer any, although the head itself was still intact, covered in wavy brown hair.

Mackenzie cleared his throat. "If you've no objections, gentlemen, I'd better keep at it," he said. "I've today's floggings to supervise at the prison at four, and then some house calls to make to kiddies with this flu that's going round, which doesn't leave me—"

"You just carry on, Doc!" said Terblanche.

"You're actually *staying*, Hans?" said Mackenzie, showing great surprise. "But I thought you—"

"No, no, the Lieutenant prefers to work this way, and I agree with him." So saying, Terblanche moved over to stand beside Kramer at the postmortem table. "Erggggh!" he exclaimed, before hastening to add: "But highly interesting . . ."

Mackenzie reached into Kritzinger and came out with what looked like a radiator hose plus attachments, until a second glance revealed it to be the windpipe and lungs. "Here we go again," he murmured. "The characteristic signs visible to the naked eye even before I section it."

"Such as?" inquired Terblanche brightly.

"When high explosives go off, there's a peak of high pressure followed by a trough of low pressure, a sort of suction effect," explained Mackenzie, obviously quoting from the blood-smudged text he had left propped open near the sink. "The violent compression-decompression strain stretches and tears tissue, disintegrates the capillary network and so forth."

"Blah, blah," said Kramer, and went over to have a look at what he imagined would be Annika Gillets. But he'd hardly taken hold of the sheet when a hand gripped his elbow.

"Tromp," said Terblanche, now very whey-faced. "Er, I've just realized something: you can't have had any lunch today, can you? How about if I nip up to one of the wards and get a nurse there to make you a sandwich?"

"Hell, I don't know how you can think of food at a time like this, Hans," said Kramer. "But maybe a cheese and tomato, plenty of red pepper."

Terblanche turned and made a hasty exit, leaving Kramer to finish drawing back the crumpled sheet covering the other postmortem slab.

At first what he saw lying there left him quite cold. The heaped collection of assorted bits and pieces seemed unrecognizable as anything, let alone a human. Then, very gradually, like recalling tantalizing snatches from some wet dream or other, Kramer found himself picking out various delights. There was a pretty foot with plump little toes, a chubby right ear pierced for a diamond stud, a sensuous right hand with burnished, long, unpainted nails, and a good solid flank with a delectable curve to it. God Almighty, Kramer thought, I've definitely missed out on something here.

And his sense of loss, however irrational, made him suddenly very angry, the way wanting to relive a dream can sometimes do. For an intense moment, he wanted this young lady back, wanted to feel her warmth against him, and even to hear, perhaps, what she would cry out near his ear.

"I suppose I could have tried to arrange that in some semblance of anatomical order," remarked Mackenzie, glancing across at him. "But if I know the undertakers, they'll just tip the whole lot straight in its coffin, and so . . ."

Kramer took a moment to adjust. "Ach, I'm sure you're right," he said. "Done a dental check?"

"First thing I thought of, Lieutenant. I had her card picked up this morning, and the teeth match perfectly."

"Oh, ja? I've not seen any . . ."

"Niko's popped the jaws in a jar in case they're needed for the inquest."

"Careful you don't leave it by your bedside," said Kramer.

Then he went back to examining the clammy jigsaw spread out before him. He tried to make sense of each and every part, flipping over the fleshy pieces to see if there was skin on the reverse that would yield a clue to where they had once fitted together. It was like attempting a puzzle that was all sunset. Then he chanced across a well-tanned section, possibly from an upper arm to judge by its oval vaccination scar, that bore the bruises of what looked like three big knuckle marks.

"These bruises, Doc," he said. "What did you make of them?"

"Bruises, where?"

"Right here, on the female deceased."

"Oh, those," said Mackenzie with a shrug. "Frankly, I'd not noticed them, but no harm done. They're immaterial."

"Immaterial? How's that?"

"Can't you see? They must be at least two or three days old, Lieutenant—nothing at all to do with the explosion."

Kramer just stared, unable to quite credit for a moment what he had just heard. "I'd like, Dr. Mackenzie," he said very softly, "to see that postmortem report on Mrs. Gillets. Pass it over, please."

"But I've already—"

"*Give!*" barked Kramer, putting out his hand. "Let's see what else you decided was bloody 'immaterial' in a murder case—Jesus Christ, man!"

The scribbled report was difficult to scan in a hurry, so Kramer turned to the summary section. Here he read:

Fragmented, no organic disease. Generative and other pelvic organs/tissue, including stomach, not present.

"But how come all this is missing, when we've still got a nice chunk of bum right here?" he demanded. "Have you *looked* for the stomach?"

"I certainly did, but hold on a moment . . ." Mackenzie went over for his textbook. "Explosions can be very strange," he said. "Might I read you this, Lieutenant, from *Taylor's Medical Jurisprudence*? '1940—violent explosion at a small ammunition factory—some 339 fragments found— um, representing only a small part of three persons.' So you see, the fact the stomach's missing isn't in itself of any particular significance, not when establishing the cause of—"

"No, I don't bloody see!" cut in Kramer. "You seem to think all I'm interested in is knowing what killed these two people. Hell, we all know that already, so who needs you to state the bloody obvious? Let me explain something to you, Doc, about postmortems. They are not about blood and guts, man, they are about *time*—and I don't mean the split second these two went to their Maker, hey? I mean hours, days, even weeks . . . the things in their lives that led up to that moment. Understand me?"

Mackenzie frowned, as though trying to focus on a revolutionary concept, and Claasens kept his eyes averted.

"Then let me put it this way," said Kramer. "I can see for myself that at least Kritzinger's still got his stomach, because you've stuffed it between his feet here, but why haven't you looked inside it? You had a go at most things."

"Um, well, because it hasn't any penetrating wounds that could add to our knowledge of the explo—"

"Ach, open it up, man! Come on, right now!"

For an instant Mackenzie hesitated, rebellion clear in the lift of his narrow shoulders, then they fell, with what looked like the practiced ease of the born loser. He carried the stomach over to his dissecting slab by the sink, selected his longest knife, and shakily divided the organ in two.

An immediate aroma of brandy was detectable, if only to be overwhelmed an instant later by a stinking sludge that included, quite plainly, lumps of part-digested curried meat, boiled rice, diced carrot and tomatoes, plus fragments of tinned peaches and, perhaps, pineapple.

"Excellent!" said Kramer. "Here we have his last meal, a proper sit-down dinner, not some snack snatched in a hurry or scoffed while he drove. Any idea of how long that had been in his stomach before the bomb went off?"

"Um, I can't be certain, my experience being a bit limited in these matters, but everything is still so intact it can't have been in his digestive juices for long, can it? Shall we say half an hour at the most?"

"My guess exactly," concurred Kramer, "based on all the street drunks I've seen puke up, hey? But you'd best still send it to the lab for a double check."

"Of course, Lieutenant!"

"Now do you see what I was making all the fuss about? This evidence makes it clear that one of the last things our friend did was to have a late supper. If we find out *where* he had that late supper, then we could also discover who tipped him off about Fynn's Creek. A man doesn't sit around stuffing his face when he's on his way to stop a juicy little popsie being blown to buggery, does he? No, he—"

"Ach, meat curry you can get anywhere!" cut in Niko Claasens with surly impatience, speaking for the first time. "You'd go bloody mad trying to track that down."

"I'm not sure," said Kramer. "Maybe Kritzinger kept the bill for his expenses or something. Anyone know what was in his pockets?"

"No idea, I'm afraid," said Mackenzie. "All bodies are stripped, with a sheet over them, by the time I—"

"What *bill*?" grumbled Claasens. "You tell me where you're going to find a place that sells meals after nine in the country district! This isn't Jo'burg, you know, it's—"

"Just a bloody minute . . . !" said Kramer, who had been flipping back through the reports attached to the clipboard. "There's no clothing listed here, not for either body. Why's that? Did CID take it at the scene?"

Mackenzie flinched away from Kramer's glare. "Niko?" he said. "This is more your department . . ."

Claasens glowered. "Ach, I did the usual when stiffs come in, Doc. I cut off and chucked it in the incinerator bag, same as we always do. Hans would have already done the pockets at the beach."

"*What?*" said Kramer. "Clothing in a murder case can—"

"Look, Niko," Mackenzie said hastily. "Be a good fellow and pop through to the refrigeration room and bring the bag back here for the Lieutenant to—"

"Bag'll be gone by now," said Claasens, with a shrug. "The boiler boy came down for it at ten. Anyway, it was just rags, not clothes. You know, filthy, useless bits of—"

"*GONE,* you bloody thick-head?" echoed Kramer, in total disbelief, his fists clenched. "Then you better get after it faster than my foot can reach your fat arse!"

Claasens ignored him, keeping his sullen gaze fixed on Mackenzie, like a wronged dog expecting his master to set things right, and this made Kramer so angry he lunged forward.

"Wait!" said Mackenzie, stepping hurriedly between them. "What Niko is implying, Lieutenant, is that the bag will have long since been incinerated by now—okay?"

"Okay?" echoed Kramer. "How can that possibly be—"

"Er, what I meant was, never to worry, there must be other ways of skinning the cat!"

"The cat, Doc," said Kramer very softly, "is going to get off bloody scot-free in this business, compared to you and shit-for-brains here. There'll be a report, concerning both of you and your conduct in these matters, going to Colonel Du Plessis, head of the division. Furthermore—"

"But, Lieutenant, surely—"

"Furthermore," Kramer went on, "should I, at any stage of this investigation, decide that my inquiries have been impeded by the behavior of you two persons, and the course of justice obstructed, then I will be compelled to regard your actions in a very different light, and to charge you both with accessory to murder after the fact—ja, a hanging offense, for which there is evidence already available."

Claasens certainly seemed to pale slightly, and Mackenzie went quite white, as Kramer then strode past them and made for the door.

"But—!" Mackenzie began. "But you simply can't do that, Lieutenant! We're doing our best for you! I'd take you for a fair man, but that's not being fair on us at all!"

Kramer turned back for just a moment. "Doc," he said, "the only thing that's fair about me is the color of my hair. People should remember that."

7

Terblanche was ambling back from the main hospital building, carrying a wrapped sandwich, when the mortuary doors crashed open. "Let's go!" snapped Kramer.

"Heavens, what's happened, Tromp?"

"Those two bloody baboons gave the boiler boy the deceaseds' clothing to burn this morning!" he said. "I don't know what the hell's going on around here, but the Colonel's going to hear about this!"

"Hold on a minute," said Terblanche. "Here's your—"

"Lost my appetite!"

"No, listen. You know what kaffirs are like, Tromp! Just because the boiler boy fetched the clothes bag this morning, it doesn't necessarily follow that he's remembered to put it in the incinerator yet, does it?"

Kramer hesitated. "Ja, but—"

"Then at least let me put it to the proof, hey?" said Terblanche, leaving the sandwich on the Land-Rover's roof and starting back toward the main hospital. "Oi, you!" he shouted out, beckoning. "Quick! Over here!"

A Zulu hospital guard in a khaki uniform three sizes too large came shambling up at a half-run, knobkerrie in hand, and delivered a salute that would have taken the top off a dinosaur egg. "*Yebo, nkosi?*" he said.

"The big boss here wants to talk to the boiler boy."

"Please, *nkosi*, this way, *nkosi* . . ."

As they began following him, Terblanche said: "Er, these clothes, Tromp, what especially—"

"I want a good look in the bloody pockets, for a start!"

"But I saw Sarel go through them at the scene—just a wallet, with his warrant card and a few rand in it, plus his ballpoint, car keys, and a hanky. That was all."

"You're certain? No little slips of paper? Meal receipt? He turned every pocket properly inside out?"

"Well, maybe not exactly, but I mean you've got to bear in mind what a mess there was and it being a colleague and—"

"Ach, forget it!"

The boiler boy, a lean Zulu in his fifties, was bouncing an old tennis ball off the far wall of the boiler house, using his forehead and bare feet to return it with such vigor that, from a short distance, the steady *pock-pock-pock* sounded like an outboard engine.

"*Baa-bor!*" he exclaimed, mortified to have been caught at play, and bolted into the boiler room, where he came stiffly to attention beside the main boiler, the sweat pouring from his bare chest.

"Right," Terblanche said to the hospital guard, "ask him what he did with today's bag of clothing he took from the mortuary . . ."

The guard launched into what sounded like a long haranguing in Zulu, augmented by mime.

Kramer found this gave him plenty of time to note the spotless state of the boiler room's concrete floor. He also noted the way in which each heap of coal had been neatly swept into an exact circle, and how brightly the copper piping gleamed. This meant he was not in the least surprised to hear, at the end of it all, that the boiler boy swore blind he'd instantly hurled the bag of disgusting rags into the flames that morning.

"Just how big a fool does he think I look?" roared Terblanche. "Ask him that! And tell him he'll go to prison if he tells me another untruth! I don't believe a word of it!"

There was a further outburst of Zulu, followed by a few hesitant words of evident denial, and then the hospital guard reported back: "Boiler boy says, true's God, he not lie to the boss, boss. He say all clothings go in the fire *mningi checha*—very, very quick."

"Well, Tromp, what do you think?" asked Terblanche. "Is this cunning monkey telling the truth or what? Is there anything you'd like to say to him?"

"Ja, there is—catch!" said Kramer, tossing the man his tennis ball.

Twice on the way back to Jafini, Terblanche tried to begin a conversation; twice it got him nowhere. His third attempt carried a hint of desperation.

"This widow I've fixed you up with is a good woman," he declared, apropos of nothing. "Big and cheerful, but a nice figure."

Kramer flicked a cigarette end out of the window and dug in his shirt pocket for another Lucky. He was still seething over the Jafini shambles, made worse by the time wasted in the boiler room.

"Terrible what happened to the widow's late husband," Terblanche went on. "It was at the mill where Annika's pa worked. You've seen the big vats they've got there of sugar all boiled up, swirling around. The poor bloke must have tripped—he went headfirst straight in, death instantaneous, came out coated in sugar as hard as anything. The DS we had at the time said it was like trying to do a postmortem on a giant toffee apple!"

Kramer shielded his match flame.

"She was left with four kiddies, and one just a babe— imagine that," Terblanche added, with a doleful shaking of his head. "No family of her own to rally round, just the neighbors to help, yet never once did anyone ever hear her complain. She simply—"

"This previous DS," said Kramer, exhaling, "the one who carried out that postmortem you've just mentioned, what happened to him? Is he still in the vicinity? Could we get him in to double-check Mackenzie's reports on Annika and Kritz?"

"Ach, no, Doc Abrahams retired and went to live with his daughter in the Cape. Anyway, as I was—"

"What we need is a good map of the district, hey?" interrupted Kramer. "You've got one?"

"Er, large-scale, you mean?"

"Bigger the better."

"We've got a map that shows farmhouses—is that big enough?"

Kramer shrugged. "It's a start," he said. "We'll get the others together, and then I want you to draw a big circle on it showing twenty minutes' car drive from anywhere within that curved line to Fynn's Creek."

Terblanche raised an eyebrow. "Excuse, but what has 'twenty minutes' to do with anything?"

"A proper, sit-down meal's been found in Kritzinger's belly, which means we can work on the basis that Kritz must have eaten no longer than half an hour before he got the chop, okay? So take off the ten minutes it must've taken him to get from his car to the house, even if he bloody ran, and twenty minutes is the maximum traveling time you've got left. That's why we're going to consider *any point* within that circle as his possible starting point—or in other words, where he ate his last curry."

"Bet it was a meat curry."

"Why say that?"

"Maaties would never touch it if it was chicken or fish, but meat curry, yes—especially mutton! It was his most favorite food."

"Oh, ja?"

"You know, he would always ask for it, without even looking at the menu. Hettie wouldn't have curry powder in the house, see? She said it was coolie swill. Next, you'll be telling me he'd had tinned peaches as well."

"Another big favorite of his?"

"Very definitely—pineapple also."

"Well, I'm buggered," said Kramer. "You've just narrowed things down again, hey?"

"But how does that narrow down anything?"

"For the obvious reason that whoever provided him with that meal must have known Kritz pretty well to make sure he had his favorite scoff—it can't have been some stranger, someone unknown to him."

Terblanche, throttling down on the last straight before Jafini, nodded slowly. "Ja, that makes sense—it makes *good* sense," he said. "Now, why didn't I think of that?"

Because CID isn't your bloody department, thought Kramer.

Back at Jafini, Bokkie Maritz claimed to have been through Maatie Kritzinger's desk three times with a fine-comb tooth, as he insisted on calling it, without coming across anything of interest, and so he had turned instead to listing the dead detective sergeant's most recent cases.

"You're sure you could find nothing of interest?" said Kramer, pulling open the desk's top drawer.

"Apart from this," said Maritz, pointing to a row of irregularly shaped pieces of colored plastic arranged along the typewriter's roller. "It makes a Scottie dog you can hang on your key chain—provided you can work out how to fit them back together, hey? I'm going to try again in a minute."

"You do that," Kramer murmured, glancing through a small stack of box camera prints.

They were all of the same four freckle-faced little kids, and in three, true to the tradition of amateur snapshots, the photographer's shadow was visible. In each instance, however, this shadow was that of a woman—which possibly explained why Ma Kritzinger appeared in none of them. This did not explain, however, why a supposedly devoted father had never seemed to be around much.

Nothing else of a personal nature came to light as Kramer went on to search the two other drawers in the desk. This struck him as only slightly odd, given Kritzinger's reputation as work-obsessed. There was certainly plenty of proof of that: time and again, Kramer came across sheets of carbon paper, some used so often they were full of tiny holes that made them look like the black lace that panties were made of.

"Anyway," said Kramer, pushing the last drawer shut, "how's that list of cases going? Can I see it?"

"Actually, I'd like a little more time first to, er, perfect it," said Maritz, hastily putting aside two pieces of the key-ring puzzle. "But what I can tell you already is, old Maaties was one hell of a worker, even if it was almost all the usual Bantu rubbish: faction fights, stabbings, assault, arson, robberies, murder, theft, one rape—"

"'Almost,' you say," interrupted Kramer. "With what exceptions?"

Maritz floundered, sending a pile of dockets cascading off the desk to the floor as he sought the one he was after. "Here's one, Lieutenant!" he said, handing over a slim folder upside down. "But as you'll note, there's nothing special about it either."

Kramer turned the papers the right way up and saw that one Hendrik Willem Schmidt, white adult male aged forty-six, had been charged with the culpable homicide of an Asiatic male who had trespassed on his land. Schmidt, according to his sworn statement, had shot the man with a single round from a .303 rifle in the belief "the coolie after my chickens." According to the statement made by the wife of the deceased, her husband had been approaching the farmyard with a sack in his hand because he had hoped to beg any old clothing the family might have for his children, and that she had witnessed this from where she was standing with the aforesaid offspring. A third statement, sworn by a Bantu farm worker, said that it was true, nobody in his right mind ever came to beg at that house because of its reputation, and so his employer had acted in a reasonable manner entirely in accordance with the known facts at the time, unaware the Asiatic male was new to the area.

"Uh-huh, nothing special," said Kramer, "apart from the date—Christ, man, this thing is *months* old! What's all this I've been hearing about the famous Kritzinger efficiency?"

"Which case is that?" asked Terblanche, who had just entered the CID office to peer over his shoulder. "Ach, the Schmidt one. My guess is he probably thought it'd get watered down to justifiable homicide in court and so he just couldn't be bothered to pursue matters. That Schmidt is always a big pain to deal with, let me tell you."

"Fine," said Kramer. "All set for the briefing yet?"

Terblanche nodded. "I've got the map stuck up on the wall of my office, duly marked as you requested, and both the blokes have just got back from Fynn's Creek, so we're ready and waiting for your instructions."

"Keep up the good work, Bok!" said Kramer, palming two pieces of the Scottie dog puzzle to keep his interest up.

Ash-smeared Sarel Suzman and Jaapie Malan looked ready for a shower, half a dozen Castle lagers each, and ten hours' sleep, which made getting them to concentrate more than Terblanche could apparently handle.

"No, *listen*," he said. "The map shows a total of thirty-three possible addresses within the twenty-minute area at which curry *might* have been served, so we'll now divide it equally and *each* of us will do a group, not go round them all together, hey?"

"I still don't get it," whined Malan, rugby stockings at half-mast and one knee grazed.

"Ach, what don't you get, Jaapie?"

"How we're going to divide this list up."

"Surely, that's obvious. We—"

"But four doesn't go into thirty-three, sir!"

"Oh, yes, it bloody does," intervened Kramer. "I take the first eight addresses, Suzman takes the next eight, Lieutenant Terblanche the next eight, and you, Malan, the last lot. After which we—"

"But that means I get nine to do and—"

"Look, have you forgotten my warning earlier on, hey?"

"What *I* don't get," cut in Suzman, fingering a trouser crease morosely and finding it no longer had its knife edge, "is why Maaties should have eaten out at all last night, when his own home is less than twenty minutes from Fynn's Creek. Are you sure Hettie hasn't changed her mind about this curry business?"

"Absolutely sure," said Terblanche. "I sent Blackspot down to have a word with her kitchen boy just quarter of an hour ago, and he confirms not only that but also that his boss didn't come home again at all after he left at breakfast time."

"Nice thinking, Hans," said Kramer. "But can we get back to—"

"I still don't see the point of all this," grumbled Malan. "If Maaties was at one of these places beforehand, and the people there told him the explosion was going to happen, then they're not going to tell us that, are they? I mean, if they *were* going to, they'd have done so already—not so?"

"No, not necessarily so," said Suzman unexpectedly. "Maybe they're frightened to get involved now, with a proven killer on the loose. It could be a different story once we actually catch him."

"Correct—except for one thing," said Kramer. "We're cops, hey? It's our job to get people to talk when *we* want them to talk, not just when it suits them, so get out there and start twisting a few arms. You follow, Malan? Show them what a real man is like when he does business!"

Suzman and Terblanche exchanged amused glances as Malan, tugging those stockings up, went over to the map and started earnestly jotting down addresses as though now hell-bent on terrorizing half of Northern Zululand.

8

*B*arely two minutes later, Kramer was alone in his Chevrolet, heading out of Jafini back down the Nkosala road to the first address on his share of the list. He'd been warned that half a mile short of Fynn's Creek turnoff, he should start watching out for a sign which came and went rather suddenly, pointing to the way to Moon Acre Farm, the property of a Mr. Bruce Grantham.

Grantham, so Terblanche had explained, was about as close as anyone had ever become to being a friend of Maaties Kritzinger, chiefly on account of the particularly savage bunch of coons living in his farm compound. Kritzinger had spent many hours—even whole days—at Moon Acre, dealing with everything from murder to serious assault, petty theft, and arson. Afterward, he and Grantham would often booze half the night away, talking it all over and coming, more often than not, to a mutually satisfactory arrangement. "Mind you," Terblanche had added, "those boys of his do some really crazy things, even for kaffirs, and I often wonder what goes on up at that big house of his. He sometimes goes so far out of his way to look after their interests you'd think he was a kaffir-lover."

Kramer narrowed his eyes. An oddly familiar figure had come in sight, back turned, walking along the verge of the road ahead of him. Then, an instant later, the inside-out jacket and the pair of tennis shoes registered. Short Arse was on the move, as jaunty as ever, chewing on a length of sugarcane. He took absolutely no notice as the Chevrolet went by, enveloping him in a cloud of red dust that hung in the air for several seconds before disappearing.

By then, Short Arse appeared to have disappeared himself, but the Chev was into the next corner before Kramer knew it, making it too late to verify this fleeting impression without reversing.

"Ach, no, the bastard can't have vanished," Kramer told himself, not dropping speed, "but one thing's for certain: I *have* seen that same walk before somewhere—and it *wasn't* some other coon doing it . . ."

MOON ACRE FARM—KEEP OUT warned the snazzy sign, and forced a quick turn to the left. The cattle grid between the gateposts clattered loudly under the Chev and then came the hiss of a wide drive, laid with gravel.

Listen, Kramer told himself, you've already got too much on your mind to start worrying about this Short Arse nonsense, so just forget all about it until later, when there's time.

But he went on searching obscure corners of his memory for a matching mug shot until the farmhouse came in view, framed by the last rows of sugarcane. Beyond them stretched a lawn so green and neat a carpet would certainly have been cheaper, provided you cut holes in it for the trunks of the English trees scattered everywhere like in a park. Keeping the grass so green were more water sprinklers than Kramer had ever seen off a racetrack, and squatting kaffirs moved in lines, plucking out imperfections with watchmaker's precision and placing them in burlap bags tied to their waists. The huge farmhouse itself was every bit as neat as the lawn, what with freshly painted columns holding up the verandah roof and bright, striped canvas making the deck chairs and other outdoor seating as cheerful as toffee wrappings.

Kramer drove right the way up to the front steps, and switched off his engine after a quick, loud rev to announce his arrival. Two wolves—or rather, two creatures that looked very like wolves—immediately sprang over the verandah railing and hurled themselves at him, snarling with astonishing ferocity. He felled the first with his car door as he stepped out and got the other in the throat with his toe cap, snapping its head back.

"Well, that's buggered the bastards as watchdogs," said a cool voice in English. "I'll have them destroyed."

Kramer looked around. Coming down the front steps was a man in his early sixties, lean as a whip and with a beak-nosed head that seemed a sunburned version of the busts printed on the Roman-Dutch lawbooks at Police College. He wore an elephant-tail bracelet on his right wrist, a fiddly watch filled with little extra dials on his left, and carried a fly whisk. The rest of his appearance was standard English-speaking farmer: short-sleeved, open-necked white shirt; khaki shorts to midthigh; long khaki stockings and tan desert boots.

"Mr. Bruce Grantham?"

"The very same. You're obviously a police officer—poor old Kritzinger's replacement? I'd been hoping it wasn't true, the guff I heard this morning on the bush telegraph."

"Depends on what it was you heard," said Kramer.

"That Maaties had become involved in some god-awful explosion or other at Fynn's Creek, and that young Mrs. Gillets had died with him. He'd been trying to save her, I believe?"

"It certainly looks that way," agreed Kramer. "You'd say that would have been in character?"

"Oh, utterly—brave as a lion! Maaties has saved my bacon more than once, I don't mind admitting, when my laborer wallahs have got a trifle out of hand. But what happened to him exactly? I think I was enough of a chum to be entitled to a few details."

"There really isn't much to add," said Kramer, "which is why I've come to see you, hoping you can come up with some ideas."

"Damned if I can see how, but I'd be delighted to help where I can—er, what did you say your name was, Sergeant?"

"Lieutenant Kramer, Trekkersburg Murder and Robbery Squad."

"A lieutenant! I do beg your pardon. They really are bringing in the big guns! We'll pop up onto the stoop and I'll see to some refreshments. But first, if you'll be good enough to carry on ahead of me, I've a spot of tidying up to do . . ."

Kramer, at ease in a comfortable verandah chair, lit a Lucky and watched Grantham supervise the removal of the two unconscious dogs by four of his kaffir weeding team, all of whom seemed to have difficulty in not grinning as they did so. This was especially true, he noticed, of one with a scarred left arm that hung slack.

"So you see, Lieutenant," said Grantham, raising his gin and tonic, "Maaties and I go back quite a way—a small toast to his memory . . ."

Kramer nodded. "Did this mean you'd count yourself as a friend of the late lamented as well as a customer, hey?"

"I'd most certainly like to think so! Many's the time the pair of us have sat out here in the evening, just chewing the fat."

"How about food?"

"Did we ever dine together, d'you mean? Oh, indeed yes, on any number of agreeable occasions."

"He was a hell of a bloke for a certain dish, wasn't he?"

"I can't remember his having a particular preference for anything," said Grantham, shrugging. "Always ate what was put in front of him. Very partial to a brandy to round things off with, though, now I come to think of it."

"Oh, ja? And when was it he last ate here, Mr. Grantham?"

"Let me see . . . Tuesday last week? We went on until

after midnight. I could always double-check with my cook boy if it's important. Servants tend to remember this sort of thing rather better, God knows why."

"Ach, no, forget it for now. All I wanted was to be able to put a tick on my list of the nights when his movements aren't accounted for. That's our problem, you see—and here I'm trusting you to keep things to yourself—we don't know the reason for Maaties being out and about last night. We've nothing to connect it with."

"And an explosion of all things! How bloody bizarre! What was it? A homemade bomb?"

"Something of the kind."

"Intended for the Gilletses?"

"Must have been, only Lance Gillets had been unexpectedly called away. Talking of Tuesday, though, I don't remember Maaties' list of recent cases saying anything about trouble here at Moon Acre last week . . ."

"It wouldn't," said Grantham, taking Kramer's empty glass to refill it with another bottle of Castle lager. "A purely social call on his part. If you ask me, he was simply escaping that frightful, neurotic wife of his. Poor chap seemed a bit down."

"In what way?"

"Well, our conversations are usually fairly lively and wide-ranging—*were*, I should say—and touch on many topics of local interest. For once, Maaties hadn't much to say for himself, and I was left scraping the barrel a bit. Mark you, he cheered up a fraction when I told him about my little clash with the Parks Board and that jumped-up box wallah they've brought in to boost, as they call it, the tourist trade in these parts. Sent *him* packing, by Christ! I'm having nobody bugger about with my cane fields."

"Ta," said Kramer, taking his refilled glass and having a sip from it. "That sounds interesting."

"Far from it: a lot of bureaucratic balls. That's also my land you see, down there between Nkosala road and this ridiculous game reserve they're creating, and they wanted to do something about widening the track leading through. Only it's my road, a private road, and I'm damned if I'm prepared to lose two feet off either side for improvements out of sheer public spiritedness. Have you any idea how much land those two strips would add up to in *acres?* So I simply named my figure, watched him go an ungodly green, and that was the end of the bastard. Maaties had a damned good laugh over that, and so did I. He said he must take a look at the reserve sometime, now his curiosity had been aroused in it—Good God, something's just struck me . . . !"

"Fire away," invited Kramer. "What is it?"

"There was a point, toward the end of the evening," said Grantham, glancing at that cockpit of a watch of his, "when dear old Maaties, frightfully pissed by then, started to tell me something he didn't finish. He was obviously upset by it, but started getting bolshy when I couldn't follow his drift and said never mind, I was too damned drunk to understand and we'd best change the subject. I said, 'The hell with you, Kritzinger!'—and said I'd show him which of us was too damned drunk by thrashing him at snooker. I think we'd reached the third frame when he put up his hands, was sick into a spittoon, and toddled off home." Grantham paused, shook his head, and gave a three-gins sigh. "Last time I ever saw the poor sod."

Kramer frowned, slightly confused. "So you'd left here and driven to some hotel somewhere?" he said. "At approximately what time did this—"

"Hotel? What hotel? Don't quite follow . . ."

"You know, where they had the snooker table, hey?"

Grantham laughed. "What a sheltered life you've led in the Orange Free State, Lieutenant," he said. "I've a full-size table of my own in the billiards room immediately behind you, should you ever feel up to a frame!"

Now that, thought Kramer, is what you really call posh, and it called to mind the jokes he'd heard told about Natal farmers driving Rolls-Royces because the glass partition behind the driver stopped livestock breathing down your neck on the way to market. He was also beginning to see why Maaties Kritzinger had felt so attracted to Grantham's company, having only a detective sergeant's pay and a large family to provide for, yet a chance here to share in the good life whenever he fancied it. What else was on offer at Moon Acre, he wondered——and what did Grantham himself get out of this unusual liaison of the cop and the sugar baron? Some bending of the law, when it came to his labor force, that much was already apparent . . . But was that all? And what was it about Grantham's coons that they caused so much mayhem?

"Lieutenant?" prompted Grantham. "We appear to have become sidetracked . . ."

"Maaties was getting 'bolshy,' you said, because you couldn't follow what he was talking about."

"Well, I'm damned if anyone could have made sense of it, and that's why, until now, I'd dismissed the whole thing as a bit of drunken nonsense. Thing was, Maaties muttered something about some native whose name I didn't catch and then started getting worked up over something he kept saying in Zulu. I've had a fair knowledge of the lingo myself, but the best I could make of it was: *the song dog*. I'd just asked him whether this was a flowery sort of reference to the jackal, with its well-known weakness for howling at the moon, when he lost his temper with me, silly sod, and now we'll never know. I'd like to have, though, because as fearless as he was, this brute had very definitely put the wind up the poor fellow."

Hell, I'm going to be dreaming bloody dogs tonight, thought Kramer.

9

The police station at Jafini looked a lot better after dark, almost welcoming, in the way its unshaded bulbs thinned the thick surrounding hedge of Christthorn, filling it with speckles of bright light.

Terblanche must have heard the Chevrolet, which had somehow lost part of its exhaust pipe, approaching from quite a distance, for he was there to meet it, hands on hips and his mouth pursed tight, more than ever a picture of utter fatigue.

"I must get that exhaust fixed for you in the morning, Tromp," he said. "You can't go sneaking up on bad guys with that!"

"Ja, it's a bit obvious," agreed Kramer, climbing out. "The last place I visited, they thought I'd come to bloody bulldozer the house."

"Oh, ja, that'd be those poor white squatters awaiting eviction down on the edge of Ma Murdoch's place—what is their name again?"

"Bothma. Man, you only had to take one look at their

cooking arrangements to know Kritzinger never ate there! Christ, he'd have been dead *long* before midnight."

Terblanche gave a weary chuckle. "We shouldn't really make jokes," he said, "but, to be honest, I thought something very similar a couple of times myself. Listen, I've got bad news for you. I came up with nothing from my eight, and the same goes for the others; both Malan and Suzman scored a duck. Apart, that is, from one family who told Malan they are sure they saw his car pass by at about seven-thirty last night."

"They did? Whereabouts was this?"

"It's easier if I show you on the map . . ."

As they started walking up the path to the police station, Kramer asked: "Ever heard of something called the song dog, Hans?"

"Sorry?"

"The song dog."

"Meaning a jackal or something?"

"No, it appears not."

Terblanche turned to him. "Has someone been pulling your leg?" he asked.

"Hmmmm, I beginning to wonder about that myself," said Kramer. "This place has gone bloody quiet!"

"Oh, I hope you don't mind, but I said to the others they could get off home once I'd heard they had nothing to report. They'd been on their feet for more than—"

"Fine," said Kramer, glancing into the white CID office. "The same went for Bokkie Maritz?"

"No, Bok had already gone by the time I got back. Left a note to say he'd found out where I fixed you two up with rooms and that he didn't want to miss supper there."

"Uh-huh."

"What about you, Tromp?" asked Terblanche, opening the door to his office. "Any luck with your eight addresses?"

"Not really," said Kramer. "Apart from getting a bit more background on this thing Kritzinger had going with Grantham. I've a feeling that another visit to Moon Acre could produce a few interesting details about both of them, but I doubt how relevant they'd be to the case. Now, show me this spot on the map and then get yourself off home—you're so buggered you're walking like a bloody hippo with a hernia."

"Here's where our only witnesses live," said Terblanche, positioning a grimy forefinger on the wall map. "As you see, their homestead isn't anywhere special, apart from being near the junction of where all these cane-lorry tracks go through the fields, and not far from the little railway line which carries cane, too. Maaties was traveling south in this direction, they say, and fast."

"Why the hell should he being doing that?"

"Well, while I was waiting for you, I stood and stared at the map for a while," said Terblanche, "asking myself the same question. The only sense I could make of it was that he had been over here, on the Mabata road, and had decided to take a shortcut right over to the other properly made road down here, connecting us with Muilberg."

"At about what time was this, did you say?"

"Approximately seven-thirty."

Kramer rubbed the stubble on his chin. "Kritz could also have been going to meet someone down any of these tracks that branch off into the cane," he said. "It grows high, so it would have hidden them from the road, and there'd be no kaffirs still out working to see them . . ."

"That's true," agreed Terblanche. "You couldn't wish for better countryside—a big crisscross maze."

"This investigation doesn't get any easier, does it?" remarked Kramer. "But, look, it's high time you called it a day, Hans. In fact, I'll even drive you home, because I want to borrow your Land-Rover and take another look at Fynn's Creek."

"*Tonight?* Out of the question, Tromp! Not only have you also done enough for one day, but the lady wife has prepared a very special meal of welcome just for you, and—"

"Hell, really? A special meal for me? You mean, someone has tipped you off I'm vegetarian?"

"Vege—" echoed Terblanche, the acute dismay in his face as plain as custard pie. "Ach, look, if you'd really rather not come round tonight, that's okay, hey? Louise will surely understand, and we can have—er, the um, pumpkin fritters another time, never worry!"

"On second thoughts, seeing she's gone to . . ."

"No, no man! Here are my Land-Rover keys—don't even bother to drive me round! I'll get the van boy to take me!"

And Terblanche was already half out of his office, when he hurried back to scribble quickly on a scrap of paper. "Er, that's the widow woman's name and address where you room is, okay?"

"Perfect," said Kramer.

Fynn's Creek also looked different after dark, but hardly welcoming. Instead, it lay bleak and forbidding, making it inevitable that Kramer should ponder the character of Annika Gillets, who had felt sufficiently undaunted by it to send her kitchen boy off on an all-night drinking spree, leaving herself entirely on her own out there. Not many white women that he knew would do that, not unless they lived in bloody great castles with fiery dragons to guard them against the terrifying Black Knight. Granted, Mrs. Gillets had boasted crocodiles in her moat, so to speak, but her house, as amply demonstrated, had rated little better than that built by the first little pig, the huff-and-puff bugger.

"It was one hell of a huff-and-puff, though," Kramer reminded himself, picking his way through the outer ring of debris by moonlight. "Where's the bloody twenty-four-hour guard this place is meant to have?"

Then he heard a rumbling laugh, and looked inland beyond the razed house to where he recalled having seen the cook boy's hut. There, two figures sat crouched over a small fire, obviously the kitchen boy and the errant Bantu constable, passing a beer pot back and forth between them and having a fine old time of it. Well, that lazy bloody cop was definitely in for a shock, Kramer decided, and began moving silently toward them.

That was a mistake, perhaps, for the move brought with it a nasty shock of its own. Suddenly, what Kramer had taken to be just a heap of roof thatch, a yard or so to his right, heaved itself up on short, bent legs, gave a hissing cough, and propelled its armor-plated length with astonishing swiftness toward the estuary, followed by five or six others. These dark shapes plunged heavily into the water, one after another, with a sound like a false start at a swimming contest for paralytic drunks.

"Bastards!" exploded Kramer.

Then came his second shock, when a deep Zulu voice, right at his elbow, said: "Bantu Constable Cassius Mabeni reporting, my boss!"

"Jesus!" said Kramer, turning. "Where the hell did you spring from?"

"By the beach, my boss. Boss Terblanche say I must be very strict and let no fishing men come by that side—I was looking carefully-carefully for them, but there are no men present, my boss."

"Then who was that sitting over there a second ago with the . . ." said Kramer, turning back toward the hut. "Shit, now there's no one! What exactly is going on around here?"

"Cook boy jump in the bush, my boss!" said Mabeni, with a happy laugh. "You give him big-big fright! But must not worry, my boss, soon he come out again."

"But who was that with him, hey?"

"Elifasi Ndhlovu, my boss, he come to give money from cook boy's uncle over by Jafini. I think the boss give him such a big fright he run away for good!"

"Oh, ja? What money was this that he brought?"

"Cook boy money he forget last night by big beer drink, my boss. Forty-two cents, my boss, and the uncle is asking Ndhlovu to return it to cook boy."

"This messenger bugger, he's known to you personally?"

"*Yebo*, I have seen him many times in Jafini, my boss. A good man, no trouble."

"Okay, fine, er—what did you say you were called?"

"Cassius—"

"What sort of bloody name is that, hey?"

"A new name, my boss!" Mabeni said proudly, puffing out

his chest. "Boss Terblanche give it to Mabeni when he is reading newspaper about big-big boxing *ndoda* Cassius Clay Tops Hivvyweight Emerican, my boss!"

"That's a hell of a lot of names for one kaffir," observed Kramer, starting toward the kitchen boy's hut. "Where does this Cassius do his boxing—up in Johannesburg?"

"*Ngasi,* my boss, I do not know," admitted Mabeni, as he took up a respectful position, marching one pace to the rear.

The kitchen boy turned out to have fled no farther than the farthest corner of his hut. He emerged again on all fours, peering first around the doorjamb, and gave a nervous laugh.

"Tell the stupid bastard to tuck his tail in and stand up like a man," Kramer ordered Mabeni.

"The translation was swift; so swift, Kramer had a shrewd idea not everything he'd just said had been repeated.

"Now, just so he knows that this is official, ask him for his full name, age, address, pass book, the usual . . ."

Mabeni made a start on this, and reported back: "The true-true first name of this man has many tongue-clicks, my boss, but his mission name is Moses, Moses Khumalo."

Kramer nodded. "Moses, hey? Then tell Moses I want to know where his friend is."

"Elifasi has run far away," Mabeni translated. "He run so fast, he will soon-soon be back in Jafini by now, my boss, this man say."

"Oh, ja? So Moses thinks he's truly a prophet, does he?"

The cook listened to the translation and then gave a tipsy guffaw, slapping his thigh, before letting fly a string of long, happy sentences, his bright eyes on Kramer.

"He is full of joy," Mabeni told Kramer, "because he did not know there was such a truly honest man as his uncle, who returned to him money he was so very drunk he had no knowledge he had dropped by the ground, my boss. Do I tell him to 'Shut up, kaffir'?"

"No, I want to hear from him what went on here at this house yesterday."

Mabeni nodded and began a tedious interrogation, not

helped by the subject's lack of sobriety, and passed on to Kramer the main elements of the verbal statement as they slowly emerged. At least, thought Kramer, he had the consolation of that old saying "*In vino veritas,*" or whatever the proper bloody French for it was.

Then, when the great, long outpouring finally came to an end, Kramer rearranged it in chronological order, threw out the total irrelevancies, and decided he had more than justified his intuitive urge to visit Fynn's Creek by moonlight.

"You've done well," he told Mabeni. "Maybe tomorrow I will find another job for you to do—okay?"

"*Yebo, nkosi!*" said Mabeni, beaming, his chest puffed right out. Then he added, sounding disappointed, "The boss is going now, boss?"

"Too bloody right, this boss is going! Hell, I'm totally shagged out—in all but the nicest sense."

How very true, Kramer thought, as he headed for Ter-blanche's Land-Rover, Mabeni following at his heels. Dear God, he could really do with a woman now, to wipe all these conundrums from his mind, and fill him with peace and a sense of well-being—just as that silent young nurse in the linen room had once done.

Then it happened a second time. Up rose a huge crocodile, a few feet in front of Kramer, and off it went with a great lashing of its tail toward the estuary, followed by several others.

"They're back *already*?" he said.

"Always come straight-straight back, my boss!" responded Mabeni, with an oddly indulgent chuckle. "You give them big-big fright, they all run quick-quick, they forget quick-quick!—they come back. When you are piccanin, your *baba* teaches you such things—it is very dangerous for small piccanin to play by river, my boss. My *baba* he tells me this many, many times."

"Hmmmm . . ." said Kramer, staring at Mabeni. "You know, there's something about this case that doesn't exactly make sense any more . . ."

"My boss?"

"Ach, it's bound to hit me sooner or later, hey?" said Kramer, shrugging.

The rough track back through the sugarcane to the Nkosala road seemed to go on and on forever, and it all looked the same—even the bit where those crazy workers of Grantham's had stood so still, razor-sharp cane knives raised in their hands.

So, to divert himself, Kramer went over in his mind the statement made by the Gilletses' kitchen boy, savoring its undoubted significance.

According to Moses, the previous, fateful day had begun with his white master working on his Parks Board Land-Rover, which was to be seen still standing where he'd left it, near the two petrol drums and well clear of the blast area. Then, at roughly ten-thirty, one of the Parks Board's Piper Cub spotter planes had landed on the beach, and the pilot had told Gillets that he was wanted to help with a rhino capture—and to bring an overnight bag, as a second rhino was possibly scheduled for the next day. Moses had packed this bag for him and carried it for him out to the small plane, while the master took leave of the young madam. Like all Zulus of his generation, Moses believed that kissing was something people should do unobserved, it being an act no less intimate than intercourse.

Half an hour or so later, while Moses was serving the young madam her morning tea, a car had appeared, coming slowly down the track; at the wheel was a white detective known to Moses as Isipikili, the Nail. The detective had climbed from his car to stand looking around, until he had been called over by the madam, who ordered that a second cup be brought for him.

On the kitchen boy's own admission, his knowledge of Afrikaans was very slight, but Moses claimed he'd understood enough of the subsequent conversation to know that the detective had begun by explaining he had driven down to Fynn's Creek simply to have a look at the new game reserve. For her part, the young madam had asked after this name and that, as though catching up on news of different people she knew. There had been laughter at first between the two whites, then his madam had said something very softly that made the detective look most surprised. It was at this point that the kitchen boy had been instructed to leave the veran-dah, where he had been putting the jam on their scones for them, and to go and collect driftwood for a barbecue planned for the weekend. Nevertheless, he had kept an eye on the two whites, in case they wanted something brought to them, by peering at them over the sand dunes. They had continued a serious conversation for some time—or at least, this was how it had looked from a distance. All the way through, his madam and the detective had remained facing one another, the way people do when intent on what is passing between them. Finally, the detective had glanced at his watch, nodded, and left.

When next the kitchen boy encountered his madam, her whole demeanor had seemed different, as though some great weight had been lifted from her shoulders. At lunch, she had not picked at her food, wasting most of it as usual, but had eaten well, greatly pleasing him. She had also complimented him on his cooking, and told him that, as a reward, she was giving him the night off to get drunk with his uncle at Jafini. When the kitchen boy hesitated, unsure what the master would think of his leaving the property and her alone, the young madam had said he was being "a fool of a kaffir," pointing out that the master need never know, and had later insisted that Moses go off duty at five, reassured by her that she would make herself a light snack for her supper—some cheese on toast, maybe, or she could warm up something.

"Oh, ja, Maaties," murmured Kramer, reaching the Nko-sala road. "So far, so good, but what *was* the great weight that you lifted from 'little Annika's' shoulders, making her seem a changed woman? It sounds to me very like she let you share in some dark secret and you promised to do something about it! Furthermore, what made you return to Fynn's Creek at midnight? Did someone else, over a curry supper at which you discussed this conversation, suddenly give you a fresh insight into what Annika had told you, sending you hurtling out there? Uh-huh, it certainly sounds that way . . ."

Kramer was perfectly aware that talking to himself could be construed as the slippery slope to raving insanity, but what else was a man to do in bloody Natal, for Christ's sake, if he felt the need of intelligent conversation?

Still turning over the events of the day, and kicking himself for ridiculous oversights—he should, for example, have remembered to ask Moses if he knew how the young madam had got those bruises on her upper arm—Kramer continued his musings. Not simply all the way back to Jafini, but right to the address where, if memory served him correctly, Terblanche had rented him a room for his stay in Jafini.

Still preoccupied, he was barely aware of taking his suitcase from the Land-Rover, and quite without thinking, thumped loudly on the freshly painted front door of 23 Jacaranda Avenue as though leading a police raid.

A fragrant, dressing-gowned silhouette opened up and scolded: "Shhhhhhh, you'll wake the whole neighborhood!"

"Sorry, lady," muttered Kramer, belatedly checking the address on the scrap of paper Terblanche had given him. "But you are the Widow Fourie, hey?"

"For your sake, I certainly hope so," she said.

10

Kramer slept badly that first night in Jafini.

He had several dreams that woke him with a start, and then, once awake, he was unable to go straight back to sleep again, having so much pressing on his mind. None of the dreams had dogs in them, which was something. The most disturbing dream of all, however, kept repeating itself: in it, a slight, shadowy figure walked jauntily down a twisting road, and then turned to shout something he couldn't quite catch.

After waking, and between attempts to get his plans for the day ahead in order, Kramer kept going over again and again his first hour in his new lodgings, during which the Widow Fourie had made him a light supper of scrambled eggs. She had said hardly a word as she moved about that small kitchen, but had appeared content with his silence as he'd sat at the table, drinking her in; she was a heady peach brandy, matured to bloody perfection.

Bullshit, Kramer had admonished himself, she's simply a big blonde with a good figure—just as Terblanche had described her. Moreover, Kramer had added, just remember,

Tromp, that the only other female you've been near *in a whole month* was lying around in the nude but in about four hundred pieces, old son.

All of which went by the board when, by accident, the Widow Fourie brushed the back of his hand as she set his plate down, making her drop it with a thud in front of him, and sending a shock through Kramer as decided as any cranked in an interview room. Immediately, she had turned, listened with her head tipped, and then disappeared down the corridor.

Left alone in the kitchen, he tried to review the events of his day, but couldn't, not for the life of him.

"I heard a noise and thought one of my kids had fallen out of bed," said the Widow Fourie, on her return. "But it wasn't that. It was your colleague, going through to gargle in the bathroom. He says he's developed a really bad sore throat."

"If it shuts the stupid bastard up for a change, who are we to complain?"

"That's not very nice!"

Kramer shrugged. "Hans Terblanche tells me that you've got kids—how many?"

"Three boys and a girl."

"Really? Exactly the same number as—" And there he bit his tongue, dismayed by his oversight.

But the Widow Fourie simply nodded. "Ja, the same as Maaties' widow," she said. "Hettie's been a lot in my thoughts today, poor woman, because losing your man suddenly can be such a terrible shock you don't think you'll ever survive it."

"You obviously knew Maaties, then?"'

"Hard not to, in a place this size, and besides, he was nearly as kind as Hans after Pik had his accident. I've always been meaning to thank him properly some day, but now it's too late. Isn't that ever the way?"

"I suppose so," said Kramer, having rarely had occasion to feel grateful to anyone. "You know something? Everyone keeps telling me Maaties was 'one of the best'—maybe he was, but when people say things like that it always worries me."

"I have the same problem," admitted the Widow Fourie, taking his dirty plate over to the sink. "I need to see some sin in a person before I can relax!"

Kramer smiled. "What sins could you see in Maaties?"

The Widow Fourie began washing up. "Practically all of them, I suppose!" she said. "He was very human."

"What else?"

She shrugged. "A loner, strong, a man who went his own way in this world. But there was also a little kid inside there who couldn't stand seeing tears, you know, and would do almost anything to help stop them—making him quite a mix-up!"

"Could that have led to his death, do you think?" asked Kramer.

"In what way?" asked the Widow Fourie, looking round.

"Ach, let's say somebody told Maaties a sob story. That she alleged, for instance, her man was beating her."

"Ja, that would probably make him want to rush to the rescue. You must mean Annika Gillets, I take it?"

"Why say that?"

"Ach, rumors," said the Widow Fourie, "about Lance and what he's prepared to do to people. He has a terrible temper, you know, and really runs amuck when he's upset. Even my maid knows that the worst kaffirs won't go anywhere near where he lives, he's given it too much of a reputation. Just after they first moved in, he caught a burglar on his front steps, tied him with rope to the back of his Land-Rover, and towed him all the way to Moon Acre, where he came from. My maid says that kaffir's never been seen since."

"Hmmm," said Kramer. "Then perhaps it's no surprise Annika didn't seem afraid to stay out there overnight on her own, especially as his Land-Rover was still parked there, making it look like he was at home."

"She'd have felt safe as houses! But where was he, hey?"

"He'd been picked up by plane earlier in the day to go

catching rhino. What else did these rumors say? That he was knocking Annika about?"

The Widow Fourie nodded. "Before they were moved to Fynn's Creek, they were up at the main rest camp. We had one of the other rangers' wives in with amebic dysentery—I work at the hospital—and she let slip there'd been trouble based on Lance suspecting Annika of flirting with guests. She often wore long sleeves on boiling hot days, as though she was hiding marks or something. In fact, the *real* rumor is that they got moved to Fynn's Creek to keep her out of trouble, and if this didn't work, Lance was facing the sack from the Parks Board."

"Had she kept out of trouble, do you know?" asked Kramer.

"I don't see what option she had," said the Widow Fourie. "There haven't been any guests yet at Fynn's—"

"Ja, but blokes must come fishing along the beach—and what if I told you her body had bruises on the left shoulder?"

"Interesting," said the Widow Fourie, sitting down on a stool. "Although, personally, I'm still not a hundred percent convinced she was as bad as some make out. It could all have been just in Lance's mind, couldn't it?"

"That we'll have to try and find out," said Kramer. "Okay if I ask a few more questions? This is the first time today I've started to get somewhere, hey?"

The Widow Fourie glanced up at the kitchen clock. "Just five minutes more," she said, "or I'll feel a total wreck at work in the morning!"

"Any idea how the two of them got together in the first place?"

"Oh, that," she said, getting up and going back to the sink. "The story is, Lance met Annika when she was hitchhiking to Eshowe—she was always doing mad things like that!—and the pair of them finished up instead two hundred miles away in Durban that night, going to a show and getting drunk on the beachfront. Her father nearly went berserk when she got back next day—he thought kaffirs must've raped her on the road and thrown her in the sugarcane—and went straight to

Lance's boss, wanting him sacked. But Lance turns up at the camp in the game reserve, tells his boss it's okay, it was just a little engagement party, and in no time at all they're married! The whole district was amazed because of her reputation and the fact this Lance bloke comes from a good Durban family—his pa's a posh lawyer and his ma was an Oppenberg. I know Hans tried to stop the marriage. He said he'd only met Lance the once, but he wasn't good enough for Annika; that he was a spoiled, private-school kid with a mean streak in him."

"Terblanche always seems very quick to rise to Annika's defense," said Kramer, lighting a Lucky. "Think there could have been something on the go between those two?"

The Widow Fourie gave a surprised laugh. "That's like asking if I think Santa does rude things to little kids!" she said.

Kramer smiled. "What's got me puzzled," he said, "is why Annika didn't take the advice of an old family friend— why she allowed herself to become entangled with such a well-established little bastard."

"You get people like that," said the Widow Fourie, with a shrug. "I don't know whether it's the excitement, the risk, or what, but it could also be they want someone else to take charge of them, someone who will not put up with promiscuity, say. She was wild, of that there is no doubt, and maybe it scared her, this wildness, because she knew she couldn't properly control it."

"Man," Kramer said, with a laugh, "have you noticed the irony? What sort of husband did this wild creature choose to look after her?"

"A game ranger!" said the Widow Fourie, laughing too, as she turned from rinsing the sink. "No, I'd never thought of that before . . ."

Their smiles locked, lingered, then faded together.

"Look at the time!" said the Widow Fourie, snatching up a tea towel to dry her hands, turning from him. "I don't know what I think I'm doing still up at this hour."

"Suggesting a few answers that could go a long way to

solve a mystery," said Kramer, rising from his chair. "If there was still trouble between Annika and Lance, and it was now threatening his whole livelihood, a man could find in that a motive for murder—especially a violent man, who might have reasons of his own not to want evidence given in the divorce court."

"But," said the Widow Fourie, with a final glance at the clock, "although I can see what you're getting at, Lance Gillets must have been miles away when the whatsit went off."

"Which is surely the whole point of using a timing device," said Kramer. "It allows the killer to get to hell and gone from the scene, and concoct himself a cast-iron alibi."

"You mean it was a *time bomb* that went off last night?"

"No proof as yet, but ja, I expect that to be confirmed tomorrow."

"Tomorrow is today," said the Widow Fourie very firmly, moving to the passage doorway, "and I've an early start with masses of bed linen to check at the hospital, so—"

"You do *what* there?"

"Ach, you know, supervise the linen rooms, count the pillows—all of that. Let me see, is there anything else you need? I've put a towel in your bedroom and the maid'll give you breakfast in the morning."

"N-no, I'm fine, thanks!"

"Good," said the Widow Fourie, adding a quick, impersonal smile. "Sleep well, hey?"

"That wasn't you singing in the shower was it, Lieutenant?" Bokkie Maritz croaked hoarsely, peering into Kramer's room at seven-thirty the next morning.

"Me? Sing? That'll be the day, Bok! How goes it?"

"I've got a sore throat you wouldn't believe," said Maritz, clutching his pajama collar even more tightly. "Also, my forehead is hotter than—"

"Straight back to bed for you!" said Kramer.

"Ach, no, I can struggle on, hey?"

"Bullshit, man! I need you well again quick. You get

yourself under a pile of blankets, sweat it out, and I'll get the DS to come and see you, give you some stuff."

"Er, I'm not too happy about seeing a doctor I don't know," said Maritz.

"Doc Mackenzie's one hell of a good bloke, Bok—all the cops around here swear by him."

"Oh, ja?"

"You couldn't be in better hands," said Kramer, and went off to breakfast, whistling.

"I'm Piet," said a small boy seated at a table on the back verandah, eating toast and marmalade. "What's your name?"

"Tromp," said Kramer, sitting down opposite him. "And in answer to your next question, I was four hundred and ninety-one last birthday."

"I'm six *and* a half," said Piet.

"Uh-huh. Where're your brothers and sisters?"

"They've gone. Ma's taken them to the hospital to play with the other little kids in the *nursery*."

"Real baby stuff, huh?"

Piet nodded. "I'm the man of the family," he said. "Ma told me."

"So how will you spend your day? Mending tractors or doing some accounts?"

"First," said Piet, "I'm going to feed my animals." He paused while the maid placed a plate of fried eggs and bacon in front of Kramer, and then said, "All right if I have your bacon fat?"

"Of course."

"Ta," said Piet. "Ma's already given me hers, so I've got quite a lot."

"What sort of pets eat bacon, hey?"

"Animals, not *pets*," said Piet, using the same note of scorn he had reserved for the word *nursery*. "Dingaan the iguana is my biggest. Smallest, I've got some cane mice, and in between all sorts: rabbits, guinea pigs, a tortoise, and three mole snakes. Dingaan's the one who likes the bacon."

"I had a pig once," said Kramer. "He hated bacon."

"But they usually eat anything!" exclaimed Piet in some

surprise. Then he laughed. "You tried to trick me," he said, getting down from his chair to go out into the backyard. "Or was it a joke?"

"My third of the day," confirmed Kramer.

And his mood was still uncommonly good when he drained his coffee cup, lit a Lucky, and decided to wander out and see how Dingaan was enjoying his tidbits.

Piet was standing under an avocado tree that gave shade to a crudely built hutch of sorts in the center of a chicken-wire enclosure.

"Where's Dingaan?" Kramer asked.

"Hiding," said Piet. "Watch . . ."

He tossed a morsel of bacon fat into the enclosure, there was a pause, and then out from under the hutch came an iguana, its little bent legs scurrying beneath a long, tail-lashing body. In a trice, the bacon had been snapped up, and the iguana was back under cover again.

"Man, that was quick!" said Kramer. "Have you ever timed it?"

Piet shook his head. "I haven't got a watch," he said. "But you couldn't time it anyway, Dingaan's too quick once there's meat near him."

"Hmmm," said Kramer.

"You want a turn feeding him?"

"Er, no, I'd best be getting to work," said Kramer. "But thanks, hey? See you later . . ."

" 'Bye, Tromp," said Piet, carefully selecting the next piece of fat.

Kramer walked away with a smile that died in seconds. He still couldn't put a finger on it, but something was wrong, very wrong, in the way he was seeing things—and now somehow young Piet had just drawn his attention to this.

11

*A*n overnight shower had done for Jafini, in Kramer's
opinion, what embalming did for a corpse. The
dead-end dump didn't look any less dead, but at least
its coloring had much improved, now all the dust had been
washed off; the faint odor of decay had gone too, swept down
the storm drains.

Two vehicles attracted his attention the instant he turned
into the main street. He saw that his Chevrolet was already at
the garage, having its damaged exhaust pipe repaired, thanks
no doubt to Hans Terblanche. He also saw Grantham at the
wheel of a diesel Mercedes pickup, and that he had one of his
mad, bad kaffirs seated right beside him in the cab, and not
on the back among the cornmeal sacks, where he properly
belonged. Didn't the man know that the only whites and
blacks who ever rode together were cops? Was he really so
thick, or just trying to be bloody provocative?

"Lovely day, Lieutenant!" Grantham shouted across, as
they passed, adding something Kramer missed.

He'd been distracted that same instant by a glimpse of an
inside-out jacket, vanishing into the Bombay Emporium.

"Short Arse!" he said to himself, gunning the Land-Rover over to the curb, ready for another hard look at the bastard when he came out. But the coon who emerged six long minutes later in an inside-out jacket was elderly, rather stooped, grinning idiotically, and had the fast shuffle of an advanced syphilitic.

"Shit," said Kramer, and drove on.

He parked round the back of the police station and used the rear entrance to reach Terblanche's office.

"Morning, Tromp!" said the station commander, pouring the stale water from his carafe out of the window. "Guess what—we've got the army with us!"

"So that's it," said Kramer. "You've been given until two hundred hours to clean up, or face a court-martial, hey?"

Terblanche looked quite hurt. "I *always* do a tidy when I get a moment," he said. "Besides, Field Cornet Dorf hasn't been in here yet. He's been down at Fynn's Creek since first light with Jaapie Malan, getting his bearings. Oh, ja, he's not one to stand twiddling his thumbs, this explosives expert of ours—he arrived about four, straight from some sabotage."

"Good," said Kramer. "This could speed up things, now I've a few ideas to work on."

"You have?" said Terblanche. "I thought you were looking a bit more cheerful this morning! Did you discover something new at Fynn's Creek last night?"

"I learned that Kritz was there yesterday afternoon and had a long, intimate chat with the female deceased which seemed to lift a big weight off her shoulders."

Terblanche frowned. "Just him and little Annika?" he said. "An *intimate* chat? This is news to me. I didn't know that he was—"

"Ach, no, I think it happened quite by chance," said Kramer. "Grantham told me he'd suggested to Kritz that he ought to take a look at the reserve some day, and from what the kitchen boy states, it sounds to me as if Kritz simply pitched up there. As for intimate, he wasn't to know Lance wasn't also going to be there—not with his Parks Board Land-Rover parked in full view."

"Ja, ja, I get you," said Terblanche, losing some of his troubled look. "But what was this long chat about?"

"Here, read my notes of the interview with the cook boy," Kramer invited him, "and then you'll know as much as I do about it."

Terblanche worked his way ponderously through the three pages. He had just finished, and was looking up to say something, when there came a rap at the door and Jaapie Malan poked his unlovely head round the jamb.

"Morning, Lieutenant!" he said. "Morning, sir! I've got the army bloke waiting to speak to you about the—"

"Ach, send him in, man," said Terblanche. "Send him in."

Field Cornet Sybrand Dorf of the South African Defence Force looked like an experiment carried out by a mad zookeeper. He had the head of a bat-eared fox, shoulders like a gnu, and his long, spindly legs gave him the gait of a giraffe. His camouflage fatigues did nothing to hide any of this, but at least his army boots had a reassuring, unhooflike high shine to them.

"Let me say at the start," Terblanche told him, after the introductions and handshaking were over, "that we're both impressed, very impressed by your application to duty— you've certainly wasted no time, hey?"

"Just obeying orders, sir."

"Oh, ja?"

"Troubled times, sir. Devices being detonated all over, political. Must take priority, sir, but we do our best, sir."

"So you've ruled out this one being political?" asked Terblanche. "Only one of my blokes did have a theory that a saboteur from a sub could've—"

"Ruled out, totally, sir. Excessive-quantity explosives, sir. Sufficient, sir, for three acts of terrorism against the state, sir, and terrorists well trained, sir, but explosives in short supply.

Other signs of amateurism, too, sir. Civilian, definitely, doubts none, sir."

"Oh, ja?" said Kramer. "Exactly how much dynamite are we talking about here?"

"Must have been seven sticks, minimum, sir," said Dorf. "In all probability, blasting dynamite, plain, same as road and dam builders use. I need to request extra assistance to make a proper search for the wrapper fragments and other items."

"Of course," said Terblanche. "You can have any help you want, hey? Only what 'other items' are you searching for?"

"Source of primary detonation, sir, timing mechanism, batteries, wires, and so forth."

"Timing mechanism?" echoed Terblanche. "So you have reason to believe that this *was* a time bomb?"

Dorf looked slightly bemused for an instant. "Naturally, sir. Is not that the whole point of using explosives?"

"In what way?"

"Well," said Dorf, shooting Kramer a glance, "an explosive charge, detonated by timing device, allows the perpetrator to be removed from the scene of the crime at the time it is actually committed, yet rest assured the deed is done."

"And so?"

"Alibi, cast-iron, sir, can be concocted."

"But why would someone miles away be asked for his alibi in the first place, hey?" said Terblanche.

"Ah," said Dorf. "That's what they hope people will think. But there is invariably some known connection with the target, sir. Case of political act: known activist and state target. Case of civilian act: known associate and deceased target—business partner, spouse, established enemies, sir."

"Spouse?" said Terblanche, his fists bunching.

"Themes, variations on, sir," replied Dorf.

"Seems to me," said Kramer, "the only bloody alibi with any relevance is the one pertaining to when the bomb was *placed* and not when it was set to go off, hey?"

"Very true, sir," admitted Dorf. "Hence all the more important, sir, to establish nature of device, timing, sir. In case of clock, ordinary alarm, for instance, maximum delay time equals one full rotation of the hands, hours twelve, sir."

"And so," said Kramer, "knowing that the blast went off at ten past midnight, the earliest the bomb could have been positioned—if an alarm clock was used—would have had to be just after midday on Monday?"

"Correct, sir. Alarm clock, ordinary, can be adapted to allow for greater delay, but would call for expertise not reflected in use of excessive quantity of explosive material, sir."

"Uh-huh, so the chances are we're looking for someone who was at Fynn's Creek within those twelve hours before the explosion?"

"Everything points that way, sir," agreed Dorf.

"Then our first job is to check on the movements of any known—er, associate?"

"Exactly, sir, pending a fuller—"

"Listen, man," said Kramer, rising from his seat on the edge of the desk, "I know you're pushed for time, so we won't detain you any longer—you're going back down to the beach?"

"As soon as I have the personnel to—"

"All the officers are at your disposal, hey? Just tell Sergeant Suzman to organize things, and Lieutenant Terblanche here and me will join you later. Okay?"

Dorf drew himself to attention again. "Very good, sir! Much obliged, sir!" The explosives expert did an about-turn and left the room, closing the spring-loaded door so carefully it suggested he hated the thought of anything banging behind him.

There was the long silence Kramer had expected, and then a hiss, which he hadn't. Terblanche was on his feet the next instant, and smashed his right fist into the side of the filing cabinet. "Bastard!" he seethed between gritted teeth. "Bastard! Gillets, you—you—you—you *bastard*!" He was plainly allowing himself just the one forbidden word, but making the most of it.

"Steady, Hans—you've only just started tidying up the place," murmured Kramer.

Terblanche looked round with an expression so distorted by pain it was terrible to look at. It was an expression only to be imagined in the ordinary course of events—the expression of a child, say, being crushed beneath a bus. Then it was gone.

Quite gone.

"I'm sorry, Tromp," mumbled Terblanche, straightening his tunic with a couple of tugs at his waistline. "Truly sorry, my friend. That was . . ."

"Only natural, Hans! You can't keep bottled up forever."

"Hey?"

"Don't tell me the thought Lance Gillets might be responsible hadn't already occurred to you," said Kramer. "You knew Annika better than most people, all her troubles and woes. You even tried to stop the wedding taking place, and so—"

"Who's been telling you all this?"

"You know damn well who," said Kramer. "You obviously spent a lot of time with the Widow Fourie after her man had his accident. You know her mind, how it works, what interests her, how bright she is. And so, when you had to find me some accommodation, your first thought was to get her to leak the information to me in a—"

"Listen," said Terblanche, raising an indignant finger to him, "so far as the Widow Fourie was concerned, my *only* thought was that she and the kiddies could do with the extra money. Nothing more than that! For heaven's sake, I didn't even *know* you then, which makes your—"

"You didn't have to know me," cut in Kramer. "So long as you made sure the investigating officer lodged with her, then you could be fairly certain that in this way, if in none other, he would soon learn a lot more about the whole Annika Gillets affair, including a possible motive. Come on, man— try and deny it!"

Terblanche shook his head. "No," he said. "I *can* deny it.

I'm not clever that way. I'm not CID, I've told you so—how many times?"

"Then tell me this," said Kramer, growing impatient. "Why, when we spent so much time together yesterday, did you never once tell me what the Widow Fourie told me last night? And yet you knew it! Because if she knew it, then you—"

"I said to you, Tromp, I said that you must always check with me anything anyone told you about Annika. I would have got round to—"

"Ja, but *then* you gave me the impression it was all old stuff, going back to when she was so-high to a bloody grasshopper! You never once implied anything up-to-date in your knowledge of her, any of the worries you had about her. Not one. Now explain that."

Terblanche retreated to his seat behind the desk and sat down heavily, crossed his arms on his blotter, and rested his forehead on them. He stayed in this position a full two minutes, not lifting his head again until Kramer's Lucky burned too low and he had to light another.

"I can't explain it, Tromp," he said. "I can only tell you that, since the moment I met Sarel down near Fynn's Creek, my mind has been—well, I don't know how to describe it. I've felt in shock, man. Real shock, like the time I found my ma dying in the small paddock, and thought at first she was a new foal trying to stand up, until I got nearer. Ja, shock like that, which is crazy! I'm a policeman, ja? I'm not meant to—"

"Fine," said Kramer. "That's all I wanted to know. I'm getting the picture and—"

"But *I'm* not!" protested Terblanche. "I don't ruddy know what's happening to me—I just watch. Do you know that? I just watch, and see everything happening far outside of me. I knew I should tell you everything when you came yesterday, but that meant I'd have to think properly about what had happened, about *what I knew would bloody happen eventually* and had tried so hard to prevent. Oh, ja, that writing has been on the wall since the very beginning! But I couldn't do it, couldn't talk about her, it was all over. I also *knew* it had to be him, that Lance must've done it, but I couldn't see *how* he'd done it. You know what? I even wondered, ja, when I got so angry there beside Kritzinger's body, whether he'd been party to doing it, only he got caught short somehow—isn't that terrible?"

"No," said Kramer, "not really. It's the way we in the CID think, hey? Maaties would have been proud of you."

Terblanche gave a surprised laugh.

They traveled north within the hour, taking the Chevrolet. An apparently casual telephone call to Madhlala Game Reserve had established that Lance Gillets was still at the main rest camp. No longer drunk, but sunk in a deep depression, the game warden in charge had said. The doctor was about to pay a visit, and Gillets' parents were expected at around eleven.

"Oh, shit," Kramer said suddenly, several very muddy miles beyond Nkosala. "Didn't someone tell me his pa's a big-shot lawyer back in Durban?"

Terblanche nodded.

"Then, my friend, we better really step on it, before the bastard starts informing sonny boy of his rights or something."

"But, Tromp, it's nearly sixty miles of dirt road from here to there, hey? And we're already going as fast as—"

"Ach, no, a better idea! I'll ring and get the local cop shop to pick Gillets up right now and put him on ice for us."

"But that could be really chucking petrol on the fire! What if we're wrong? What if—"

"A lawyer ought to know the husband is always the number one suspect in a wife murder, hey? That should make Pa Gillets keep things in perspective, and not—"

"No, Tromp, he'll be a father first, man! I know I would. There's really no way around this."

"Except to go like the bloody wind, hey?"

12

*T*he family cars in line outside the game reserve's main entrance looked every bit as respectable as their neat and tidy occupants, who gave details of their reservations to a Zulu game guard with a wide, welcoming smile. The Chevrolet joined the line like a drunken bum, hotfoot from the forces of law and order, crashing a PTA meeting: steam hissing from under its bonnet, another hubcap gone, and minus a wing mirror. Terblanche had to roll down his mud-splattered window before the game guard was able to see and recognize him.

"*Hau*, greetings, *baba nkosi*!" the game guard said, shedding his frown to snap off a smart salute. "Straight through, suh! Straight through!"

And up went the barrier, which bore a warning that the speed limit within the reserve was 15 mph, and the next sign read "Caution: Rhino."

"They should get a few more like that for outside the Colonel's office," grunted Kramer.

Terblanche chuckled. "Ja, only *bigger*," he said. "Well, it isn't much farther now, so can we have a quick recap? I didn't, er, quite catch all you were saying on that last stretch . . ."

Kramer nodded. "We have a murder," he said. "We have a known hard-case, we have motive, and we have method. All we're lacking now is the opportunity—not so?"

"Opportunity?"

"To set a crude time bomb ticking. That is our one real problem. According to the cook boy, Moses Khumalo, Gillets left Fynn's Creek in midmorning, so *theoretically* it was impossible for him to have used an alarm clock to trigger an explosion that happened more than twelve hours later—which it did."

"Ja, but he could have sneaked back somehow," said Terblanche.

"Exactly," said Kramer. "Which is what we now have to find evidence to prove . . ."

As Terblanche had predicted, it did not take Kramer long to reach the main rest camp, his progress through that last mile or so of long, dry grass and flat-topped thorn trees being completely uneventful. He found this disappointing, never having been in a game reserve before, and having rather hoped he'd spot at least one species of lumbering brute he wasn't accustomed to handcuffing.

The main rest camp turned out to be a bit of a letdown, too, being no more than an orderly collection of round, thatched rest huts, empty stockades, rock gardens, and a dozen or so larger cement-block buildings, also with thatched roofs, all set about with the same flat-topped thorn trees. Kramer had once visited a secret detention camp out on the edge of the Kalahari Desert very nearly as boring, but at least there every one of the shuffling inmates had been worth a second look, as opposed to what now confronted him: an asinine assortment of city dwellers, padding about in their shorts with red knees, flip-flop sandals, and garlands of bloody long-lensed cameras, looking like each had a multiple hard-on.

"Park over there where it says 'Reception,'" said Terblanche. "The Parks Board have got Gillets in that hut just behind it."

"Like so, you mean?" said Kramer, bringing the Chevrolet to a sudden, sliding halt.

"Very nearly," said Terblanche, opening his eyes again.

Almost immediately, as they climbed out, they were approached by a stocky individual in game ranger's uniform, who said in English: "Lieutenant Kramer, I presume?"—and smiled for no apparent reason at all, although he could have been trying to make some kind of joke.

The man was so deeply tanned that he was surely, however posh his English accent, in imminent danger of racial reclassification. As for his age, it was difficult to guess, late fifties to sixties, perhaps, but his background was obvious. Only an ex-military type would have known how to angle his Parks Board green beret quite so nonchalantly, while the cut of his khaki uniform suggested he was still using the same coolie tailor who'd kitted him out like a Boy Scout for the Battle of El Alamein.

"Ralph Mansfield, warden, chap in charge," he said, extending a hand that was like taking a grip on an off-cut of pine. "Excuse fingers!" And he barked a laugh at what had to be a very old joke, intended to make him a bit of a character and to put people, new to amputees missing a set of digits, at their ease.

"Where's Lance Gillets?" said Kramer.

Mansfield turned and pointed. "He's in that hut over there, doped to the eyeballs. Still in shock, so the quack said, when he popped in about half an hour ago and gave him something to take. Quite wrong, in my opinion: the sooner the chap sobers up and is made to face what's happened like a man, the better."

"Ja, but is he all right to talk to?" asked Terblanche.

"Help yourself, my dear chap! I'll be over in my office if you need anything, and—oh-oh, look who's arrived . . . The Gillets Seniors, to judge by the pinstripes."

"Then keep the buggers busy for the next ten minutes, okay?" said Kramer.

Lance Gillets was lying under a sheet on the bed in the rest hut, facing the whitewashed wall. It took him a count of six to become aware of the fact he had company, and a lot less to roll over, coming up on his elbows at the same time. "Who the fff—oh, hello, Hans! Good to see you," he said, not making it sound at all convincing.

Then he turned to gaze at Kramer; a cocky look, superior man views inferior man, the way he had probably been taught to do at private school. You could almost hear his mind putting the ticks against its checklist: cheap, off-the-peg suit; frayed shirt collar; brown tie patterned by blue horseshoes; great, clumping black shoes with rubber soles like tractor tires; a broad, inelegant belt that had cracks in its mock-leather surface and far too big a brass buckle—*another bloody Boer, another bloody hairy-back*. Or perhaps Gillets had applied some other form of test, Kramer couldn't be sure, but he did know that the result was the same: he still ended up feeling dangerously like a kaffir.

So he did his own looking, hard and unwavering. Gillets' dentist, he concluded, must have bought himself one hell of a swimming pool on the strength of all the correction work he'd done, bringing those exquisite teeth neatly into line and closing the gaps between them. They certainly hadn't simply grown that way, not from that kind of jawline. And then someone equally artistic must have set the pace for all those who followed him, by sculpting those brown curls into a Rock Hudson haircut that can't have been cheap either. As for the tanned, smoothy bit in the middle—the straight nose, fine cheekbones, and striking, long-lashed tawny eyes—they helped a lot to complete the first impression he gave, that of undoubted officer material, a jolly good fellow. It was only at a second glance that Lance Gillets looked as unreal as those bloody poofters modeling sweaters in adverts.

"Meet Lieutenant Kramer of the Murder Squad," said Terblanche, making the introduction with ill-concealed relish. "He's going to get the one who killed little Annika and see he's strung up good and high, hey?"

Gillets' face remained deadpan.

"What's the matter, man?" asked Terblanche. "Aren't you pleased?"

"I'm not—not anything," said Gillets, his Afrikaans so unguttural it bloody *minced,* and lay back again.

"But don't you want the murderer caught?" Terblanche persisted, moving closer to him.

"Of course I do—it's just that I know it won't make any difference," retorted Gillets. "Annie'll still be dead."

"An-*nika,*" said Terblanche.

"Dead," said Gillets.

"Now listen here, hey? You—"

"What *will* make a difference," said Gillets, closing his eyes now, "is when *I* get my own back. I just need time to think, that's all. Things are so jumbled."

"Time to think about what?" asked Kramer.

"Who could have done this, you clown!"

"Hey, just a minute!" began Terblanche, very indignant. "You can't talk to the Lieutenant in that—"

"He can talk how he likes, Hans," Kramer cut in. "It's the privilege of every condemned man . . ."

Gillets showed very little reaction, a slight movement of his hands clasped on his chest beneath the sheet, that was all. "What makes me a condemned man?" he asked.

"That's obvious," said Kramer. "Your Land-Rover was still parked at Fynn's Creek, nobody local was aware you'd flown out of there, and so the killer must have thought he had *you* in his sights as well—only he chose the wrong night for it."

"Christ, so obvious it hardly needs stating," sneered Gillets, looking up at him. "By being 'condemned,' are you insinuating that this 'killer' still has me down for the chop on his shopping list?"

"Uh-huh. Or are you suggesting there could have been a good reason for someone wanting to kill just your lady wife? I believe she did have a bit of a reputa—"

"Don't talk shit! Of course I'm not! Annie's never harmed, never hurt anyone! Jesus, she's dead only because of *me,* you sodding idiots!"—and as he said this, Gillets grabbed up a tumbler from his bedside locker and hurled it at the opposite wall, sending orange juice and broken glass flying everywhere.

"Ooops," murmured Kramer, gratified he'd provoked an outburst that gave him some idea of how this spoiled, overgrown brat could behave. Then he went on to picture him in a tantrum, turning like a deadly three-year-old on the woman who threatened his career. "Anyway, as I was saying, you must be on the killer's list still. Would you like police protection? It could happen at any time."

Gillets gave an amused snort. "Crap. He's a total bloody coward or he wouldn't have used dynamite—he'll keep well clear for a bit. Long enough, anyway, for . . ."

"For you to do your thinking?"

"There can't be many bastards who hate me as much as that."

"I wouldn't be so sure—" began Terblanche, before Kramer's hard nudge silenced him.

Gillets sighed. "Not *still* trying to put me down, are you, Uncle Hans? Isn't it a little late for the rampant jealousy bit now?"

Terblanche bristled. "What are you trying to hint at?" he demanded. "I'll have you know—"

"Take it easy, hey?" said Kramer, now wishing to Christ he'd not brought the station commander with him. "We're here to hear what Mr. Gillets has to say . . ."

"Mr. Gillets," said Gillets, "has nothing to say. I'm meant to be in deep shock, so just leave me alone or I'll tell my father when he comes and there'll be trouble, I can promise you!"

"Hell, no need for any hard feelings," said Kramer apologetically. "Come, Hans, my friend, it's time we were on the road again, hey?"

"But," said Terblanche, getting no further before Kramer motioned him to leave ahead of him.

He was still looking bewildered, half through the doorway, when Kramer turned at his side and said: "You're meant to be in deep shock, did you say, sir?"

"Jesus, you heard!" stormed Gillets.

"Then here's some of the real thing," said Kramer. "Will you hold your hands up nicely so I can see them, please?"

"What the hell for?"

"You're refusing to do it?"

"Here, look all you like—so what?"

"Uh-huh, they should fit some interesting bruises we've found among the bits and pieces," said Kramer.

The look on Gillets' face at the moment was enough to put a spring into the step of any man, all the way back to the Chevrolet. Terblanche almost capered.

"Hey, Hans, cool it, man!"

"Ja, ja, Tromp! I'm sorry, okay? But all the time we were in there, I thought you had changed your mind, that he was going to be let off scot-free, and *then* you—"

"Listen, we had only a few minutes, we couldn't really start anything," said Kramer. "But we have given him something to think about."

"Ja, and we did elicit that reference to dynamite, didn't we? How would he know a thing like that?"

"Well, to keep things in perspective," said Kramer, "explosions and dynamite do sort of go together in most people's—"

"What's up?" asked Terblanche.

"Shhh, turn away, the parents!" said Kramer, having glimpsed the game warden emerging from his office with a smartly dressed couple in their fifties. "I don't want us getting involved at this stage . . ."

The hiatus also provided him with an opportunity to review how he truly felt after meeting Lance Gillets for the first time. Something was wrong, something was missing, of that he was convinced, despite a strong gut feeling he had just confronted a nasty, dangerous little bastard. Perhaps gut feelings could be led astray in the presence of someone unusually violent by nature, picking up on not a single act but a whole range of them, showing no discretion, he reasoned. And perhaps, to extend this logic a pace further, the cold-blooded murder of Gillets' wife had not been among them.

"The parents've gone now," said Terblanche, peeping.

Kramer's gut feeling, when tested, was now coming up either null and void or numbed by an onslaught—he just didn't know what to make of it. "Look, let's sidle round that way and back up to the boss's office," he said. "There are a few questions we've got to ask him . . ."

13

*T*he game warden's office opened off the main reception area. Its furniture was plain, set square on a carpet of coconut matting. A huge map of the game reserve, divided into areas shaded different colors, hung to the right of the desk, and the rest of the walls were taken up by framed paintings and photographs, every one of which appeared to have an animal in it, ranging from warthog and flamingo to white rhino and hippopotamus. In one of the pictures, Mansfield was feeding a baby elephant, using a rubber teat attached to a beer bottle.

He saw Kramer peer at it, and said: "No, that *isn't* milk, I fear, Lieutenant. Poor old Winston grew up to be a *dreadful* soak, I'm afraid . . ."

"East Africa?" guessed Terblanche.

"Uganda—no, I stand corrected: Kenya. I'm afraid I've rather dodged about a bit!"

"Ja, it's the way the bastards keep chucking their bloody spears at a bloke, isn't it?" said Kramer. "But can we get back to the business in hand, hey?"

"Of course! Take a seat, gentlemen. Coffee?"

"Ta, but no," said Kramer. "We'll have to be on our way in a minute. First, though, I wondered whether, regarding Lance Gillets—"

"Rather distinguished couple, his parents, what? Frightfully well dressed and well spoken. Did you see them?"

"No, not really," said Kramer. "Can we stop this getting off the subject and—"

"I say, old chap," said Mansfield, scratching his stump with the fly whisk held in his left hand. "I've been doing a spot of thinking. Not at all sure I can be of much assistance after all—might not be in order, y'know! Got to remember my lords and masters on the board, adverse publicity, all that sort of thing. I'm sure you'll understand . . ."

"Anything I ask you to do will definitely be in order, believe me," said Kramer. "The adverse publicity and that sort of thing will begin only the moment you don't cooperate—understand me?"

"Ah," said Mansfield, glancing predictably at the rather distinguished cigar stub left in the ashtray on his desk.

"Listen, those two must have had bad times with him before, so don't fall for all Pa and Ma Gillets had to tell you," said Kramer. "I bet they're experts by now at making people feel sorry for them, and getting them to keep their traps shut."

"That's a bit steep! What on earth makes you say that?"

"Because, if it wasn't so, they would have been here yesterday," replied Kramer. "Like any other parents whose young son's wife has been murdered, only a few hours' car ride away."

"But Ralph Gillets explained he'd had to appear in court before the Judge President on behalf of—"

"Ach, no, there's no hearing that can't be adjourned, not in these circumstances! What really happened was, the lady first had to have her hysterics—you know, cry and scream and scare the shit out of the servants, saying she just couldn't take any more. Then, when she finally woke up to the fact that she'd *better* go—or what would her friends say?—the old man, who'd been using her as his excuse, had to come, too."

"God preserve me," murmured Mansfield, after quite a pause, "no bloody wonder I prefer animals . . ."

And Terblanche, nodding, silently concurred.

"Fine," said Kramer, lighting a Lucky. "First, I want to know whether if at any time it has crossed your mind that Lance Gillets could have been behind what happened early yesterday morning at Fynn's Creek."

"What an extraordinary idea!"

"Is it? How would you describe them as a couple?"

"Well, um, rather ill matched, I suppose, and things were bound to get a bit sticky eventually—but that's it. I've never *dwelt* on the matter, if you know what I mean."

"Why not, sir?"

"No idea. Better things to do, I suppose."

"You're sure you are not being evasive because suddenly you feel partly responsible for what's happened?"

Mansfield did a double blink. "Good Lord, no!" he said. "What on earth do you mean by that?"

"We understand that you'd put Gillets under a lot of pressure recently, telling him that Fynn's Creek was his last chance to get his private life sorted out and make good."

Mansfield's face darkened. "Who the Devil's been—"

"Is it true?"

"To some extent."

"Meaning?"

"I would have been recommending we got shot of him anyway, once I had someone to take his place."

"Oh, ja? You'd better expand on that."

"Difficult. I suppose it could have been partly a certain, er, unpleasant streak in him that regrettably surfaced."

"*See?*" said Terblanche to Kramer, looking vindicated.

"What sort of streak exactly?" asked Kramer.

"Put it this way," said Mansfield. "It's always been a deuce of a business, getting any of my game guards to work under him."

"Meaning boys, Bantus," explained Terblanche, in case Kramer had missed the distinction between game guard and game ranger. "Can you quote any specific examples of—"

"Ach, never mind about that," cut across Kramer. "Let me ask you the *opposite* question now, Mr. Mansfield: why did you hire this man in the first place?"

"I didn't, as a matter of fact," he said. "That sort of thing is done by our headquarters staff. And he came to us most highly recommended, the right sort of background and all that. Awarded his gymnasium's Sword of Honour during—"

"Ah, so he's another former army man, like yourself?"

"Not army, no—he was at the Navy Gymn in Simonstown, as I recall."

"Bugger!" said Kramer.

Mansfield raised a bushy eyebrow. "Have I inadvertently said the wrong thing?" he asked. "I was simply—"

"Too right, you have!" replied Kramer. "Because, so far as I know, sodding sailors don't usually receive training in preparing explosive charges—do they?"

Both bushy eyebrows now rose. "I say, you really are rather drawing a bead on Gillets, aren't you? Is that wise?"

"Meaning what, sir?"

"I mean I had him under my eye the whole of Monday, from the moment I had him flown in until well after midnight, when we finally called it a day and took to our beds. Put him up myself, a shakedown in my living room, and shared a nightcap with him, explained I'd been glad of a chance to see how well he could work in a team, in view of odd complaints I'd had. Now *that*, Lieutenant, was the only moment in all that time he looked a trifle on edge: for the rest of that day, he'd been perfectly cheerful and agreeable—almost a changed character, in fact!"

"I see," said Kramer. "Like a man might act who'd fixed to secure himself a happy release that very night from a bad situation?"

"Good God, no!" replied Mansfield, taking out a large khaki handkerchief to mop his brow with. "Like anyone glad to be away from his better half and all that damned bickering for a while, I'd imagine."

"So what time was he picked up from Fynn's Creek?"

asked Kramer, rising, having become increasingly frustrated by this line of inquiry. "Morning or afternoon?"

"Morning, definitely. Can't have been much later than half past ten, because the plane only—"

"Fine," Kramer said, turning to prize Terblanche out of his seat.

"Is that all, dear boy?" said Mansfield. "Because I—"

"Just a sec," said Terblanche, "there's something *I* want to ask. This business of the plane going to fetch Gillets from Fynn's Creek—was that all a bit sudden, as we have been led to understand? Or had he some prior warning you might be needing him for a few days?"

"Oh, no, I'd have had him drive up, had I known properly in advance he'd be needed," said Mansfield. "Thing was, Jonty Armstrong had a sudden malaria attack that morning, leaving us a bit light on the ground, and Lance, being one of the chaps on three days' standby for special duties, was—"

"Ah, so Gillets could have at least *planned* for the time he might be away?"

Mansfield gave a little frown. "Why, of course," he said, nonplussed. "That's the whole point of the standby thing, surely? He was married staff, with his good lady and her own life to consider, the necessary arrangements to make."

"Precisely," said Terblanche, looking hard at Kramer.

The journey back to Jafini seemed to take forever, made all the more tedious by the station commander's repeated claim to have found the chink in Gillets' armor.

"Christ Almighty, Hans, how many more times must I say it?" growled Kramer, growing very impatient as they left Nkosala behind them. "Nothing up at that bloody game reserve gave me cause to feel confident we'd picked the right chief suspect; in fact, the reverse happened. Gillets wasn't right somehow as the killer, and almost everything Mansfield told us was totally inconsistent with—"

"Ja, *almost* everything, Tromp! Except for—"

"You're clutching at straws, man!"

"You wait and see, Tromp. Gillets could easily have positioned that time bomb on the off chance of his being called to do standby duty, and then just switched it on when the plane came for him."

"Oh, ja? Before eleven in the morning? What about the maximum delay of twelve hours between—"

"The clock must've had something wrong with it; maybe it stopped or slowed down for a while."

"Huh! That I can believe!"

"Or maybe he didn't use an alarm clock for a timer, but something with a longer delay on it."

"Such as?"

"I've no idea, Tromp! But who knows what Dorf has discovered while we've been away, hey?"

"He could have discovered there never was a time bomb," said Kramer, slowing down. "But that somebody had just taken that dynamite and bloody lit it!"

Terblanche chuckled. "Wait and see!" he said again, at the risk of having his neck wrung.

"Tell me, Hans," said Kramer, determined to distract him and selecting a surefire means of doing so. "Reference little Annika . . ."

"Oh, ja?" said Terblanche, turning around. "What about her?"

"We've seen one lot of parents today, but where have the others got to? Has Doc also got them under sedation? In fact, I can't remember anyone mentioning them since I—"

"They're dead, a big tragedy last year," explained Terblanche. "Man, it happened only two weeks before the wedding. They were on their way home one night when Andries somehow lost control coming round this sharp left-hand bend—his car shot off the road and went smack into two cane trucks, killing both her parents instantly."

"Where was this?"

"On Grantham's land along a track back that way, which Andries used as a shortcut down from the mill to home— they'd been to the boss's for a barbecue. There was a theory

Andries had swerved to avoid a kaffir or some animal in the road."

"Wasn't he just full of jungle juice?"

"The medical report did say he'd drunk quite a bit, ja, but naturally the magistrate, who was also at the party, was keen to find some other reason. Maaties was asked to look into the kaffir angle, but I don't think he went to much trouble—road traffic accidents he never saw as CID work. Mind you, they often can involve just as much forensic as any—"

"Ja, ja," said Kramer, anxious not to be drawn into that old argument, "and you say the wedding went ahead just the same?"

Terblanche sighed. "More's the pity," he said. "But at the time, even I could understand it. Poor little Annika felt suddenly so alone in the world, it was somebody to cling to. Plus, she also knew how keen her parents had felt about the marriage, and called it granting them their 'last wish'—which was true, I suppose."

"What about his parents, were they as keen?"

"Weren't at the wedding, Tromp—which is how today was the first time I've ever set eyes on them. I think that gives you some idea of how violently they were against it, against their son marrying into a family so far beneath them."

"Hmmm," said Kramer, momentarily entertaining a very bizarre suspicion regarding the elder Gillets pair.

Everyone at Jafini police station seemed to be trying to talk to him at once.

"Oh, *there* you are, Lieutenant!" said Bokkie Maritz, waving a piece of paper. "The Colonel's just been on the phone—he's worried you could have been upsetting some big-shot lawyer who rang him from the game reserve. He wants you to—"

"How's the throat, Bok?"

"Hell, a thousand times better, sir! He really is a good doctor, isn't he—that Doc Mackenzie? Man, I'd hardly swallowed one spoonful of the mixture he gave me when I—"

"Your turn, Malan," said Kramer, looking at the detective constable waiting behind Maritz, red-faced from a day at the beach. "How are things going at Fynn's Creek?"

"Fine, sir! Dorf awaits your presence, he says. He has fresh information for you, but hasn't let on exactly what."

"We're on our way! Hans, did you hear that? Dorf's—"

"But the Colonel wants you to ring him immediately, sir!" bleated Maritz, shaking the piece of paper. "I promised him you would!"

"Then you mustn't make promises you can't keep, Bok," admonished Kramer. "And what is it that *you* want, Cassius? Aren't you meant to be off duty now?"

The big Zulu nodded and smiled shyly. "*Yebo,* my boss, that is true," he said. "But Boss Terblanche he tell Cassius he must first give message to Moses cook boy to come here to Jafini station to make written statement, boss."

"Oh, ja, I remember. Has Moses remembered something else—come up with something new?"

Cassius shook his head. "No, but very strange-strange thing is happening, boss. Moses say, boss, he must be wearing his Sunday bests to do such a important thing as make statement, so Cassius he tells him, 'Make it snappy, kaffir!' Much-much noise, my boss, because Moses cook boy cannot find Sunday bests in his hut, no trouser, no ee-shirt, no belt, no shiny shoe. *Hau,* bad-bad thief has come by his hut and—"

"Ach, really!" said Maritz. "Sir, you could be on the phone instead of wasting time on kaffir petty theft and—"

"Finish what you were saying, Cassius, hey?" said Kramer.

"My boss," he said, trying to ignore Martiz' glare. "Moses cook boy absent from his place of work only one time—same night he go for big-big beer drink with his uncle."

"You're saying his things were stolen the night of the blast?"

"*Hau,* correct too much, my boss!"

"Then, presumably, the thief must have been some sly bastard who saw Moses getting pissed out of his brains in

Jafini and whipped down to the hut while his back was turned," said Kramer. "Good, let's catch him and quick, hey? You never know what *else* the bugger might have noticed that night, right? This could be our big break-through!"

14

*I*t was late afternoon, with sunset about to blood the sea, when Kramer and Terblanche returned to Fynn's Creek, bringing Bantu Constable Cassius Mabeni with them, riding in the cage on the back of the Land-Rover.

"Jiminy, just look at that!" exclaimed Terblanche, as they topped the last incline. "What on earth has Dorf been up to? Playing chess or something?"

It was indeed an unexpected sight: that neat grid of thatching string, stretched taut between freshly fashioned wooden pegs, and covering the entire blast area. Even more extraordinary in its way was the fact the place was now as tidy as a chessboard, too, with every piece of debris, every article of clothing, every item of kitchenware, for example, neatly stacked around the periphery in carefully categorized piles.

"Just what it needed, a woman's touch," murmured Kramer. "And a worse old woman I've never bloody come across . . ."

"Ja, but I bet he's found a twenty-four-hour timer somewhere in there," said Terblanche. "Come and see!"

"Huh!" said Kramer.

They climbed from the cab and found Cassius Mabeni already disembarked, standing stiffly to attention and awaiting further orders.

"Right," said Kramer. "You're to go to Moses, get him to go over the facts of the theft again, and—most important—you're to get a bloody good description of his Sunday best, understand? We're going to have to be able to recognize his missing clothes the moment we find them or see them on anyone. Okay?"

"*Hau*, Cassius will try, my boss!"

Then Kramer and Terblanche carried on down to where the Parks Board Land-Rover still stood. Beside it was a pile of recreational items—fishing rods, a pair of frog flippers, two tennis rackets, a smashed-up phonograph, and so on—while the next pile was given over to bathroom items, including two bars of Lux soap, two sponges, two nailbrushes, two pumice stones, two loofahs, and a rubber duck. Kramer picked up the duck and squeezed it, expelling a stream of small, sweetly scented soapy bubbles from the squeaker hole in its beak.

"Little Annika!" gasped Terblanche, caught off guard. "Dear God above, you can *smell* her . . ."

"Lieutenant Kramer?" said Dorf, right behind them.

"Ja, Sybrand?" he said, handing Terblanche the duck as he turned. "We were just admiring your work, hey? We understand that you've found some fresh evidence."

"Very little, but all the more significant for that," replied Dorf, motioning Kramer and Terblanche to follow him. "It's assembled over here, on my field table, folding."

And it was very little, by the look of it. Four tiny scraps of brown paper, in a cellophane envelope, labeled; three cigarette lighters, labeled; a can of lighter fuel, labeled; an envelope with two twists of wire in it, both covered by red plastic insulation, both labeled; a heavy, square battery, labeled; a small, coiled spring, brass cogs, steel spindles, and other clock parts, labeled and carefully stowed in a small cardboard box.

Everyone crowded round while Dorf, standing on the far

side of the display like a market stallholder going through a particularly lean time, and with much the same eager glint in his eye, pointed first to the scraps of paper. "These," he said, "are fragments from the waxed wrapping used around sticks of D14, the most common blasting explosive. The paper's fine diagonal watermark pattern is very distinctive."

"What sort of blasting would that be?" asked Kramer.

"Quarrying, road construction, dam building—call it civil engineering, if you like. It's also the type, because of the circumstances in which it is often stored, most commonly stolen. I'm sure you've had instances of that around here."

"True," said Terblanche. "But not for some time, hey?"

"When last?" asked Kramer.

"Three, four years ago, Tromp. Mind you, I've heard these thefts are not always reported, because of the trouble the owners can get into for not following regulations about their safekeeping."

"That used to be the way," agreed Dorf. "But people are a bit jittery now that such a theft could have political implications—I'm sure you'd have heard if this little lot had been stolen locally."

"Then we'd best request Pretoria for reports of stolen dynamite nationally," said Kramer. "Next?"

Dorf pointed to the three cigarette lighters. "Two of those have lighter fluid in them," he said. "The remaining one, which your Bantu CID sergeant found near that line of bushes directly behind the detonation point, contains plain petrol. The conclusion I draw is that these two were filled from this can of lighter fuel, recovered from Square F23 on my grid, and thus the property of the householders, while the *third* lighter could have been dropped by the killer—anyone recognize it?"

There was a general shaking of heads.

"Ach, come on, tell us about the time bomb," demanded Terblanche. "First of all, *was* it one?"

Dorf nodded, pointing to the small cardboard box. "Ja, I think we can call that more than a reasonable assumption, Lieutenant. Detonated by this little alarm clock here—the traveling variety, to go by the reduced size of its components. We have yet to find the case, but I'm sure it can't be very far away. Those wires and the battery were obviously part of the same crude setup. Maximum setting, a twelve-hour period."

Terblanche frowned. "But what proof have you," he asked, "that the spring and the rest of the stuff weren't from a traveling clock owned by the deceased and her husband? I—"

"These items were embedded in the mud *below* the blast," explained Dorf. "Not only that, the various parts show not the slightest sign of corrosion, which indicates they can't have been exposed to the sea air for long. Contrast them with these parts from a clock that must have once stood in their—"

"Be that as it may," said Terblanche, "it still looks to me as though you assume too much from too little, man—no offense intended!"

"But that's my point, Lieutenant," said Dorf. "There *is* so little, even after a most intensive search, that I can be virtually certain the alarm clock could not have been modified, for instance, to give a time delay in excess of—"

"Ach, I give up!" muttered Terblanche, raising his hands in mock surrender. "I'm going to see how Cassius is getting on, Tromp—okay?"

And with that, he stumped off.

"Hope it wasn't me that upset him," said Dorf.

"It was the time factor," said Kramer, lighting up a Lucky. "You're one hundred percent certain the bomb could not have been activated any earlier? We have a possible suspect, you see, who could have done it at about eleven but not later."

"What did I tell you, hey?" Malan whispered to Suzman. "*That's* why they went to the reserve! Gillets is obviously their number one—"

"Malan!" barked Kramer. "Forgotten my warning?"

"Sorry, Lieutenant! I'm really sorry, hey?"

Then Dorf spoke, reclaiming everyone's attention. "No, Lieutenant, nobody can be one hundred percent sure of anything in this world. Very early this morning, in another place, I lost a colleague who forgot that and clipped the wrong wire without first tracing its path properly. Therefore, I can only say that I'm ninety-nine point nine percent certain of the twelve-hour limit—unless, of course, an accomplice was used by the suspect you've mentioned."

"An accomplice?" echoed Kramer. "No, sorry, I can't see it, not in this context."

"Tromp!" came a distant voice.

"It's Lieutenant Terblanche, sir!" said Malan, puppy-eager to make amends. "Shall I go and see what the matter is?"

"No, I've a better plan, Jaapie," said Kramer. "You take Field Cornet Dorf here to the Royal Hotel in Nkosala and see he has a bloody good meal with you. Only the best for one of the best, hey?—he's more than deserved it. As for the rest of you, you can forget this little lot now and go home—bugger off!"

That had been an uncharacteristically kindly gesture on his part, Kramer knew full well, but, at the close of what had turned out to be a miserable, balls-aching, frustrating day, he'd needed something to raise his spirits a little, such as the thought of what would happen to the Colonel's piles the instant he spotted an extravagant dinner for two on expenses. With any luck, it'd probably be a full, merciless hour before his sphincter finally unclenched itself.

"Tromp! Didn't you hear me?"

"I'm coming, man, I'm coming . . ." said Kramer, hopping over the last strand of taut thatching string. "What's the problem?"

"No problem, it's just we seem to have solved the theft of the garments—only I'm afraid it isn't good news."

"Oh, ja?" Kramer reached the bare patch outside the cook boy's hut and saw a second Zulu squatting subserviently there, beside Moses. "Who's this, then?" he asked.

"Moses cook boy's uncle from Jafini, my boss," explained Cassius Mabeni. "He come to bring food because police say Moses cook boy must never-never leave this place."

"Uh-huh—and so?"

"Well, Cassius was questioning the cook boy, just like you

told him to," said Terblanche, "when all of a sudden, the uncle here starts chipping in. They had just got to where Cassius was asking if the cook boy remembered anyone leaving the beer drink, and the cook boy had answered he could remember nothing, not even dropping the money that had been so kindly returned to him. Then his uncle says, 'What money?'—and they started arguing."

"About what?" asked Kramer.

"Uncle man say Elifasi Ndhlovu was not drinking beer with them that night, my boss," said Cassius Mabeni. "He says it is all one damn big lie."

"Ja, that's right," continued Terblanche, "and so the cook boy here says to him, 'Why would a man give to me money out of his own pocket that I had not dropped? That doesn't make much sense, you old buffoon!'—or words to that effect."

"No, it doesn't make sense," agreed Kramer. "Unless—"

"Ah, but the uncle had his own answer for that! He says that this Elifasi must have used the money as an excuse to come down here and see what he could steal. But, because there was a police guard on the property, he had stolen from the cook boy instead, taking his Sunday best."

"Hmmm, not a bad theory. It wasn't until today that Moses noticed his suit had gone, was it?"

"Exactly," said Terblanche. "So the garments could have still been here in his hut on the night of the explosion, only to be taken the *following* night, when Elifasi came by."

"Hell, I was here myself then," said Kramer. "No wonder the bastard took off like a clockwork meerkat! You remember that, Cassius?"

"*Yebo*, my boss—too very-very damn quick!"

"But didn't you tell me he was a good bloke, this Elifasi character?"

Mabeni looked embarrassed. "That is true, my boss," he admitted. "A man who had caused no trouble."

The cook boy started shaking his head and making a long protest in Zulu.

"Ach, no, what's that all about now?" demanded Kramer, his patience wearing thin. "Just tell this Moses that, as far as I'm concerned, the matter is no longer of any interest to me, and that he can sort it all out with Cassius in the—"

"He's saying," interpreted Terblanche, "that he is certain the garments were not taken by Elifasi, who did not have the eyes of a thief but sat with him the whole time and just talked and asked questions and everything."

"Questions? Such as what?"

"Oh, I suppose the usual kaffir things, how many children he had, how many wives, but I'll ask him," said Terblanche, and did so with some abruptness, as though intent on keeping the cook boy's answer short.

Moses could not have kept it shorter: he said nothing in reply, just looked suddenly very uncomfortable and played dumb.

"*Hau!*" said Mabeni, looking at Kramer and Terblanche in surprise. "Cassius now kick this cheeky kaffir, my boss?"

"Ja, I think that's an excellent idea," said Terblanche, drawing his truncheon. "What the hell does he think he's playing at?"

"*Yega, yega!*" pleaded Moses, crossing his arms over his face and backing away. "No hit, boss, no hit!"

Mabeni bellowed at him in Zulu, grabbed his arms, pulled them down, and yelled in his face, making him screw up his eyes. Still with this eyes tight shut, the cook boy began a babble, holding Mabeni's huge hands at bay.

Terblanche listened briefly, then turned to Kramer: "Ach, it's nothing," he said. "He's just worried that we will inform Gillets he's been disloyal, telling personal details about his master and madam, the way servants do. Apparently, this Elifasi character once worked for a boss just as hard, and this gave them much in common, stories to joke about." Terblanche paused, listened again, and said: "Now he's even more worried that *we* will not be too pleased with him also telling his visitor about the CID sergeant who came here, plus what action he'd seen the police taking since the explosion.

As I said, normal servant's tittle-tattle, only we've really scared him and he—"

"Hold it!" said Kramer, so sharply that not only Terblanche but the cook boy, too, were stopped in their tracks. "I thought the word 'questions' sparked this off, hey? Tittle-tattle just flows, but questions are another bloody matter entirely! It's a point that needs clearing up." A very nasty feeling was beginning to emerge, like a maggot hatching in the pit of his belly.

Between them, Terblanche and Mabeni interrogated the cook boy, changing tactic and addressing him quietly, allowing him to squat beside his uncle. His replies were faltering and he frequently seemed to have difficulty in grasping what was required of him.

"Ach, come on," Kramer growled, flicking aside a half-smoked Lucky. "I can't wait half the—"

"Yirra, Tromp," said Terblanche, looking shaken now as he turned to him. "He says they just talked at first, anything and everything. The questioning itself seems to have started when he began asking the cook boy about *us*, the police, hey? All very casual, ja, but the coon wanted to know the description of who was in charge of the case, what had been found, where we were looking—luckily the cook boy's such a raw kaffir he couldn't tell him much. But what does this all *mean*, hey? Was this Elifasi Ndhlovu spying on us? I tell you, it's like nothing I've ever experienced in the whole of my service before!"

Kramer shrugged, his mind racing.

"You know what, Tromp?" said Terblanche. "I'm beginning to think this case *could* be political . . . Don't you think we'd best stop and call in the Security Branch?"

"And make fools of ourselves if it isn't? You heard Dorf say it couldn't be. No, Hans, first we find this Elifasi bastard ourselves and have a little chat with him."

"But—"

"His name probably means bugger all, so what we need now is a description—have you got one?"

"Ja, I asked for it earlier," said Terblanche, nodding and

taking out his notebook shakily. "It's not much, hey? Bantu adult male, average height, slim build, speaks country-boy Zulu, late twenties maybe, wears old tennis shoes, inside-out jacket, matches in his ears, and—"

"Short Arse! I can't tell you why, *but I bloody knew it*!" said Kramer.

15

*T*he day changed note then, like a guitar string breaking.

Another went as the Land-Rover reached the point, just south of the Moon Acre turnoff on the Nkosala road, where Short Arse had disappeared in a cloud of the Chevrolet's dust the previous day, not to be seen again.

"That sly little bastard!" muttered Kramer, making Terblanche and Mabeni, who sat between them, look round. "He's been playing silly buggers with me the whole time!"

"You mean Elifasi has?" asked Terblanche.

But Kramer was too preoccupied by the exact science of hindsight, as he'd once heard it described, to reply.

How painfully obvious it now seemed to him why Short Arse had done his vanishing trick. Wary that he could be stopped and questioned, as might any kaffir male when a white woman had been murdered, he had taken a nosedive through the dust cloud into the dense sugarcane and hidden there. Then, once it had seemed safe to do so, he'd emerged again and continued on his way to Fynn's Creek to see Moses the cook boy, much amused to note, no doubt, that the law was elsewhere, wasting its time on bloody Grantham.

On top of which, it had now also occurred to Kramer that his first encounter with Short Arse, within only a minute or so of his arrival in Jafini, could not have been the coincidence it had seemed at the time. Rather, the cunning bastard had been bent on making an immediate check on every newcomer who looked as though he might be part of police reinforcements.

"This Short Arse, this Elifasi bugger," said Kramer, "must be caught before this night is over—understood?"

"But how?" asked Terblanche. "I've already asked Cassius here if he can remember his current address from his pass book, and he—"

"Forget it, it'll be a fake anyhow," said Kramer. "Our main advantage is that presumably he doesn't know we're on to his little game, or we'd have been out looking for him sooner. My bet is, he'll be still hanging around somewhere, trying to find out what we—"

"But why, Tromp?" said Terblanche. "Why is he doing this?"

"My guess is that he's somehow part of what happened at Fynn's Creek," said Kramer. "He may even have been the bloody accomplice that Sybrand Dorf believes could have been involved, the one with the petrol lighter that got dropped."

Terblanche gave a low whistle. "You mean Lance Gillets could have paid this kaffir to plant the bomb for him? But that's terrible!"

"Been done before, using kaffirs as murder weapons," Kramer reminded him. "You remember that cop in Pretoria whose wife hired two wogs to—"

"Ja, I know, but to think little Annika was . . ."

"Say that *is* what went on here," said Kramer. "And now Short Arse, alias Elifasi, is shitting himself that he could be caught and held solely responsible. Hence he's tried to find out the state of the game from the cook boy, hence he's—ach!

I don't know all the ins and outs yet, but I do know this: that little black bastard *is* mixed up somehow in this business."

"Only . . ." began Terblanche.

"Only what?" said Kramer, changing down to go into the last bend before the long straight leading to Jafini.

"We're still left with the basic problem, Tromp. Who stole the cook boy's clothes? Shouldn't we also be looking for another coon who—"

"Elifasi could have stolen them himself after all," said Kramer. "The same night he planted the bomb—simple, man."

"But why would he want to?"

Mabeni stirred, clearing his throat. "My boss?" he said.

"You have an answer for the Lieutenant?" said Kramer. "Good, then speak up, let's hear it, man!"

"Elifasi maybe need new clothings description, my boss," he said cautiously. "Maybe last night he run far-far away."

"Now, there is a thought," said Kramer, not liking it one bit. "You haven't seen him today, for instance?"

Mabeni shook his head.

"I thought I had, just for a moment," admitted Kramer, "outside the Bombay Emporium early this morning, but it turned out to be this ancient kaffir with syphilis. Same type of jacket, same shiny lining."

"Syph . . . ?" repeated Cassius Mabeni.

Terblanche translated for him, and the Bantu constable gave a short, merry laugh. "Mad-mad, that one," he said. "He say he is Prime Minister of South Africa two times over."

"Oh, ja, old Two Times?" said Terblanche, chuckling. "He used to do some odd-job garden work for me, until the day he decided he was going to take out all my roses and return them to this tribal homeland he had set up for them. Can you imagine? Holes left all over the place, and my poor roses struggling to grow, stuck in a pile of broken bricks I had?"

Mabeni laughed, covering his mouth politely with his hand, but Kramer still turned to frown at him. "What the hell's the matter, kaffir?" he said. "I want you thinking, not playing at silly buggers, hey?"

And if Terblanche, now a bright red, liked to consider himself also rebuked, all well and good, thought Kramer.

Bokkie Maritz was sitting in the brightly lit CID office, slurring into the telephone, watched by a gleeful Sergeant Sarel Suzman, looking a lot less angular and morose for once.

"What's going on?" Kramer paused to ask him.

"I think Bok's had too much of his sore-throat mixture," said Suzman. "You've got to watch Doc Mackenzie, hey? He's a terror for prescribing lots of alcohol in everything— when Lieutenant Terblanche had flu, his cure for it nearly gave him the DTs, hey?"

"Ja, but who's Bok talking to?"

"The Colonel, Lieutenant."

"Didn't I order you to go home?"

"Ja, but—"

"Then go!" hissed Kramer, impatient to strike while the iron was hot.

Suzman went, glowering but obedient, one of nature's lapdogs.

"Hey, Bok!" Kramer said loudly, advancing on him. "Man, don't tell me it's whiskey now! And only half the bottle left? What the hell are you *doing*? First it was gin, then it was—"

"Shorry, hold on jush a sec," said Maritz to the Colonel, turning round in utter bewilderment.

"Oh, Christ!" said Kramer. "You're not talking to that same lady again? The one you upset this afternoon with your remarks? For God's sake, *stop now*, Bok! That kind of call can be traced, man, and this is a police station! Here, give that to me—!"

And he whipped the receiver from Maritz' hand, before the idiot had time to stop boggling, and said into the mouthpiece: "Hello? Operator, here—sorry, madam, we seem to have a crossed line. Replace your phone on its hook, please!" And he did just that himself, knowing the Colonel would ring back as fast as he could be reconnected.

"Hey, wash you think you're—" began Maritz.

"Out!" snapped Kramer. "Go and wait in the station commander's office, where we will find out what you've been up to today! And that is an *order*, Sergeant—so *move!*"

"But I—"

"Go, before my boot does the job for you!"

Maritz stumbled to his feet, wide-eyed, looking as though he now believed every canteen story ever told about this lunatic from the Free State, and fled the room, bumping into two desks and a chair on the way. He had just lurched from sight when the phone gave a shrill ring.

"Jafini CID, Kramer speaking . . ."

"Lieutenant, is that you?"

"Good evening, Colonel! Hell, it's nice to hear your voice again—I thought we'd been totally forgotten up here!"

"Hey? Didn't you get my messages? What the hell is going on, man? Bok's—"

"Messages, Colonel?" said Kramer.

"Ach, you know! To ring me about Advocate Gillets and his complaint about—"

"News to me, Colonel! What has he got to complain about?"

"So you haven't been using threatening tactics on his son Lance, then? Only Mr. Gillets alleges—"

"Hell, no, Colonel! Me and Hans pick on a poor kid still in deep shock under the doctor? Ring Mr. Mansfield, the bloke in charge at Madhlala, and he'll tell you that we only paid a courtesy call, ten minutes at the most. Mansfield in fact thanked us for our discretion, Colonel—honest. You could try reminding him of that and see what he says."

"You were accompanied by Hans Terblanche, you say?"

"Every minute of the time, sir! We work as a team."

"You do?" said the Colonel, unable to keep the surprise from his voice. "A good, steady fellow, Hans, although Maaties found him a bit slow. But, listen, no more visits without a call to me first, okay? Advocate Gillets is not a man we want to—"

"Promise, Colonel," said Kramer. "Otherwise, things are starting to progress nicely, sir, I'm glad to report! The funny thing is, I was just about to phone you. Field Cornet Dorf of the Defence Force was here today, and has given us a few leads we can start working on."

"I'm very pleased to hear it, hey?" Du Plessis paused and cleared his throat. "Er, Lieutenant . . ."

"Ja, Colonel?"

"You make it sound as though all is well up at Jafini."

"So it is, Colonel! Your Press clampdown is working perfectly. Not one reporter in—"

"No, it's not that, Lieutenant. It's, er, Bok . . . Just how are things with him, exactly?"

"Oh," said Kramer, then switched to speaking far too lightly and airily: "When did you last speak to him, Colonel? He's just a bit, er—shall we say, feverish?—at the moment. Also been a bit out of sorts, a bit low, that's all, but I'm sure he'll soon get over it. He's been telling you about his bad sore throat presumably?"

There was quite a pause. "You say, Lieutenant, that Bok is, what—a bit low?"

"Er, yes, sir, in a manner of speaking. Perhaps it's because he's, er, not used to being so far away from home, sir, and away from his lovely lady wife and all the usual restrictions—I mean, away from the usual routine, sir. Admittedly, I've been out all day, so I'm a bit out of touch with—"

"You can't, er, explain the situation a little more clearly, Lieutenant?"

"Colonel?"

"Listen," said Du Plessis, "I respect a man for his loyalty, as you well know, Tromp, but perhaps in this instance it might—"

"Look, sir, wouldn't you like to have a word with Bokkie himself?" said Kramer. "He's right here at Maatie's old desk, playing with his little Scottie dog puzzle and—"

"No, no, that won't be necessary!" said the Colonel hastily. "Just tell him from me . . . Look, maybe it's best since he's, as you say, feverish, if Bokkie gets a lift back tonight, hey? There's a Firearms Squad vehicle leaving Nkosala at eight for tomorrow morning's conference. Then Bok can get that sore throat properly seen to and be in the bosom of his family, which is a man's proper place when he's sick."

"Colonel, sir, you're one of the best, hey?"

"It won't leave you too short of men?"

"Hell, no, we'll manage, Colonel—good night, sir!"

Kramer let the receiver slide from his fingers back into its cradle. Right, he thought, now I have you all to myself— although when, how, or where I'm going to be able to take wicked advantage of this, I don't bloody know.

He meant of course the Widow Fourie.

"Look, I've managed to find that old dynamite theft," said Terblanche, coming into the CID office. "Sorry, are you about to use the phone? Because I—"

"No, just finished!" said Kramer, turning. "The Colonel wants Maritz back, so I've just arranged a lift for him. Any chance of the van taking him round to pick up his suitcase?"

"Ja, I'll fix that in a moment, hey?" said Terblanche, placing a bulging docket on Malan's desk. "I thought it worthwhile a quick check, in case the dynamite has been stolen from the same place again."

"Good thinking," said Kramer, moving to look over his shoulder. "Who investigated?"

Terblanche pointed to the name at the foot of the list of exhibits: *J. J. Mitchell*. "Joe did, but in the end, he didn't have much luck—Joe was Malan's predecessor here, before he went on to higher things. All two dozen sticks of dynamite were recovered, as you can see from this list, but nobody was arrested and the case still lies open. Now, where was it that this happened exactly . . . ? It's on the tip of my tongue."

Kramer plucked a yellow form from the mess of papers. "Shaka's Halt," he said.

"Ach, of course! A nothing sort of place way up, you know, near the mountains. Sort of a quarry, where they get gravel for roads."

"You're right," said Kramer, studying the form. "There's the name of the contractor here, Barney Sherwood, Umfolosi Quarry Company—and a phone number. I'm going to try him . . ."

The dialing tone lasted for barely two rings. Sherwood thought at first that the police were calling to tell him that the case had at last been solved, then became irritable when he realized they hadn't. He said that *nothing* further had been taken from his explosives store, thank you, and pointed out that this was undoubtedly *just as well*, considering how totally incompetent the police had proved themselves to be. Furthermore, he wanted to lodge a complaint about the police seizure of a man's lawful property, leaving him seriously out of pocket.

"I don't know what the hell you're talking about, sir," said Kramer. "And I don't *want* to know. Just see you go and check your store once more, right now, and ring us back by half past eight, confirming it is secure, or there'll be trouble, hey? I'm the world expert on examining gravel lorries for serious infringements of roadworthiness regulations."

"That'll put him in a panic!" said Terblanche, as the receiver clattered down.

"Never failed yet with one of those bastards," said Kramer. "You'll see, he'll ring again by eight-fifteen at the latest."

The contractor rang at eight, just as Maritz, looking most bemused, made his maudlin farewell and departed in the company of three very silent Firearms Squad officers, temporarily stationed at Nkosala.

"Well?" said Terblanche, turning his attention back to Kramer. "Any luck at Shaka's Halt?"

Kramer shrugged. "Nice idea of yours, Hans, but a big fat zero, the man says—all his dynamite is accounted for. Best we put that dynamite docket away and stop buggering about, hey? Our job tonight is to catch Short Arse. Nothing else must get in the way of that—*nothing*."

"Ja, but how, Tromp? Where do we begin?"

"We could try a ride around, see if—"

"But what if he spots us doing that, and—"

"True. Ach, we'll just have to sit down and do some hard thinking first, see if we can't come up with a better plan."

16

*T*he Widow Fourie came out of the kitchen, carrying a glass of water, just as Kramer opened her front door at a quarter after midnight, doing his best to make not a sound.

"Hello," she said. "You're up late . . ."

"And you."

"Ach, no. I was fast asleep until a minute ago—little Piet woke up, wanting a drink."

"I could bloody do with one," muttered Kramer, before adding: "Good night, hey?"

"Top shelf, pantry," she said. "Behind where the box of birthday-cake candles is kept."

Kramer watched her go down the corridor. She looked tired, but walked with none of the unsteadiness normally associated with someone just roused from slumber, which intrigued him.

Then he found, behind the box of birthday-cake candles, a large, untouched bottle of Oude Meester brandy, its seal still intact. There was a holly-leaf label attached to the neck of the bottle which read: *To my beloved Pik, Happy Christmas! XXX*.

Kramer poured a good measure into a tumbler and sat down at the kitchen table, propping his feet up. He saw no harm in drinking a dead man's booze. He had read somewhere that people did this to Napoleon's brandy all the time—and then boasted to their friends about it.

"So you found the bottle okay," said the Widow Fourie, returning to the kitchen with an empty glass.

"Like some?"

"No, not for me, thanks."

"Have just a drop," he insisted. "One tiny drop! It'll help you get straight back to sleep again." And he looked her in the eye.

"No, honest," she said, turning quickly away.

"Suit yourself!"

"You sound upset," she said, rinsing the glass in the sink. "Why's that?"

"All right if I have another?"

"It's there to be drunk."

"So am I," said Kramer.

She sat silently with him, sorting the children's freshly laundered clothes into four neat piles on the tabletop, while he sank that first tumblerful. His gaze kept returning to her and especially to that wide, generous mouth with its bracketing of laughter lines.

"If you're staring at these spots," she said, "it's my time of the month, that's all. You don't have to be so blatant about it."

Kramer dug out a Lucky. "Ach, no!" he said. "I was thinking of something else entirely: Short Arse."

"I beg your pardon!"

"Hell, not you, hey? Just some kaffir."

"What kaffir?"

So he told her, speaking freely, too freely maybe, but he'd hardly eaten all day and the brandy was coursing strong through his veins. He let slip that he had a hunch about this kaffir that made the hairs at the back of his neck stand up, a sort of destiny thing.

"Oh," she said, and became silent again.

"Don't just sit there—talk!" he said. "Keep on talking. Tell me how bloody stupid I'm being!"

"I can't," she said. "The day that Pik got killed, he kissed me good-bye at the door, same as usual, then he came back and kissed me and the kids again, a second time. There seemed to be no reason."

They were both quiet after that, while the kitchen clock kept its ponderous loud ticking.

"This native," said the Widow Fourie, abruptly brisk and businesslike, pouring herself a small tot of brandy. "You'll just have to look for him, find him, see for yourself how plain and ordinary he is, and put an end to—"

"Look for him?" echoed Kramer. "What the hell else do you think Hans and me have been doing half the night?"

"You didn't tell me that. How am I supposed to know?"

"We searched everywhere, high and low. Gone! Vanished, just like that . . ."

The Widow Fourie downed her brandy in one, grimacing at the taste, then placed the glass very carefully on the tabletop. "You say," she said, "that he's probably changed by now into the suit of clothes he stole from the kitchen boy at Fynn's Creek. Were you able to give people a good description of them?"

"Oh, ja," said Kramer. "Excellent."

"You're sure?"

"Cassius got it directly off the kitchen boy. One black jacket, black pants with shiny seat, and a white shirt that has a patch on the left shoulder made out of the shirttail. A belt that's black on the outside, grey on the inside, and the buckle has a five-pointed star on it, real trading store. Also, a pair of size eleven, black, imitation lace-up shoes. Thick soles with a crisscross pattern, a nick in the left toe cap from a falling penknife, and a blemish on the right shoe that's an area of roughness in the shape of a half-moon. Oh, and the shoes hadn't been dyed evenly: the left one had a bit of purple in the black, when you held it to the light."

"Yirra," said the Widow Fourie, "that really *is* a description! The cook boy told you all that? He must've been in love with those blessed shoes of his!"

Kramer nodded. "My reaction was the same," he said. "Only Cassius pointed out that there are over three hundred words in Zulu you can use to describe the different colors of a cow. On top of which, there are even more words for every kind of horn, hoof, et cetera. I think what he meant was, when a coon around here is too poor to own any cattle, then a shoe—even one that's not real hide—just has to do, hey?"

"Hmmmmm," said the Widow Fourie. "So this native hasn't been seen since—can't he just have gone? Y'know, back to wherever you think you first saw him?"

"Ja, outside the magistrate's court," muttered Kramer, then realized what he had just said.

And he was back in Trekkersburg, on his very first morning, in the alley beside the courthouse, which had been thronged so solid with worried kaffir wives and their families that you had to force your way through them. Then, all of a sudden, the crowd had parted of its own volition, and through it had come a coon version of Frank Sinatra making with the jaunty walk. The snap-brim hat, padded shoulders, and zootsuit larded with glinting thread were all secondhand ideas from a secondhand shop. Yet with them went the feeling that here was an original, even if someone, somewhere else, had thought it all up before. The man walked that way because he thought that way, and the crowd had sensed this—just as it had sensed that something special, perhaps even deadly, walked with him.

"Tromp?" said the Widow Fourie, sounding very concerned. "Trompie, are you all right?"

"Ach, fine!" he said, blinking, reaching for more brandy. "You think the kaffir's gone back? Why the bloody change of clothes if he was going to do that? No, my feeling is that he's still around, lying low, still keeping a watch on what we're—"

"But why?" asked the Widow Fourie. "That's the part I don't get. I can't see how a native could possibly have been mixed up in—"

"Then I'll have to just bloody ask him!" said Kramer testily, needing time to think, feeling the pressure. "Find a way to get my cuffs on him, and ask him lots of things—ask the two-faced bastard what the hell's going on here!"

"I know a way," she said.

"Pardon?"

"I know a way of catching him, if he's still in the area," said the Widow Fourie. "It's what my Uncle Koos did, that time he had all the trouble with the leopard. You know what sly, cunning creatures leopards are, hiding away so you never see them—leaving you just to find another of your flock has been taken in the morning? Well, Uncle Koos knew the leopard was out there somewhere, hiding in the foothills, and so he just got a goat and—"

"Ja, ja, set a trap!" said Kramer, nodding.

He did not sleep much after that. Every time his eyes closed, and his mind lost its grip on the day, slipping into strange half-dreams, mostly seascapes, it took only the slightest sound to jolt him wide awake again. Then he would lie staring at the ceiling, trying to grasp the actual implications of Short Arse and Zoot Suit being one and the same bastard, until eventually his eyelids drifted shut once more, restarting the cycle.

"Can Dingaan have your fat, please?" Piet asked him at the breakfast table.

"I'd sooner he had my head," said Kramer, waving aside the milk that the maid had been about to add to his coffee. "Ja, of course he can—he can have the whole of my bacon, if he likes. I'm not in the mood for it."

"Ja, my ma warned me," said Piet, forking the bacon over onto his bread plate.

"Warned you about what?"

"She said you'd probably be like a bull who had backed into a big cactus this morning."

"That ma of yours . . ."

"She's nice, isn't she?" said Piet. "Sometimes I think Fanie Kritzinger's got a better one, but not always."

"Oh, ja? Any view on his pa, then?"

"He's dead. Kicked the bucket. Everyone knows that."

"Who told you, hey?"

"I don't know—one of the kids, down by the river."

"Was his pa a nice man?"

Piet shrugged.

"Come on," said Kramer. "What was he like?"

"He wasn't like that other policeman who used to come and see my ma a lot, Herman's uncle. He was like . . . well, a bit like you, I suppose, and they didn't let *him* have a uniform either."

Kramer wasn't sure why, but as he drove to Jafini police station shortly before nine, he kept thinking about that little conversation.

Then he became preoccupied by other things, and in particular by the trap he would set that day for Short Arse. Try as he might, he had not been able to improve on the trick that the Widow Fourie's uncle had played on the leopard, and had finally decided there was probably no need to. Just as the leopard had been attracted by the sheepfold, Short Arse had his own known center of interest: the Fynn's Creek murder scene. Granted, now that all the activity had died down there, most of its appeal must have gone, too, but some form of tethered goat could soon change this.

"Goat, goat, goat . . ." Kramer murmured, trying to think of something simple.

Simplest of all would be to renew police activity at Fynn's Creek and then make a mystery of what exactly they were up to. But how? Now that Field Cornet Dorf had been over the site with such care, it was difficult to see what there was left to act as a fresh focus of attention. Hell, the whole place had been scrutinized and every last morsel of possible evidence had—no, wait! There *was* still one part of the scene as yet unexamined: the hut of Moses the cook boy, where Short Arse himself had come calling!

"Perfect," said Kramer.

Terblanche had on his harassed look. "Morning, Tromp!" he said, scraping a splash of maize porridge from his tie. "Goodness, what a start to the day . . ."

"You should try eating slower, Hans."

"No, no, not this! I've just had the station commander at Nkosala on the phone, reminding me I've got to be in court there at ten in the middle of all else! And if I don't find my statement soon to memorize, I won't know what to say! I did try for an adjournment on account of assisting you in this matter, but—"

"That's fine, man! I'll see you after. I just need to borrow one of your blokes and a boy."

"Take Malan—I prefer Sarel to be in charge of the station whenever I'm away—and any Bantu that's going. What's this in aid of?"

"To help me find Short Arse."

"Ach, I'm sorry, of course! Just shows what a muddle I'm getting myself into. Let's hope today our luck changes, hey?"

"Man, I know it will."

"How can you be so sure, Tromp?"

Kramer almost told him about the trap, then realized something just in the nick of time. Above all, the renewal of activity at Fynn's Creek had to appear wholly authentic in order for his plan to work, but if transparent rustics like the station commander and his little gang of half-wits were allowed to know what was really going on, they'd be very unlikely to play their roles convincingly enough to fool a blind man tied up in a sack with carrots stuck in his ears.

"Let that be my surprise, Hans," he said, straightening the station commander's tie for him and tucking it in neatly.

17

Kramer liked it when things began to happen quickly. Malan, on the other hand, looked as though he'd prefer things to be happening very, very slowly and exceedingly gently.

So dreadful was his hangover after the previous evening's junketings with Field Cornet Dorf at the Royal Hotel, Nkosala, that, pale and shaky, with his rugby socks down around his ankles, he accepted his orders without question for once, and went in search of One Ear, practically tiptoeing from the station commander's office.

"That must have been some meal you had at the Royal with Sybrand," said Kramer, as they headed for Fynn's Creek with the Bantu detective One Ear riding in the cage on the back. "And he looks such a quiet type."

Malan grunted. "Only until his third beer, Lieutenant. He's been under a big strain lately."

"How many beers did he have?"

"Er, eight or nine, same as me, and three brandies, Lieutenant."

"Uh-huh. Much broken furniture on the bill?"

"Hell, no, Lieutenant! None, hey?"

"Pity," said Kramer, thinking of the Colonel.

"Lieutenant," Malan began afresh, clearing his throat, "you must forgive me if this sounds a stupid question, but why exactly are we going down to the beach again?"

"I told you: to take a look at the cook boy's hut."

"Ja, I thought so, only Sarel said he can't see what possible relevance—"

"Suzman? Who asked him to stick his nose into this?"

"Er, it was just I was explaining to him where I was going today and he—"

"Uniform should learn to mind its own business," said Kramer. "Just as CID should learn to keep its trap shut!—you hear? I don't like having my movements being debated by all and sundry."

"Sir, I only—"

"Then don't," said Kramer.

It was wild, down at Fynn's Creek. A high wind, slanting in off the whitecapped ocean, plumed the tops of the sand dunes, filling the air with fine, stinging sand. The debris from the explosion flapped and skidded, slithered, tore apart the neat grid of thatching string set up by Field Cornet Dorf, and the door of the hut belonging to Moses the cook boy was, not unnaturally, tight shut.

Kramer banged on it with his fist. "Moses, you in there, hey?" he called out, his words whipped away by the wind.

The cook boy poked his head out an instant later and greeted him effusively.

"He offers his most humble greetings to the Great Bull Elephant, sir," One Ear translated, "and says—"

"Tell him less of the bull and more of the just-listen," said Kramer. "Tell him his hut could be very important to the case and it has to be thoroughly investigated forthwith."

"Hau, hau, hau!" responded Moses, immensely flattered.

Kramer then entered the hut and took a good look round. There was nothing to see, really, other than an iron divan, a twist of threadbare bedding, a mine boy's cheap tin trunk, some square biscuit tins, a shaving mirror, a candlestick and candle, a walking stick, a few cooking utensils, and a length of string, fixed between the rafters, from which dangled three wire coat hangers used for servant-boy canvas shorts and tunics. It bothered him there might be bedbugs running loose, ready to launch a major offensive, but nonetheless he closed the door firmly behind him and resolved to stand there in semidarkness, pretending some form of intensive search, for the next twenty minutes.

He lasted five, but given the buffeting effects of the weather outside, he calculated it would have seemed a lot longer than that for the others, and opened up again.

"Is that it, Lieutenant—you've finished at last?" asked Malan, who had got sand in one eye and was poking at it with a corner of his handkerchief. "Man, this wind is—"

"Ask Moses for me," Kramer said to One Ear, "where he kept the clothes that were stolen. Were they in his trunk?"

"*Yebo, nkosi gakulu!*" replied Moses, nodding vigorously.

"Ja, I thought as much. Well, that might as well stay here and be fingerprinted with the rest of the stuff. Tin like that can take a good palm impression when the lid is being closed again. Oh, ja, and ask him if the trunk is usually kept there, under his bed. The intruder must have pulled it out?"

Again, Moses nodded.

"That settles it," said Kramer. "Fingerprints will have to pay a visit—I'm not dragging whole beds back up to Jafini, bugger that for laughs."

"Hell, this is a bit thorough, isn't it, sir, for a Bantu petty theft?" remarked Malan, his eye streaming by now.

"Ach, no, it's much more than that, man!"

"In what—"

"Malan, you're fishing, hey? Didn't I say all would be revealed to you at the appropriate time?"

"Sorry, Lieutenant! It's just—"

"Tell me," said Kramer, "how good are you with your hands?"

Malan frowned. "In what sense?" he asked cautiously, making a knuckle pop. "You mean like in karate or—"

"This hut needs to be made secure," Kramer explained, "and this silly little latch on it is far too flimsy. What I want instead is something tough with a bloody big padlock. Can you see to that for me, chop-chop?"

"I, er . . ."

"Excellent!" said Kramer. "And while you're away, buying the necessary and picking up the tools, One Ear here can stand guard. This place must be kept one hundred percent secure at all times until the lock is on—understood?"

Malan nodded enthusiastically. "Only wouldn't it be simpler, sir," he ventured, "if Botha came straight over now from Nkosala and did his fingerprint check while we—"

"Ach, I'm not having some half-baked scene-of-the-crime idiot work on a case of this magnitude!" said Kramer. "Who is this Botha, a CID who does fingerprints part-time? Same as Suzman takes murder-scene snaps I *still* haven't seen?"

"Er, ja, we don't really have the proper—"

"Exactly," said Kramer, "but *I'm* Murder Squad and I'm going to arrange for our top bloke from Trekkersburg to come up here." Then, turning to One Ear, he ordered: "Tell Moses to collect his pass book—I'm taking him back to Jafini with me right away, where he can go and stay with his uncle for a while."

This announcement made Moses clap his hands in delight, but Malan looked no happier, as he eyed the door to the hut, sizing up the problems with which it would present him.

"Here," said Kramer, tossing him the Land-Rover's keys, "you'll be needing these. Just see you make a bloody good job of that, you hear? Take lots of measurements."

Malan caught the keys. "But how are you—"

"Ach, man, it's obvious! I'm going back in Kritz's car—it's high time something was done with it."

Kritzinger had been issued with a Chevrolet the same make and model as Kramer brought up from Trekkersburg, only black instead of cream. It was also missing its hubcaps, and there was a long scratch in the paintwork down the left-hand side. Closer inspection revealed a dent in the front fender, bloodstained and matted with animal hairs, black and white.

"Goat . . . !" murmured Kramer, savoring the irony and wondering if he should not have used the car for setting his trap instead—it had also escaped any previous attention.

"Just sit here a moment and wait," he said, turning to Moses the cook boy, who had been following obediently at his heels. "*Sit!* You understand that?"

Moses nodded and squatted down on his haunches quite contentedly in the lee of the thorn trees hiding the vehicle.

Kramer tried the driver's door and found it unlocked. He then slid in behind the wheel and deduced, from the position of the seat, that he and Maaties Kritzinger would have been pretty well the same size, certainly when it came to leg length. He checked the controls. Although the Chevrolet was parked on a level piece of ground, it had been left in gear and with its handbrake on. These were the unthinking hallmarks of a habitually cautious man, and entirely in keeping with the long approach on foot which Kritzinger had then made to the game ranger's outpost. Kramer pulled out the ashtray, discovering it packed to the brim with Texan stubs—Lucky Strike's main rival.

Next, Kramer opened the glove compartment and searched it thoroughly. Apart from the handbook which went with the Chev, and a pair of cheap, women's sunglasses, he found nothing. He started on the seats, front and rear, digging his fingers deep into the spaces between the cushions, and came up with seven burnt matches, a spent ballpoint, and a bent paper clip.

That's when he started to look for actual hiding places, more typical of a thoroughly cautious man. He ran his hand along behind the dashboard, checked beneath the carpeting, and prodded the upholstery lining the doors. Nothing.

He climbed out and went round to inspect the trunk. It was locked, but Terblanche had thoughtfully provided him with a spare key, kept on the station's keyboard. The trunk was showroom clean, having never been used, by the look of it. Even so, Kramer pulled back the matting, inspected the spare wheel, and dug into every nook and cranny. Still nothing.

With a frown, he closed the trunk lid and returned to sit in the driver's seat, lit a Lucky, and took the pair of cheap sunglasses from the glove compartment. Logically, they had to belong to Mrs. Kritzinger, he reasoned, as she must surely have been the only female to have occasionally ridden up front with Maaties in his work car. Moreover, it they *weren't* hers, would Maaties have left them lying about like that, on show? But what if he had been unaware of them being there? Say someone had slipped them into the glove compartment, unnoticed by him as he drove into the final twilight of his life, heading for a curry dinner somewhere. The same someone who had later told him something that had sent him racing to meet his death at this godforsaken spot.

"Ach, I'd better do a check," muttered Kramer, not persuaded he had made a major find, but uneasy now at the thought of dismissing the damned things out of hand. "Moses? You ready to go, hey? Then jump in the bloody back, kaffir—I've got a lady to see!"

And he barely noticed the cane cutters this time, some working all alone, others in groups, blacker than black, hooded by their sacks, long knives motionless, watching him drive by, just the whites of their eyes showing.

Back in Jafini, Kramer turned and said to his backseat passenger: "Okay, so where the hell does your uncle live, hey?" He wanted to make a door-to-door delivery, so that Short Arse was almost bound to hear of it.

"Uncle?" Moses repeated, baffled.

"Ja, man, your bloody uncle, hey?"

"*Hau, EEE-uncle! Yebo, yebo yebo, nkosi gakulu!*" said Moses in a happy outburst of comprehension. "*Eee-uncle* down by that side, *nkosi*!" And he began giving what seemed like quite contradictory directions, pointing in several directions at once.

"Look, Moses, man," said Kramer, "I'm going to drive down into shantytown, go slowly all around, and when we're near your eee-uncle's place, just give a yell—okay?"

And that was how things finally worked out, with Moses

being dropped off outside a small mud-walled house, its tin roof held down by ripening pumpkins. In moments, his uncle was out to receive him, and even before Kramer had been able to make his U-turn, a crowd of astonished neighbors had gathered, all bursting to hear how he had come to ride in the well-known car of a detective sergeant everyone thought was dead.

"You tell them, kaffir!" muttered Kramer, as he picked up speed a little. "And make it one hell of a story, you hear? I don't want Short Arse to be disappointed . . ."

Then he shot round to the police station to exchange Kritzinger's Chevrolet for his own, and almost ran down Suzman in the yard, coffee mug in hand and his mouth wide open.

"Jesus *Christ*, Lieutenant, I thought I'd just seen a spook driving up!"

"Oh, ja? That's why I'm doing a swap—high time I called on Hettie Kritzinger, wouldn't you say?"

"Well, sir, I'm not too sure about that," said Suzman. "The same thought had occurred to me—that maybe I should go say hello—but Doc came in for a minute this morning and he's not too happy about her."

"Ach, I'll play it by ear. What's the address?"

"Forty-four Sunrise Street, about two blocks farther from where you're staying."

"Uh-huh. See you later, then."

"But where's Jaapie gone, Lieutenant?"

"Malan's doing some carpentry for me down at Fynn's Creek," said Kramer, twisting his ignition key. "Any bits and pieces he wants can come out of petty cash, okay?"

"*Carpentry?*" echoed Suzman, looking bewildered.

"Love to stay and chat, Sergeant, but duty calls, hey?"

Outside the red-brick bungalow where Maaties Kritzinger had once lived with his little snapshot family, there was a poker-work nameplate on the garden gate that read: *Happy Haven*.

"Total Neglect" might have been more appropriate, for the

place was in one hell of a state. This was not true of the garden itself, which had been tended as carefully as any in the care of a garden boy wanting his wages, but the house was another matter. Lengths of storm guttering hung loose, the off-white paintwork had bubbled, one window had a cardboard patch Scotch-taped over the sort of hole made by a cricket ball, and the front door's varnish was faded and streaky. Accentuating all this drabness was a scattering of brightly colored toys, most of them near a tipped-over swing and an upended tricycle.

Yet no children came running out to peer at the tall stranger, as Kramer advanced up the crazy-paving path, his trouser legs whipped by the wind. Neither was there any sound from within after he rapped loudly on first the front door and then on the one leading from the back verandah into the kitchen.

Then a lavatory cistern flushed, and into the kitchen shuffled a small, bedraggled-looking woman, wearing a candlewick dressing gown clutched tight across her flat chest. She gave a violent start when she noticed Kramer, squash-nosed at the window in her back door, and he hastily took out his warrant card to press it against the pane for her.

"So you've come," she said, in a whispery voice, opening up. "I knew you would one day. I've been waiting for it for years."

18

A *hungry* kitten mewed and pressed itself against Hettie Kritzinger's bony ankles. She glanced down and frowned a little, as though it reminded her of something. "The children," she added, "aren't here. They've been taken by neighbors, I think. The Widow Fourie has rung. Twice. Everyone has been so kind."

"I suppose this is where you must keep the milk," said Kramer, stepping into her kitchen and swinging open the refrigerator door. "Ja, there's plenty . . ." And he filled the kitten's saucer. "Like a coffee or something yourself, Mrs. Kritz?"

She shrugged, conveying a sense of utter indifference. "I always knew you would come," she said. "But people have been so kind. Some, because it interests them. They want to know all the details of how he died. He died a hero, so they tell me."

"Er, ja, Maaties was attempting to—"

"One of the best. They tell me that, too. They always have and I always knew."

Kramer thought it advisable to say nothing further until he

had placed two cups of coffee on the kitchen table, and had pulled out a chair for her, having first removed from it a Mickey Mouse coloring book.

"The good die young," said Hettie Kritzinger, taking a different chair. "That made the first part of our marriage the worst years of all. It made me so afraid. Every day I expected this. Then I discovered he wasn't always good, but could often be quite bad in a way, and that made things easier. I thought he'd at least reach forty. Now this . . ."

"Sugar?" offered Kramer, holding out the bowl.

She ignored it. "Now this," she said, touching a skinny-fingered hand to her frizzy ginger hair, looking at him with empty eyes that seemed disproportionately huge, like a bush baby's.

Kramer stirred three heaped teaspoons of sugar into his coffee. "I never knew Maaties," he said. "I'm from the Free State, only just arrived in Natal—Trekkersburg Murder and Robbery Squad. Tromp Kramer."

"Are you married?" she asked.

"No, I'm not—no ring, see?" And he held out his left hand. "Come to think of it, your husband didn't wear one either, though, did he?"

"Only at first. He had it specially inscribed on the inside with our initials. 'You see that, Hettie,' he would say, 'what that means is: wherever I go, you go, too.'"

"A nice thought, hey?"

"Frightening," she said. "A policeman goes to some terrible places. I made him leave it with me eventually." And she began playing with the big, loose gold ring that covered her own wedding ring.

"By the way," said Kramer, placing the sunglasses on the kitchen table between them. "Do you know whose these are, hey?"

"Mine," she said, barely glancing at them. "Oh, ja, some terrible, terrible places. It gave me nightmares."

"You mean Maaties occasionally let slip what his work involved?" asked Kramer.

"He never let slip," she said. "He always told me, told me

everything, told me in detail the things that troubled him, and afterward he could sleep. Often I'd lie there and get the stomach cramps. Then he stopped, said things had become too serious, too dangerous to talk about."

Kramer tried not to lean forward. "What sort of things made him stop?"

"Obsessed," she said, taking her first sip of coffee. "For months, he's been obsessed."

"Obsessed by what?"

"I've tried asking him. A killer, he says, but he must have the proper facts first. He can't believe it. He doesn't say any more."

"And how long has this been going on?"

Again, a shrug. "Since last year sometime," she said. "All I ever hear now is what he shouts out in his sleep."

"Such as?" prompted Kramer.

"Oh, it's just gibberish."

"Can you remember any of it?"

"It seemed like the name of something. Some kind of animal . . ."

"Wild or domestic?"

She looked down at the kitten, still lapping. "A dog," she said. "Some kind of dog, I think it was. It really scared him."

"What sort of dog?" urged Kramer.

"Can't remember," said Hettie Kritzinger.

Ten minutes later, Kramer was back in the yard at Jafini police station, still finding it difficult to relax his shoulder muscles. Even after making allowances for the woman's present circumstances, he felt pretty sure that she would have always had much the same effect on him—and he couldn't imagine how Maaties Kritzinger had been able to stand such intensity, year after year. No wonder the poor bastard had spent all his time working! Or was it that, being the kind of man he was, she had slowly lost any lighter side to her, becoming eclipsed by the dark shadows he cast in their marriage bed, where she had implied he'd done most of his talking?

"Ach!" said Kramer, getting out of the Chevrolet. "You are a bloody detective, Tromp, man! Just stick to those sort of deductions!"

Not that he had much to work on, but at least he now knew that something, dating back to the previous year, had wrought a decided change in Maatie Kritzinger's behavior, leaving him incredulous and secretive and apparently afraid to divulge even a suspicion for fear of its enormity.

"What I must do," Kramer told himself, starting toward the rear entrance to the station, "is go and take a look at all those papers of his myself, try to work out what set him off like this. I must've been mad to make that Bokkie Maritz' department!"

Malan was lying in wait for him, just inside the building. "Lieutenant, sir," he whined, "that lock-and-bolt thing is turning out a proper disaster—I've been trying to get it right for hours!"

"What's the problem exactly?"

"The wood of the door isn't thick enough for the screws that a big bolt takes, so they go right through and—"

"Then just add a bit more wood to it, make it thicker, man!"

"I've got to go down there *again*? That's six trips I've done since—"

"You haven't left it unguarded, have you?"

"Never, sir! But I thought maybe Suzman could have a go. He's quite handy with tools, you know, and quite prepared to give me a—"

"No chance," said Kramer. "Lieutenant Terblanche wants him here to deputize, and I'm not going to even argue."

Suzman, hovering in the charge office door, must have overheard the entire exchange, and very wisely said nothing about it.

One by one, Kramer went through every docket in or on the desk of the late Maaties Kritzinger. This took hours, but he had plenty of time to kill—his trap could not be set until after darkness fell.

As Maritz had claimed, almost all of Kritzinger's cases had been routine Bantu matters, save the one concerning the shooting of an Asiatic male begging clothes for his children—and this other, rather weird investigation that Kramer now had open before him.

According to the postmortem report, the deceased, an elderly white female living alone on a farm, had in effect died of fright during a burglary with aggravated circumstances—to wit, she had been tied up in an eiderdown and left to utter muffled cries while her home was ransacked. That in itself was nothing special—Bantu gangs risked the gallows carrying out this kind of raid all the time—but Kritzinger had scribbled something rather unusual on the exhibits sheet. A pair of spectacles had been found lying at the foot of the deceased's bed, and Kritzinger had noted:

> *Not hers, a male's. Not a Bantu's either I bet—don't these frames cost a bomb? But Colonel won't take the point so local inquiries continue.*

And the great sheaf of attached statements were all from Bantu males in the Jafini area, leading nowhere.

"I wonder if he was right?" muttered Kramer. "And what is he bloody hinting at?"

The door to the station commander's office opened and Suzman entered with a cup of tea. "You really have had your head down for the last three hours, haven't you, sir?" he smarmed. "I just thought you might like this."

"What's up? Are your boys all out?"

"Er, no, Lieutenant, but I didn't like to send one in on account of the fact you could be—well, engaged in confidential matters."

Kramer nodded. "Talking of which, where do I find a key to the exhibits cupboard?"

"Just tell me what you require, and I'll fetch it for you right away, sir."

"I require the key," said Kramer very firmly.

Even then the toadying bastard would not leave him alone,

but reappeared at his elbow just as he was digging about in the cupboard, amused by the bizarre objects he kept coming across. Kramer particularly liked the teddy bear in some sort of jockstrap, a relic of an unsolved case of sending offensive matter through the post.

"Sis!" said Suzman, with a shudder of disgust. "You'll find the shelves go in years, Lieutenant, with the solved cases, ready for court, on the top one."

Kramer uncovered, on the middle shelf, a neat parcel that contained what looked like bits of broomstick, wrapped in a greasy brown paper, and which the faded ink on its exhibits label described as "1 doz. sticks dynamite." "Where the hell did these come from?" he said, turning the label round. "Oh, ja, that quarry place I rang up last night. So that was what the old bugger was complaining about—not getting his stuff back! Someone should have explained the position regarding evidence, hey?"

"Lieutenant?" said Suzman.

"Ach, never mind, man, ancient history!" said Kramer, pushing the parcel aside and digging deeper. "Is it safe to store like that, by the way?"

"Fine, sir, so we were told."

"Gotcha!" said Kramer, his right hand closing on a pair of spectacles, well hidden by a pile of almost new clothing.

One glance at those frames was enough to see immediately what Kritzinger had meant: no coon in the world, unless he'd stolen them, could ever have worn glasses like these—hell, they'd have taken more than a month of Kramer's *own* wages to pay for.

"Not those again," said Suzman. "Maaties suspected the grandson, you know: a car salesman from Durban, very flash—too flash, was his argument, for a bloke with the kind of bad breath he had."

"Oh, ja?" said Kramer. "But the case never got any further?"

"It's still open, Lieutenant," said Suzman, shrugging. "Any particular reason for your interest?"

"Uh-uh, I'm just snooping around, trying to get the feel of

Kritz's last year. Tell me, Sergeant, any recollection of his suddenly changing in manner? Getting tense about a case, becoming even a bit obsessive?"

Suzman thought for a few seconds. "No, sir, I can't," he said. "Would you like some toast, maybe, to go with your tea?"

"Ta," said Kramer, convinced by now his only hope of making any progress was through the capture of Short Arse.

And then, almost before he knew it, the seemingly endless wait was over: a ragged sunset, which showed how hard the wind was still blowing, pinked the blotter on Terblanche's desk, and it was time to visit Fynn's Creek again.

"Suzman," said Kramer, rapping on the door of the privy out in the yard, "I've a message for Lieutenant Terblanche when he gets back from Nkosala. Tell him I'm going down to make sure the cook boy's hut is secure, then I'm going to take an early night for once. Maybe we all should—nothing new is likely to emerge before tomorrow, hey?"

"Is it true there's a fingerprint expert coming?"

"Who told you about that?"

"Er, Malan, Lieutenant. He was explaining why the lock had to—"

"Ach!" said Kramer. "What's important is that you relay my message to Lieutenant Terblanche the minute he gets here."

"Er, very good, sir," came Suzman's muffled voice. "And what about—"

"I'll be seeing Malan myself, so don't you worry about him, hey?"

"No, what I was going to ask, sir, was where will you be if you're suddenly needed?"

"The Widow Fourie's of course, but I might decide to eat at the Royal in Nkosala first. I'll see how I feel after I leave the beach."

"Very good, Lieutenant! Er, 'bye for now, hey?"

Commandeering the last remaining Land-Rover, Kramer took the cellophane wrapper from a fresh pack of Luckys, made sure he'd have plenty of matches, too, and set off, hoping that Malan and One Ear would not meet him halfway, having left the cook boy's hut secure but not under surveillance. Granted, it was still daylight, which meant Short Arse was highly unlikely to be abroad yet, nosing round to discover what all the fuss had been about, but you could never tell with a kaffir, least of all with one as sly and devious as this little bastard.

19

*T*he sound of Kramer's arrival at Fynn's Creek went unnoticed, so great was the noise being made by the wind now, as it battered at the coastline. Malan, watched by One Ear, was trying to close a large padlock and have it stay closed, but it kept falling open.

"Ach, try turning the key at the same time!" suggested Kramer, making both men jump. "Massive locks like that sometimes have a different way of working."

And he was right: the padlock stayed closed, securing a bolt robust enough for a Robben Island cellblock.

"Here, Lieutenant," said Malan, handing the key and its duplicate over. "Sorry it took so long, hey?"

"That's okay, man. You can scoot now."

"Meaning I can bugger off, Lieutenant?"

"Ja, and your Bantu also. Time we all packed it in for today—there'll be plenty to do tomorrow."

Malan didn't need telling twice and neither did One Ear, who grabbed up a bag of tools that had been borrowed somewhere, gave Kramer a nervous, polite nod, and hurried off in his master's footsteps, leaning forward into the wind.

In two shakes of a Land-Rover's exhaust pipe, they were gone.

A quarter of an hour later, having spent the time in pretended close examination of the area immediately in front of the cook boy's hut, Kramer started up the other Land-Rover, swung it round, and followed in their wake along the track that led to the Jafini road.

"Sssssssss-bang!" he said softly, imitating the sound of a puncture as he reached the point where the cane fields began, and then he let go of the steering wheel, allowing the Land-Rover to swerve off the track, plunge into the cane, lurch to a stop, and stall there.

He got out, muttering under his breath, and went round to inspect the right rear wheel, crouching down beside it with a matchstick hidden in his right hand. He pressed the matchstick into the valve of the tire and deflated it, the hiss being lost in the noise the wind was making.

Then he took the spare tire from the bonnet of the Land-Rover, propped it up, and left the matchstick to deflate it, too, while he got out the jack. He jacked up the rear of the vehicle, took another look at the spare tire, removed the matchstick, and swore. He looked around him, turned up his jacket collar, and started on foot down the track, confident he had left behind him a sorry tale told in pictures, should anyone chance upon it. He was fairly certain that Short Arse would not be abroad yet, while the light still lasted, but felt it was wiser to take what precautions he could to disguise his actual intentions.

Fifteen yards farther on, Kramer left the track, undoing his fly as though about to relieve himself. Instead, he pushed on through some young cane, hoping to God he would not meet a mamba, and then doubled back toward the sea.

Reaching the line of scrub vegetation, just short of where the dunes began, Kramer paused, weighing up where best to position himself for what might prove a long vigil. There was definitely something to be said for staying in the scrub, which offered both cover and shelter from the wind. By edging along five hundred yards or so to his right, he could align himself with Moses' hut and have a grandstand seat when Short Arse finally made his appearance. The snag was, however, he could find himself at the very spot where Short Arse might choose to emerge from cover himself, and frighten the little bastard off, before he even had a chance to realize it.

"No, it's got to be the beach side," Kramer muttered.

Once on the shoreline, he could again move south, line himself up with the hut, and approach up the side of the huge dunes bounding the outpost. In fact, by lying flat just below the summit of the biggest dune and peering over it, he would have an unparalleled, panoramic view of Fynn's Creek, making it virtually impossible for anyone to come creeping out of the sugarcane without being seen first.

It wasn't difficult, something like two hours later on a surprisingly chill night, to feel that the whole ramshackle, overconfident, ill-founded scheme had been the biggest mistake of an otherwise moderately successful career. The wind had apparently been trying to make this point right from the outset, when Kramer, belly-down on the biggest dune, had reached the top and taken his first look down the far side. A moment later, a cloud had been blown in front of the moon, making it impossible to see a damn thing, and then enough sand had been blasted up both his trouser legs to form the basis of a cement mix.

Worse still, the wind had again and again craftily drawn breath each time Kramer attempted to light a consoling Lucky, and then puffed out his match at precisely the moment the flame reached the tobacco. And even when, after dozens of tries, he finally managed to get a cigarette alight, the wind still had a trick up its sleeve: it made the tobacco combust so fiercely the whole lot was consumed in a fraction of the time it usually took, leaving a very nasty aftertaste.

"All I can say for you, you bastard, is that you're keeping any bloody fishermen away," grunted Kramer, as he closed his eyes to another sudden bluster, wondering what in God's name he was doing, a fully fledged CID officer in the South African Police, lying here *sober* and addressing the elements.

He'd had words with the sea earlier. It had seemed so huge and unreasoning, poised there behind his back, filled with dark mysteries and horrors, showing off its immense strength in breakers that boomed above the shriek of the wind, that he had become not at all sure that it would remain much longer below land level, but might decide tonight was the night for a little slap and tickle among the sexier ladies of Jafini, sparing not a thought for the poor bugger it drowned on the beach on its blundering way there.

"So watch it," he had warned. "Any more of your nonsense, hey, and I'll come and bloody piss in you!—and that'll change you *worldwide*, you hear?"

Now, in a different mood, waiting for the next all-too-brief gap in the scudding clouds, Kramer gradually became aware that the sea in fact made him edgy in much the same way as when there was a woman behind him who kept staring, yet turned her face away whenever he looked round.

Suddenly he stiffened, holding his breath.

In that instant, the sea, wind, the very universe itself, personified by the great, dizzy dome of star pricks wheeling overhead, ceased being of the slightest importance; Kramer had just seen, without the shadow of a doubt, something man-size scuttle like a huge crab across the mud behind the cook boy's hut.

Then the biggest cloud in the sky hid the moon.

Without even pausing to curse, Kramer heaved himself forward, nosedived down the far side of the dune, and started doing a form of breaststroke, propelling himself as fast as possible down that slope of fine, slithering sand. The stuff began to pack the inside of his jacket, fill his top pockets, work its way even into his mouth as he gasped silently, quickly breathless with such sudden exertion. Yet he hardly noticed this, so intent was he on reaching the bottom of the dune undetected.

There, he had barely recoiled from the clammy feel of the

mudflats when a flashlight came on, directed at the new padlock and bolt which Malan had fitted to the hut door that day, unwittingly inviting just such a covert inspection.

"Christ, it's worked!" said Kramer, in the softest of whispers. "It's bloody worked! *I've got you,* Short Arse, you bastard . . ."

And he knew his words would be safe with the wind, which blew hard, harder, began to howl, shriek, to whip up flapping debris, slam it against the Parks Board Land-Rover, making the flashlight whip round. Seconds later, however, the bright beam was back on the padlock, and Kramer advanced swiftly to crouch behind the Land-Rover's tailgate, pistol in hand.

Then a great, thick crowbar could be seen, in that wavering circle of light, being pushed in behind the padlock and levered violently upward. Because of its size—Short Arse must certainly have assessed the situation earlier—the crowbar made very short work of the bolt, ripping it out of the door, still attached to a fair bit of splintered wood, and a split second later, the flashlight moved inside the hut, to be directed at something on the floor there.

"April fool," murmured Kramer, standing up just as the moon broke big, bright, and beautiful behind him.

It sent his shadow like an assegai into the hut, and left him in clean-cut silhouette, like a combat target on a shooting range.

"Police!" he bellowed, bringing his pistol up, two-handed, aiming for the center of the hut's doorway. "Come out backward with your hands on your—"

Vvvvvvit-ting

Curiously, he didn't hear the firearm actually being discharged, only the sound of the bullet ricocheting off the Parks Board Land-Rover to his immediate left. He did, however, see the muzzle flash within Moses' hut, and diving into the prone position, he instantly took aim and squeezed the trigger.

His Walther PPK didn't even go click. He squeezed the trigger again, but it seemed to have locked solid. His heart hammering, he tried to work the cocking slide, but the slide barely moved before it also jammed, grating on an intrusion of fine dune sand. This wasn't something Kramer heard but *felt*, sickening him to the pit of the stomach, and leaving him, in that terrible, terrifying instant, with bluff his only weapon.

"Hold your fire!" he shouted as calmly as he could. "You're totally cornered in there, you have no escape route, so be sensible, hey? Just chuck your weapon out and— *Jesus!*"

Kramer ducked as another muzzle flash lit up the inside of the hut, to be followed by two others; the bullets struck either side of him, stinging his cheeks with fragmented debris. He rolled twice to the left, tugging frantically at the cocking slide, and came up on his elbows again, aware of one thing: if he didn't manage to return this fire within seconds, then the next muzzle flashes would be from outside the hut—and the bastard would come straight for him. Cornered men were men with few options; cornered kaffirs—who could hang for aggravated burglary, let alone murder—had no options at all: it was kill or be killed, and Short Arse bloody knew it.

"Your last chance!" Kramer yelled out, wishing to God he knew how to say this in Zulu. "I don't want to shoot unless I have to!"

The moon hid its face, plunging everything once more into total darkness, and he took swift advantage of this by again rolling over, changing his position, trying to wrench back the slide, not bothering to take aim, tugging with all his strength on the trigger anyway, knowing it wouldn't work, getting ready to *throw* the bloody thing.

The next bullet seared Kramer's right shoulder even before he was aware of seeing the muzzle flash, so near and so bright it almost blinded him. Hurling his pistol as hard as he could into the lingering dazzle, he made a bid to leap up, turn, and run, but missed his footing and fell, his left knee hitting his chin so hard that, half concussed, he ended up sprawled groggily, flat on his back, his arms and legs no longer seeming part of him. At which precise instant the wind seemed to catch its breath, for there was sudden silence that lasted just long enough for an abrupt, chesty cough to be heard, followed by the unmistakable hammer click of a double-action revolver cocking itself, perhaps only a yard away.

"No!" snarled Kramer, trying to heave himself up, his head swimming. "Don't you bloody dare, you little black—"

There was a deafening bang, a gasp, someone shouting out an order to "Drop your gun!" in Afrikaans, and the next two muzzle flashes came from behind the hut. They were answered immediately by three more deafening bangs, just before somebody running full pelt tripped over Kramer's right foot and landed heavily beside him, completing his sense of total confusion.

"That was—a big help, Lieutenant!" wheezed a voice in the darkness, sounding winded. "I hope—you realize—he's—got clean away now . . ."

"Who the hell?" demanded Kramer, trying to raise himself on an elbow only to flop back, dizzy and nauseous, his eyes impossible to keep open, his jaw feeling broken in a dozen places. "Is that you, Malan?"

There was a low, rumbling laugh from his rescuer. "No, sir, not Malan. I am—a detective sergeant."

"Oh, ja? stationed where?"

"At present, sir? Nkosala."

"Then what in buggeration are you doing here, man?"

"That, Lieutenant, is a long story, which can wait for now. How badly are you injured?"

Kramer, who detested being like this, as helpless as an upturned dung beetle, and with his head still behaving as though he'd just drunk a Cape wine cellar dry, merely grunted.

"Look, sir, maybe it's best if I help you into that hut over there and—"

"No, wait, let's hear this long story of your first, hey?" insisted Kramer, playing for time, determined to force himself unaided to his feet the moment his sense of balance stopped playing silly buggers. "How did you guess there might be trouble with Short Arse here tonight? Nobody knew—"

"Short Arse, Lieutenant?"

"Ach, you know, the coon who was doing all the shooting—alias Elifasi Ndhlovu, the bastard who killed Maaties and the nympho!"

The detective sergeant laughed the same low, rumbling laugh as before, but this time there was an odd edge to it.

"Listen, what's so bloody funny about that, hey?" growled Kramer, willing his eyes open and twisting round to see what sort of expression went with such a laugh.

He timed this well, because, just as he turned, the moon came out again, lighting up the man's features.

Kramer never forgot that moment. It was Short Arse.

20

"Y OU!" Kramer said, thunderstruck.

"Me, my boss: Bantu Detective Sergeant Mickey Zondi—the Lieutenant wishes to see my warrant card?"

And I'm meant to bloody believe this, thought Kramer, trying to reconcile the faultless Afrikaner accent with the kitchen matches poked through each earlobe, or indeed the Walther PPK with the burlap-sack hood and cane knife, but making sense of only the pair of well-fitting tennis shoes, ideal for hard, fast running across the Fynn's Creek mud flats.

"Boss, my warrant," said Zondi, holding out his opened wallet.

Kramer knocked it aside. "Then who in Christ's name was that, taking potshots?" he demanded, his senses still reeling from the blow he'd given himself on the chin.

"No idea, Lieutenant—I did not see the face."

"Bastard! Me neither. Oh, *shit* . . ."

A splatter of fat raindrops had swept over them, as a sudden squall came rampaging in off the sea, and Kramer tried to rise, but lost his balance. Before he knew it, he had been hauled up bodily and was being hurried over into the cook boy's hut, most of his weight being borne by a spare, muscular frame, not all that much shorter than his own, which then quickly and discreetly disengaged itself, leaving him to crash down in a heap on the sagging divan.

"Now, listen, kaffir!" Kramer began, attempting to get his feet back on the floor.

"*Hau*, my boss, give me a minute first, okay?"

"Like hell, I will! I want to know exactly what is going on around here, and I want to know *fast*. Have you got that?"

There was a nod, and Kramer slumped back, disguising his giddiness as nonchalance. It was only after he heard the hut door close and a match being struck that he realized his orders were being totally ignored. Infuriated, he heaved himself up on an elbow.

"Cigarette, Lieutenant?" asked he who had been Short Arse, handing him both a Texan and the bedside candle to light it from. "Not your brand, I know, but Boss Kritzinger, to judge by the ashtray in his car, thought very highly of it."

Kramer heard himself give a surprised laugh. "Christ, man, what sort of kaffir *are* you?" he asked, touching the Texan to the candle flame.

"Black, same as all the others, Lieutenant."

"But what else?"

Zondi took off his burlap-sack hood, tossing it into a corner of the hut. "I'm also from Trekkersburg Murder and Robbery, Lieutenant, sir; Bantu section; seconded to work solo undercover in Zululand on the Mslope case."

"Never bloody heard of it."

"Bantu male Matthew Mslope, Lieutenant, wanted in connection with the murder and rape of three white nuns, one charge of arson, and the illegal possession of firearms. He led a mob that destroyed a mission school in a valley far up in the mountains last Christmas Day, sir."

"But why you, hey? And why undercover?"

"Because all other attempts to find Mslope have failed,

Lieutenant. The people must be protecting him. Another problem is the fact Mslope is a raw native, sir, of whom no photographs have ever existed—to track him down you must have someone who knows him well by sight so he can recognize him, even if he has taken the necessary steps to alter his appearance."

"And you think you could do that, hey?"

"Yes, my boss. I am certain of it."

"How come? You've arrested him in the past?"

"Mslope has never done any wrong before, Lieutenant. I know him because I was a pupil at that mission school many years ago, the same time as he was. He is my cousin."

Kramer raised an eyebrow. "You would send your own cousin to the hangman in Pretoria?"

"I would prefer to kill Mslope myself, sir," said Zondi, touching his shoulder holster. "There would be some dignity in such a death, which would greatly benefit the spirits of our ancestors."

Giddiness again overtook Kramer, forcing him to lie back, half aware that this clammy coldness he felt was possibly some form of delayed shock. "But what the hell has all that nuns nonsense got to do with this business?" he demanded.

"Nothing, Lieutenant, except that it brought me down into this district from the mountains three weeks ago in search of Mslope," replied Zondi. "And tonight I just happened to be passing this way when I–"

"Don't give me that bullshit, man. You've been treading on my bloody shoelaces from the start! Why was that? You'd better start explaining yourself, hey?"

Zondi lifted his cigarette to his lips to hide a smile and said, with a shrug: "I was made curious, sir."

"Oh, ja? By what?"

"By the enormous explosion three nights ago, Lieutenant. Only I was on surveillance at the time, and so I had to wait until morning before I could go along to Jafini police station and see what there was to be overheard in the charge office. I soon—"

"Why didn't you just ask them straight out?"

"Mslope has excited much sympathy, even among those duty-bound to report his whereabouts, Lieutenant, and so I am under strict orders from Captain Bronkhorst not to allow anyone to know that I am a police officer until the time an arrest has been made—or whatever."

"Then you've made a total balls of things tonight, haven't you, hey?" said Kramer. "But never mind that for now. What happened when you got to the police station?"

"I told the Bantu constable on counter duty that I was seeking advice concerning my pass book, sir. He said I must sit and wait because he was very, very busy. So I sat with an old woman whose fowls had been stolen and with a man who had come to report there was a penknife in his back. Slowly, slowly—we sat on that bench many hours—I learned some of the details of these killings and I was made shocked and angry, for Lieutenant Kritzinger had seemed a very good boss, very fair."

"Ach, not you, too, hey? One of the best?"

"I knew they spoke very highly of him in the reserve, Lieutenant. He would come to them quietly and alone, sit many hours and hold a proper *ingxoxo,* speak with courtesy to the people and in their own language, and explain why he had to do such and such, for it was his duty. Many times, the suspect he was seeking would come forward with his hands held out like this for the cuffs, because the chief had turned to this offender and asked him to show the proper respect. There were times, too, when Boss Kritzinger did not take a man to jail, but he gave him a good beating instead, allowing him to be at work the next day so his family would not suffer. *Hau,* he could hit hard, the people say! They called him *Isipikili,* the Nail, because with one blow he could join together a man and a wife who had been fighting!"

"So this was an old weakness of his?"

"Sorry, Lieutenant?"

"Just go on, hey?"

"There was much talk, Lieutenant. Fortunately, my earnest request for advice was not seen as too urgent, so I was allowed to wait ignored and unattended for many hours, overhearing many things."

"Such as?"

"About how the body of Boss Kritzinger had been found just after four o'clock in the morning, and that it had not been badly mutilated, although that of the white madam had been torn into many pieces. For a while it was wondered whether Boss Gillets had been made into even smaller pieces, then someone said no, he was away, working at the big game reserve. Everyone was much puzzled to know why this thing had been done. Another thing to puzzle them was that it seemed a new CID lieutenant was being sent up from Trekkersburg to take charge of the case. Everyone was greatly surprised, for they had expected Captain Bronkhorst to do this work. One man said maybe Captain Bronkhorst was afraid he would look bad if he failed to catch the person who had made the explosion. But later, Mtetwa, the Bantu sergeant, said no, it was not like that. He had spoken with a former CID colleague in Trekkersburg and had been told that Captain Bronkhorst was busy with a very big investigation, assisting the Security Branch to find a certain Bantu male, Nelson Mandela."

"Who?" asked Kramer.

"Oh, some Xhosa," said Zondi, with what seemed a very Zulu gesture of dismissal for someone belonging to a lesser tribe. "I seem to remember he is also ANC, once a lawyer."

"Oh, ja? Why didn't the Colonel just tell me that?"

"Lieutenant?"

"Ach, never mind," said Kramer, motioning for him to continue.

"Then, in the afternoon, Boss Bokkie Maritz arrived at the police station, sir, driving a Trekkersburg Chevrolet, and I was afraid he might see me and say something to identify me to the others, and so—"

"Which would have been bloody typical!"

"And so, in great haste, sir, I made off with many questions still unanswered in my head."

"Uh-huh, and somehow took yourself into the Bombay Emporium just after I went in there . . ."

"I had great need of cigarettes, sir."

"So getting a close look at me within minutes of my arrival in Jafini was just a coincidence, hey?"

"Indubitably, Lieutenant."

"Don't you bloody try lying to me, hey?"

"*Hau,* would your most humble servant ever do such a thing, my master?"

"Damn right you would, kaffir!"

And they both laughed, as though they had just invented a new kind of joke together.

"The truth is, Lieutenant," said Zondi, dragging out Moses' tin trunk to sit on, "I thought I recognized the boss from somewhere, and wanted to double-check on this."

"And?"

Zondi shrugged. "I still wasn't sure, boss. I just knew I had this strange feeling that the Lieutenant and me—"

"Ja, ja, ja," interrupted Kramer. "How come the next time I saw you, you were sneaking along the Nkosala road, heading for Fynn's Creek?"

"Sneaking, Lieutenant?"

"Ach, you know what I mean! Or are you going to deny taking a bloody big dive into the cane to avoid me?"

Zondi smiled. "I took a shortcut to the sea, that is true, boss."

"But why?"

"I wanted to speak with Moses Khumalo, Lieutenant."

"For what reason?"

"Something had begun to interest me greatly, boss. Something that did not make sense at all."

"Oh, ja? Explain."

"After you left the trading store, boss, I wanted to find out more, for such is my nature, and so I went to Mama Dumela's shebeen, down in the shantytown. I had begun to wonder whether Moses Khumalo had not returned to Fynn's Creek much sooner that I remembered, and so might possibly have seen something that—"

"So you *had* been drinking with him the previous night?"

"Not exactly with him, Lieutenant, but in the same room, correct. I was seated at another table with different menfolk. Mama Dumela pours her illicit liquor very freely and so naturally her customers talk very freely, making it a good place for finding out many useful secrets."

"Any bloody excuse, hey?"

Zondi smiled. "When I returned to Mama Dumela's, boss, many people were already gathered there, to speak with much excitement about the killing of the whites at Fynn's Creek, and to mourn the passing of Boss Kritzinger. In the center was the old woman from the police station whose fowls had been stolen, retelling all that she had heard. Mama Dumela said that plainly these killings had been born of such great evil that even the crocodiles had been too afraid to come back out of the water."

"You've lost me, man . . ."

"What Mama meant was, Lieutenant, why had the bodies not both been eaten up during those four hours it took to find them?"

"Shit, she's right!" exclaimed Kramer, suddenly seeing again, in his mind's eye, Dingaan the iguana snapping up the morsels of bacon fat thrown to him every morning by little Piet Fourie. "Christ, I've kept being nagged by the feeling I was overlooking something! Those crocs zoom back pretty quick!"

"Maybe not always, Lieutenant," said Zondi. "It is hard to know how a creature like that will behave. Such a big explosion could have frightened them very, very much, making them hide in the water and—"

"Ja, but it's a good point nonetheless. I wonder why nobody else has come up with it?"

Zondi said nothing, but concentrated instead on stubbing out his Texan on the sole of his tennis shoe.

"Here," said Kramer, producing his pack of Luckys and shaking the dune sand from it.

They both lit up again.

"What else did you learn at the shebeen?" asked Kramer.

"Nothing, boss—not even the approximate time Moses the cook boy had left to go back to Fynn's Creek. Nobody could remember. And so I decided to make up some excuse to come here to the beach, and that's when the Lieutenant saw me."

"Bloody caught you in the act, you mean!"

"Right!" said Zondi, chuckling. "*Hau,* you came up very suddenly, Lieutenant!"

"And did you find out why the crocs hadn't had their midnight feast?"

Zondi shook his head. "No, Lieutenant, that was to remain a big mystery. I still have not solved it."

"But what did you make of all that stuff you got Moses to tell you about Sergeant Kritzinger's visit?"

"The Lieutenant knows I—? *Hau,* I had not expected anyone to take such an interest in a raw kaffir like Khumalo!"

"Ja, your second big mistake. But I still want to know what conclusions you drew, man . . ."

"It seemed Boss Kritzinger's words had gladdened the young madam's heart in some way, but I was not sure how, boss. Is there any investigation Boss Kritzinger could have been conducting that involved the interests of the young madam?"

"Christ, is that the best you can do? No other ideas?"

Zondi shrugged. "I suppose Boss Kritzinger could also have brought her news of a visit from her lover that night—something of the sort to greatly excite her."

"Ach, now wait a minute! Remember, this is a white madam you're talking about, hey? So watch it!"

"Lieutenant, when I was young, before I could join the police at sixteen, I worked two years as a houseboy . . ."

"So what?"

"I am thinking of Moses Khumalo, Lieutenant. In my experience, white masters and white madams almost never give you time off unless they want you out of the way to afford them full privacy. For example, boss, many have a mating custom after the big lunch on Sunday, and so their servants are always permitted to take the rest of the——"

"Damn it, man, I understand what you're hinting at," said Kramer, "but it's a bullshit theory that doesn't fit the facts. Boss Kritzinger was the only other person killed by the blast; I don't know of any pieces of some bare-bummed bloody 'lover' blown all over the place!"

"Then it could have been Boss Kritzinger himself who——"

"Ach, no! Had Moses ever seen him at Fynn's Creek before, hey?"

"No, that is true, Lieutenant," said Zondi, shaking his head. "And it is also true, boss, I have heard nothing at the shebeen of a scandalous nature concerning Boss Kritzinger. *Hau*, you should hear how some white masters and madams in this district behave! One houseboy was saying——"

"Enough!" said Kramer. "Almighty God, who'd have thought you kaffirs were such bloody gossips? Can we get back to more serious matters?"

"Gladly, Lieutenant," said Zondi. "Which means, boss, I must repeat my question."

"Which one was that?"

"I asked the Lieutenant whether Boss Kritzinger had been investigating a case that could have lifted a weight from the shoulders of the white madam, making her——"

"And the answer is, ja, possibly, but there could be a lot more to it than that. I hope you're not expecting me to start reeling off to you the whole of my bloody investigation so far!"

"Are we not both Murder and Robbery, my boss?"

"Jesus wept, you really are the cheekiest damn kaffir I've ever bloody come across!"

"*Hau*, Lieutenant, *very nearly* Sister Theresa's exact words to me on many, many occasions," said Zondi.

21

*F*inally, the squall outside the hut hollered for help, and
its big brother came running, a God Almighty storm,
which hammered at the hut door and started trying to
tear off the roof thatch.

"A pity this didn't happen three nights ago," remarked
Kramer, forced to raise his voice. "Would have put a bloody
dampener on things, hey?—might even have blown the fuse
out!"

Zondi nodded, but clearly he was still preoccupied by the
résumé Kramer had just finished giving him. His eyes had
that unfocused look, although directed at the candle flame,
and he remained motionless, hands deep in his jacket
pockets.

"My uncle used to have a pet baboon who sat just like that,
dead still for hours," said Kramer. "His excuse was old age
and constipation—what's yours, hey?"

"Lieutenant?" said Zondi, turning, and his broad smile
caught up a second later. "*Hau!* I'm sorry, my boss, but
many, many things have begun to fit together, making
everything so much clearer!"

"Oh, ja?"

"But, er, with respect, the Lieutenant will allow me to correct one of his possible theories? Boss Kritzinger could not have eaten that last meal of meat curry with Boss Grantham."

"How the hell would you know that, hey?"

"Because, Lieutenant, Moon Acre is a place of employment for many, many runaway men, and it was there that I was on surveillance that same night, hiding from the dogs in a treetop near the compound. I can swear to you that Boss Grantham ate alone at round about eight o'clock, and then listened to his radio on the front verandah, drinking gin and tonic, until close to eleven, when he told the chef and the other staff to go off duty. He then retired to his bedroom, and there he remained reading until the explosion, when he came running out with a rifle in his hands, calling out in an alarmed manner for his *induna*."

"The big bang took him by surprise, you say?"

"I am sorry, Lieutenant."

"Ach, no! Let's get at the facts, man! That could save me a lot of time, as it tends to bugger any case against Grantham, doesn't it?"

Zondi shook his head. "I see no reason for that, my boss. Clearly, there are many strange things that happen at Moon Acre of which we have still much to learn."

"Incidentally, did you spot Cousin Nun-Shagger there?"

"No, boss, but the possibility remains. I must make further inquiries."

"Uh-huh. Where else have I gone wrong so far, that you know about?"

"It was not I, boss, who took the Sunday-best clothes of Moses Khumalo, the cook boy."

"Oh, really? Who did, then? Any ideas on that score?"

"I think it was probably a Bantu quite unconnected with this case, my boss—somebody also drinking in the shebeen that night. Someone who overheard Moses saying he had been given the night off because his boss was away, and who would have known, by watching Moses, that it would be many, many hours before he returned to Fynn's Creek. This someone could have slipped away then, and gone to see what he could steal from him—or even steal from the house, boss. The point is, Lieutenant, those clothes must have been taken the same night as the explosion, because the next night, when you caught me speaking with Moses Khumalo, they were no longer there."

"Hell, Moses couldn't be sure of that, when I last asked him!"

"Maybe not, Lieutenant, but during my visit, when Moses went to make water, I gave this hut a quick search, just as a test of his honesty. This tin trunk, boss, was quite empty."

Kramer sighed and shook his head. "On second thoughts, *Smart* Arse might have been a better name for you," he said, holding out his Lucky Strike packet, two cigarettes protruding.

"Many thanks, Lieutenant! Actually, in this matter, I thought exactly the same way as the boss did: I also started a search for the clothing thief, thinking he might perhaps have witnessed matters of interest at Fynn's Creek that night, but without success, sir. I would think that since the explosion he has been very, very afraid of those clothes, and has probably buried them deep in some ant-bear hole."

"Then here's an order, Bantu Detective Sergeant. The next bloody ant bear you see with a patch in its best shirt and shiny seat in its pants—you arrest the bastard, okay?"

Zondi chuckled, and they shared the fluttering candle flame, lighting up and each inhaling deeply.

"Now your turn," said Kramer. "Let's hear what you been up to the past few days—especially what you've discovered."

"Starting from where, boss?"

"From where you left off. You know, I'd just caught you talking to Moses Khumalo, the cook boy . . ."

"*Eh-heh*," said Zondi, rising to pace about again. "Well, boss, I felt no wiser after that, except I had a suspicion that Boss Kritzinger had come on Monday to discuss some case in which the young madam had an interest. I wanted to seek more information while I had the chance, and so, seeing the Lieutenant was very busy with Moses, using Cassius Mabeni as his interpreter, I decided to examine the vehicle which Boss Kritzinger had left behind."

"Christ, and there was me, thinking you had hightailed out of Fynn's Creek, like a buffalo with its bum on fire!"

"Which is true, Lieutenant. But I also circled right round and came cautiously back. And when I reached the vehicle, I was at first disappointed. I had hoped to—"

"Hold it a sec!" said Kramer, having had a sudden, nasty thought. "I hope you're not going to tell me you removed anything from it? Because, when I searched it, there was bugger all to be found, hey?"

Zondi shook his head. "No, I took nothing, boss. It was all very bare, as you say, except for the ashtray."

"Jammed full, as I remember."

"To the top, boss. But there were many more used matches than there were old cigarette ends."

"You *counted* them? But what could that tell you? When my ashtray gets too full, I do what Kritz must have done—start chucking my cigarette ends out of my window!"

Zondi nodded. "Me, too, boss—and when I am sitting parked somewhere. So, just on the off chance of learning more about Lieutenant Kritzinger's movements that night, I took a look around. You know that small fever tree hiding the car which had the big bend in its trunk? Eight freshly smoked Texans lay close beneath it. Boss Kritzinger must have been flicking each one away in the same fashion, through his car window, just like the Lieutenant does, which was why they had all landed in almost the same place."

"Oh, ja? And?"

"Remember, there were eight of them, Lieutenant. Eight times the eight minutes a Texan takes to smoke, and you have sixty-four minutes spent there, minimum."

"Impossible!"

"Not if Boss Kritzinger had been chain-smoking, sir," said Zondi. "Sitting there very worried, trying to make up his mind whether or not to do something."

"Such as?"

"Well, whether to reveal to the young madam some news that could be very upsetting, boss."

"But this can't be right! Didn't you hear me saying earlier that the curry had to have been eaten within twenty minutes or so of his death? There is no way he could have done that *and* sat around smoking eight bloody Texans!"

Zondi shrugged.

"You don't follow what I mean?"

"It's like this, Lieutenant," said Zondi. "From that first night, when all the cook boys were talking at Mama Dumela's shebeen about the curry search, it seemed plain to me that every kitchen within a certain area had been eliminated, leaving only one. I then naturally assumed that the remaining kitchen was where the meal had been prepared, for there could be no other explanation."

"Now I'm the one who doesn't follow!"

"I mean the kitchen here at Fynn's Creek, Lieutenant. Is that not correct?"

"Can't have been! Look, apart from everything else, let me repeat that the curry et cetera was Lieutenant Kritzinger's favorite meal, and so it must have been prepared for him by someone very familiar with his ways. You're not trying to suggest he and the young madam were bloody intimates on the quiet, are you? There's certainly no evidence for thinking that!"

Zondi blew a careful smoke ring. "What I do suggest, boss, is this," he said. "Say Boss Kritzinger and the young madam agreed that morning to meet again in the evening, when he would have further news for her, and this was what made her so happy. Is it not possible she offered to serve him a meal then, to have while they talked, and she asked him what kind of food he'd like best to eat? His request would have been easy for most households to find; he favored very ordinary things."

"Hmmmm."

"*Hau*, I know what's troubling the Lieutenant!" said Zondi, smiling. "It must of course never be assumed a young madam can cook for herself. But I double-checked, sir. At Mama Dumela's shebeen, I discovered the whereabouts of the old woman who used to be cook girl in the young madam's parents' house, and yes, the young madam could make simple dishes like stews and curries and even—"

"Okay," said Kramer. "All this sounds very logical, but how do you explain the fact Boss Kritzinger was killed as he *approached* the house that night—with a full belly?"

Zondi shrugged. "The Lieutenant," he said, "has told me that some noise or other must have attracted the attention of the young madam, bringing her through into the guest room. Could not that same sound have also attracted the attention of Boss Kritzinger, who then decided to *leave* the house and investigate the noise another way—despite a full belly?"

In the silence that followed, a silence made all the more acute by the storm having died away as swiftly as it had arisen, two owls hooted, one high and one low.

Kramer rose unsteadily to his feet, tried a couple of steps, waited until his sense of balance adjusted, and then tried a couple more. "I'm having to reshuffle all kinds of things in my head," he said. "But you know something? I think we might be getting a bloody sight closer to the truth of what happened that night, hey?"

Zondi nodded.

"So finish telling us what else you've been up to, and then we'll put the whole lot together and see where that leaves us."

"*Hau*, I do have not many more things to say, my boss," replied Zondi. "I have really been a mere observer in these matters—which, I must confess, have greatly intrigued me, but I have also had my own job to do."

"Ja, ja, but *was* that you I saw go into the Bombay Emporium just after breakfast?"

Zondi grinned. "I fear so, Lieutenant! *Hau*, that was a bad moment for me, until I could persuade Two Times that his own jacket would look much better inside out, and quickly sent him off home to show his daughters what a handsome fellow it made him!"

"You're not to be bloody trusted, are you?"

"With respect, Lieutenant," said Zondi, "I had a feeling the boss was becoming too interested in my presence, and that this might lead to my being exposed as a police officer before I found my cousin Matthew Mslope. After that, I tried hard to disappear from view."

"Until tonight, hey?"

"Naturally, the Lieutenant's activities today greatly aroused my interest, for I could see no reason why, having searched this hut myself, it had become the center of much attention. On account of which, I decided to come and watch to see what—"

"Ja, ja, the rest we can take as read. But, in between disappearing and tonight, did you pick anything else up? Any more information that could be pertinent?"

"What I did, boss," said Zondi, "was go to the shebeen to see if I could find out if there was a case that Boss Kritzinger would want to discuss with the young madam. Mama Dumela suggested a road traffic accident in which both the young madam's parents had been killed, allegedly through the carelessness of Boss Grantham's cane boys. When I asked her why she should think of this, she told me there had been talk in the shebeen of Boss Kritzinger having been to see a *songoma*, high in the mountains, to inquire further into the matter."

"What the hell are you talking about?" asked Kramer.

"A famous witch, Lieutenant," said Zondi. "Surely there were witches and wizards in the Orange Free State?"

"Of course there bloody are! Half of the bastards on police retainers to find lost and stolen Bantu cattle, through their usual trick of frightening the shit out of half-witted kaffirs! So what?"

"This witch is also on a police retainer," said Zondi. "Mabata police station pays it each month, and that is maybe how Boss Kritzinger got to hear of her, if he did not already know she was the greatest *songoma* in the area, able to give any man the answer to the question that most vexed him."

"Christ, was sodding Maaties bloody white or wasn't he?"

"I think Boss Kritzinger had been forced to heed only his heart, Lieutenant, like any man who had grown desperate," said Zondi. "And because he was so close to the People of Heaven, there are many who said he—"

"The people of *where*?"

"Heaven, boss. That is what 'Zulu' means: the People of Heaven."

"Christ, they never taught us *that* in bloody Sunday school!" said Kramer.

"Anyway, Lieutenant," said Zondi, "Boss Kritzinger went up in the mountains to see the *songoma*, he asked his question, and she passed it on for a reply from her great spirit, the Song Dog."

"Oh, shit," said Kramer, "there's something else maybe I should have told you . . ."

For an instant, the high, shrill zzzzzzzzzzzzz of a mosquito could be heard in the hut, above the croaking of mangrove frogs, then the sound ended abruptly.

Zondi, distracted, looked round to see where it might have landed, then back at Kramer, with one eyebrow raised.

"You'd just got to this Song Dog business . . ." Kramer reminded him.

"Ah, yes, Lieutenant! I was told Boss Kritzinger had been inquiring after the circumstances of a fatal collision last year when—"

"So you've already said. And?"

"Regrettably, that is all I learned of the matter, Lieutenant," said Zondi, "but at least it gave me a link between Fynn's Creek and Boss Kritzinger."

"Surely to God, there must have been more to it than that!"

"Trouble was, boss, this information had reached me in an old, ragged whisper, passed on from one mouth to the other, starting with some person who was very, very sick, and who had gone to this *songoma* for special medicine. The *songoma* is now nearly deaf, boss, and that is the only reason we know as much as this, for Boss Kritzinger had to state his troubles in a big, loud voice. But her reply was given in an old woman's mumbles, I'm told, making it impossible to hear what her words were from outside the cave entrance. Consequently—"

"Ach, never mind what *she* said, which was bound to be bullshit anyway!" said Kramer. "What interests me far more is the exact nature of the questions Lieutenant Kritzinger put to her, because questions themselves can be every bit as revealing as answers, you know!"

"I am sorry, but as I say, that is all that I know, Lieutenant. The trouble being, this cave lies far away, and—"

"What if I drove you there? How long would it take?"

"Just to Mabata, boss? Because the rest of the way, a man has to walk many, many miles."

"Ja, ja, to wherever. Two hours? Three? Because if we—"

"*Hau!*" exclaimed Zondi, startled into his first and only interruption. "The Lieutenant does not understand! Mama Pelapela, the *songoma*, is like a true doctor, boss, in that what a person says to her is meant to be secret. It is considered a most sacred matter."

"Then ask the old bitch how sacred her bloody retainer is," growled Kramer.

22

*T*he dirt track to Mabata could well have been built by
a farmer determined to deter traveling salesmen
intent on seducing his nubile young daughters, decided
Kramer. The bloody thing wasn't simply an obstacle course,
boasting everything from falling boulders to the sort of dips
and turns that perverted roller-coaster designers only dreamed
about, but it also had a deeply rutted, corrugated surface
which proved an absolute ball-breaker, numbing everything
from the waist down, with side effects on the brain.

But Zondi drove well, to Kramer's surprise, pushing the
Land-Rover to its limit, and all he had to do was sit back,
keep himself braced hard against the dashboard, and hope to
God that the shocks, half-shafts, and diff would hold out. He
also hoped even harder that he would soon be rid of the
dizziness that had again overtaken him, while helping to
reinflate the tires.

Then, quite suddenly, Mabata finally appeared in the
Land-Rover's jolting headlights, and presented him with a
fresh set of preoccupations. Two Alouette helicopters stood

parked on the open space in front of the tiny, stone-walled police station, surrounded by policemen in camouflaged battle fatigues, sprawled on the ground drinking beers, and Zondi had to brake violently to avoid making a sticky mess inside someone's sleeping bag.

"Hey, watch it!" bawled a bullnecked sergeant, leveling his Sten gun as he advanced angrily. "You want some holes in your windscreen so you can see better, you dumb-head?"

"Not if they're going to be the same size as that bloody great mouth of yours," said Kramer, getting out. "What the hell is this? Boy Scout Week?"

"Tromp!" exclaimed the sergeant, his ugly face lighting up like a warthog's at the sight of wild melon. "Tromp bloody Kramer! Well, I'll be buggered! Long time no see, hey?"

Kramer shook the extended hand. "How goes it, Aap?" he asked.

Aap van Vuuren shrugged. "Not bad," he said, "although I'd rather be back home in the Free State most days, to be honest. But I've got married, you know, and she doesn't want to live too far from her folks."

"So she's Natal-born? An English-speaker?"

"God forbid, man! You'll want to know if she's got a lick of the tar brush next! Do I *look* a bloody liberal?"

"Well, you've got your safety catch on," pointed out Kramer.

Van Vuuren grinned and set the Sten gun aside on the Land-Rover's hood. "So, to what do we owe this visit?" he asked. "You're actually promoted lieutenant now, I hear—still CID?"

"Murder and Robbery. How about you?"

"Ach, still Uniform, still trying to stop these mad kaffirs from killing each other. Faction fights every weekend in the reserves is one thing, just a few hundred huts burned, a few bodies. But this business between the Sithole clan and the Shabalalas is turning to war, man, and the Colonel has suddenly ordered us in, following reports that hundreds of bloody servant boys are buggering off on compassionate leave to come home and take part in one big final battle. It's supposed to start first thing in the morning, and we're one of the three groups going to come down hard on the bastards, put a quick stop to it. Man, I'd booked a court to play tennis."

"Another new face?" said an amiable voice, and Kramer turned to see a portly, grey-haired man in an SAP raincoat, his pajama trousers and slippers showing beneath it, come waddling across. "Sergeant Stoffel Wessels, sir, station commander here at Mabata. You can't know how good it is to have company, hey? Eleven months of the year, the best conversations I have are with billy goats!"

"*And* with the Oude Meester, Stoffel!" said Van Vuuren, with a wink for Kramer.

Wessels smiled beneath his walrus moustache. "Very true, Aap, very true. And a most cultivated old gentleman he is, to be sure—a brilliant philosopher! What profound thoughts he encourages in a man! What profound thoughts!"

"Oh, ja?" said Kramer. "But right now, my interest is more in witch doctors and other such tomfoolery. You know one hereabouts with a 'song dog'?"

"Of course, Mama Pelapela! What a character! What a character! Is this to do with poor Maaties?"

"Uh-huh. I want to know if—"

"Poor Maaties! Difficult to believe! Difficult!"

Perhaps, thought Kramer, billy goats needed everything said twice to them before it sank in properly, but Wessels was beginning to get very definitely on his nerves. "How far is it to her place?" he asked. "Could I get there tonight?"

"Tonight? Ach, no, not a hope, I'm afraid! It's three hours on foot there, and three—"

"Shit!" said Kramer.

"Can I help?" offered Van Vuuren. "I mean," he said, turning to Wessels, "can you point to this place on a map?"

"Now what?" Zondi murmured to himself in Zulu, left alone on the front seat of the Land-Rover, pinned down there by a dozen pairs of hostile eyes wondering what in Christ's name this strange black thing was doing in their deeply tanned midst.

He lit a Texan and sat back, tipping his hat down over his nose.

It had been quite a night, one way and another, and very little of it could be said to have had anything to do with his own quarry, cousin Matthew Mslope.

Poor Matthew. Whenever he thought of him, he could smell again the eucalyptus scent of the blue gums surrounding their mission school, deep in that remote Zululand valley. There the best dreams of his life had been dreamt; all you had to do, the white nuns had said, was to learn your lessons well and then, when you grew up, you would be the equal of any man and could do whatever you wanted to do. They had been wrong, those stupid, kind women, who believed all men were brothers, totally wrong, but Zondi still could not feel bitter. Unlike his classmate, his cousin Matthew Mslope, who had gone back with a mob to burn, pillage, rape, and wreak his revenge. Which had also been wrong, and meant that he, too, had to die now.

Or rather, once this intriguing business of explosion at Fynn's Creek had reached some sort of conclusion. Zondi had always derived a particular pleasure from a white killing. Not for the reasons that many might suppose, being quick to suggest racial, political, even arithmetical implications well worth a lick of the lips—but because nonwhite killings tended to be so banal, so straightforward: hot-blooded outbursts of violence that left nobody guessing. Here was the hacked-up body, here was the kindling axe, here were thirty-six eyewitnesses, and here was the murderer, still hanging around, looking a bit weary, but quite prepared to go to his fate in order to spare the spirits of his ancestors any further turbulence.

A white killing, on the other hand, almost invariably— possibly because there had been so many ingenious books and films made about them—contained a strong element of mystery, making a man really "put his thinking cap on," to use one of Sister Theresa's favorite expressions. Yes, it was as though most white murderers felt they had a tradition to maintain, certain standards to uphold, and so acted accordingly. Or was it because they tended, in the main, to be less passionate, less impulsive, and far more cold-blooded in their killing, more calculated, and certainly more conscious of the possible consequences?

"Interesting . . ." murmured Zondi, tapping his ash into his other hand and then sending it, with a puff, out of his window.

"Grantham wasn't bullshitting me," said Kramer, sliding into the driver's seat of the Land-Rover. "Stoffel Wessels, the station commander here, says that Kritz came back from seeing this old witch-doctor crone in one hell of a state. All he wanted to do was get drunk and he flattened nearly a case of Castle lagers before saying a bloody word to him."

"And, Lieutenant?" prompted Zondi.

"Apparently, Kritz really did go to find out about something he was investigating—what he described as a 'series of fatals.' "

"A *series*, you say, boss?"

"Well, the impression he gave Wessels was definitely of more than one."

"*Hau!* Did this include the young madam's parents?"

"Wessels wasn't given any details."

"But what other 'fatals' do we know of, Lieutenant?"

"Buggered if I can tell you!"

"What else did Boss Kritzinger let slip, boss?"

"That he was very worried by something the Song Dog had warned him about."

"Which was, boss?"

"No idea, he wouldn't tell Wessels, and then tried to turn it all into just a joke. Listen, you and me are going to be at this cave place first thing tomorrow, and we're going to find out exactly what—"

"First thing, boss? That cave is many, many—"

"Ach, I know! But it's all fixed up. You see that old

colleague of mine over there? He'll have us whipped in and out in no time."

"You mean, Lieutenant, we are to ride in a helicopter? I, er, would rather . . ."

"Hell, you're not afraid to fly, are you? You, a bloody Zulu warrior, the bravest of the brave, scaring everyone shitless in your monkey skins and snazzy leopard trimmings, hey?"

"The Lieutenant has placed his finger *right* on the problem, boss! As he can see, I am simply not dressed for the occasion," said Zondi.

23

*A*n hour after first light, an Alouette helicopter rose with a high whine and clatter from the bare patch in front of Mabata police station, tipped forward, and headed westward, climbing.

"Hey, Tromp," Aap van Vuuren shouted in Kramer's ear, "you must introduce me to this new girlfriend of yours, when you get the chance!"

Kramer frowned. "What the hell do you mean by that?" he demanded.

"You obviously don't realize what a state she left you in last night! Grass stains, ja, that's one thing, but Jesus, your clothes were covered in mud and blood, man! She must be a proper bloody tigress!"

"Hell, no," Kramer shouted back, "she's a librarian."

Van Vuuren grinned, and then leaned over to check that the Defence Force Pilot had the right map strapped to his thigh, showing the wax-penciled course the helicopter was to follow.

Kramer glanced back at Zondi, crouched behind them,

grim-faced but intent on the scenery below. "Well?" he said. "This beats bloody walking, kaffir, you've got to admit!"

"It makes me frightened about God, boss," said Zondi.

"Oh, ja?"

"From up here, Lieutenant, a man is *nothing* . . ."

"Maybe that's what improves the view."

Which was remarkable in its way, if you liked mountains that resembled sections of browned backbone exhumed from a shallow grave, complete with the usual snail-trail patterns of footpaths and the snails themselves, represented here by pointy-roofed Zulu mud huts adhering to the steep slopes in village circles. Later, slow coils of smoke would rise from the fireplaces outside each main hut, but presumably it was still far too early for even the youngest wives of a sub-chief to be stirring. Cattle panicked, though, starting skinny stampedes at the sound of the helicopter's rotors, and tiny herd boys, roused from their half-slumber, shook feeble fighting sticks, as the giant dragonfly shadow skidded over them.

"The general idea is," said Van Vuuren, still shouting in Kramer's ear, "we'll drop you off at this witch doctor's, knock some sense into these bloody kaffirs, then come back and pick you up again on the way home, okay?"

Kramer, who had already agreed to this plan at least five times that morning, nodded.

"In other words," said Van Vuuren, "we should be back no later than twelve noon."

"Ja, ja, so you said."

"Give or take a few minutes."

"Ja, fine."

"Depending on how things go."

"Of course."

"About noon, then?"

"Ideal."

"Or maybe a little after, who knows?"

Dear God, thought Kramer, no wonder Van Vuuren had a reputation for getting the suspects he interrogated to sign *anything*.

* * *

Zondi chose his footholds on the steep path with care, aware that his legs were still a little shaky after that helicopter ride. As interesting as it might have seemed at times, a man had to draw the line at what was natural.

Pausing to catch his breath, he looked back down at the landing place but failed to spot the Lieutenant, who must have found himself somewhere comfortable to sit out of sight and smoke his Luckys.

"This witch-doctor business is kaffir's work," the Lieutenant had said after the helicopter had gone. "Just see that I'm not disappointed."

And Zondi had been greatly relieved, because visiting a *songoma,* more especially one of such extraordinary repute as Mama Pelapela, called for a show of respect that most whites would find too humiliating even to attempt, thus jeopardizing everything.

"Which again poses the question: what sort of man could this Maaties Kritzinger have been?" Zondi said to himself, continuing his climb. "Unusual, to say the least . . ."

Then the mountainside began having the strangest effect on him. Perhaps it started with the crow which swooped suddenly, cawing, making him turn and watch it rise again into the sky. For several seconds, he felt a child again, always fearful when a crow warned him about something—as his grandmother swore they did—yet never knowing what it was. And when his gaze returned to the path ahead, he kept on seeing that differently, too. Like a child, his eyes picked out creatures he'd so far not noticed: a grotesquely faced grasshopper bobbing on a grass stalk, two bustling dung beetles, a praying mantis gorging itself, spiders, ants, lizards . . . no snakes, although he did come across the sloughed skin of a puff adder, which made his heart beat faster. How *alive* that slope now seemed, how filled with stings and bites and certain death, and how much more alive he himself felt, how much more at home, a million miles from the sidewalks of Trekkersburg, the alleys, shantytowns, and city stench.

A goblin sprang up in front of him, hideous, prancing,

waving its tiny cowhide shield and assegai, uttering a long, wavering cry, barring his way in a kilt of monkey tails.

For an instant, Zondi froze.

"Who is it that travels this path?" came the shrill challenge. "Who is that *dares* approach the cave of She Who Hears the Song Dog?"

Then Zondi laughed. "Tokoloshe!" he said, recognizing the Zulu dwarf in that instant. "Man, I've often wondered where you'd got to!"

"Oh, shit," said Tokoloshe in English, letting his arms drop. "Not *you*, Sergeant Zondi . . ."

"The self-same, my friend! Where was it that we met last? Ah, I know! At Trekkersburg bus station—you were pick-pocketing a crowd of white school kids."

"Never!"

"Oh, ja? That isn't how I remember it. But tell me, why the change of occupation?"

"An honest living, Sergeant . . ."

"That I can't believe!"

"You're right, it was a bit more complicated than that."

"I wish I had time to listen—later, maybe?"

"Perfect!" replied Tokoloshe, with resounding insincerity, and then switched back to Zulu to say: "The *songoma* will want to know why you have come to see her. What should I tell her this is about?"

"If she's any good, she'll know already," said Zondi, holding out a ten-rand note.

Snatching it from him, Tokoloshe went leaping up the footpath like a goat, beckoning to Zondi to follow him.

Ridiculous! thought Kramer, coming to his senses in the shade of an overhanging rock. I must be mad. No wonder Van Vuuren and his cohorts had lifted off in a state of snide giggles, at last able to express their amazement that any white man, let alone a senior CID officer in the SAP, should take some black bitch of a witch so seriously he would go to these lengths to include her in his investigations.

"Totally ridiculous!" he said aloud, stamping on the Lucky

Strike he had only just lit. "Zondi, you come back here, you hear?"

But when he looked up the side of the mountain, Zondi had vanished, leaving just an old crow stropping its beak on a boulder.

The cave mouth, invisible from the air on account of surrounding foliage, mostly an out-of-place granadilla vine, had an unexpectedly homely appearance. Two empty milk bottles stood just outside the entrance, as though the National Co-operative Dairies milk cart was likely to call by at any minute, and a pair of pink, knee-length bloomers had been hung out to dry on a thorn bush.

"Wait here," ordered Tokoloshe, pointing his spear at a spot just beside the fireplace, which was defined by a ring of baboon skulls. "I must first announce your presence!"

Zondi, who suspected that the helicopter had already done all the announcing necessary, nonetheless squatted down as directed.

That was when he noticed that the milk bottles each contained something after all: pubic hair suspended in fine spiderweb.

"Sergeant," said Tokoloshe, emerging from the cave on all fours, "you are deeply honored! The *songoma* will see you straightaway . . ."

"Out here?"

"No, inside. You must crawl."

So crawl he did, aware that Tokoloshe must be savoring the moment; he crawled over two bath mats, a welcome mat, an off-cut of purple carpeting, and finally three cowhides before coming to a halt where the dry, silvery sand of the inner cave began, trying to make his eyes adjust to the dim light.

"Greetings, Michael Zondi!" a crone's voice cackled, followed by a wheeze of laughter. "Servant of the white man who steps from the sky . . ."

"Greetings, Wise Mama!" said Zondi, gritting his teeth in the face of gratuitous insult. "I am a servant to no one."

Another wheezing laugh.

And then he saw her, gap-toothed, face wrinkled like the knee of a rhino, flat withered breasts, three inflated bladders knotted above her left ear, a long black skirt, and dozens of copper rings around her swollen ankles. She was eating sardines and condensed milk, mixed, from a tin plate with a dessert spoon.

Unbidden, the Widow Fourie stepped lightly into Kramer's thoughts, smiling at him the way she had done when offering him that bottle of brandy, and he closed his eyes for an instant, hoping to keep her there.

But already she was gone again, shouldered aside by the work he still had to do, and by the increasingly agitated frame of mind in which he found himself, as he waited for Zondi to return from that cave somewhere high above him.

Zondi had now been gone more than half an hour, and the sky was clouding over.

Zondi's eyes had begun to smart. The *songoma* kept on adding pinches of herbs to a small clay pot containing hot coals, filling the cave with strange aromatic smells and far too much smoke. While she did this, she rocked back and forth on her haunches, muttering away to herself, and repeatedly cast at her feet a set of bones that included, unless he was very much mistaken, at least three human finger joints. She had told him to remain quiet.

"You have come," she said eventually, "with a man who has dreamed a dream."

That could be confidently said of anyone, thought Zondi, remembering Sister Theresa's oft-repeated homily on sorcerers, but his reply was respectful: "I hear you, O Wise One."

"You have come," she said, "to ask me many, many questions . . ."

That didn't call for much by way of a clairvoyant gift either, thought Zondi, given Tokoloshe would have told her he was a detective, but again he merely said: "I hear you, O Wise One."

"Then get on with it, let's hear what you have to say," she snapped testily, still rocking, setting the bones aside. "Since you drew close, my ears have filled with the sound of women weeping and children grieving."

"You must know, O Wise One, that Detective Sergeant Kritzinger is dead—Isipikili? News of that kind would surely travel swiftly, far and wide."

"Yes, I know of this matter, Michael Zondi, and my heart is sore."

"Isipikili came to visit you here, Great Mama—is that not true?"

"He has been here many, many times, Michael Zondi."

"He has? When was the last time, Great Mama?"

"On Sunday."

"This Sunday that has just gone, Mama?"

She nodded. "He had much troubling him, and came again to seek the wisdom of the Song Dog."

"I need to know the nature of his troubles, Mama."

"Then why not read what he has written?"

"I know of no such writing, O Wise One."

"Yet it exists! He has told me. He has written down all he knows of this matter, and has read through it many times, seeking enlightenment."

"Yet I have not found these writings, Great Mama. Can you tell me where I might lay my hands on them?"

"Bah! Do I *look* like a nursemaid?"

"No, Great Mama, but what else can I say when you speak in riddles?"

"You consider that a riddle? Before you leave, you will certainly hear a riddle from these lips, for what the bones tell me about you is greatly disturbing! But I will *tell* you when I speak in riddles—in the meantime, with regard to this matter of things written, I thought I had made my meaning quite plain!"

"Forgive me, Great Mama. Please go on, repeat to me what Isipikili came here to request of the Song Dog."

"Huh! Why should I, Mr. Policeman? I can see in your eyes that you doubt my great powers, and besides, you have not flattered me sufficiently. Where do you think you are, at the damn doctor's? You have not marveled at my wondrous sorcery—or at least my astonishing memory—and not a word have you uttered in praise of my remarkable alertness for a wizened, wrinkled old woman."

"That is only because, Great Mama, you have the light in your eyes of a young maiden, compelling me to see you with breasts ripe and full, and your thighs plump and shiny . . ."

"*Hau!*" she exclaimed, a delighted cackle escaping her as she clapped a hand over her mouth. "So you are not altogether the mission boy I first smelled when you entered my cave, Michael Zondi!"

Kramer, pacing up and down, incessantly checking his watch and trying not to, gritted his teeth as yet another half hour crawled by.

"What the hell's going on?" he demanded of the crow, which had swooped down to take a closer look at him. "Listen, you evil black bastard, I'm talking to you! Is the old bitch turning that stupid kaffir of mine into next year's patent remedy or what?"

The crow tipped its head, the better to keep him firmly fixed by its beady eye.

"Ja, I can just see it," Kramer went on, lighting his third-to-last Lucky. "Essence of Bantu Detective Sergeant bloody Zondi, four rand a small ointment tin, just rub it in. Perfect for lumbago, for talking bullshit, for frightening off—"

At which very moment, the crow gave a squawk, rose into the air, and went flapping away, startled by a shower of pebbles and loose lumps of clay. Seconds later, Zondi appeared, slipping and sliding, almost losing his footing every yard or so, as he came hurrying back down the path. His face was surprisingly somber and his fists were clenched hard.

"Hey, Mickey, what's up?" asked Kramer. "You don't look too happy, man . . ."

"Who, me, Lieutenant?" said Zondi, plainly forcing a

smile. "Oh, take no notice, boss—I was wanting to leave long ago, but the *songoma* held me back, insisting on telling me what the bones had revealed to her earlier, and wanting to talk about stupid dreams. Kaffir nonsense."

"Such as?"

"Believe me, Lieutenant: irrelevant."

"Oh, ja? But was *anything* she said relevant, hey?"

"It was indeed, boss!" said Zondi.

24

Zondi, seeing Kramer was down to his last two Luckys, raised a hand and said: "No, boss, the Lieutenant must have one of mine, please." They lit up and then sat side by side beneath the overhanging rock, with the crow edging up again.

"This is how things were, Lieutenant," said Zondi, pausing to pinch a crumb of tobacco from the tip of his tongue. "The *songoma* has known Boss Kritzinger many years. He would come to her because he wanted to learn the story of the Zulu people—she claims her memory goes right back before the Zulu wars with the English, and that her father was at the kraal of Shaka when the Voortrekker leaders were killed there after being warmly welcomed. Boss Kritzinger said one of his ancestors was among that number, and he wanted to understand why Shaka had suddenly—"

"Whoa!" Kramer interrupted. "History lessons later, okay?"

"The point I was hoping to make, Lieutenant," said Zondi, a trifle stiffly, "is that the *songoma* was surprised when Boss Kritzinger came to ask her to intercede for him in seeking the wisdom of the Song Dog. It was not his way—he had never done such a thing before."

"Ah, I get you. And this was when, last Sunday?"

"Uh-uh—last October, boss."

"Hey? But I thought . . ."

"Boss Kritzinger paid two visits concerning this matter, Lieutenant, that's what is confusing you. On the first of these occasions, during the last part of October, Boss Kritzinger came to tell her he was deeply troubled by the death of the two whites whose car had hit a sugarcane truck on land belonging to Boss Grantham."

"Christ, so at least we were warm, hey?"

"Lieutenant?"

"Just go on, Mickey!"

"Boss Kritzinger told the *songoma,* boss," said Zondi, "that he wanted the Song Dog to confirm whether his belief was correct: that the crash had not been an accident. He also wanted the Song Dog to let him know how close he had come to identifying the culprit. In reply, the—"

"Hey, hang on a moment!" said Kramer, frowning. "There's something I don't get. If Kritz was prepared to shame himself by crawling to a witch doctor with questions like that, then why not go the whole hog? Why didn't he ask the Song Dog straight out to name the guilty party and have done with it?"

"The *songoma* is no fool, she wondered the same thing," said Zondi. "But she suspected, she says, that Boss Kritzinger *already knew the answers* to the questions he was putting."

"Ach, no, this is getting too complicated for me, man!"

"Not really, boss. A man may know something, but making himself believe it is often another matter entirely— especially if it is a bad thing. I remember going as a young policeman to the house of a family where the smallest child had been missing for a month, and although I was carrying the smallest child's dress, all torn and bloodstained, the parents simply would not—"

"Ja, ja," said Kramer, reminded of a similar incident he'd

give a lot to forget. "Point taken. You're saying that Kritz wanted something or someone outside him to confirm that some unthinkable thought of his was justified, right? But he was a *detective*, for Christ's sake! Why didn't he just check it out in the normal way?"

Zondi shrugged. "Maybe that was impossible to do, boss, without risking a terrible calamity if the idea proved wrong. Maybe the only action he dared take at that time was to consult the *songoma*, who was just an old kaffir living many miles away—at least she was someone he could talk over his problem with quite freely."

"Hmmmm," said Kramer, close to scoffing at the idea before conceding that he himself had felt much the same way lately. "But that of course raises the interesting possibility that Kritz could have said a lot more to her about this business than she let on."

"Agreed, boss, and that is part of the reason I was with the *songoma* for so long," said Zondi. "But I could not budge her from one story—*hau*, she was like a rock stuck in a dry riverbed!"

"Back to her story then. We'd got to where Kritz had come to her with those questions for the Song Dog . . ."

"The *songoma* told Boss Kritzinger that he must return after nine days and she would have the Song Dog's reply for him. But Boss Kritzinger did not keep that appointment. Many months were to go by before she saw him again."

"Which was on Sunday?"

"Correct, Lieutenant."

"Hmmmm," said Kramer. "I can understand Kritz having second thoughts and not going back those nine days later, but why change his mind again? Was it because he was suddenly no longer confident he knew what those answers were after all?"

"*Hau*, you show great insight, Lieutenant! The *songoma* says he was in an even more troubled frame of mind, and mumbled something about things being probably much more serious than he had imagined. Having written down all he knew about the matter, and then having stared at it many times at his desk, he had begun to wonder whether some of his ideas had been wrong and the real truth lay in another direction. He wanted to know if she could remember anything of what the Song Dog had said in response to his original questions."

"That can't have been very difficult, seeing she makes the bloody stuff up herself, hey?"

"I don't think she is aware of that, Lieutenant, but she did say to remember was easy, because the request had been so unusual and the Song Dog's reply had been so brief."

"Huh!"

"You don't wish to know what its words were, boss?"

"Of course I do!" said Kramer, flinging a stone into the gorge below. "Bullshit or not, they could well have influenced the silly bastard's thinking at the time of his decease."

Zondi nodded and said: "Then here are those words of the Song Dog, Lieutenant: *Your path is righteous, Isipikili, but beware: he who hunts in long grass may step on the mamba . . .*"

"And that's *it*?" said Kramer, jerking his head back. "Jesus wept, I didn't expect much, but you can hardly call that a bloody money's worth, can you? It doesn't even match up properly with his questions!"

"Yet the *songoma* says that Boss Kritzinger was greatly encouraged by the reply, boss."

"In what way? Shit, it's the sort of mumbo jumbo that could be applied to practically any situation! All it boils down to is go for it, but watch your bloody back, hey? It could be the CID motto!"

Zondi nodded. "Broadly speaking, I must agree, Lieutenant, but here was a man taking every word very personally. Boss Kritzinger told the *songoma* that the Song Dog was right: for months he had 'hunted buffalo in the long grass,' completely overlooking there could be a deadly serpent right at his feet—and yet, that very morning, he had caught what could have been a glimpse of it. *Hau,* he was very pleased."

"Did she ask him what he meant by 'serpent'?"

"My belief is that they discussed this at great length, boss, but all she would say to me was that she had added her own caution to the words of the Song Dog. She had told Boss Kritzinger that he must 'hunt only man' and 'heed the least of messengers' whenever he felt in danger."

"*Hey?*"

"I know, Lieutenant, all very puzzling, but this is how these people speak. We could spend much time debating the meanings."

"Only if we thought it was worth the trouble, Mickey! But our sole concern is the *effect* this bullshit could have had. How did Kritz leave this place? What mood was he in?"

"He was troubled, boss, and the *songoma* was afraid for him. His shadow was growing faint, she said."

"Oh, ja, the finest prophecies are the bastards of hindsight, not so?"

Zondi grinned. "*Hau*, you too could be a great *songoma*, Lieutenant, famous for your wonderful sayings!"

"Watch it, kaffir—a bit of respect now!"

Their laughter drove the crow away.

Kramer rose and looked at his watch. "Christ," he said, "it's only just gone nine. I'm buggered if I'm sitting here, twiddling my thumbs until twelve for Aap and his bloody helicopter. How about you, man?"

It was a good thing Zondi had spent so much time staring at the ground during the flight from Mabata to the sorcerer's mountain. Without the mental map he had made, the confusion of footpaths, especially in the many deserted valleys where there was nobody to help with directions, would have led to a great deal of wasted time and energy.

As it was, it still took them more than two hours of steady trudging, up slopes and down slopes, over wild country and through occasional semicultivated areas, to come within sight of Mabata. The second helicopter had disappeared from in front of the little stone police station, and the only sign of life, detectable at such a distance, was some movement at the rear of two white vehicles parked beside the flagpole.

Zondi, who had been leading the way in companionable

silence, paused and glanced round, his eyebrows raised as though asking whether Kramer wanted to stop and rest for a minute or two.

Kramer shook his head. He had ceased talking, ceased thinking to a degree; now was the time for action, and all he cared about was getting back to Jafini. Sweating profusely and with his jacket slung over his back, he kept his eyes on the flip and fall of Zondi's heels, no longer bothering to look up. He'd had more than his fill of picturesque rural scenes typifying Zululand: the mud huts and the aloes, the drought-stunted maize and the potbellied piccanins, the donkeys with rocks tied to their tails, which was said to inhibit nocturnal braying. His legs, which had begun protesting, found themselves having to work harder and harder as the incline grew steeper.

Then he noticed some empty Castle lager bottles, glinting in the dry grass on either side of him, and seconds later he and Zondi reached level ground again, only yards from where they had left their Land-Rover, outside Mabata police station.

In front of it stood the station commander, Stoffel Wessels, still in slippers, his shoulders slumped, staring vacantly at the horizon behind them.

"Stoffel, what's up, hey?" asked Kramer, then realized that the two long white vehicles in the background were ambulances. "Somebody's been injured?"

Wessels turned to him, refocused slowly, and said, with an odd sort of chuckle: "Chopper chop-chop!" he said.

"I'm not with you, man," said Kramer, glancing at Zondi, who responded with a shrug, indicating an equal sense of bewilderment.

"Got the chop!" said Wessels, striking himself on the back of the neck with the edge of his hand. "Chop, chop, chop!"

"Listen, uncle," said a young ambulance driver, hastening over and putting an arm around Wessels' shoulders. "You must come and sit inside quietly for a while—you are in shock, hey? Don't worry, everything is being taken care of, and there is more help on its way."

"That's nice," said Wessels, nodding.

"You'll come with me, uncle?"

"So long as I don't have to see those—"

"No, uncle; promise, uncle; we'll go round into your house the other way, uncle. Here we go, no need to hurry . . ."

The second ambulance driver, a burly middle-aged man with an Elvis haircut, long sideburns, the lot, came over to Kramer, sized him up, and said in foreign-sounding English, "You all right, guv? Bit of blood there on yer shirt, I see."

"Ach, no, that's nothing! What the hell's going on here? Do you know?"

"Simple enough, squire. According to your lads in the other helicopter, who saw the whole thing, the first one down landed in a bit of a hollow, with a steep bank to one side, like. This was right where them wogs was fighting, see? Bullets and bleedin' spears flyin' all over the place, and some nig-nog givin' it the old one-two with a flippin' shotgun, dancing around up on a rock. Score was about Shabalalas fifteen, Sitholes fourteen, playin' for a draw, and the crowd's *lovin'* it, the women all making that special you've-got-no-balls sound, eggin' 'em on. Y'know, the usual, and normally, no problem. Only it looks like nobody in the copter realized how close to that bank they'd come, and so when the first three jumped out and legged it for cover, they went straight up the bank and *whack, whack, whack*, rotors caught 'em, decapitated the lot! Oh, aye, dead nasty but they'd not have known what hit them, mind. Trouble is, the copter tipped a bit as this happened and rotors caught the ground on t'other side. Next thing, these other lads see, is the whole caboodle doing a sort of a cartwheel, up out of that hollow and straight over this bloody cliff them Shabalalas had got their backs to! *Boom!* One big ball of flame and every nig-nog for miles is leggin' it, fast as their feet'll carry 'em. Second copter goes in, gets through to our control via its radio, and brings out the first three. It's gone back now for the others before bits of 'em is pinched to be made into *muti*. Wouldn't have yer job for a big clock, I'm tellin' yer! Fancy a bit of gum, chief?"

Kramer declined the proffered stick of Wrigley's with a shake of his head, glanced into the back of the nearest ambulance, then turned and went over to the Land-Rover, followed by Zondi.

"Can't see what help we'd be, hanging around here," he said, starting the engine. "You heard all that?"

Zondi nodded and sighed. "The crow, boss," he said.

"Come again? What was that?"

"I've never liked helicopters, Lieutenant," said Zondi.

25

*F*irst of all, Mickey," said Kramer, as they started cautiously down the zigzagging, hazardous track leading from Mabata to the coastal plain, "I'm going to have you formally seconded to this investigation, okay?"

"Boss?"

"Well, any damn fool can see your undercover role has been blown to buggery by now, so we'll just have to catch Cousin Nun-Shagger later on, when we have the time, hey? For expediency's sake, however, to avoid a lot of nonsense from Bronkhorst, the Colonel, and the rest of the bloody red-tape brigade, I'm going to bullshit them that the mission murders and the Fynn's Creek ones are possibly connected. That way, I can have you start work for me officially almost the minute we get back to Jafini. The 'officially' aspect is important, of course, because of technicalities such as the continuity of evidence et cetera, once we finally drag this bastard, kicking and screaming, to bloody court."

"*Hau*, this is very good news, Lieutenant!"

"And as for what we do next, it seems we have a simple choice. Either we go looking for whoever took potshots at us last night, *or* we start poking into what the Song Dog's sicked up on the carpet. Myself, I favor the latter plan, because at least we know where to bloody begin, hey?"

"Boss?"

"Didn't the witch-doctor female tell you that Kritz had been fretting over what he'd written about the cane-truck fatal at his desk?"

"That's true, Lieutenant. Only I—"

"And she did say 'desk,' didn't she? Not 'table' or something similar?"

"No, 'desk' for definite, boss, because I was surprised that someone so raw would know the term. Then I realized she was repeating part of Boss Kritzinger's speech word for word, showing off to me how good her memory was. But I thought you said—"

"Then obviously if we can find those case notes of his, a hell of a lot of time could be saved! Sounded to me as though Kritz had already done most of the groundwork."

"But, I thought, boss," Zondi finally got in, "I thought the Lieutenant had already made a thorough search of Boss Kritzinger's desk and found nothing?"

"Ach, maybe I didn't look as hard as I might have. After all, I didn't know at that stage he'd been committing his big secret to paper, creating a document he'd not want anyone else to see. I just hope to God he didn't destroy it!"

"Or maybe the desk that the *songoma* spoke of was a different one he had back at his own house, boss."

"Good thinking, hey? I'll do a check on that. Anything else she said I should know about?"

Zondi smiled. "Well, there was what Mama Pelapela told me, Lieutenant, when I tried to trick her into telling me more, by asking if she had any advice to give us."

"Oh, ja, what was that?"

"Mama Pelapela replied, boss: 'I say to you both, revenge is your gift to the unjustly dead; go forth and be generous! For even when you are wrong you will be right, and when—' "

"Cheeky old bitch!" said Kramer. "When have I ever been

wrong, hey? But that first part I *like*—oh, ja, very definitely!"

"Me, too, Lieutenant," said Zondi.

They came down out of those mountains like two-up in a fiery chariot, billowing a great plume of red dust behind them, and fell upon the Bombay Emporium like wolves upon a fold—or at least, that was how an astonished shop assistant seemed to view it when they bought up every Texan and Lucky Strike pack in sight, aware that they could have a long, hard haul ahead of them and no time to bugger about shopping for essentials in the middle of it.

They were on their way out of the trading store when Zondi nudged Kramer and said: "Look, boss . . ."

Hans Terblanche had just double-parked his Land-Rover beside their own, and was lumbering with a frown toward the store's verandah.

"Wait here while I find out what he wants, Mickey," said Kramer.

"Tromp!" said Terblanche. "Where in heaven's name have you been, hey? And look at the state you're in! You've had me and the Widow Fourie worried sick about you, imagining all sorts of things!"

"Oh, ja?" said Kramer, reaching the top step. "None of them too filthy, I hope."

"Pardon?"

"Ach, I've just been following up a few leads, doing this and that, bumming a helicopter ride off Aap van Vuuren from Mabata."

"Mabata?" repeated Terblanche, taking a pace backward, his color draining. "You surely don't mean you . . . !"

"Relax, Hans, this isn't a ghost you see! I got off the stop before, hey, so no harm done."

"Isn't it terrible what happened to those blokes? I've never known such a week!"

"Terrible," said Kramer. "And you? What have you been doing?"

"Me? I've been waiting for that fingerprint expert of yours

to arrive from Trekkersburg—in between five hundred other things! You know Malan's off sick today? An infected thumb that he got from some hammer yesterday, and now Sarel's got to go and relieve Stoffel Wessels up at Mabata. He's packing himself a suitcase at his ma's house right now, and the Colonel says I'm to drive him up there chop-chop—I'm on my way round now—on account of Stoffel's having a nervous breakdown or something, and then I've got to bring Stoffel back for a proper checkup at the hospital, leaving only a raw Bantu in charge here, referring all important calls to Nkosala, while I—"

"Would it help if I kept an eye on him?"

"You actually mean that?"

"Of course."

"Wonderful, man! You don't know what a weight that is off my shoulders!"

"Fine, then I'll see you later, hey?"

"Many, many thanks," said Terblanche, hurrying back to his Land-Rover. "I owe you a favor, hey?"

No, we're quits, thought Kramer, very heartened by having been told how much the Widow Fourie had missed him.

And then, as the station commander's Land-Rover went backfiring off up the street, its tailgate flapping, Zondi emerged from the Bombay Emporium and murmured: "Why the sly little smile, Lieutenant?"

"Ach, didn't you hear, hey? I've just been put in charge of Jafini, which means *we can bloody tear the place apart* in our search for Kritz's stuff, if we need to . . ."

After just fifteen minutes back at the police station, that was no longer the idle threat it might have sounded. The dead detective sergeant's desktop, awash in dockets, old carbon papers, and everything else once stored in its drawers and pigeonholes, had yielded nothing that seemed worth a second glance.

Zondi dropped to his knees and started looking under the desktop itself.

"I've already done all that!" said Kramer. "Can't you come up with something more original, man?"

"In a minute, boss," said Zondi, pulling the drawers right out and turning them over.

"And I've already explored those as well—you won't find a damn thing stuck to them, I bet you!"

"Hmmmmm," said Zondi.

"Listen," said Kramer, "time to test your idea of the desk being one he had at home. I'll go and find Kritz's number in the boss's office, ring the house, and pick up the inquest papers on the Cloete road traffic fatal while I'm there."

An unfamiliar female voice answered the Kritzingers' telephone and explained, rather sharply, that she was Hettie's sister, newly arrived from Durban to gather the bereaved family together and take them back with her.

"I'm afraid Hettie's under sedation again," she said.

"Can you just tell me if Maaties had a desk at his house?" said Kramer. "Somewhere he kept his personal papers et cetera?"

"No," she said, without hesitation. "The family live cramped enough as it is, what with there being six of them." And something in her voice implied she had *never* approved of the marriage.

"What about a table with a locked drawer he could've—"

"No," she said. "Frankly, I'm quite shattered by the conditions I've found here! Do you know, the toilet doesn't even flush properly? That man acted as though—"

"Er, well, give Mrs. Kritz my best, hey?" said Kramer, and dropped the receiver back into its cradle.

Then he began another hunt, this time for those inquest papers. "You fight dirty, Hans, you bastard!" he growled, having rooted about on the windowsill in the station commander's office, and then among the piles of other documents stacked all over the floor, only to find what he sought in its proper place in the filing cabinet.

The inquest docket contained no more than an average amount of paperwork. Just a pro forma accident report, filled

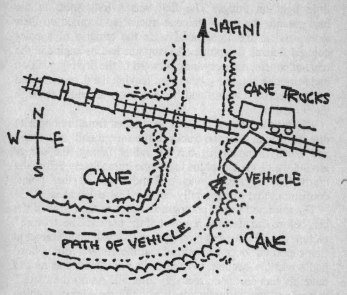

in and signed by someone called W. D. de Klerk, a couple of poor carbon copies of the two postmortem reports, more carbons of the seven statements De Klerk had taken, the standard set of photographs, shot at night using a flash, and a sketch plan of the scene.

The sketch plan showed a right-angle turn in a dirt road that ran through acres of mature sugarcane. Several arrows indicated the path of a vehicle that had gone round the bend safely enough, but had failed to straighten up properly. Instead, it had plunged off the road, through a thin screen of cane and into two cane trucks, standing on a railway track which crossed the road at that point.

In short, it was just another classic example of a partygoer cornering too bloody fast on his homeward journey, and so innocent of mystery that it only made Kritzinger's interest in the affair all the more puzzling.

Perhaps, thought Kramer, the photographs would throw a

little light on things. The first was a long shot. In the background, the two sugarcane trucks lay derailed on their sides, and in the foreground were the remains of a pale-colored Renault Dauphine. A Dauphine had its engine in the rear, of course, so everything forward of the driving position had scrunched up like a bean can, leaving the driver impaled on his steering column and his passenger shredded through the windshield.

The second photograph had been taken from the opposite direction, with the cane trucks in the foreground, and didn't add much, although it showed, rather faintly, the corner around which the Dauphine had come immediately before the crash. The sugarcane was tall and dense at that point, confirming that it had totally obscured what lay ahead.

The third and fourth photographs were of the inside of the car, before and after the removal of the bodies. The "before" picture was slightly less grotesque in its detail than Kramer at first supposed, once he realized that the driver's lolling head had somehow become twisted right round and that he *did* have his ears on the correct way after all. As for the "after" picture, it was virtually identical, offering almost nothing new to look at, aside from a few details like the sticky-topped steering column; the ignition key still in the ignition lock, complete with fancy key ring; and a lurching statuette of St. Christopher, looking *I bloody told you so* on the top of the dashboard.

Zondi wandered in at that moment. "The Lieutenant has found the inquest papers?"

"Uh-huh."

"Do they give any indication of foul play having—"

"Not so far; all very straightforward. Kritz didn't have a desk at home, by the way—you have his sister-in-law's word for it."

Zondi sighed. "Six times I have been through all the contents of Boss Kritzinger's desk here, boss—nothing. I am beginning to wonder if maybe what we were told by the *songoma* wasn't all just a big nonsense. I had thought, *hau,* wait till we get to Jafini! The pieces will start coming together fast!"

"Ja, and maybe they will, man," said Kramer, preparing to move on from the photographs to the accident pro forma.

"But does the Lieutenant realize that so far we do not even have corroboration of Boss Kritzinger having any interest at all in that fatal? We could be wasting—"

"Hey, *wait a minute . . .*" said Kramer, rising, the last of the six photographs in his hand. "Come round here, quick! What do you make of that, hey?"

"Make of what, Lieutenant?"

"There, where my finger's pointing. What shape would you say that thing was?"

"I think it is possibly a dog, boss."

"Damn right, it is! But what kind? What breed, I mean?"

"Lieutenant?" said Zondi, very warily.

"What if I told you that Kritz kept a Scottie dog key ring, exactly like this one, tucked away somewhere in his desk— until Bokkie Maritz unearthed it last Tuesday?"

"*Hau, hau, hau . . .*"

"You can say that again! You know why? Because I'll bet you bloody anything *it was the same key ring,* confirming that Kritz certainly did have an interest!"

It was good to see Zondi with his smile again.

Then, to clinch matters, Kramer remembered the two pieces of the key-ring puzzle he had palmed, with the sole intention of making life more interesting for Bokkie Maritz, and produced them from his trouser pocket. One was white, the other red, and it proved simple enough to match the latter, from which the Scottie's tail jutted, with the image in the photograph.

"But how would Boss Kritzinger have come by this key ring, Lieutenant?" asked Zondi. "He was not the investigating officer, and even if he had been, why—"

"All sorts of ways! Simplest of all, he could have gone to the car dump to inspect the wreck, after being told to take an interest in the case, and have taken it as a memento or something."

Zondi snapped his fingers, as though a sudden idea had struck him. "Perhaps Boss Kritzinger had considered giving it to Mama Pelapela to hold in her hand while she addressed the Song Dog," he suggested. "That is a thing many *songomas* do."

"There you are, then! Man, we just keep getting warmer and warmer, don't we? So back you go, try taking a fresh approach to the problem, and I'll whip through these statements, see if I can't spot what got Kritz's Y-fronts in a knot, hey? Tell you what, my son, I'll bloody *race* you!"

26

O n his own in the station commander's office once more, Kramer sat down and took up the accident pro forma, his eyes alighting on "Cause of Accident (if known)," where he read: "Apparent loss of control, no other vehicle involved. Strong smell of alcohol vicinity driver's abdominal injuries."

The obvious place to look next was at the "Forensic Report Summary" overleaf: "Gross Multiple injuries, fatal in both cases. Driver had consumed roughly the equivalent of a bottle of wine, passenger ditto."

"Shit, what's new?" said Kramer, tossing aside the pro forma and picking up a sworn statement made by someone called Daryl Gordon Taylor, hoping he would provide some hint of what had aroused Kritzinger's suspicions:

> I am a white adult male, aged fifty-two years, residing at the Manager's House, Jafini Sugar Mills Ltd., Jafini, Northern Zululand. My occupation is mill manager and I have been employed by Jafini Sugar Mills Ltd. in this capacity for twenty-seven

years. Throughout this period, I have been acquainted with the deceased, Andries Johannes Adolf
Jeremiah Cloete, who was employed at Jafini Sugar
Mills Ltd. as the European foreman with a labor
force of thirty-five non-European mill boys under
him. He performed his duties well and responsibly
at all times. I have also known the deceased on a
social basis for twenty-five years and consider him a
good friend and colleague meriting respect for the
moderation he showed in all things.

On the night in question the deceased and his
deceased wife were present in my garden for a
barbecue. Also in attendance were Mr. and Mrs. G.
T. Taylor, my aged parents, Mr. J. G. H. Geldenhuys, the magistrate from Nkosala, and Mrs. J. G.
H. Geldenhuys, Miss Susan Truscott-Smythe, who
had come to buy a horse from me, and Mr. Roberto
Fransico, who I was given to understand was her
uncle and benefactor. We assembled at seven
o'clock for drinks and the servants had the meat
ready by eight o'clock. It took over two hours to eat
after which coffee was served. At no time did either
of the deceased consume more wine than was offered
to the rest of the guests being too well mannered for
that. By the time of their departure at approximately
eleven o'clock I was confident they were as sober as
Mr. J. G. H. Geldenhuys, the magistrate, who left
just ahead of them although on a different road. The
track the deceased used is generally used only by
employees of Jafini Sugar Mills Ltd. and of course
Mr. Bruce Grantham registered owner of the land.
The deceased always used that track for visiting my
place. I estimate he must have traveled up and down
it more than 1,150 times over the period I have
known them including every Christmas and New
Year without once having an accident. I totally
reject the rumor the deceased was speeding and
misjudged a corner he knew so well. My belief is

*that he must have seen some animal or native in the
road and tried to avoid it making his big mistake
that way for he was a tenderhearted man who could
not bear to see a creature that was suffering. In
conclusion I would like to state that the deceased
always took extra special care while driving a
vehicle belonging to Jafini Sugar Mills Ltd. as was
the case when this tragedy occurred.*

"Man, oh, man," murmured Kramer. "With friends like
that, who needs attorneys?"

Even so, while such a statement might indeed encourage
any reasonable man to suspect that Cloete could have driven
home safely from a booze-up at Taylor's place blind drunk
with his head in a bucket, it still contained nothing to suggest
that anything other than one of the more banal vagaries of fate
had finally caught up that night with a very boring-sounding
couple.

"Damn, damn, *damn* . . ." said Kramer.

Zondi, seated in Kritzinger's chair, was trying to imagine
himself in the dead man's shoes as well.

"Here I am," he thought, "and over there, directly
opposite, in front of the window, is Jaap Malan. I have a
secret document I don't want him or anyone else to find. If I
hide it here, in my desk, there is a chance he might stumble
across it—perhaps looking for some statement or other,
during one of my many absences . . . My only way of
keeping it from him would be to place it somewhere he would
never dream of looking, and yet, at the same time, it would
be somewhere that provides me with ready access. Such as?"

He looked all around him, and then back at the desk across
the way from him. "Ah!" he said.

How wonderfully simple: Kritzinger must have hidden his
secret papers somewhere on *Malan's* side of the room—not in
a drawer or anything like that, of course, but somewhere just
as easy to get to.

* * *

"That looks an interesting idea, Mickey," said Kramer, strolling back into the CID office. "What are you doing to Jaapie's desk—changing the gearbox?"

Zondi, flat on his back beneath the desk, began to extricate himself. "Just wait, boss," he said, "I could have a big surprise for you . . ." Then he crawled round to the far side and started removing drawers.

"Thought you'd like to know," said Kramer, dropping the inquest docket on Kritzinger's desk, "that Colonel Du Plessis has just approved your secondment to the Fynn's Creek case. Mind you, he was in such a bloody tiz-woz, what with the chopper crash and the arrest of this Mandela character, he'd probably have given me permission to ravish his lady wife *and* the pedigree cocker spaniel."

"I am very happy for you, boss."

"You bugger! You're not listening!"

"Please, Lieutenant, I'm engaged in—"

"Some bloody weird behavior! Ja, I'm well aware of that."

Zondi pushed both drawers back. "Ah," he said, "another even more brilliant idea, boss! Will the Lieutenant please move over this side and use Boss Malan's desk instead?"

"Why?"

"So I can test my brilliant idea, boss."

"Bloody hell," sighed Kramer, doing as he was asked, taking the inquest docket with him. "I just hope you—"

"My reasoning, boss, is based upon the fact that Boss Kritzinger had in his desk a Scottie dog key ring of special significance that he had not made any actual attempt to hide, or else such a person as Boss Bokkie Maritz would never have found it."

"So what?"

"Surely that is the key to Boss Kritzinger's handling of secrets, Lieutenant? *He did not hide what was hidden.* He simply relied on others being unable to grasp a special significance."

"Oh, ja? So he hid his notes by not hiding them either—is that what you're saying?"

"Precisely, boss! With the big advantage he could look at them very easily whenever he wanted."

"Hmmmm. Maybe you're making a mistake by imagining things on Kritz's behalf without having any real idea of how bright he was. Personally, I think you overrate him, kaffir."

"But what was it that cost Boss Kritzinger his life, Lieutenant?" asked Zondi. "What he knew—or what he did not know? Was it intelligence or stupidity?"

"Ach!" said Kramer, sitting down behind Malan's desk. "It's your bloody theory, man—you prove it." And he took up the next of the sworn statements.

It had been made by Jacob Gerhardus Hendrik Geldenhuys, the Nkosala magistrate, and apart from the preamble, giving his race, age, and all the rest, it appeared mercifully brief, running to no more than two paragraphs:

> In my view the deceased was not inebriated to the degree it had affected his ability to drive a motor vehicle correctly at the conclusion of the evening, having imbibed his liquor slowly over a period of more than four hours in conjunction with the consumption of a considerable quantity of protein, which is known to alter the nature of alcohol and and inhibit its absorption into the system. (See State v. Koekemoor, et al.)

Well, he would say that, wouldn't he, the self-serving bugger, thought Kramer, for the magistrate must have been in exactly the same state when he drove Mrs. Geldenhuys home from the party.

> As a magistrate I am of course more ready than most to condemn drinking and driving, but here, I believe, we have seen occur nothing more than another inexplicable tragedy, such as has already befallen this concern this year and over which I had the sad duty to adjudicate.

Kramer fell to pondering what Geldenhuys had meant by "another inexplicable tragedy" and the phrase "this concern." When the penny finally dropped, it slid chill down his spine like a chip off an ice block, causing a reflex shudder that jerked him to his feet. "Christ, the toffee apple!" he said.

Zondi looked up, a pencil clamped sideways between his teeth, and raised an eyebrow.

"Ach, Pik Fourie!" said Kramer. "Hubby of the landlady where I'm staying? He worked at the sugar mill, too, until he fell in a vat of bloody boiling sugar."

Taking the pencil from his mouth, Zondi asked: "Is the boss saying we have now another murder that links up?"

"I bloody hope not!"

"But was Boss Fourie's death in any way suspicious, Lieutenant?"

"His widow certainly doesn't act that way. She's just very sad, that's all; it shows in her laughter sometimes—but only when the kids are about."

Zondi suddenly averted his eyes, as though he might have been looking too thoughtfully at Kramer.

"Er, listen, Mickey," said Kramer, "I'm going to go and find this other inquest, hey?" And he left the office in a state of embarrassment he had never known before.

He was reminded slightly, however, of the day his silent nurse had first beckoned to him, showing she was aware that there might be more to Tromp Kramer than just the big bad cop the rest of the world seemed to see—kaffirs especially.

Unsettled, for some reason he could not identify, Zondi lit a Texan and picked up the Cloete docket, curious to see for himself what it contained. After glancing at the sketch plan and at the photographs, he skimmed through all seven statements. Five were by the Cloetes' fellow partygoers, and each testified to the mill foreman's apparent sobriety at the end of a quiet, very civilized evening. The remaining two statements were more down-to-earth and had been submitted in written form, as opposed to being dictated, coming as they did from experts asked to express an opinion.

In one, a qualified examiner from the Government Garage in Durban gave his findings regarding the roadworthiness of the Renault Dauphine before impact, and said in his summary:

> As to be expected in a company-owned and maintained vehicle, everything including brakes, lights, and steering was in good order, suggesting human error was the deciding factor.

And in the other, the district surgeon, Dr. Abrahams, had written:

> Mr. Andries Cloete was a private patient of mine although I saw little of him, his health being excellent for a man of his age, as was evidenced by the fact he had been on another of his long hunting trips only a week before his demise, bagging his thirty-seventh elephant, also a leopard at night, which speaks volumes for his reflexes and eyesight. He had no drinking problem that I was aware of; his liver and kidneys supported this view on postmortem examination.

"Hmm," said Zondi, now sharing Kramer's perplexity, for he could see nothing in the inquest report to suggest there had been foul play whatsoever—nor why there might have been cause for even suspecting any.

Then he heard a white woman's voice out in the corridor, surprising him a little, and he hurriedly swept the crash pictures out of sight, extinguished his cigarette, and wondered if it would not be discreet of him to slip quickly through the open window.

"Mickey, you'll never guess who that was, hey?" said Kramer, returning to the CID office moments later. "Kritz's sister-in-law has just called by quickly to hand this in before taking the family down to Durban." And he placed a battered imitation-leather briefcase on Malan's desk. "She said my phone call had set her thinking—'a man must have *somewhere* for his personal papers'—and she came up with this."

"Is there anything in it which—"

"Christ, kaffir, give us a chance!" said Kramer, as eager as he was to discover what the case contained. He undid the clasp and began removing everything tucked into its three divisions. "This year's income tax form, mortgage agreement, insurance policy, insurance policy, pension details, more pension details, birth certificate, same, same, same, same, same, marriage certificate, firearm license, savings bank, Barclays Bank statements—ah, what's this?"

"A statement from an accused in a stock theft case, taken down in Zulu, boss," said Zondi, looking over his shoulder. "And that next one is another old case concerning a grave opened up to make *muti* from the corpse. They look to me like unsolved cases."

"Uh-uh, and what have we here?" Kramer took out a heavy, lumpy, sealed envelope that had a couple of Zulu words scrawled on it. "More of the same?"

"That reads 'His' and 'Mine,' boss."

"Oh, ja? I hope it's nothing rude, hey?" said Kramer, slitting open the envelope with Malan's paper knife.

"How strange . . ." said Zondi.

"Two shoe-print casts," said Kramer, laying them side by side. "Both right shoes, sunk in soft mud or clay, and plaster of paris poured in. Could this 'his' be the bastard we're looking for, hey?"

"But which is which?" asked Zondi. "If one of those shoes is supposed to be Boss Kritzinger's?"

"They look almost identical to me, except one's a bit longer."

Zondi examined the casts more closely. "A strange thing for a detective to do, boss: put his *own* shoe forward for comparison."

"Not really. Kritz could have been plodding around in a

certain area, looking for clues, and then suddenly noticed there was another set of prints there, forcing him to make some distinction between them."

"Then surely the first step, Lieutenant, is to clear up the 'which is which' problem by getting one of Boss Kritzinger's shoes and measuring it?"

"True," said Kramer. "Only his house will all be locked up, now that his sister-in-law's moved everybody to Durban—and I bet she's taken even the servant's bloody keys with her."

Zondi shrugged. "Wouldn't it be simpler, boss, to put a ruler to one of the shoes Boss Kritzinger was wearing when he was blown up the other night?"

"You don't understand, man—that's not *simpler* at all," replied Kramer. "The mortuary at Nkosala is run by Bud Abbott and bloody Lou Costello: all Kritz's things got chucked in the bloody incinerator!"

"*Hau!* Is the Lieutenant sure that—"

"Listen, I was present when the boiler boy swore on his God's oath that 'all clothes' had been chucked in his fire."

"The boss believed him?"

"Jesus, what would you do if you were handed a stinking pile of rags like that, all soaked in blood and shit and Christ knows what else?"

Zondi screwed up one eye, while he appeared to calculate the odds of something. "Lieutenant," he said, "it is time for a kaffir to do a bit more kaffir's work. Have I your permission to borrow the Chevy?"

27

Kramer took very little notice of the Chevrolet leaving the yard. He wasn't even quite sure why he had agreed to Zondi using it. Ever since the name of Pik Fourie had come up, his mind had been fighting off a thought he really did not want to think, and all else had become a little unreal.

For once, upon first opening an inquest docket, he did not start by looking at the set of police photographs, tucked into their glassine envelope. Neither did he stop to examine the reason.

Kramer began instead with the postmortem report, immediately flipping over it so that the details of the deceased's height, weight, hair color, eye color, and general physical condition vanished from sight.

Then he zeroed in on: *Death would have been instantaneous due to vagal inhibition alone, setting aside asphyxiation, shock, etc.*

"Thank Christ," he said.

Zondi had left both desks in a mess, but Kritzinger's looked the quicker to tidy. So Kramer sat himself down at it, swept some picked-over rubbish back into the top drawer, slammed it, and then pushed aside the litter of used carbons to make room for the Fourie docket.

More muddle. Some of the statements had been put back upside down, and the pro forma had wandered off into the middle somewhere, instead of acting as the introduction. Kramer licked a fingertip and started searching through Kritzinger's carbon copies of the statements. They were all rather faint, something he had always found intensely irritating.

"Ach, no!" Kramer muttered under his breath. "What the hell were you bloody playing at, Kritz?"

He was certain he'd just seen several perfectly good, hardly used sheets of carbon paper on the man's desk, and looked round for one to prove his point. Noticing that the once-only typed impression was not reversed in its black, waxy surface, he had to smile; Kritzinger had plainly made the same mistake he himself kept on making. You put the damned carbon paper the wrong way into your typewriter, typed away unaware of this, and ended up with a blank copy, a mess on the back of your top sheet, and having to start all over again from the beginning.

Then, with a jolt, he suddenly registered what those lines of typed words actually *said:*

> **Cloete and his wife. But if I am wrong? That could be my job and MY wife and family right down the drain! So check and double check and take no action until you are one hundred percent absolutely certain you hear. The main trouble is I can't work out the reason although I am pretty sure this wasn't the first time he**

Kramer could read no further. He had first to stand up, light a Lucky, start pacing about, get himself under control, stop his hands shaking so bloody much that he had difficulty extracting a match from its box without spilling the others.

"Jesus, Mickey, you choose your bloody moments to disappear, hey?" he muttered.

There proved to be eight sheets of carbon paper, scattered about on Kritzinger's desktop, that had been used only once; one was a CID requisition list, broken off halfway through, and another three were ancient duty rotas. Setting these aside, Kramer took the remaining four sheets and placed them in sequence, by noting how the sentences broke between one page and another. That done, he lit a fresh Lucky off the cigarette he was about to stub out, and began again at what looked like the beginning.

> De Klerk phones me and says the magistrate has been going over the Cloete fatal statements and he wants a theory in them checked out. Taylor's put forward the idea C crashed because he tried to avoid a native or animal in the road. I say a bloke that kills so many animals as he does is not going to think twice about what he runs over. De Klerk says ja but we're interested in finding the native so we can prove it wasn't drink that caused the accident. I say I can't see what difference running down a native would make to C who has shot a few of them also in his time besides elephants. I tell De Klerk that the only thing that would make C swerve in my opinion is seeing something in the road he can't hit and hope to live like a brick wall maybe.
>
> He tells me that isn't my worry. I am the man with the native contacts so he has been instructed to tell me to find the native and see he gives the right evidence. I am sorry for little Annika regarding her ma and pa but I am too busy with genuine cases to bother with a nonsense like this and so I do nothing.

De Klerk bells me again. To get him off my back I go to G's farm. We have a few beers then I go to the compound. Naturally none of his boys owns up to staggering around drunk in front of C's car. Do you think we are MAD Isipikili? That is NOT the way home Isipikili! And so on. G and me had some more beers. We agree C was unlucky there were those two cane trucks hidden in the cane because otherwise no real harm would have been done by leaving the road at that point. We also agree C can't really complain because he had always been a terrible driver and had got away Scot free far too many times already. G says surely my time is being wasted and I tell him too right it is.

Next morning De Klerk rings up and says cancel the order. The case will be heard by a magistrate specially brought in so that Geldenhuys can give evidence and make sure no slur is left on the memory of C and Annika won't have any trouble getting paid the insurance. I say fine suits me.

I have almost forgotten about it two days later when I am on foot in the street and Bhengu greets me near the Bombay. He is the oldest boy G has got with some wonderful memories of Zululand before the sugar came. He calls it The Sweetness That Turned Sour A People's Dream and had better watch out the SBs don't hear him. A long salutation and then he starts talking in a big mumble. I put him in my car and I ask him what the problem is.

He tells me that he was the boy in charge of the cane trucks at the side of the road where the accident happened and now he is much troubled. I say he is being an old fool and to just put the whole thing from his mind. He says he cannot do this because that is the section where G appointed him to work and he is afraid of the evil spirit which has come to dwell there.

I ask him to describe the form the evil spirit takes but he says he has not seen it yet. He knows it is there though because at night it moves the cane trucks about. My reaction is to laugh and ask how often this has happened. So far only once is his reply. The night Boss Cloete left this world he says and expects me to believe that.

I tell Bhengu that there was nothing the matter with where the trucks were left but if he wants to blame an evil spirit for putting them there it is fine with me. He wants to go on talking about the spirit but I get cross and put him out of my car as I have lots of work to do.

I am driving back from near Mabata that night when a thought occurs to me. I ask myself why has Bhengu

The telephone rang, and with a growl of irritation, Kramer broke off to snatch up the receiver: "Ja? Who is it? Speak quick because I'm bloody busy right now!"

"It is only Zondi, boss, at Nkosala police—"

"And so?"

"I have just had another idea, Lieutenant, that I thought I must tell you very fast."

"Then don't bugger about, man! Out with it!"

"The Lieutenant knows those carbon papers I had in my hand from Boss Kritz's desk? If I may make a suggestion, the boss should maybe check them to see if he hid—"

"Nine out of ten, Smart Arse," said Kramer, adding, just before he put the receiver down: "Come straight back here right away, you hear me?"

And had to find his place again, beginning that paragraph afresh:

I am driving back from near Mabata that night when a thought occurs to me. I ask myself why has Bhengu brought ME a problem that has to do with spirits? He knows I am not a witch doctor and cannot give him a charm to protect him even though I know a lot about the subject and study it at first hand in my spare time. No it must be because Bhengu knows full well what I am and because he does not really believe in this spirit either or he WOULD go to a witch doctor.

It is late but I head straight for G's farm. G is not there so I ask the induna to fetch Bhengu out of bed. I take him to one side and say I have come to drive out an evil spirit for him and tell him to get in the car. We go to where the crash was and I make him follow me over to where the two trucks still are lying on their side. I say to him fine show me where these trucks were when you left them and before the spirit moved them to here. Bhengu says they are not the trucks he is talking about. The trucks moved by the spirit are the upright ones on the other side of the road.

Show me what you mean I say. We start to cross over the road but Bhengu stops in the middle and points to the railway line the trucks go on. He says that the upright trucks had been moved to this spot and then moved back again. I naturally ask him how he can possibly know this and he asks me to put on the headlights of the car.

Bhengu then shows me all the small slugs and similar creatures that come out at night and crawl over the railway lines to get to the other

side. Cane has millions of slugs in it as I know
from boyhood and they all seem to like cold
surfaces. Bhengu tells me that when he came to
work at this place in the morning he had felt sure
the trucks were not standing in the same place as
the day before because some firewood he had left
propped against one end had fallen over and was
now separate from it by two strides. That had
made him look at the railway and he had seen
slugs squashed flat to smithereens where the
truck wheels had passed over them. He had
followed the squashed slugs to a point just past
the center of the road and had seen from this that
the trucks had been there the night before and
then pushed back again to almost their original
spot.

I felt sure I was looking at Mr. C's brick wall in
the middle of the road. No wonder he had tried to
steer around it only to hit the other trucks hidden
by the cane.

But naturally I wanted to be sure of this so I
asked Bhengu what other proof he had the trucks
were moved. He said he could show me a mark
made by the spirit. He showed me a footprint
pushed in the mud by a man straining to start the
trucks moving. This footprint was between the
two lines near his firewood. I noted that it was
the print of a man wearing a shoe and quite like
my own footprints I had made in the mud.

I thought I knew then why Bhengu kept calling
this a spirit. No cane boy wears shoes so this must
have been a print made by a white man but he
could not bring himself to say it to me being of
the old school. I thanked him and told him to tell
no one and dropped him off at G's compound.

That footprint really worries me but I don't know why. I do not want to report this matter until I have more time to think. I have not handled a white-on-white murder before but somehow this could be even more serious. It has begun to rain again and soon the footprint could disappear. Perhaps I should make plaster casts which is easy enough.

In the morning I do not ring De Klerk. I have not enough evidence yet to support what I am think-ing. It is best the inquest just goes ahead because if I am right that will not matter and at least I will not have made a fool of myself by speaking out too soon.

Okay now I think I know how the crime was planned. As the noise of C's car approached the bend the trucks were put in the road. If he had hit them then a cane boy could have been blamed for leaving the brakes off. If he did not hit them but went round then he would hit the trucks in the cane instead and the other trucks could be put back again. The perfect murder because it was only an accident happening to a terrible driver who had been drinking and it worked lovely.

But what worries me is that I do not know WHY it was planned. What could the motive have been? I need also to supply the motive if I am to be believed. I do not believe myself sometimes and my wife has started to shout at me. She wants to know why I go to G's so much. It is strange but I have a feeling that there I will find the answer.

I delve into C's past. I learn he was once farm manager to G but they had different views on how boys should be handled and there was a big bust-up only this was 28 years ago. Too long I think for a grudge. I think G is letting his boys brew illicit liquor in some room under his house and distilling it properly. He looks at the young ones too much. Perhaps this is what upset C and for that I cannot blame him.

I also delve into C's life at the time of his decease. His main concern seemed to be finding enough cash to pay for a big wedding for Annika and I learn from G that he has been to him asking for a loan which was turned down flat. C apparently ended up using threats and this gave me the idea it could be blackmail. I have

The telephone was ringing again.

Plucking the tennis ball from the air, midflight, Zondi smiled as the boiler boy spun round, exclaiming: "*Yeee-ba-bor!* I thought you were—"

"Who, my brother?"

The boiler boy became immediately tongue-tied, shrugging so emphatically that his bony shoulders almost touched the plugs in his earlobes.

"I see," said Zondi, beginning to bounce the ball off the ground, stepping up the rhythm, "you would have me believe you are too stupid to answer a simple question, is that it?"

The man smiled idiotically.

Zondi switched to bouncing the ball off the wall of the boiler house. "Pretend what you like about yourself to the whites," he said. "But because a man is a boiler boy that does not mean he is also a damned baboon—take good care you do not insult the memory of my father!"

That brought a second look of surprise to the boiler boy's face. "Your father, chief?"

"Of course! Was he not head boiler at Trekkersburg

General from before he was married until the day we carried him to his grave in the high hill?"

" 'General' is a hospital?"

"Where else does a man get a death-house contamination so bad his whole arm swells up before the poison grips his heart?"

"*Hau, hau, hau!* It pains me to hear this, chief!"

"Good," said Zondi, directing the ball at the wall so that it would bounce back toward the boiler boy. "Perhaps we can now converse in a more sensible fashion."

"Your esteemed father, chief," said the boiler boy, catching the ball and using the wall to return it to Zondi, "had opened up a bag sent for incineration? Is that how he contracted—"

"*Eh-heh*. You know how it is, the job pays so very poorly."

Then Zondi appeared to become absorbed in the movement of the ball, as it bounced back and forth off those baking red bricks, traveling faster and faster between him and the boiler boy.

28

"**Y**ou sound distracted, Tromp," said Terblanche, barely audible on the crackly telephone line from Mabata. "Did you get all that?"

"Ja, ja, Stoffel's still a total, gibbering wreck and you're about to take him to the hospital at Nkosala. Fine, then, if that's all, I'll—"

"The Bantu I left in charge is coping all right?"

"He's doing a great job, Hans—honest!"

"And you? Are you likely to be there for a while yet?"

"I've plenty of paperwork to keep me busy, of that I can assure you!"

"Well, in that case, I'd best leave you to—"

"Ja, do that," said Kramer, slamming the receiver down. "Jesus Christ—and I called *Dorf* an old woman? I'll bloody kill the next bastard who interrupts me!"

This time, however, he had kept his place on the carbon.

blackmail. I have to find out the nature of these threats. My only hope of this is finding some way of getting to talk to G's servant boy Nyembezi

who brings the drinks out onto the verandah. I
have noticed the way he often hangs around close
enough to hear when G wants him to fetch more
and must be able to hear other things as well
although I do not know how good his English is.
The trouble with Nyembezi is that he never seems
to leave the farm. I don't want to question him
with G's knowledge for obvious reasons.

!!!!I have suddenly realized I could be finding the
answers I need by looking somewhere else for the
person who could have done this thing to Cloete
and his wife. But if I am wrong? That could be
my job and MY wife and family right down the
drain! So check and double check and take no
action until you are one hundred percent absolutely certain you hear. The main trouble is I
can't work out the reason although I am pretty
sure this wasn't the first time he

Unwilling to believe he had come to the end, Kramer
re-examined the sheets of carbon paper he had discarded and
then started searching all three desk drawers again.

Nothing. "Shit!" he said, thumping a fist down.

Then he went through the charge office and out onto the
verandah, wondering what the hell had become of Zondi.
With a lot to discuss and some fast planning to do, it was
hardly the time to start buggering about, ignoring a simple,
straightforward order to return to base and creating further,
quite unnecessary problems. If he had hoped to see Zondi
arriving back at that very moment, then he was disappointed,
although in all truth he wasn't at all sure what he was doing,
striding about the place, fit to be tied, achieving absolutely
nothing.

So he returned to the CID office, took up the first statement
to hand from the Fourie inquest, and began reading it, seating
himself only as an afterthought. The statement had been

made by George Wauchope Sullivan, a white adult male of forty-three whose occupation was described as industrial chemist at Jafini Sugar Mills Ltd.

> I have known the deceased for the past six years ever since his appointment. He was a dedicated family man of sober habits at all times. With so many kiddies to provide for he had to be. He could make one bottle of brandy last from Christmas to Christmas he once told me. I say these things because it is just not true he must have been drunk to be at the mill on a Saturday and to have fallen into Primary Cauldron Three. I was the one who discovered the body. The mill is usually not operative at the weekend. We leave everything on tick over and just the night watchman on guard. However I am occasionally required to make a special sample check and for this purpose I proceeded to the mill at approximately 3 p.m. on the Saturday in question. I left my wife two children mother-in-law and our neighbor seated outside in my station wagon thinking I would only be a minute. I noticed on arrival that the door to the wages office was standing open and my curiosity was therefore immediately aroused. I knew no large sums of money were kept on the premises but I still wondered if someone had tried to burgle the safe. I entered the wages office and saw Pik's jacket was over the back of his chair. So that is it I thought. Pik has come in to do some overtime as it was near the end of the month. It is true that near the end of the month the deceased often put an extra couple of hours in. We had met on several such occasions in the past. My assumption at the time was that he had gone to relieve himself leaving his jacket behind. I went out of the office and along the catwalk leading to the

cauldrons to get my sample. One and Two were switched off. My interest was Cauldron Three. It was sticking out above the surface just a hand with a ring on looking hard and shiny. I recognized the ring instantly. I said My God Pik what are you doing here. My imagination said that he must have been working in the office when he thought he heard a noise or something and came to Three to take a look and slipped and fell in or something. There is no proper rail around Three and it could happen I suppose although the Bantu workers seem to manage OK being barefoot. I then returned to the wages office to use the telephone to ring the authorities as this seemed to be a business call and not a personal one and in compliance with company regulations.

"Oh, Jesus!" said Kramer, sickened by such arse-crawler's mentality, and reached for the next statement.

I am an adult white female aged 28 and the wife of the deceased. On the Saturday in question the deceased informed me that he had his usual end of month bookkeeping to do at the mill. The deceased said he would be gone only an hour or two, after which we could take the kids to the beach for a picnic. The deceased left the family home in Jacaranda Avenue at 2 p.m. exactly. Up until that time he had consumed three cups of coffee and then one cup of tea with his lunch. I know this for a fact. At 2:15 p.m. approximately he rang me from the mill. He said he had been thinking about the picnic on the beach and wondered if the kids would not prefer going to the game reserve as that at least would be something a bit different. I agreed with him and he said he would be back to get us at 3 p.m. He sounded his normal self. At 3:50 p.m. I was contacted by Sergeant Suzman of the SAP who came to the house with the news of the accident. The deceased had

"Hello, boss," said Zondi.

"Listen, you bugger!" exclaimed Kramer, swinging round on him. "Where in Christ's name have you been for so bloody long? I've been coming up with all kinds of things, hey?"

"Me, too, boss," said Zondi. "Here . . ." And held out a brown-paper shopping bag.

"What the hell is this?"

"The shoes Boss Kritzinger was wearing the night he died—also his belt, boss."

Kramer took the bag. "But the boiler boy swore to me that he'd—"

"Lieutenant," said Zondie, "with respect, there is white man's rubbish and there is black man's rubbish—and the poorer the black man, the bigger is the difference. A boiler boy, boss, is a very poor man indeed."

"And so?"

"The boiler boy swore he had destroyed the *rags*, boss, but I wondered about the rest of what Boss Kritzinger had been wearing. Leather is not cut the same as clothing in a mortuary, and no matter how dirty it had become—blood, excrement, anything—it is also very easy to clean up and make pure again. Does the Lieutenant know how many months a boiler boy would have to work to save up for one pair of shoes from the trading store?"

"He had these hidden in his sleeping quarters?"

"Uh-uh, the boiler boy had given them, boss, to his mother for his brothers to borrow and help them find work. That is why it took me a little longer to recover the goods, or else I would have been back much sooner and —"

"Ach, never mind," said Kramer. "You did well there, hey? Now we've got the shoes, that gives us the same start as Kritz had when he was shown the print at the murder scene."

"What print at what murder scene, Lieutenant?"

"Here, take a look at this stuff on the Cloete fatal and tell me what you think," said Kramer, passing him the four sheets of carbon. "I'm going to go and get us a couple of meat pies, hey? For once in my life, I feel bloody starving."

"Hello, Tromp!" said someone at waist level. "How goes it?"

"Piet!" he said, suddenly becoming aware of the Widow Fourie's eldest, standing right there at his side in front of the counter at Jafini Bakery along the main street. "Shopping for your ma, hey?"

Piet shook his head. "For me," he said.

"Fine. Best you go ahead, then—the lady's waiting."

"Two bubble gums, please," Piet piped up in English, holding out his money.

Surprisingly, the bakery sold the horrible stuff, plus "nigger balls" and the equally strangely named "tickey sherbets" that made up the rest of Piet's order. It did, however, appear to be clean out of toffee apples.

"Tell your ma," said Kramer, as Piet was handed his purchase, "that—well, that I'll be along later, hey?"

"Good," said Piet. "She was very grumpy last night and didn't read to us properly because she kept looking out the window for your car. Got bloody fed up with it."

"Language, young man!" remonstrated the snooty-looking old cow behind the counter, slamming shut the drawer of her cash register.

"Well, that's what my ma said," added Piet, before disappearing.

Kramer bought two meat pies and two bottles of coke, topping off his order with two jam doughnuts.

The bakery woman possibly made an attempt to engage him in conversation—there were noises-off of a coquettish and inquisitive nature—but apart from noting her breasts were so covered in talc that the exposed part of them looked like two unbaked loaves stuffed down her dress front, he ignored her.

He just put down his money instead, and went striding back, feeling purposeful at last, to the police station.

Zondi was one hell of a fast reader. He had already gone through the four sheets of carbon, and having set them aside, had made a start on the Fourie file.

"Well?" said Kramer, handing him his pie and doughnut. "What did you think of Kritz's little message to us?"

"*Hau*, Lieutenant, I do not think there can be any doubt left that the Boss Cloete fatal was definitely a murder!"

"Uh-huh, and would you agree that the shoe print should provide us with a shortcut to whoever did it?"

Zondi nodded. "But so far, boss, I have not seen anything in this other matter, concerning Boss Fourie, to make me feel as certain that—"

"Ja, ja, I haven't either, apart from it being another so-called accident which seems a bit inexplicable," said Kramer, opening the Cokes on the edge of the desk. "I suggest we put that business to one side for the moment and concentrate on the shoes, hey? They're our one solid lead among so much talk and bloody supposition. Here, this drink's yours—see you don't spill it on anything!"

After taking a pull at his own Coke and a bite from his doughnut, Kramer cleared a space on Malan's desk for the plaster casts of the shoes, and laid Malan's boxwood ruler beside them. "Shoe," he said.

Zondi dug into the shopping bag, felt around, and handed him the right shoe of the pair he had brought back from Nkosala, giving a little sigh.

"Why the sigh?" asked Kramer, measuring the shoe.

"Once before, boss, I had to look for the owner of a brown boot—*hau*, it took a very, very long time to find out who it had belonged to."

"Just a bloody minute . . ." murmured Kramer, measuring the shoe again and then checking its length against both of the casts. "I expected this bloody thing to be a bit shorter than the cast made from its impression, to allow for the spread of mud under pressure, but this item of footwear you got from the boiler boy is *over an inch longer than both of them*, hey? It can't ever have been Kritz's!"

Looking most perplexed, Zondi moved around to check the measurements over his shoulder. "But that shoe was certainly taken from among Boss Kritzinger's effects, Lieutenant—the boiler boy had actually confessed to it, knowing he could be landing himself in big trouble."

"His ma could have given you the wrong pair, though—had you thought of that?"

Zondi shook his head. "Impossible, Lieutenant. I took the boiler boy with me, and he had already described these shoes to me before we arrived at her house, citing certain identifying marks that I was then able to verify."

"Such as?" demanded Kramer.

"A roughness the shape of a nail clipping on the right one, a little cut on the toe of the left, and the blackness not quite even, so that the left one has a touch of purple in it."

"Shit, why has life got to be so complicated, hey?" protested Kramer. "Just for a few seconds there, I thought we were at last— *Jesus, I know whose bloody shoes these are!*"

"Lieutenant?" said Zondi.

29

"Y ou are never going to believe this," said Kramer, finding his mind in such a bloody boggle that his words weren't coming easily, "but these are the shoes stolen from the cook boy!—night of the explosion."

"*Hau!* From Moses Khumalo?"

"The very same, Mickey. I swear it."

Zondi shook his head. "No, boss, it makes no sense," he said.

"Bugger sense! It's *true*, hey?"

Zondi again shook his head, infuriating Kramer. "Listen, kaffir," he said, "what else did you say you'd brought back?"

"Er, a belt, Lieutenant."

"Fine! Have you seen me look in this bag?"

"Uh-uh, you have not looked in that bag, boss."

"Here, take it!" said Kramer, tossing the bag over. "And I'll tell you what you'll find inside: one black belt with a grey side as well, and a buckle that's a gold color with a five-pointed star in the middle."

Zondi removed the belt from the bag, inspected it, and gave a low whistle.

"Am I right?" demanded Kramer.

"One hundred percent, boss! How did you know this?"

"Because I remember what Cassius gave as the description of the cook boy's stolen items, that's how!"

"But, boss," began Zondi, rather hesitantly, his brow furrowed, "does that mean the Lieutenant is saying that Boss Kritzinger arrived at Nkosala mortuary dressed in the clothes of another man, of a *Bantu*—not his own?"

"He must've done!"

"Maybe the boiler boy could have become confused between the clothes of a dead thief and—"

"Impossible. No other fresh stiffs in the place."

"*Hau*, the implications could be very strange, boss!"

"Too right," agreed Kramer. "Shit, I'd better check this out first, before we do anything else, hey?"

He managed to reach Nkosala remarkably quickly, give or take a few impromptu detours that undoubtedly left the other drivers involved pale, shaky, and deeply reflective. The "Welcome to Nkosala" sign didn't so much go by in a blur as appear to duck hurriedly.

"Easy, man, easy . . ." Kramer told himself, throttling back as he approached the hospital driveway.

Then, out of the corner of his eye, he spotted Terblanche, leaning against his police Land-Rover round the back of the white wards, reading a newspaper, and a sudden thought occurred to him. He made a sharp left turn, crossed some lawn, and came to a sliding halt beside the station commander.

"Tromp!" said Terblanche. "What brings you here, hey?"

"Lots," said Kramer through his car window. "Only you know those photos Suzman took of Maaties *in situ* down at Fynn's Creek? I want to know where I can get hold of them and—"

"Funny you should say that!" said Terblanche, looking very pleased with himself. "Not five minutes ago, when I went to buy this paper, I remembered the snaps and so I picked them up at the chemist's where Sarel took them for developing."

"Give," said Kramer, holding a hand out.

"I'll come round," said Terblanche, and seated himself in the front of the Chev before passing over a Kodak print wallet marked *For Jafini Police/Urgent.* I hope they're okay. I haven't had the stomach for a peep myself yet."

"So how's our friend from Mabata doing?" asked Kramer, opening the wallet. "Are they keeping Stoffel in hospital?"

"I'm waiting to find out, hey? Only I hate the smell in these places and Doc Mackenzie isn't finished with his tests yet."

"Hmmm," murmured Kramer, not really listening.

He had started going through the twelve contact prints made from Suzman's roll of 120 film. Uppermost were three out-of-focus snapshots of a grim-faced old bitch in a deck chair on a crowded beach, shading her eyes against the sun with one hand while using the other to keep a merciless grip on the collar of a small mongrel, cowering low at her side.

"Ach, those are just Sarel's private ones; it's his own film, of course, which he had to interrupt for us," explained Terblanche. "He must've been trying to get one of his ma smiling but she wouldn't—typical, really!" And he laughed.

Kramer returned them to the wallet and fanned out the remaining contact prints like a hand at poker.

"A real dragon, his ma," Terblanche went on. "I remember the time their cook girl smuggled her piccanin into her quarters to spend the night when it was sick, whereupon she—"

"Hans, can you just shut up a sec?"

"Sorry, Tromp! Sorry! Looking for anything special?"

Kramer ignored him and went through the rest of the prints one by one, dealing them into his lap. They were a typical amateur balls-up; two weren't in focus, three had Suzman's shadow falling over Kritzinger's body, obscuring detail, and the whole lot were too contrasty, making it impossible to distinguish certain shapes or to guess at the color of things—the jacket, for instance. Even so, a set of properly lit, properly taken pictures by Fingerprints would probably have proved equally disappointing; the half a bucket of gut spilling out of the body was enough to hide any belt buckle.

"Well," he said, stuffing the prints back into the wallet and then pocketing it, "I'd best get down to the mortuary for a minute." And he threw open his door.

"Doc's not there, Tromp. He's busy with—"

"Ja, you said. Only I'm looking for Niko."

"Oh?"

"You've seen him today?"

Terblanche nodded. "He wanted me to come and have a coffee, only I couldn't, could I? Not while I'm—well, sort of on duty here, hey?"

"Hell, no," said Kramer.

"My beautiful shoes! *Hau, hau, hau!*" exclaimed Moses Khumalo, clapping his hands in delight, as Zondi brought him into the CID office. "And look, my belt also. *Hau,* you are a very great detective, Sergeant Zondi!"

"Glad you think so, my brother," said Zondi, pulling over a chair for the rustic to perch on. "Want your black suit back as well?"

"*Hey!* That is possible?"

"Very possible. Or at least, a new one very like it."

"*Hau!*"

"Seat yourself and I will do the same. We will talk, Moses Khumalo."

"No, I must stand, Sergeant Zondi. I am but a humble man in your presence."

"We will sit, my friend, and we will share this fine American-blend cigarette together, while we speak further on the subject of young madams. Would you not like that?"

"*Hau,* very, very much, Sergeant Detective!" said Moses Khumalo.

Niko Claasens was making the hummy sounds a man makes when he thinks he is all on his own, pottering around his little kingdom, building new castles in the air. He gave a tremendous start when he noticed Kramer watching him from just inside the double doors to the refrigerator room.

"Hello, Niko," said Kramer. "Having a quiet afternoon, hey?"

"Er, ja, sir," replied Claasens, his expression wary. "I'm afraid the doc's—"

"Ja, ja, I know. But this is just an informal visit—Hans tells me you're serving coffee?"

"Sorry, Lieutenant? Oh, I see! You would like some?"

"If it isn't any trouble—I'm bloody parched, hey?"

"Of course not, sir! It'd be a pleasure—here, let me switch the kettle on."

Kramer stood back to allow him to get past and reach the wide shelf where the coffee-making things were kept. "So you didn't get Aap and the rest of those buggers?" he said.

"No, the Colonel wanted them all taken straight back to Trekkersburg for the sake of the relatives, thank God," replied Claasens, switching on his electric kettle. "Man, most things you get used to in here. Last week, for instance, there was that Bantu female, stabbed to death by the mother-in-law, and her baby stabbed, too, when it started to come out the womb afterward, but—"

"If it's one of your own, that's very different," said Kramer. "Ja, I know. Talking of which, remember those clothes of Maaties you chucked in the—"

"Ach, not that again!" said Claasens, turning with his big fists bunched. "How many more times?"

"Hey, hey, hold on a sec!" said Kramer, holding out a hand to fend off the porter's indignation. "You're going off half-cocked, you know that? I was about to make a perfectly innocent observation that was no reflection on you or the way you do your job, man."

"You were, sir? Ach, I'm sorry, hey?"

"No need for an apology either," said Kramer, ready now to conduct a little litmus test. "All I was going to say was, Kritz certainly did have one hell of a strange taste in clothes for a white man, don't you think?"

The healthy pink began to drain from the mortuary porter's

cheeks, although his stance remained casual. "I'm not sure I—er, follow your meaning exactly, Lieutenant," he said.

"I'm talking about what the body had on when it came in here," said Kramer. "Christ, how on earth had poor old Maaties ended up wearing a worn-out pair of scruffy shoes three sizes too big for him, hey? And the kind of bloody belt only kaffirs buy from trading stores? Not to mention a frayed old shirt with a big patch in the back and a buggered charcoal suit that didn't fit properly either?"

Ashen, Claasens just stood there, and then, to Kramer's surprise, he took a pace forward. *"How the HELL do you know that?"* he hissed.

Moses Khumalo took his fifth drag on the shared Texan and passed it back to Zondi, using both hands as a clear mark of respect, while he nodded vigorously.

"Eh-heh, that is true, Sergeant Detective, the young madam was always friendly in her nature when white men came to the house. I think she liked them."

"Who were these men?" asked Zondi.

Khumalo shrugged. "Men that came with the master," he said. "Maybe they were the men he worked with—nearly all wore the same uniform."

"So the master was always present?"

"Eh-heh, to the best of my knowledge, Sergeant Zondi. I work from six in the morning until ten at night and fall asleep very fast."

"You have never seen any other white men at the house?"

"Once, a fisherman, who came when the young madam was alone to ask if he could have water for his bottle."

"Did you see what he looked like?"

"Eh-heh, I filled his bottle for him."

"Was he anything like this man?" asked Zondi, showing Khumalo a head-and-shoulders photograph of Pik Fourie, enlarged from a wedding picture, that he had found in the inquest file's glassine envelope.

Khumalo nibbled his lower lip, concentrating hard on the image. *"Hau,* it is hard to say," he said finally, "but maybe yes, maybe no, Sergeant Zondi. You know how it is with these white faces which can grow darker and then lighter, depending on what time of year it is."

Wish you were here, Mickey, Kramer was thinking, just so I could see your expression, man. The behavior of Niko Claasens, mere mortuary porter at Nkosala, was becoming more and more extraordinary every second—anyone would think he was a bloody Boss agent, suddenly blowing his cover.

"I asked you a question, Lieutenant!" barked Claasens. "I've asked it how many times? Ten? Twenty times? Where did you come by this knowledge?"

"On the back of a Post Toasties box."

"Don't try being clever with me, man! Let me warn you, if you value your bloody job, me and the Colonel go back a long way—oh, ja, a very long way!"

Kramer shrugged. "Me and my arse go back a long way," he said. "But not everybody's all that impressed, to be honest."

Claasens stared at him, then gave a low, grudging laugh. "I told the Colonel," he said, his whole manner changing, the bluster giving way abruptly to a grim matter-of-factness. "Ja, I *warned* him you'd be bloody trouble, right from the start."

"Oh, ja, when was that, hey?"

"The very first day you arrived, after all that fuss you made here at the postmortems, teaching Doc to do his job properly and everything—*that* was unexpected. I said then he should never have sent you."

"Why not?" demanded Kramer.

"You were—well, not the kind of outsider we had need of, in the circumstances. In fact, ever since then I've maintained you should either have been withdrawn or be told the delicate position we're in at the moment. Otherwise, like I told him, you'd be the kind to go your own sweet way, snooping too far into things, leaving us wide open to all sorts of bloody complications."

"Such as?"

"You strolling in here this afternoon and deliberately letting slip that you knew things you shouldn't! Come on, tell me how you found out about the clothes—that, I've got a right to know."

"Oh, ja? Not until you fill me in on the rest of the story," said Kramer. "Hell, the whole reason I came across to Nkosala in the first place was in the hope of cutting a few corners."

"Trouble is, if I told you, it'd be for the opposite reason—to stop you doing anything," said Claasens, placing two coffee mugs side by side, next to the Nescafé jar. "Jesus, you don't know how relieved I felt when I heard this afternoon that you'd got it into your head this business was connected with those missions killings! Good, I thought— enjoy your nice wild-goose chase, Lieutenant! Then back you bloody came, not two hours later . . ."

"Ja, and I'm likely to keep doing that, hey, Niko?" said Kramer, tiring of all the half-statements, hints, and innuendos. "Only next time, man, it could be a case of *me* informing *you* of exactly what's been going on, here and at Jafini—and of what I've already done about it, hey?"

"Look," said Claasens, swinging round to face him, a cautionary finger raised, "what I said at the outset is still true: these are very serious matters! Do you realize how much is at stake here?"

"No, but I'm listening," said Kramer, leaning back against the postmortem slab with his arms folded.

30

*N*iko Claasens hesitated, glanced at the wall phone over by the door, as though he would much prefer discussing the wisdom of his next move with a superior first, then turned to face Kramer again. "Okay, this has all gone too far to turn back now," he said. "Either I put you in the picture, or the chances are you're going to do some real damage without knowing it."

"Uh-huh—and?"

"It's like this, Tromp," said Claasens, adding Nescafé to the two coffee mugs, "three of us have known all along what happened the night of the explosion."

"Ach, bullshit."

"But it's true. Also, we've known who did it and why—down to almost the last little detail."

"You mean I've—Jesus, you *bastards* . . ."

"Man, I don't blame you, feeling that way! Hell, who likes to suddenly find out he's been misled in every direction—and by his own people? But, as you'll realize in a minute, there were reasons for this which outweighed any personal considerations, and besides, it isn't as if you haven't had a crucial role to play in seeing that—"

"*Misled?* Is that what you bloody call it? It's—"

"No, wait, hear me out first! Because of what we three knew, we had no alternative. To have proceeded in the normal way with this matter would have done nothing but terrible harm to Maaties' memory, his wife and innocent kiddies, and to the SAP as a whole, especially in these times of serious unrest, hey? That's why the Colonel decided our first duty was to make sure there was no scandal, to let the case go 'unsolved' for now, and then, once the fuss had died away, we could take our own action and see justice done privately."

"What scandal?" demanded Kramer. "What kind of action?"

"The appropriate penalty for murder, Tromp! Make no mistake, the swine certainly isn't going to get away with it. But before I tell you his name, you have to understand that, from now on, you are part and parcel of the Colonel's plan, and none of us must do anything that could jeopardize it, okay? Maaties and Annika were killed by Lance Gillets."

"Ach, no! That's ridiculous!"

"It isn't, you know, it's the truth."

"But Hans and me have already been through all that— which you've obviously not troubled to do! Or are you trying to tell me that little arsehole would know how to make a sophisticated delay longer than twelve hours with an alarm clock? Christ, he wouldn't know where to even begin, man! On top of which, I've already proved he couldn't have been anywhere near—"

"You didn't notice a pair of frog flippers, down at the Fynn's Creek?"

"Of course. But what have they to do with—"

"Then obviously you never took a closer look at them," said Claasens, with the trace of a smile, "before we realized our oversight and spirited them away. Because, if you had, Lieutenant, you'd have noticed they were navy issue. Gillets was at the Navy Gymn straight after leaving school, you see, to get his Defence Force training over and done with—he trained as a frogman."

"Oh, *shit* . . ." said Kramer.

"Exactly. He learned practically everything a man can learn about the use and detonation of explosives, including improvisation behind enemy lines—we've checked on that. And what is a limpet mine except a kind of time bomb, ja? Stick it to the side of a ship and—"

"Ja, ja, no need to rub it in!" said Kramer, sick to the stomach now, as he remembered a reference also having been made to Gillets' naval background by his boss, the game warden. "But how can you be sure he actually did it? There's a bloody big difference between having the know-how and—"

"Don't worry, we—"

"But have you interviewed bloody Gillets—or even seen him since that night? Because I have, and my instincts—"

"Tromp," said Claasens, switching off the kettle, "how often have you had to deal with rich-kid English-speakers of that kind? Coming, as you do, from the Free State?"

"Well, never, I suppose, but—"

"Then wait until you know them better before thinking you could have anything in common to base a feeling on, hey? Christ, they're a race apart, man! You know what they call an Afrikaner bloke like you? The nice ones say 'hairy-back'— Gillets would say 'fucking rock spider.' "

"Even so," cut in Kramer, "my impression was of—"

"Listen," said Claasens, "I'm just going to have to tell you the whole thing, but you mustn't repeat it to another soul, not ever. Do you promise? Only the Colonel, me, and Suzman were meant to ever know this."

"Why not Terblanche as well?"

"Huh! Hans is such a bloody Christian these days you can't trust him with *anything,* hey? Do you promise?"

"Fine, not another soul," said Kramer.

"Well, the start of it all was just after midnight on what was actually last Tuesday morning," said Claasens, pouring boiling water into the two coffee mugs. "Sarel was out on patrol, three or four miles to the north of Fynn's Creek, when there was this huge bloody bang and he saw the flash reflect off some low sea cloud. That's how he knew straight off where to go, and he got to Fynn's Creek, about twelve-thirty."

"Hey? I thought he got stuck in some sand, trying a shortcut, and it was four before he—"

"No, no, four was when he left again, having had a hell of a lot of things to see to first."

"Ah," said Kramer, "so that was what spoiled the crocodiles' picnic!"

"Sorry?"

"No, no, nothing important—just you go on."

"Ja, well, Sarel drove up, and you can imagine what a shock it was, finding the whole place blown to bloody pieces! Then he had a much bigger shock: poor old Maaties lying there, stone dead, in his headlights—but that wasn't all: he was as bare-bummed naked as the day he was born, hey? Ja, all he had with him was his bloody gun! And not five yards away was the bedroom of the biggest little nympho Zululand had ever—"

"*Five* yards?"

"That's right, man! I tell you, Sarel really had his work cut out, trying to quickly put a very different complexion on things! Can you imagine, a father of four and a senior SAP officer being found in such a situation? Never mind the fact Maaties had always been one of the Colonel's favorites! But do you think Sarel could find Maaties' clothes anywhere? Not a chance! There were fires all over, he didn't know how much time he had before others reached the scene, none of Gillets' stuff was big enough, and so he just—well, you've obviously somehow guessed that part already, hey? The hardest decision he took was to move the body back another twenty yards, and the Colonel nearly had a cardiac when he heard about this, but I told him not to worry, Doc wouldn't be able to tell in a month of Sundays, especially not if I gave him the right books and—"

"You got to the body first, right?" said Kramer. "The same as you did a quick sorting job on the lady's digestive-stroke-generative organs, trying to make sure the rest of us would never know what she'd been eating *and* bloody doing, just before blast-off?"

"Christ," said Claasens very softly, his wary look back as he turned round with a mug of black coffee in each hand. "It really is a good thing we're having this little talk, I can see that. Here, this one is yours—sugar's in the tin there."

"Ta," said Kramer, accepting the mug. "Carry on, man—it can't have taken Sarel until four just to do what you've described, can it?"

"Not the initial adjustments, no, but he still had old Maaties' shoulder holster to find, and when still nobody came, he just carried on, looking and looking for it," said Claasens, pausing to take a sip of coffee. "That's when he got his next big shock."

"Oh, ja?"

"His flashlight was getting really weak, but it caught a glint off something chrome like a holster rivet. Hell, no, it was just the thing in the middle of a gramophone you fit the hole in a record over. Annika had an old wind-up model, you see, because there was no electricity, and—"

"Ja, ja, I saw it lying there, all buggered and the wooden case split open. She'd stuck some pictures on the lid—weren't they of that bugger Cliff Richards who got our police dogs in trouble down in Durban?"

"That's the one," confirmed Claasens. "Only when Sarel got to it, the first thing he noticed was—you know that sort of trumpet-thingy gramophones have inside them?"

Kramer nodded.

"Well, half sticking out of this one was a rolled-up school exercise book, as though that's where someone had been hiding it. Not a bad place either! Only three little screws to undo and then you lift—"

"Ja, ja, but what was it? A diary, right?"

"But not like one Sarel had ever seen before! That Annika's thoughts were worse than a man's, he said—far worse. So dirty in parts—she wasn't interested in length, she said, only in *diameters*—it made his hair stand straight up on end! Then, skimming quickly through, he noticed references to a certain 'Martinus' beginning to appear, which was Maaties' proper name, of course, and that was another big shock he had. Only it had got so late by then, almost four o'clock in the morning, that he didn't dare waste too much time on reading it, in case Hans or Jaapie turned up and caught him with it, so all he really took in were the very last things she'd recorded. These were to the effect that she was sure now that Gillets knew what had been going on between her and Maaties, every time he'd been called away, but that he actually *liked* the idea—it was what had been making him extra randy each time he came home again! Oh, ja, apparently he'd just kick the servant boy out, pull all her clothes off, and start sniffing for Maaties' scent, like some bloody animal! He'd tell her she was a bloody bitch on heat who needed to be reminded who was master. You remember that big bruise on her arm at the postmortem?"

"Uh-huh," said Kramer, "*and* how it made you squirm, you bastard! But 'Martinus' isn't an uncommon name, not by a long chalk, so how certain are you that she was referring—"

"Completely certain, I'm afraid," said Claasens, with a sigh and a shake of his head. "Right at the end, on the very last page, she started wondering is she hadn't made her husband too bloody jealous. And she said that perhaps she had better warn Maaties that Gillets had started to say some very strange things about her days of 'fooling around with a certain cop' being numbered. Presumably, she can't have passed on that warning in the event, or Maaties wouldn't have hung around the other night."

Kramer shrugged. "Who can say? Maybe he liked a little extra bit of excitement—the bugger was always too perfect. There weren't any other names that Suzman recognized?"

"No, as I explained, he just—"

"And where's the diary now? Any chance of—"

"Christ, you can't keep a thing like that hanging round— what if it fell in the wrong hands, hey? It wasn't as though it was ever going to be needed as an exhibit. No, naturally the Colonel ordered Sarel to destroy it, the minute he heard of its existence!"

"So it's gone, gone for good?" said Kramer, experiencing a sense of relief he had not expected.

"Gone for good, Lieutenant," confirmed Claasens. "As soon as Sarel could hand the scene over to Hans, he went straight back home—not to the police station, where he could have been overheard—and got through to the Colonel. The diary went into his mum's kitchen stove straight after, it's an Aga."

Kramer nodded. "And then you were roped in? An old and trusted friend, to bugger about with the forensics?"

Claasens smiled. "That's broadly it, Lieutenant," he said, with a nod. "But no hard feelings, hey? You must be able to see by now that you have had a very vital role to play, even if it was just going through the motions for appearance' sake. In fact, it's a role far from over! Can you think of some way of passing a few more weeks up here?—because I don't think we can consider the case 'unsolved' much sooner than that?"

"Ach, a man can always find ways of killing time," said Kramer, suddenly quite determined not to leave Jafini before he and the Widow Fourie had become better acquainted. "What if I switch to helping look for this mission rapist that my kaffir's been trying to track down?"

"The perfect solution!" said Claasens. "I'll tell the Colonel that it's certain to keep you out of mischief from now on, hey?"

I bloody hope not, thought Kramer.

31

Zondi, dozing in the late afternoon sun, his feet propped on Kritzinger's desk, sat up with a jerk, looking in some puzzlement at the empty doorway. "Lieutenant?" he said.

"Ach, I'm right behind you!" said Kramer, addressing him through the yard window. "I just gave you an order: get the hell out of there—we're going for a drive, hey?"

"Sir!" said Zondi, coming straight out over the windowsill and landing neatly, heels together. "*Hau*, there is a great urgency in your voice, boss!"

"Oh, ja? And for good reason, let me promise you, but first we need someplace to talk where no bastard's going to start sticking his nose in."

"But, boss—"

"Just get in and shut up, hey?"

Zondi slid down in his seat, tipped his hat forward right over his eyes, and sighed.

As the Chevrolet left the police station and plunged out into the road, Kramer slowed down for a moment, flipped a coin in his head, and turned right. Just beyond the Bombay

Emporium, he swung left, traveled five shady blocks, and then entered the driveway of the Widow Fourie's house, taking the car right round the back and onto the lawn there. Dingaan the iguana shot out of sight, and so did two white rabbits, but otherwise there were no signs of life, even though it was after five o'clock.

"Must've taken the whole tribe out with her someplace, hey?" murmured Kramer, switching off the engine. "Even better than I'd hoped."

Zondi sat up and looked around him. "It's okay for me to speak again, Lieutenant?"

"Ja, fine," said Kramer, pulling his tie loose and undoing his collar. "But be prepared, hey, to answer the Big Question . . ."

"Which is, boss?"

"Tell me, when the Almighty made kaffirs, did he give them souls, hey?"

"The boss means the same as the white man?"

"Uh-huh, of course."

"*Hau*, God would never do such a terrible thing, Lieutenant."

"Excellent," said Kramer, "no man who likes to break a solemn promise. Now you just listen to this, kaffir, and don't you bloody interrupt until I'm finished, you hear?"

Dingaan the iguana ventured out some twenty minutes later, so quiet had everything become, and went over to where various fly-covered scraps of meat lay scattered in the far corner of his run. The rabbits were already out, wrinkling their pink noses at him like upper-crust neighbors watching the street's recluse on his way to browse through downtown trash cans.

"But, boss," murmured Zondi, ending a long, reflective silence in a voice so low that barely an ear twitched in his direction, "we have thought all along that Boss Kritzinger was killed because of what he *knew*—now we are being told it was because of what he was doing . . ."

"Couldn't it have been a mixture of both? Couldn't it have

been through Kritz's investigations into the Cloete business that he grew to be on intimate terms, shall we say, with their daughter, little Annika?"

"That could well have been the case, Lieutenant," agreed Zondi. "But the point I am trying to make, based on all you have just told me, is this: it seems we are no longer hunting one killer here in Jafini, as we previously thought—but *two* killers, boss."

"Unless, of course, Gillets was also responsible for the Cloetes'—"

"I'm sorry, that I cannot believe, Lieutenant, with all due respect! True, there is an obvious connection between Boss Gillets and Boss Cloete, that I admit, but in what possible way could those deaths have benefited him? We know Boss Cloete had given the marriage his blessing, because of how hard he tried to see it began in fine style. And what about Boss Fourie, who also suffered the same kind of strange accident? I tried hard this afternoon to see if Moses Khumalo knew whether he was known to either Boss Gillets or the young madam, but a definite link I could not establish. We do not even know if Boss Gillets ever knew Boss Fourie, so why should he want to—*hau*, now I see!"

"See what, Mickey?"

"The Lieutenant thinks Boss Fourie might also have been a name in the young madam's schoolbook?"

"God forbid!" said Kramer. "When he had a lady like the Widow to go home to? The thought had never crossed my mind, man!"

But Zondi plainly had the bit between his teeth now. "I thought Boss Fourie's wife was heavily pregnant shortly before his death, Lieutenant? Perhaps he had not been able to lie with her for many weeks, and so, maybe he sought release with—"

"Ach, no! That's bullshit, I'm sure of it!"

"One hundred percent sure, boss?" asked Zondi, raising an eyebrow. "Or is the Lieutenant doing what Boss Suzman did on Monday night? Trying to protect the deceased's widow and family from—"

"You fight dirty, kaffir!" protested Kramer. "And if I had that diary, I'd bloody prove to you how wrong you are!"

"It's just a theory, boss."

"What is? The idea Fourie died for the same reason that Kritz did? Do you realize man, you've just talked yourself right round in a complete circle—and we're back to the belief there's only one murderer involved?"

"Not quite, boss. What of the Cloete case? I cannot get that to fit."

"Hmmmm," said Kramer. "If you consider the methods used in each case, that gives us two killers again: one using 'accidents,' the other being a bit more blatant—you can't call a time bomb a bloody 'fatal,' can you?"

"Boss, boss, boss," said Zondi, with a long sigh. "One minute, so many things make sense; next minute, so much totally contradicts!"

"Which could mean we're probably wrong about everything, couldn't it, hey?"

Zondie nodded.

"Ach!" said Kramer. "You know what I'm beginning to think? It's high time we stopped buggering about, playing these guessing games, and got some bastard just to give us all the right answers."

"But how, Lieutenant?"

"By getting hold of bloody Gillets and making *him* tell us what he did and didn't do!"

"A fine idea, Lieutenant! Only how exactly—"

"Ja, that's the other Big Question," admitted Kramer, and accepted one of Zondi's proffered Texans.

But he didn't seem able to give his mind to the problem as he should; he simply couldn't concentrate. He was still very distracted by the idea that Pik Fourie might have been one of little Annika's lovers. On one hand—chiefly for the Widow Fourie's sake, although not entirely—Kramer utterly repudiated the notion; on the other hand, an element of gnawing doubt persisted, fed by the deep cynicism that came with the job he did. Once again, how he wished he could have seen that bloody diary, just to put his mind at rest. Because what Kramer feared most in this world, he suddenly realized, was the Widow Fourie having her illusions shattered by some chance revelation, and then finding that she had lost her capacity for placing her trust in a bloke again, henceforth and forever. In fact, rather than risk this ever happening, he would *kill* any bastard who harbored such knowledge—and this brought him back to Gillets, only with a greater sense of urgency.

"Mickey, man, the hell with the Colonel, Claasens, the lot of them!" he said, turning to him. "We've *got* to think of some way of getting to Gillets chop-bloody-chop, hey? Are you game?"

"Er, right, Lieutenant . . ."

"You don't sound too happy—why's that?"

"No, no, boss, a different matter," said Zondi, with a shrug. "I have just realized that the boiler boy will think me a great liar. I had promised him that if he told me everything, he would not be prosecuted for the technical theft of the belt and shoes, Lieutenant. But if you've revealed to—"

"Hell, the boiler boy's got no worries!"

"But I thought the Lieutenant had told Boss Claasens about the clothing? How the shoes—"

"Ach, no!" said Kramer. "As far as Claasens is concerned, I'd studied Suzman's snaps of the murder scene very carefully, and had noted how the deceased was dressed, from the belt buckle downward. Claasens was never at the beach, so I don't think he'll get the joke."

"What joke, Lieutenant?"

"Here, look for yourself," said Kramer, handing him the Kodak wallet, and was rewarded moments later by a deep, rumbling laugh when Zondi spotted the great spill of intestines.

"*Hau*, the boss better find some way of losing these pictures before Boss Claasens sees them!"

"Could be dropped somewhere completely by accident, I suppose," said Kramer, starting the engine. "Ach, no, Mickey! Don't tell me you're developing your cousin's taste for old white women with moustaches, man? Sis! Or does it run in the bloody family?"

Zondi was examining the three prints of Suzman's mother, with one eyebrow arched.

"Besides which," added Kramer, "the old bitch isn't even in focus."

"Although the background is nice and sharp, boss."

"Ach, Suzman's a total bloody clown with a camera."

"I don't know, Lieutenant . . . I must admit I much admire the young madam with the broad pelvis."

"Where?" said Kramer, taking the print from him. "I'd not noticed any—dirty little bugger, you can see straight up her bloody skirt!"

"And in the background of this next one, boss, the young madam is bending right forward so that her big breasts can be clearly—"

"Eyes off, kaffir! No, it's okay, you can look at the last one: I think the lady must've twigged what he was up to—you can see how she's frowning at him over her big sunglasses and turning her head away. Well, I never . . ."

"A sly man, boss."

"Ja, *and* a creepy bastard, too, to be getting his cheap thrills this way! I bet he's got a special album for these, hey? Holds it one-handed."

Zondi laughed.

"No, seriously," said Kramer, switching off the engine again. "Makes you bloody wonder whether Suzman really did get rid of that diary. Personally, I think there could be a fair chance it's actually hidden in some private library of his in the back of his wardrobe . . ."

Nodding, Zondi reached over to stub his Texan out in the car's ashtray. "I have known such hiding places, boss—*hau*, when I was a young houseboy, I was warned by the cook boy I must never touch them or the master would kill me."

"So you also think this might be worth looking into?"

"It could be, Lieutenant, although the boss did say that Boss Claasens seemed certain the diary had been truly destroyed by Boss—"

"Ja, but Claasens was also the silly bugger who thought the boiler boy had destroyed everything Kritz came dressed in, hey? He relies too much on bloody hearsay! Besides which, I really *want* that thing . . ."

"But how, Lieutenant, do we go about—"

"You any good at really pissing off small, unhappy dogs?" said Kramer, twisting the ignition key.

Then he backed right out of the Widow Fourie's property in one go, jerked the steering wheel into a left lock, and did a tail-wagging takeoff up Jacaranda Avenue, just missing a black cat that tore home, probably to read up on popular superstitions.

Finding out where a white policeman lived in a place the size of Jafini was no problem: you just stopped the first kaffir you saw and asked him.

The bungalow on the corner of Trichard Street and Fynn's Lane turned out to be surrounded by a stout chain link fence, and both its gates—one leading to the garage, the other to the front door—were closed and bolted. The house itself looked equally unwelcoming, with great, thick burglarproofing bars over its windows, rendered in wrought-iron but far too Spanish and frivolous for the severe lines of the rest of the building. The *BEWARE OF THE DOG* sign was big enough to give even a Bengal tiger an exaggerated opinion of itself, and the climbable trees were all thorn trees, suggesting that someone had a fairly unpleasant sense of humor.

"About upsetting this dog, Lieutenant . . ."

"Forget it," said Kramer. "If my memory serves me, there's a servant girl living on the premises."

"Further to my investigations, madam, I must ask your kaffir maid certain routine questions?"

"Uh-huh, and I'm sure that Ma Suzman, the mother of a fine, upstanding young police sergeant, will be only too happy to cooperate, my son."

32

*T*he odd thing was, Suzman's mother *still* seemed out of focus when she responded to the sound of her Yorkshire terrier's furious barking along the chain link fence, which began the moment Kramer and Zondi stepped from the car. At first, this illusion depended rather less on sight and sound, given that she slurred a lot of her words. But when she came up close, breathing the heady fumes of gin, its blurring effect on her features could be quite as readily discerned.

"Wash the hell you want?" she demanded, attempting to draw a bead smack between Kramer's eyes with the tip of her wavering walking stick. "You better look out, hey? My son's a policeman!"

"Uh-huh, and we're policemen, too, Mrs. Suzman," said Kramer, displaying his warrant card. "Known old Sarel for years."

"Oh, ja?" she said, bringing her stick back to the perpendicular just in time to stop herself falling flat on her face. "Never seen you before!"

"I'm CID; the replacement for poor Maaties, auntie."

"Sarel never said! He needsh a good hiding, that son of mine! So many secrets he keepsh from me! If only hish pa was . . ."

"Secrets auntie? Such as what?"

"Ach!" she said. *"Thinksh* he's so damn clever, but I know! Oh, ja, I know all right! I've got eyesh in my head!"

Kramer tried hard not to exchange glances with Zondi, and chanced instead a quick mind-boggler in his best English: "Preoccupy this party, partner, pending a perusal pertinent to the personal possessions of the—"

"Hey!" Mrs. Suzman said, again raising her stick, and rendering herself as unstable as a tripod that had just lost one leg. "What wash that? Can't you speak a God-fearing language that—"

"Sorry, auntie!" said Kramer. "You know what kaffirs are like, and this bastard's mission-trained, extra thick. But I'd like him to question your maid in her servant's quarters, if that's okay with you, hey?"

"That little bitch! Sarel's already had one go at her, but I still say she'sh a bloody thief!"

"Hell, which of them isn't, auntie?" said Kramer, really turning the charm on.

Zondi would have had difficulty keeping a straight face had he not noticed, the very moment he set eyes on Miriam Dinizulu, the young servant employed by the Suzmans, a deep blue bruise in the superbly brown, glossy pigmentation of her left cheek. The blow, to judge by its shape, had been a back hander delivered with considerable force.

"Listen to me, my sister!" he bellowed, raising his fist to her in her small, barely furnished room at the rear of the property. "Does your employer here understand the tongue of our people?"

The reply was a startled, emphatic shake of the head.

"Good! Then I will continue to speak it! And you will act as though you tremble at my every word, if you know what is good for you!"

Miriam Dinizulu's wonderfully large, expressive eyes rose

to meet his gaze for an instant, showing much surprise and bewilderment.

"We are here, my Lieutenant and I," continued Zondi, in a menacing, snarling tone, "to investigate matters that have nothing to do with you, fair maiden, and so this is only a pretense intended to keep this stupid old woman out here in your room long enough for the aforesaid investigations to be made."

He knew he had risked a lot by stating the facts so plainly, but his intuitive confidence in Miriam Dinizulu proved fully justified. With a sudden twinkle in her eye and a whimpering cry, she fell to the floor at his feet, shielding her head with her arms against any blows that might follow, and exclaimed: "*Hau!* Like this, do you mean, my brother? Don't you think I did that just beautifully?"

Zondi drew back his foot.

"That's right, don't you take any cheek from the bitch!" applauded Mrs. Suzman. "You bloody kick her, hey, if you want to, boy! Nobody here ish going to mind."

"I bet *you'd* mind, my sister," Zondi barked at Miriam Dinizulu, greatly admiring the width of her pelvis. "So go on, distract her—start talking! Recite the Bible, tell me all the colors of your father's cattle, *anything!*"

Miriam Dinizulu chose instead to list all the colors of her father's goats, on account of the fact he was an unusually poor man, even for Jafini native reserve. Then she went on to explain, in a wild, sobbing gabble, how she hoped one day to marry well, and to insist that, for her wedding payment, her father had to receive at least ten head of the best dairy cows ever owned by a black man in Zululand.

"What's she saying? What'sh she saying?" demanded Mrs. Suzman, bringing her straining, yapping terrier to heel with a savage tug on its leash. "Ish she still denying stealing from me? Ask her where my clock has gone, hey? Ask her!"

"In a minute, promise I to the madam tell," said Zondi, in garbled, faltering Afrikaans, giving the Lieutenant the wink he had been waiting for.

* * *

Kramer murmured something about fetching handcuffs and a rhino-hide whip from the car—earning no more than a curt, approving nod from Mrs. Suzman, so taken was she with Zondi's very noisy interrogation techniques—and then headed straight for the back verandah of the house, hoping to find the kitchen door open.

It had been left flung fully ajar. Crossing the spotless kitchen in two strides, Kramer entered the central corridor of the house, took a guess at which door to try first, and had the kind of luck that usually made him a little uneasy. The rather small, dimly lit bedroom behind that door was obviously Sarel Suzman's: his spare uniform tunic and trousers were on an old-fashioned trouser press, beside a tall Victorian wardrobe with an oval mirror, and above his mahogany dresser was a group picture taken on passing-out day at the Police College. Next to the bed, with its wooden headboard and grey candlewick bedspread, was a table with a drawer that didn't lock and an upright wooden chair with a padded leather seat. Then, about two feet away, stood the kind of marble-topped washstand that had supported a large jug of water and a hand basin in the 1800s.

At a second glance, neatness was evident everywhere in the room. The bedspread had been placed over the bed with perfect symmetry; on the washstand, the Brylcreem jar, the pair of hairbrushes and comb, the soap dish, and the green face flannel had been arranged in a straight line; on opening the wardrobe, the first thing to catch the eye was the orderly row of shiny shoes, all on parade there.

"Hmmmm," murmured Kramer, "so the maid must do his room—which means that *if* that bloody diary is anywhere here, it won't be where she might accidentally come across it when he's away and his back is turned . . ."

He moved back to the table and took the drawer right out to make a quick inspection of its contents, pressing his thumb down in the center of Suzman's papers and lifting only a corner of each document to preserve their order and relative positioning. The papers proved the usual boring, predictable collection of tax forms, certificates related to car ownership, police pension slips, and other similar bits and pieces. The one exception to this rule being the glossy holiday brochure in full color that lay on top, filled with enticing photographs of beautiful beach girls disporting themselves beside the sea in Cape Town, and including, on the back, a coupon that Suzman had begun to complete.

Kramer was returning the drawer to its casing under the table when the light from the window struck the brochure at an angle, showing up a series of indentations that made him pause for a closer look at them. Clearly, they were the sort of marks left by a pencil being used to trace an image onto another sheet of paper, and they followed the outlines of both pretty girls on the brochure's cover. The edges of the girls' bathing costumes had been left out, however, turning them perforce into nudes, and some geometric shapes—four circles and two neat triangles—had then been added, making it obvious that nipples and pubic mounds had been finishing touches.

"Bloody hell . . ." said Kramer.

But much encouraged, quite certain now that Suzman would have been the last person to throw Annika Gillets' diary away, Kramer continued his search with renewed determination.

He went back to the wardrobe and, bearing in mind that neither Ma Suzman nor the maid servant could reach the top of it, that's where he felt first, running his hand all the way round and then across its plywood surface—nothing. The inside of the wardrobe revealed nothing either, and the same was true of its bottom drawer and all the drawers in the dresser.

Conscious that time was slipping by fast, and not knowing how much longer Zondi could keep Ma Suzman at bay, Kramer began to search less logically, poking into every corner he could think of, and even lying on the floor to check to see if anything was wedged under the bed, between the mattress and the bedsprings. Then he rolled over and examined the parquet flooring itself, quickly realizing that the wooden blocks would not readily lend themselves to providing a place of concealment, being tight-fitting and glued to concrete.

"No, this is stupid!" Kramer muttered, getting to his feet again. "If it's hidden anywhere here, then it's got to be where he can get to it easily, but the women would be very unlikely—"

He turned and looked at the washstand. Its marble top was a good inch thick, while it was at least a yard wide and two feet the other way. A tall man would find it a bit of an effort to lift away; a short female would really struggle to move it at all, not having the same strength or leverage—and anyway, why should she want to do such a thing in the first place? A good wipe with a wet cloth was all that it ever needed.

For a moment, Kramer dithered, knowing he really ought to first make a quick check from the kitchen window on whether Zondi was still managing to keep Suzman's mother at bay. Then he decided just to chance it, and having transferred all the hairbrushes and all the other bits and pieces over onto the desk, he took a firm grip on the heavy slab of marble.

"Listen, boy!" said Mrs. Suzman, beginning to move toward the doorway of Miriam Dinizulu's little room. "I'm going to find your boss and get him to deal strictly with you! All this bloody talk and you've told me nothing!"

"*Hau*, missus, please not to go! Just this second this maid begin to me inform your clock regarding!"

"Oh, ja? What did she say, hey?"

"You'd better tell me *something* about this blessed clock, my sister," Zondi growled at Miriam. "We can finish getting to know each other later."

"She keeps accusing me of many thefts, my brother," said Miriam, with the right sort of snivel. "Mostly thefts of her gin and of certain foods that she can't remember having eaten herself because she is so drunk all the time."

"Has she always been such a mess as this?"

"They say it began maybe a year ago. I have worked for her only a short time, so I don't really know."

"The clock!" Zondi snapped in Afrikaans.

"She says I have taken a small one that folds shut like a little box with a hinge in it. It used to be on the top shelf in the store cupboard where she keeps her old suitcases, with also a special iron for hotels and a—"

"That's enough!" bellowed Zondi, then turned to Mrs. Suzman. "The girl she still deny all knowledgings of—"

"Nonsense! It was there, I saw it myshelf on Sunday night when I went to get a new light bulb for my reading light! Up on the top shelf? Monday it was gone! Gone, you hear? Tell her I want it back right now, hey!"

Zondi grabbed Miriam Dinizulu, hauling her to her feet. "It is good to touch you, my sister!" he yelled at her. "Your skin is very smooth and your limbs are so supple!"

"And my knee is hard, my brother, very hard, should you dare to take any further liberties!" Miriam whispered.

"What did she say then, hey? Come on, tell me!"

"Very, very soon, missus, big promise!" said Zondi, and asked Miriam: "That bruise on your face? Was it this clock that caused it?"

She nodded. "Boss Suzman," she said in the same whisper. "His mother sent him to beat the truth out of me. He said afterward he was satisfied she had just lost it herself as she loses many things, and so I was not going to be sacked. His mother would soon forget, he said—she could not remember a week ago. I was surprised, but I am already looking for another job, I can tell you!"

Zondi very nearly turned back to Mrs. Suzman then, but something made him pause, think again, and say to Miriam Dinizulu: "You say you were surprised when Boss Suzman just let the matter drop?"

She nodded. "Yes, my brother, he had not even searched my room for the clock. Just shouted, hit me a bit, and seemed content that the whole matter be forgotten. It seemed a strange thing for a white policeman."

"Too right!" agreed Zondi, feeling a sudden surge of

excitement, slightly dizzying in its implications. "This clock that disappeared sometime after Sunday night, did it look an expensive one?"

"No, cheap, my brother, very cheap, only three jewels," said Miriam Dinizulu.

Kramer, knowing now what it meant to stand stunned, went on staring down into the shallow cavity hollowed out with a chisel in the wooden top of the washstand, and usually hidden from view by the heavy slab of polished marble.

At a glance, one thing was obvious: the cavity contained nothing remotely resembling a school exercise book turned into an intimate diary by a licentious young woman. Yet that hardly seemed to matter any longer.

Neither did the tracings over on the left, topped by a picture, made from a film still of Victor Mature and Susan· Hayward embracing in the nude, to which erectile tissue had been clumsily added.

Rather, what riveted Kramer's attention, making his heart beat, his fists clench, and his breathing difficult, was the scatter of contact prints, all taken on the same 120-size film as the murder-scene shots of the dead detective sergeant, Maaties Kritzinger. The uppermost picture showed a personable young couple, arms around each other's shoulders, dressed in bathing costumes at what was obviously a beach barbecue, and smiling at the camera; Kramer could only guess who the man was, but it didn't take much imagination because, sitting beside him, thigh-to-thigh and not caring who saw it, was the Widow Fourie, looking the happiest he'd ever seen her.

She wasn't to know, of course, that the picture would finish up with a jagged, violent scribble in ballpoint all over the man at her side, canceling him out, ruthlessly ripping him from her embrace forever, and ripping the surface of the print, too, so that the crazed line ended at a fat, obscene puncture mark.

33

*K*ramer and Zondi half collided in the kitchen doorway, and said simultaneously: "It's *Suzman!*"

"Jesus, how did you find out?"

"The time bomb, boss! He—"

"Later," said Kramer. "First, we'd better get the hell out of here with the minimum of fuss and—"

The shrill scream for help had come from the servant's quarters.

Zondi spun around and sprinted off, Kramer hard on his heels, and they got there just as Mrs. Suzman took another wild swing with her brass-tipped walking stick. The maid, also trying to dodge the dog, had been forced back into the farthest corner of her room, and was stumbling about on the collapsing truckle bed, quite frantic.

"Take me away, take me away!" she begged in English. "Please lock me up somewhere safe, *po-eee-seeeee!*"

"Ta, auntie," said Kramer, plucking the walking stick from Mrs. Suzman's grasp. "Sergeant, arrest that thieving bitch and bloody chuck her in the car, hey?"

"At last!" said Mrs. Suzman, dragging the dog back. "But

why was it left to an old woman to force a confession? What's the matter with you SAP? Have you all turned into nancy boys and bloody poofters, hey? That'sh what I keep asking Sarel!"

Zondi bundled the maid out, still sobbing, and Kramer tossed the walking stick onto the bed, very aware this drunken old bitch could now cause even greater problems in the wake of his shattering discovery.

"I kept saying to that soft bloody son of mine: 'Arrest her, man!' He wouldn't hear of it!"

"Auntie, you know something . . . ?" remarked Kramer, glancing around the room, noting the thick bars over its single high window near the ceiling in the rear wall, and the hefty door lock, in which the maid had left her key. "This place looks very bare without a phone, hey?"

Mrs. Suzman blinked. "What wash that?" she said, giving a snort of amused disbelief. "*No phone in a kaffir's room?* Tell me, whoever heard of a kaffir who wanted to—"

"Ach, I wasn't thinking so much of kaffirs as of a life-form even lower," said Kramer, stepping out of the maid's room and locking her into it.

"*Hau,* boss!" said Zondi, as the Chevrolet was gunned away from the curb. "But what if the neighbors—"

"Not one of the buggers has appeared yet, despite all the row she's already made, hey? Don't you think they're more than used to the sound of her bloody ravings and think it wiser to take no notice?"

"*Eh-heh,* that is true, Lieutenant. Although the maid told me—"

"Where the hell is she, by the way?"

"I gave her bus money to go running back to hide meantime with her father in the reserve, boss—she knows too, too much, that one!"

"Not as much as *I* bloody know!" said Kramer grimly, digging into his jacket pocket. "Here, take a look at these— but make sure you handle them only by their edges . . ."

And he tossed Zondi a small packet that turned out to

contain five contact prints, wrapped in a very rude tracing. As soon as he saw the first of the prints, Zondi sat bolt upright.

"But this is the photo, Lieutenant, of Boss Cloete and the madam dead in the Renault crash, with terrible scribbles all over them! *Hau*, what kind of hatred is this?"

"We'll just have to ask Suzman, hey? The next picture shows Fourie . . ."

"*Hau, hau, hau!* But look, only the boss has the marks made on him."

"Uh-huh. He was the only one killed, see?"

"And this young madam with the young boss, Lieutenant?"

Kramer, who was making for Jafini police station with his foot down, glanced away from the road for only a split second. "That's little Annika in her bikini," he said. "I'd recognize the gorgeous curve of that bum anywhere; the hand is hers also, plus the ear with the diamond earring. The bloke in the frog flippers and carrying her in his arms is—"

"Boss Gillets, Lieutenant?"

"Uh-huh. What else do you notice about that one?"

"The mad lines go all over both, Lieutenant! Was the plan to make him *and* the young madam dead?"

"Uh-huh, looks to me like Gillets had a lucky escape that night, hey?" said Kramer, turning right onto the main street.

Zondi frowned as he examined the remaining prints, turning them this way and that. Both showed happy-looking couples, wearing bathing costumes on the beach, and each had been attacked so violently that the ballpoint had torn through the emulsion.

"Does the Lieutenant know who these last bosses and madams are?" he asked, as the Chevrolet came to a stop in the police yard beside Terblanche's Land-Rover. "More victims?"

"Kritz did hint he wasn't sure how many killings were involved," Kramer reminded him. "Or maybe, those couples haven't had their turn yet—who knows? We'd better try and identify them soon, in case we need to warn them."

"*Hau, hau, hau . . .*"

"I've also whipped the rest of the bastard's collection, hey?" said Kramer, taking out two Lucky Strikes and lighting them. "But they're not worth bloody bothering with. Unmarked, just more females catching a tan on the beach—you know, crotches and big tits, something else in the foreground. Here, this one's yours . . ."

"Ta, boss!" said Zondi, taking a long pull on the Lucky the instant he was handed it.

"And then," said Kramer, "there's a final set that looks like it was taken at various times from the scrub line behind the cook boy's hut, showing Annika Cloete doing this and that, as though the bastard's been doing a lot of spying on her, sort of a bloody Peeping Tom with a camera."

"No more couples, then, Lieutenant?"

"No, none. You've noticed there's a pattern?"

Zondi nodded. "And no pictures with Boss Kritzinger in them?"

"Uh-uh. I double-checked, looking for Ma Kritz to help identify him; looking for a bloke simply fitting Kritz's description. Nothing! No more scribbles either."

"Then we have a break in the pattern, boss," said Zondi, blowing a smoke ring. "It could mean that finally we have proof Boss Kritzinger *was* an accidental victim of that dynamite explosion."

"You know something, Mickey? You could be right! No wonder Suzman bloody panicked and tried to make as big a mess as he could of the original evidence, hey? And then got the Colonel to call the dogs off, telling bloody lies about Maaties' reputation, saying *anything* just to avoid what he knew would otherwise be the consequences!"

"What dogs, Lieutenant?"

"Ach, you know: bastards a lot harder and smarter than you and me, my son—*real* detectives. The kind you call in from Jo'burg Murder Squad when you really have a problem, something a bit personal or truly unacceptable? No-necks who just walk in, pick you up, nail you to the wall, and—"

Zondi laughed.

"You think I'm joking? Listen, they came to Bloemfontein last October, to help look for this white male who'd raped his servant girl's seven-year-old. Three days later, they went away again, and a week later, we locals found the bugger. The DS said that because of the cauterized blood vessels, done with a blowtorch, he'd not bled to death but had died choking on his own cock, very slowly."

"*Hau!*"

"Oh, ja, they don't mess around, and Suzman must have heard that. What they especially hate is any cop who does harm to another cop, no matter what his excuse is."

"Then, Lieutenant, perhaps we had better be very sure that we aren't about to make another big mistake ourselves, not so?" said Zondi, arching an eyebrow. "How strong is our evidence? Maybe Boss Suzman was very fond of these couples he took pictures of, and when they were killed, he became so upset he took his pen and—"

"Ach, no! What's this? Fairy-tale time?"

Zondi chuckled. "No, boss, that was a bad joke, but one thing does worry me a bit, and that is—"

"Hey," said Kramer, interrupting, "you haven't told me yet what *you* found out at the Suzmans'—what was it?"

"Oh, that a small traveling clock had gone missing over the weekend, which the maid took the blame for, and that Boss Suzman had come back in very dirty clothes last night, which he obviously tried to clean up a bit himself before throwing them in the wash basket."

"After you'd sent him arse over tip in the mud at Fynn's Creek with your bloody awful marksmanship? Ja, that figures! Christ, while I was setting up my little trap yesterday, it was bloody Suzman who kept poking his nose in, wanting to know what was afoot, asking questions and everything! Man, I don't know how I missed that."

"But, boss, to go back to what I was saying, there is still one thing about all this that truly worries me: would Boss Suzman have been clever enough to make a time bomb? And where would he have got dynamite from, without—"

"Hmmm," said Kramer, "now *that,* Mickey, is a bloody good question . . ."

"You see, Lieutenant, even if—"

"Got it!" whooped Kramer, flinging his car door open. "You want to stand amazed and truly mind-boggled? Then just follow me, hey?"

Trust Hans Terblanche to choose that exact moment to halt Kramer and Zondi in their tracks as they hurried into the police station, by blocking the corridor outside his office with his benign, bumbling presence.

"Tromp!" he said, with a huge beam. "Really good news, hey? Our friend Stoffel from Mabata will be allowed to leave hospital first thing tomorrow morning! Aren't the miracles of modern medicine wonderful?"

"Hans," said Kramer, "isn't there a bloody *Reader's Digest* you can bugger off and read somewhere?"

Terblanche, glancing at Zondi, allowed his hackles to rise visibly. "Ach, Tromp," he said, "that's not how I like to be—"

"No offense intended, Hans, hey? It's just I haven't time to waste. Have you got your key to the exhibits cupboard?"

"Er, ja, here it is, only—"

Kramer grabbed the key from him and hastened to the end of the corridor, where he had the padlock off before Zondi and Terblanche could reach his side. Then he threw open the cupboard doors and reached in, his right hand confident it knew exactly where to go. It disappeared under a bundle of recovered clothing, felt around, rummaged for only a second or two, then came out again, clutching the brown-paper parcel labeled *Umfolosi Quarry Co.*

"But, Lieutenant," ventured Zondi, with a wary sideways glance at Terblanche, "that label says a dozen sticks, and one look tells me that there *are* a dozen sticks in—"

"Just *listen,* though . . ." said Kramer. "Bet you they don't all make the same sound!"

"Heavens, you're not going to put a match to—" began Terblanche, stepping back sharply.

"Relax, Hans, the fireworks are later," said Kramer.

Then, one at a time, he tapped each of the twelve paper-wrapped cylinders against one of the cupboard shelves; six produced a dull thud; the rest gave the sharp rap of wood on wood.

"Look, cut-up broomsticks, Mickey!" said Kramer, stripping the wrapping off a sample of the latter. "Note also, this isn't proper dynamite paper, man. It's ordinary brown parcel paper, smeared with something like butter to give it the right greasy, translucent look." He sniffed at the wrapping and added: "Christ, it *is* bloody butter—and no watermark!"

"Six sticks substituted, Lieutenant . . ." murmured Zondi. "One less than Boss Dorf said were used to blow up the house at Fynn's Creek."

"Ach, nobody's perfect!" said Kramer.

Terblanche grunted and said: "What exactly is going on here, hey? How much longer am I going to be kept in the dark?"

"Listen, Hans," said Kramer, turning to him, "there's a lot I've got to fill you in on, but first, have you any idea where Sarel Suzman is?"

"Up at Mabata, of course—I thought I'd told you that."

"But he is still there, hey?"

"Of course!"

"The point is, man, I need a quick word with old Sarel—in person, that is—only I'd appreciate it if he didn't know I was on my way up there, okay?"

"Why?" challenged Terblanche unexpectedly.

"I'll also explain that later, once I—"

"Sorry, that's not good enough, Lieutenant!" said Terblanche, his voice hardening further, in a way it had never done before. "I also think it's high time your boy went into Bantu CID, don't you?—maybe find himself something useful to do there . . ."

"You heard, kaffir," said Kramer.

34

Terblanche led the way through into his office and motioned for Kramer to be seated. "You know what you're doing, Tromp?" he said, in a gruff, aggrieved voice, as he sank into the chair behind his desk. "You're doing to me exactly what Maaties used to do. The more I get to know you, the more I realize how alike you are—but it's really not nice that."

"*Me?* Like Kritz? Jesus, you can't be serious, man! I'm not a bloody—"

"Listen, you've been treating me as thicker than that blasted farm boy you've got seconded to assist you! But there *are* limits to my stupidity, of that I can assure you! You want a 'for instance'?"

"Hell, if you think—"

"Point number one," said Terblanche, pointing with his paper knife, "you asked me for a key to the exhibits cupboard. Such keys are only available to white noncommissioned officers and above, correct? A total of three personnel at Jafini: two sergeants and me. Only we go minus one, because one of those sergeants is now dead, killed by a

273

dynamite bomb. And then we go minus one again, because *I* know I have had nothing to with taking explosives that never belonged to me. Heavens, man, give me credit for something! Even Hans Terblanche can take two from three and see that the one who's left, the one who's got some difficult questions to find the answers to, must be Sarel Suzman! Why not just come straight out with what's on your mind? Why not treat me the same way you—"

"Fine, then take a look at these pictures Suzman kept hidden away in his bedroom, Hans," said Kramer, who really didn't have time for point number two. "I was about to show them to you anyway . . ." And he dealt the defaced prints one at a time onto Terblanche's blotter—all except for the Fourie picture, which he palmed.

There began a long, crackly silence.

Terblanche's hands shook as he lifted each print, looked at it, and then laid it gently aside again, as though trying to make up somehow, in his clumsy way, for the violence they'd been subjected to.

"No," he said in a whisper.

"Ja, Hans," said Kramer. "It's hard to accept, man, I know, but it's true. Do you know who everyone is? I'm stuck regarding the identity of those two couples in the pictures on the left."

"These—" began Terblanche, but had to swallow first. "These were good friends of mine from the tennis club at Nkosala. That's Barry Gardiner and his young wife, Sue; that's Louise and Pat Simpson, his farm manager."

"Oh, ja? Were, you say?"

"B-Barry had this big sugar farm just above Nkosala, and his own little plane, a four-seater. They—they all died in it, last Christmas, some fault after takeoff. He used to fly in, you see, bringing Pat dressed as Santa Claus, for the kiddies, and say he'd fetched him down from the North Pole. The kiddies all saw the crash, it was terrible! Even the piccanins, watching the party from the fence and asking for cake, they also cried, wept their hearts out. Oh, *man*!" And now Terblanche was weeping too.

"Listen," said Kramer, certain he had heard somewhere it was better for a bloke to be allowed to express his deep feelings than to suppress them, "get up off your fat arse, hey, and help me go get this bloody animal!"

Stumbling to his feet, the station commander dragged a forearm across his eyes to wipe his tears away, then jerked open his top desk drawer, fumbled a fifty-round pack of .38 ammunition into his right trouser pocket, followed it with a pair of handcuffs, and shoved two tear-gas grenades into his tunic's side pockets, before grabbing up a whip, a big torch, and a long truncheon. Then, without looking at Kramer, for his tears had not stopped streaming down, he barged past him, blinking, snatching up the keys to his Land-Rover on his way out.

"Be with you in two seconds, hey?" said Kramer. "First, I've got to tell my boy where we're—"

"Listen!" said Terblanche, turning abruptly, speaking through clenched teeth. "This has got to be just us. Understood?"

"You mean—"

"Just *us*. You and me only, Tromp!"

"Fine," said Kramer, "we ride alone, that's agreed. You get the Land-Rover started . . ."

Then he went down the corridor and walked into the Bantu CID office, expecting Zondi to be waiting there impatiently, bursting to hear what had happened after he'd been ordered to remove himself from the corridor.

"Mickey, are you deaf?"

Zondi, totally engrossed in a slim docket, looked up and took a second or two before responding. "*Hau*, sorry, boss!" he said, leaping up out of his chair and thrusting the docket eagerly toward Kramer. "Look, Lieutenant, see what is written here! I saw that notice over there on the noticeboard and then I found—"

"What's this? Has the bastard also been killing off—"

"No, no, boss—not Boss Suzman. The Bantu male suspect described here sounds like my cousin Matthew Mslope!"

"Ach, Christ, we haven't got no time for that now, man. We're hitting Mabata before Ma Suzman can raise the alarm or anything else happens. But I've got to ride with Terblanche so, here, grab these!"

Zondi caught the Chevrolet's keys and weighed them in his hand, an eyebrow raised. "Lieutenant?" he said.

"Ach, you'll think of something useful to do with them, kaffir, if you try hard enough, hey?"

Then Kramer turned at the sound of a Land-Rover over-revving, and tried a little stunt he'd just picked up: he did a half-vault over the wide windowsill, landed heels together, and covered the rest of the distance at a run.

Very torn, Zondi watched the churned dust quickly settle out in the yard, and then looked back at the docket, which he had still clutched in his hand. If the investigating officer in this particular case of petty theft had his facts right, it looked as though there was now every chance of Matthew Mslope finally being made to pay the ultimate penalty.

On the other hand, although the Lieutenant's parting words had been strangely ambiguous, Zondi could not help feeling that he had, perhaps, an equal duty to travel up to Mabata, there to assist if necessary in the arrest of that psychopathic pervert, Sarel Suzman.

Still in a dilemma, back Zondi went to the bulletin board in the Bantu CID office, where an efficient-looking, ballpoint *Wanted* notice demanded of Detective Sergeant Mtetwa's fellow workers:

INFORMATION REGARDING BANTU/ASIATIC MALE APPROX 28 YEARS APPROX 5'3" POOR CLOTHING NKOSALA AND JAFINI AREAS SAID TO VISIT CHURCHES SITTING STILL AND PRAYING FOR LONG HOURS UNTIL EVICTED OR DOORS CLOSED OFTEN LEAVES BEHIND SMALL BLUE WILD FLOWERS ONCE FOUND SLEEPING OVERNIGHT AND CHASED AWAY BY PRIEST ST AUGUSTINE'S RC NKOSALA WANTED FOR SUSPECT THEFT OF 1 PRAYER BOOK 1 SMALL

CANDLE 1 BOX OF VICAR'S MATCHES FROM ANGLI-
CAN CHURCH JAFINI—BDS MTETWA

The Lieutenant, of course, would have been quick to point
out that it was only through a *lack* of efficiency on Mtetwa's
part that the thing was still up there, and bound to catch
Zondi's eye as he entered the office, because the docket itself
had *Complaint Withdrawn* scrawled across it. An attached
note from the station commander, written two days earlier,
had informed Mtetwa that the vicar of St. Peter's had rung up
to say his wife had found the missing objects in their small
daughter's dollhouse.

The Lieutenant would have enjoyed that. Just as he would
have smiled, too, at the Black Mass theory advanced sepa-
rately by the church warden, who admitted to have been
reading the Sunday papers his lodger took.

But what would the Lieutenant have made of Mtetwa's
own statement, based on a large number of informal inter-
views he had conducted? These had built up a picture of a
strange, haunted figure that people kept seeing in their
churches, but could never describe too clearly, having
dismissed it as simply dark-skinned, before it could excite
their curiosity.

Obviously, however, from the frequency of these sight-
ings, this phantom of the pews had to be living somewhere
fairly near both Nkosala and Jafini, and accordingly should
not take too long to track down, especially if a close eye were
kept on all places of worship.

But before lifting a finger, the Lieutenant was bound to
say: "You're sure all this 'approx' bullshit gives us a close
enough description to confirm that this *is* the bloody nun-
shagger, kaffir?" At least Zondi had his reply ready: "Oh,
without a doubt, boss. Most especially the little blue flowers,
for Sister Theresa said she had been named thus, the Little
Flower, and when we were piccanins, we would pick them on
the way to school for her on many, many days, me and my
cousin Matthew Mslope."

This sudden memory caused Zondi's throat to hurt so

much—it was as though a hangman's noose had begun to crush his windpipe—he found his mind made up the very next instant.

When the roller-coaster section of the road up to Mabata succeeded in checking Terblanche's headlong rush, Kramer decided the time had come to do a little talking, to fill the man in, before reaching the mountain police station.

He began by describing Maaties Kritzinger's first uneasy suspicions about the Cloete affair, and then went on to the meeting with the old Bantu cane-worker, Bhengu. He skimped on only a little of the detail, but of the Pik Fourie case he said nothing.

"So let me get this straight, Tromp," said Terblanche, dropping the Land-Rover into its lowest gear to cross a dry watercourse. "Maaties was sure the Cloetes had been murdered, but he couldn't see any motivation?"

"Well, can you? I still can't—so that's one of the things we'll just have to ask Mr. Suzman! Ach, Maaties tried all sorts of ideas. He even ended up going to see a bloody witch doctoress! But that could in fact have been the big turning point for him."

"The *songoma* told him a name?"

Kramer shook his head. "But I'm pretty sure she pointed him in the right direction. You see, Maaties probably felt he could talk freely to her—just an old kaffir woman, stuck up in the middle of nowhere—and she listened to him, listened carefully. Then she saw that, between the lines of what he was saying, lay a fear he was trying not to think about, and sensing what this was, she warned him of someone dangerous very near to him—which the bastard was, of course! And that tipped the balance."

"Sorry? I'm not with you."

"Ach, she made Maaties finally face facts and try a plaster cast of his own shoe to see how closely it resembled the one he found at the crash scene. I think that all along he had been preventing himself from recognizing a print made by police issue. You know, it was something so unthinkable he'd been looking for any excuse to pin the blame elsewhere."

"Too right!" agreed Terblanche. "I can see myself doing just the same, hey? When was this?"

"We can only guess, but my belief is that Maaties didn't make the connection with Suzman until maybe last weekend, or even as late as Monday morning. But when he did, that took him straight out to see little Annika, in case she knew of any reason for animosity between him and her parents. You know how Suzman became aware of this?"

Terblanche stopped the Land-Rover on the far side of the gully and shook his head.

"I think the dirty bastard was up to his old tricks again!" said Kramer. "Playing at Peeping Toms from behind the cook boy's hut. The moment he saw Maaties and Annika together, deep in conversation, he must have realized trouble could be brewing—there's nothing like guilt for making bad bastards clairvoyant! Hans, are you all right, man?"

Terblanche had begun looking very upset again, but in a different way: pale-faced and staring at nothing.

"Tromp," said Terblanche, "I have a confession to make, hey? I think I know the reason for animosity between the Cloetes and Suzman, and I would have spoken out before, only I hadn't any idea it might be important."

"Ach, never mind that now!" said Kramer, switching off the Land-Rover's engine.

"Well," said Terblanche, shrugging, "I suppose it all started when Andries Cloete, little Annika's pa, first came to see me semiofficially, wanting to lodge a complaint about Sarel. Like lots of young blokes around here, he'd tried his luck with little Annika before she got married, only to find she wasn't that kind of girl, hey? In fact, for a time he was a big nuisance; always dodging off to her pa's place when he was meant to be on patrol, all times of the night even, and giving her so many gifts it was embarrassing. Eventually, Andries Cloete told him he wasn't welcome at the house any more, and to stop bothering her. That seemed to work, and then came the news of her engagement. Heavens, what a business that was! Suzman acted like a—well, the way he hates everyone who isn't Afrikaner *and* Nationalist Party is bad enough, but English-speaking stuck-ups who went to private school—phew! He went across to the Royal bar at Nkosala for three hours, and then drove back to the Cloetes' place, where he just walked straight in—no knock first, like he was on a kaffir raid!—and said he'd come to *save* Annika by making a formal offer of marriage. He had written it out on the back of a bar menu! Everyone was so amazed they just sat, their mouths hanging open. He started talking about racial purity, the need to honor the Boer Nation in spirit and deed, and about how marrying tainted blood like young Gillets, who was half Jew, was as bad as getting in bed with a white kaffir, and things much worse than that. Finally, Andries interrupted and said: 'All right, Sergeant, you tell me how *you* are any better. Let's hear about how much schooling you've had, what your prospects are—oh, ja, and what was the last known address of your father?' In his way, he was just as bad: he hit Suzman everywhere it hurt with words, and then, when Suzman got up and took a swipe at him, he punched him in the belly—so hard all that beer Suzman had been drinking at the Royal peed straight down his leg. '*Now* who's worse than a kaffir?' Andries is alleged to have said. 'I've got raw coons down at the mill, and not one of them's ever done a thing like that before! Sis, man! Get out of my house!' Then I was called, because naturally big trouble was expected, but no, nothing! Suzman had gone straight home, it appeared, and although his ma rang the next day to say he was sick, the day after that he was back. I said nothing, he said nothing; he just got on with his work, which improved a lot. So I thought: Good! He's learned his lesson, and is man enough to admit it in his own way. Not for a moment did I realize he was planning to take such a terrible revenge for the shame he had suffered!"

"Ach, is that surprising?" said Kramer, hoping to do something to calm the station commander's visible state of increasing agitation. "Hell, when the Cloetes were killed, it must have seemed—well, just an act of God."

"Rubbish!" snapped Terblanche. "Any fool could see that crash was the work of the Devil. *God* is who I go to avenge!"

For which, in this context, read little Annika, thought Kramer, now alert to a young man's recklessness in the station commander, who had probably been her most ardent lover since puberty, quite without knowing it.

35

A lone black crow flapped across the bloodstained clouds of sunset, its cawing impossible to hear above the bellow of the Land-Rover's engine as it charged, buffalo-like, up the other side of another steep dip in the road to Mabata. Kramer had taken over the wheel, Terblanche's nerves being too jangled, he said, to concentrate properly on a track that skirted the tops of so many cliff faces.

"Tromp," he said, chain-smoking, lighting another Stuyvesant, "in a couple of minutes, we'll be there . . ."

"Then you'd best ask Mr. S. for an ashtray."

"You mean, we'll just arrive, like normal?"

"Uh-huh, and see how long things stay normal—that could be highly informative."

"But what happens then? What's the plan?"

"Given the choice, my friend, would you rather go to a symphony in the town hall, written two hundred bloody years ago, or to a night of squeeze-box around a campfire, where the more the peach brandy flows, the better and wilder grow the tunes, hey?"

"Meaning what, man?"

"I don't read music," said Kramer.

For once, Terblanche's response was immediate. He laughed, slapping his great thigh, and said: "So if he resists, we might have to chastise him before putting the cuffs on?"

Oh, there's more to it than that, thought Kramer, but, like Maaties Kritzinger before him, he doubted the wisdom of telling Terblanche everything. He might be deeply shocked, for instance, to learn that Kramer wholeheartedly agreed with Sarel Suzman over one thing: that a widow and four orphans most certainly deserved better than to have their precious illusions perhaps shattered by overzealous police work, done by the book in accordance with the highest Christian principles.

In short, the bastard now faced summary execution, just as surely as Mickey's mad, sad cousin did, but for reasons entirely different: not only for the evil he had already done, but for what he might yet do, if allowed to make a full and frank confession in public.

"Greetings, my child," said the old priest in Zulu, reining in his horse, his dog collar white enough to still stand out like an orange rind in the last of the daylight. "Your car has broken down? Do you need any help with it?"

"*Hau!* I would be most grateful, boss!" said Zondi, close to being at his wit's end, having just established that he'd broken a half-shaft, placing the Chev completely out of action. "Would it be possible for the master to assist me by holding this jack in place a moment?"

"To be sure it would be possible for Father Tom O'Hara," said the priest, dismounting, "but not for your master—only the Good Lord is that. 'Father' is what you call me, or nothing at all, if you're not after having a heavy boot up your backside."

Zondi chuckled, touched by a nostalgic affection for such rough, kindly men as these, and said: "You are from a mission nearby?"

"Over the hills there, St. Francis'. Forgive me saying this, but you're a fool of a man to bring a decent car along this road—something was certain to happen to it. Where's that jack you spoke of?"

"In here," said Zondi, opening the trunk of the Chevrolet and reaching into it. "At the mission, you have a church?"

"Of course! And a school and clinic too!"

"Have you ever," said Zondi, handing him the car jack, "seen a man who comes by himself to pray in your church, bringing with him some small blue flowers?"

"Now, how would you be knowing that?" said the priest, very surprised. "There was just such a poor fellow with us only yesterday, and as I said to Brother Bernard—oi, just a minute, you young rascal, what do think you're up to?"

Astride the priest's horse, Zondi said, as he dug his heels in: "Forgive me, Father, but I know what I'm doing."

"Hold it!" said Kramer, when the Bantu constable behind the charge office counter at Mabata leapt up, ready to rush through and announce their arrival. "There's no need for that. Tell him to sit down and take it easy, Hans—we can do the necessary ourselves, hey?"

The constable said something in Zulu to Terblanche, who translated it as: "The boy says he thinks the boss is asleep and would not be pleased if he did not give him some warning of visitors."

"Asleep? I'm not bloody surprised, after running round the beach half the night, taking potshots!"

"Tromp?"

"Ach, later, Hans. Tell the boy it's okay, that you're expected and the boss said just to walk straight in."

Then, with a glance at three primitive-looking Zulus seated on a narrow, wooden bench near the door, waiting patiently to tell the constable their problems, Kramer motioned Terblanche to follow him, and they entered a short corridor.

"On second thoughts, Hans," he said softly, pausing after a couple of paces, "two of us suddenly pitching up here at once could be one too many. Why don't you go in first on your own, and we'll see what transpires? Do you think you could handle that?"

Until that moment, Kramer had always supposed that the lions kept by the Romans, to consume Christians as a public diversion on otherwise dull afternoons, must have been a mangy, cowardly lot, stupid enough to have been trapped and caught in the first place, and then degenerate enough to live in captivity content in the knowledge that a feeble half-roar would bring hot dinners crashing down on their knees all around them. Then he saw a glint in Hans Terblanche's eye that reversed all this, suggesting those Coliseum lions must have been the toughest, roughest, gutsiest, most foolhardy sons of bitches in the whole Roman Empire.

"Lieutenant!" said Suzman, hoarse with sleep, pausing to give an abrupt, chesty cough. "What's happened? What're you doing here?"

"Ach, I've come to relieve you," said Terblanche.

"Hell, that's really nice of you, hey?"

"Think nothing of it," replied Terblanche. "You're a good bloke, Sarel, uncomplaining."

Kramer, straining to hear every sound being made in the room, noticed something very insincere about the way Terblanche had said that, and wondered if Suzman would, too.

"Lieutenant?"

"Ja?"

"Your voice sounds a bit funny—why's that?"

"Er, could be tiredness, I suppose!"

"Lieutenant Kramer's had you on the hop?"

"Not especially. Why?"

"Ach, I just wondered what he's been doing today—I thought you could have become involved, sir, that's all."

"Er, no. He's been going his own sweet way, as usual."

"Huh! I heard he teamed up with some kaffir."

"Oh, ja, you mean the secondment? He has this new theory, you see, that the mission boy we were looking for last year is somehow mixed up in Maaties' being murdered and—"

"Wasn't murdered!" cut in Suzman angrily. "Maaties' death was entirely accidental, caused by trying to save poor Annika from—"

"Bullshit!" said Terblanche.

Which was shocking enough, coming from him, but his next sentence left Kramer convinced he had to intervene instantly, by creating one hell of a distraction, if he wanted to get anything further out of Suzman before the end came. He reached inside his jacket.

"*Bullshit*," repeated Terblanche. "Maaties was murdered by *you*, you cold-blooded, perverted little bastard, just as you murdered Andries Cloete and—great heavens!"

Kramer had touched a dynamite fuse to the glowing tip of his Lucky, seen the quick fizz of sparks, and tossed the thing into the station commander's office.

"Look out!" shouted Suzman, leaping back, breaking a windowpane with his elbow. "Someone's—shit, what's this, some kind of bloody joke?"

"No, a bloody broomstick, Sergeant," said Kramer, suddenly in the room. "Funny, I thought you'd recognize it."

Suzman just stood there, staring at him, the fuse still fizzing, and gave a cough, then another.

"What's the matter?" asked Terblanche. "Are your nerves so shot you've been smoking far too much? How my heart bleeds for you!"

"You—!" began Suzman, starting forward.

"Watch it!" warned Kramer. "My nerves are so shot it's not going to take much before I blow your bloody head off, hey?" But he left his Walther PPK inside his jacket, seeing no need for it while Suzman's Smith & Wesson was still buttoned down in its holster.

"Excuse me a moment," said Suzman. "You won't mind if I put this out?" And he crushed the end of the fuse between a paperweight and the desktop.

"We're arresting you on a charge of murdering Detective

Sergeant Martinus Kritzinger," said Kramer, "and of course, Annika Cloete, Andries Cloete, his wife, those four Santa Claus people, and—"

"*Santa Claus* people?" said Suzman, picking up a metal wastepaper bin and calmly sweeping the mess he'd made on the desk into it. "What sort of—"

"The Simpsons and Gardiners!" snapped Terblanche, bringing his revolver out surprisingly quickly. "Don't you try anything funny with that bloody bin, hey?"

"What, this?" said Suzman, with a mocking smile. "You have quite an imagination, sir, if I may say so! Oops, you've made me go and drop Stoffel's pen into it . . ."

"Who else?" demanded Terblanche. "Who else have you *crossed off* snaps you took?"

"You don't know, Lieutenant?" said Suzman, reaching into the bin. "Hell, I'd have thought you'd have at least recognized old—"

"Shoot, Hans!" said Kramer.

The bang was deafening.

Hans Terblanche dropped dead like a poleaxed bull in a butcher's yard, half his head torn away by the .357 Magnum that Suzman had fired through the bottom of the waste bin. The next instant, the huge muzzle had swung round, perfectly steady.

"Oops," said Kramer, bitterly regretting what he'd just done, quite inadvertently, to one of the best, all because he simply didn't want to hear something.

"Your gun—out!" ordered Suzman. "Out and on this bloody desk right now, or you get it, too, Mr. Murder Squad!"

The last time Kramer had been spoken to this way, he had dawdled, and two seconds later a sniper from the Security Branch had punctuated the trite little melodrama with a big, red period mark in the middle of the hostage-taker's forehead. That, however, had been by prior arrangement.

"Good thinking!" said Suzman, grabbing up the Walther PPK as it clattered across the desktop.

Then he fired again, and the duty Bantu from the charge

office, who must have rushed to the doorway to see what the noise was all about, fell face-forward, hit low in the gut somewhere, to die almost at once in Terblanche's wide-flung arms.

"Blood brothers," sniggered Suzman, "wouldn't you say, Lieutenant?"

"Shit, I'd say *anything* while you're still pointing that cannon at me," said Kramer.

Suzman smiled his thin smile. "Don't worry," he said. "You will. There are quite a few things I want to ask you."

"I can ask a few questions, too?"

"Why not, Lieutenant Clever-Dick? I think I'm in a position to see no harm comes of it! What's on your mind, hey?"

"Hell, a whole lot," said Kramer. "Such as, how did you know how to make a proper, long-delay time bomb, using your ma's traveling clock? You look too bloody thick for that."

"Not too thick to fool you, though!" said Suzman, with a laugh that could curdle viper's milk. "That was never a time bomb, you arsehole. I just tied the clock any old how to the dynamite, stuck on some wires and a battery, and lit the fuse by hand. I reckoned the blast would take care of the details and any—"

"Jesus," said Kramer, "that was genius. You must've planned all this bloody cleverly—so how come you buggered it up by killing old Maaties by accident? Your accidents had never been accidental before then."

"Ach, that dirty bastard had me properly fooled!" said Suzman, his grip tightening on the Magnum's butt. "I never knew Gillets was away, see? I thought him and Annika might start talking and I'd better do something quick. When I got under their house that night, and heard the bloody slut making the sound she always did when coming in a big way, it never crossed my mind it wasn't Gillets—Christ, Kritzinger was ten years older than she was, which is disgusting enough in itself, but his pockets were always full of his kiddies' photographs, and he—"

"Ach, no," said Kramer, shaking his head. "That's bullshit and you know it! Maaties never laid a finger on—"

"What?" said Suzman, turning very pale. "You're saying I'm a liar, hey?"

"Hell, no!" said Kramer. "It's just—"

"Oh, ja? So why had he hidden his car, hey? And why—"

"Fine, fine," said Kramer. "Let's not argue about this. I wonder what little Annika was like in bed, hey?"

"Nothing like the Widow Fourie, I bloody bet," said Suzman, his sneer back. "A bit of an old boot, isn't she? Too many snotty-nosed kids too fast? Isn't that why you had to get your nerve up by drinking all that brandy the other night? Don't think I didn't see you follow her out of the—"

"Bastard!" said Kramer, feeling a wild lurch in his belly, and only just stopped himself from taking a suicidal lunge at him.

Suzman truly laughed for the first time. "Ja, *that* you didn't like!" he said, grinning. "Don't worry, there will be more before your time is up! Man, it's a shame, you and her could have made such a happy couple . . ." And he gave another laugh, but it emerged as a very bitter sound, jagged with rage and envy.

"Just like you and little Annika would have done, given a fair chance, hey?" said Kramer, with sudden insight so close to sympathy that it shocked him, but only until he realized that the same insight offered him one last chance of creating a diversion. "No wonder you hated happy couples so much! If you ask me, you had a very raw deal, Sarel. Hell, being just a humble, uneducated cop myself, I can imagine how you felt when Andries Cloete—"

"*Turn!*" Suzman screamed at him. "Hands behind your head! You think I don't bloody know what you're trying to do? Stand absolutely still or you're dead meat!"

Kramer waited, back turned, hands behind his head, never more vulnerable in his life—but worse than that, quite without any idea of how he was to survive this predicament very much longer. He heard Terblanche's corpse sigh, as it was rolled over on the floor behind him, the rubber duck squeak, and then the faint clink of the handcuffs being take from the dead man's tunic pocket. Next moment, hard and surprisingly cold, the bands of metal closed around his wrists, biting into them deeply until the rachets stopped clicking.

"Keep those hands exactly where they are!" ordered Suzman, punching his gun muzzle against Kramer's spine so hard it might have chipped a vertebra. "We are going out now to your Land-Rover."

"What am I, hey? Your guarantee of safe passage?"

"Jesus, how long has it taken you to work that out?"

"I've had other things on my mind," said Kramer.

"And the jokes can stop, too, you hear? Start walking. We go out through the charge office."

"Ah, but what about the other Bantu cops up here?"

"Huh! They're all out with the squad looking for the kaffirs who crashed that chopper this morning. Walk faster!"

Just for one wild, irrational moment, Kramer then hoped he would step through into the charge office and find those patient, waiting figures still seated on the bench, eager to leap to his assistance. There was no one in the charge office; one of the waiting Bantu had fled so quickly he'd left his boots and a mouth organ on the bench behind him.

"Carry straight on," said Suzman, knocking the receiver off the charge office telephone, so it would give a busy signal should anyone try to call in. "Out onto the verandah . . ."

The moon was bright again, making Mabata police station seem only all the more isolated and deserted, a bleak platform jutting out above the night mists, gathering like shroud cloth in the valleys below.

"Start walking toward the vehicle," ordered Suzman. "But move slowly, a count of two between each step, same as a funeral march."

"Man, you're weird," said Kramer.

"Shut up!" snarled Suzman, smashing his gun barrel down on Kramer's clasped hands from behind. "When you reach the vehicle, climb in the cage on the back, so I can put the padlock on . . ."

"Now, that's a little twist I hadn't expected! The cage? Do I get to black-up with burnt cork and everything?"

"Move!" shouted Suzman, kicking him in the back. "Keep moving! Do exactly as I say!"

"I can do quite a nice drunken kaffir impression, or would you like me to—"

"Stop that! Stop it! My patience is running out fast! Back against the vehicle! Now turn around slowly—more slowly than that!"

"Which way will we be heading?" asked Kramer. "North? Over the border into Mozambique?"

Suzman frowned. "You can be bloody too clever for your own good sometimes, you know that?" he said, bringing the Magnum up, aiming it right between Kramer's eyes.

"So can you, shit-brains," said Kramer. "If you hadn't invented a dirty diary that'd never existed, just to totally box in poor old Maaties, then I'd never have gone looking for it and you'd not—"

"Enough!" seethed Suzman. "You've been asking for this, doing everything you can to really goad me! This is as far as you go, you hear? Christ, why the big look of surprise, all of a sudden? You've pushed and pushed me until—"

"Because I've just had a big surprise, all of a sudden, you bloody idiot," said Kramer, shrugging. "Why not look behind you, and see for yourself what—"

"Not that old trick! You must think—"

"Ja, but same as with old dogs, it's not easy to teach certain types of people any new ones, hey?"

"*Hau*, how very true, boss!"

"Wha—" began Suzman, startled into spinning round so quickly that he momentarily lost balance, and his handgun swung wide for an instant.

In that same instant, there was another loud bang, only this time it was Suzman who probably never heard it, because the 9mm steel-jacketed slug, discharged at point-blank range, had already passed through his brain and was heading due south again, very relieved to be well out of it.

Or so Kramer thought it reasonable to suppose, as he looked up from the slumped body and said: "I see, self-defense, was it, kaffir?"

"Indubitably, Lieutenant," said Mickey Zondi.

36

There was a languor in Kramer the following morning that was wholly new to him. Even though the Widow Fourie said he'd grow used to it, and further assured him that his work would not be affected, he had his doubts about this. For a start, he felt as though every question he'd ever want to ask had already been answered. On top of which, he had never felt so relaxed, so filled with a sense of well-being, nor quite so poorly equipped to go hunting a potentially dangerous killer wanted on a multiple murder charge.

But a promise was a promise, and long before Colonel Du Plessis—or any of the rest of the half-witted headquarters mob, who had booked in overnight at the Royal Hotel, Nkosala—could possibly expect him to make an appearance, he was on the move again, watching out for the turnoff to the native reserve just south of Jafini.

Zondi was waiting there, spruced up and in his silver-threaded zoot suit, flip-brim hat, the lot, just as he'd first seen him, smoking a Texan. "Many thanks, Lieutenant!" he said, climbing into the Widow Fourie's battered old station wagon.

292

"I had wondered where we would get a vehicle from. This is a fine choice, not in the least like a police car."

"The state I'm in, we need every bloody advantage we can get," said Kramer, stifling a yawn.

"The Lieutenant did not sleep well last night?"

"No, I didn't get a lot of it, that's true. And you?"

"Me neither, boss. *Hau*, I had so much to think about!"

"Such as?"

"Where I would find the money for ten head of dairy cows, first-class, boss," said Zondi. "I may even have to give up smoking."

"Shit, what's this? You're chucking the bloody job to go farming, hey? In *that* suit? Huh! And I'm supposed to believe you?"

Zondi smiled, shrugged, and settled back in his seat, while Kramer struggled to bring the speedometer needle up to the fifty mark and hold it there.

"By the way," said Kramer, "we're not going to that mountain mission you first told me about."

"You mean St. Francis, boss?"

"Uh-huh. Matthew's moved on. I gave it a ring before I left Jafini. That's the one good thing you can say about the Roman Peril: its priests have to be up bloody early for their six-o'clock mass-thingy. I wanted to find out how crowded the church might be, things like that, 'so an arrest could be made,' unquote. But I was told he had appeared at another of their places yesterday, down here on the coastal strip. If you look at the map by your feet, you'll see where—I've put a circle around it."

"*Hau*, that was most fortuitous, Lieutenant!"

"Bloody lucky, you mean, although not really."

"Boss?"

"The thing is, he seems to be going downhill, and had fainted or something, right there in the church. The priest had rung the clinic at St. Francis to ask what to do, and that's how the connection was made. Are you still sure you want to—"

"I must, boss," said Zondi, nodding. "His suffering, and

the suffering of the spirits of our ancestors, is clearly now truly terrible."

"Uh-huh," said Kramer.

He'd had a few unhappy moments with spirits himself, the night before. Sarel Suzman's had proved the least welcome, clouding the face of the Widow Fourie as soon as he'd been mentioned.

"Jeeeez, so *he* was the killer?" she had said, with a shudder, as she cleaned and dressed Kramer's shoulder wound. "Yet when Pik died, he was so kind, kept coming round here! Almost like poor, poor Hans did—mind you, I began to wonder if there wasn't more to his visits."

"Just a minute, whose uncle is Herman's?" asked Kramer, suddenly remembering something little Piet had once said to him. "Was it Hans?"

"Ach, no, Sarel Suzman."

"Damn!" said Kramer, realizing how close he had come, what seemed like an eternity ago, to having first established a link with the murderer.

"You know what, Trompie?" the Widow Fourie added. "After a time, I think I knew what his game was: he was trying to hang up his cap in my hall, thinking all I wanted was another man to look after me and the kids, that I'd not be too choosy. I had to discourage him hard after that, and finally he stopped coming." Then a horrified look crossed her face. "My God," she said, "you're not going to tell me he had anything to do with—you know, with what happened to my Pik?"

"Hell, no," said Kramer firmly, knowing his denial would have the ring of truth because this was an issue which, thank Christ and H. Terblanche, had never been finally settled.

Then another spirit, entirely benign by way of contrast, although equally disturbing, had intruded. Kramer noticed the Widow Fourie had kept her eyes closed at first, when his palm skimmed lightly down her belly, then had flinched, as though caressed by a memory that had fooled her for a moment. After that, she had kept her eyes wide open, intent on him, craning to see that it was indeed his hand she felt, and sometimes placing her hand over his hand, further reassuring herself.

But when they began to make love again in the morning, each slowly becoming aware of the warmth of the other, finding it fuse them together, arouse them, finding their limbs had minds of their own, moving, sliding, touching, thrilling in the singularity of their contact, there were only two people in that bed, and a smoothed-out dent in the pillow.

"Boss?" said Zondi, looking back at a vanishing signpost. "Did not that say it led to the place we are looking for?"

"Damn, I was daydreaming, man!" said Kramer, using the handbrake to effect an astonishing U-turn.

Within minutes, they were traveling down a rough track toward a small collection of buildings that lay huddled in a slight dip, built around a simple little church, the doors of which stood wide open.

"Listen, Mickey," said Kramer. "Two shootings on two consecutive days, both by the same Bantu detective sergeant? People could start talking. But there is a way around this: I owe you one—I'll do it."

Zondi looked tempted, but shook his head. "My thanks, boss," he said, "but that would please only the spirit of the law, not—"

"The spirits of your bloody ancestors! Ja, ja, I know! But at least borrow my PPK, so Forensic is fooled into thinking it was me, hey? How does that thought appeal to you?"

"Hmmmm," said Zondi.

"Alternatively," suggested Kramer, "last night was mine, today's is yours—we swap guns and avoid a lot of bullshit and soul-searching on the part of the Colonel. White on white, black on black, no explanations to make to the Brigadier in Pretoria."

"Done, Lieutenant!" said Zondi.

They continued down the slope and had just reached the first mission building when something made Kramer laugh softly. "I've just been thinking," he said, "about the nonsense the bloody Song Dog tried to get us to believe: that we would be wrong and yet right about Maaties' murder! Can't see where we've ever been wrong in our deductions—can you, hey? Hell, the poor bugger just went to Fynn's Creek to ask some bloody questions, got blown to buggery by accident, and forced Suz into making up every kind of allegation against him!"

"Uh-huh, boss," agreed Zondi, shaking his head but keeping his eyes fixed on the church, now only a few hundred yards away, and smelling the scent of eucalyptus trees. "In truth, the Song Dog said quite a few ridiculous things; some so very silly I did not bother to repeat them to you."

"Such as?" said Kramer, beginning to throttle back.

"The Song Dog said we must beware of the wife of the prisoner who was captured this week, Lieutenant."

"Hey? What nonsense is that? We haven't take any bloody prisoners—and certainly don't intend to! Go on, tell me, what else?"

"Oh, the Song Dog also warned that one far-off night, Lieutenant, you and me would stand alone together, arm in arm in a black township, wearing red necklaces as bright as petrol flames, on the orders of that selfsame—"

"*Necklaces?*" said Kramer, bringing the Widow's station wagon to a juddering halt. "You and me? *Us?* Whoever heard of blokes in bloody necklaces? What the hell does it take us for, hey? A couple of bloody nancy boys and poofters?"

Zondi laughed and swung his door open, cocking Kramer's pistol. "You're right, my boss," he said. "It is bad enough that the Lieutenant and me go picking the wild, wild flowers now."